House

of

Elgarroth

A Vaeldor Adventure
written by

Ronald G. Bellar

Vaeldor House LLC

Brighton, MI 48114

HOUSE
OF
ELGARROTH

Dear Reader,

House of Elgarroth is a telling of the lives of Vecnor and Tux. The story begins centuries before the *Fate of Vaeldor Trilogy,* and continues through the years the series takes place. It is **HIGHLY** recommended you first read the *Fate of Vaeldor Trilogy,* for *House of Elgarroth* assumes you are aware of many events that are told therein. For your convenience, a detailed Glossary of Names[1] and pronunciations is provided at the back of *House of Elgarroth.*

Fate of Vaeldor Series
(in reading order):

Alas! The One that Evil Brings
Might and Strength of Evil Bone
Eyes Open in Shadowy Hall
House of Elgarroth

Visit Ronald G. Bellar's website at:
   http://ronaldgbellar.com

Or his Facebook page at:
   https://www.facebook.com/vaeldorhouse

---

[1] Some entries may act as small spoilers.

CONTENTS

North
Pavan
Helmland
Balgorn R.
Lormin
Dmurr
Darum
Carumbor
Lothen F.
Lake Beldora
Benzoll
Shield R.
Onzac
Arbornum
Beit
Stone Eagle M.
Vol Maren
Rornibur
Shield R.
Zurzak
Darmoor
Maple
Lore F.
Neja
Eastgate
Casdella
Stony R.
Ellaville
Virch
Tall Pines F.
Sistama
Squire R.
Larkorn
Rivercross
Endless
Sea
Sikilaville
Korban B.
Tikken
City
King
Arman L.
Urell Coast
Dominelli
Salemi F.
Moclen
Prince
Arman R.
Garthglen Bog
Arman F.
Sarell
Desert
Queen Arman L.
Tenvale
High Riser M.
Boddrom Sw.
Windy R
Dakreal F.
W. Palidur
Fendora
Philen
Holindale

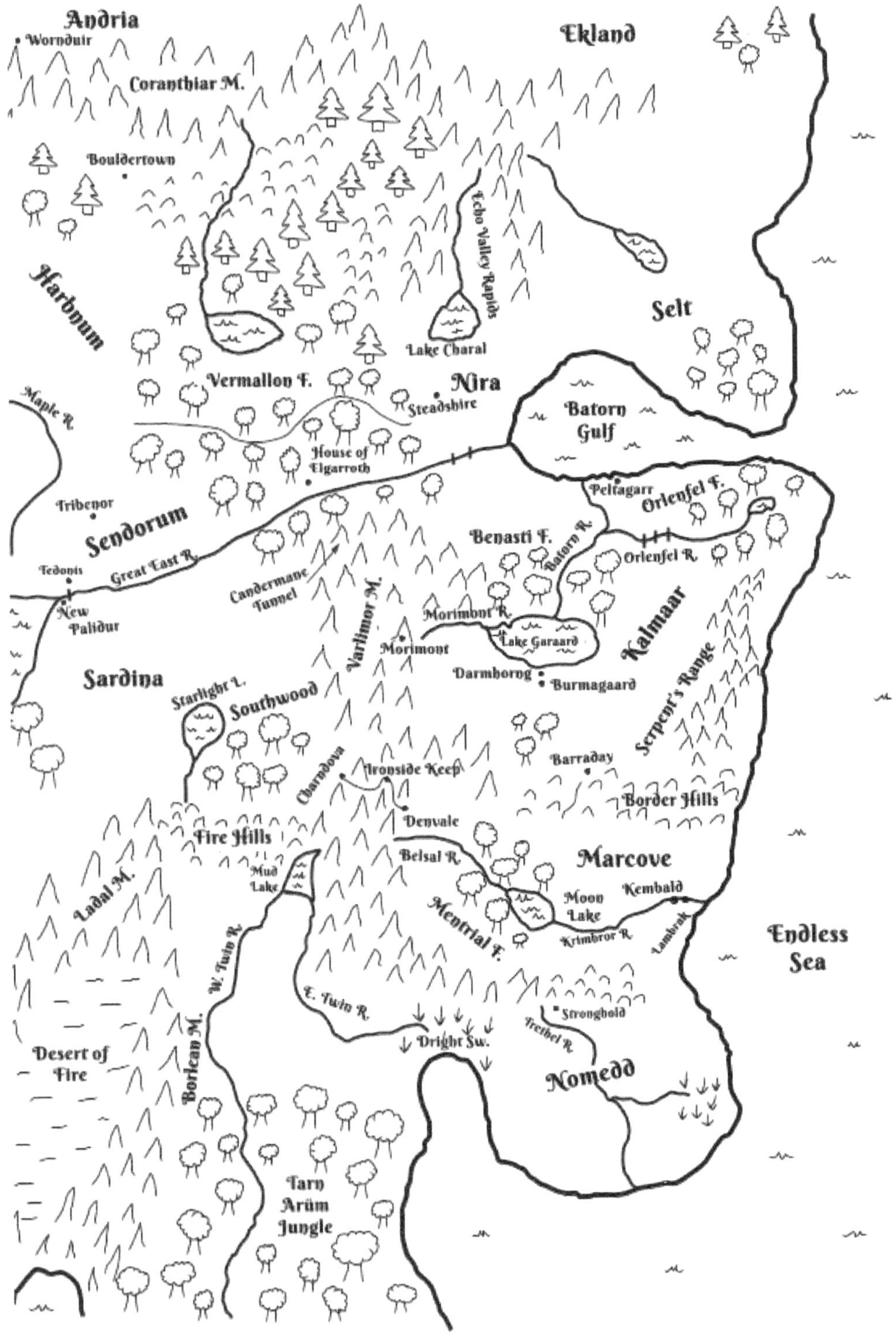

Andria
Wornduir
Coranthiar M.
Ekland
Bouldertown
Harbnum
Selt
Echo Valley Rapids
Lake Charal
Vermallon F.
Nira
Batorn Gulf
Maple R.
Steadshire
House of Elgarroth
Pelfagarr
Orlenfel F.
Tribenor
Sendorum
Benasti F.
Batorn R.
Orlenfel R.
Tedonis
Great East R.
Candermane Tunnel
Morimont R.
Kalmaar
New Palidur
Varlimor M.
Morimont
Lake Garaard
Serpent's Range
Sardina
Darmhorng
Burmagaard
Starlight L.
Southwood
Barraday
Charndova
Ironside Keep
Border Hills
Denvale
Fire Hills
Belsal R.
Marcove
Ladal M.
Mud Lake
Moon Lake
Kembald
Mentrial F.
Krimbror R.
Lambrak
Endless Sea
W. Twin R.
Borkean M.
E. Twin R.
Stronghold
Dright Sw.
Frethel R.
Nomedd
Desert of Fire
Tarn Arüm Jungle

Prologue

An Untimely Demise

What evil magic was at play? It was the middle of summer, yet the foggy atmosphere encompassing the swamp was as frigid as the harshest winters of the far north. Still, not a body of water showed the slightest hint of icing over. This baffled Palius as he trudged through the murky river, this one just as cold as the last, and its chill penetrated deep into his bones. For three days he had traversed the bog in search of... He wished he knew. He wished he had a clue where to even begin looking.

Ahead, another waterway appeared. It could not be more than fifty feet away—that was as far as the haze allowed him to see. He dreaded the thought of wading across. Mud bearing the stench of a festering corpse already covered most of his body, and the river would only add to the pungent odor. This was no place for an elf.

Times like this made Palius yearn for his former home in Vermallon Forest. There, under the shadows of the Coranthiar Mountains, survival was a constant struggle against the elements, foul beasts, and raiders of both hobgoblins from the woodland and goblins from the mountains. But they were dangers he could anticipate. He had been the finest warrior of his elfish clan for much of the first century of his life, and his parents were proud of the way he led his kin to overcome every threat; tactics and swordplay came easily to him. Who knew those talents would lead him here?

"This is vital," his master had told him before he left on this journey. *"We must find what is hidden."*

Palius would succeed. There was no other option.

As he neared the river, he detected movement through the mud. It was muffled, as were all sounds in this wretched place, but it definitely came from behind him. And *any* noise within the swamp was cause for alarm. Palius drew his sword and turned. The haze offered no clue as to the source of the noise.

"Show yourself!" he ordered.

A hiss slithered from the darkness to the right, and it repeated to the left. He looked back at the river. Silhouettes emerged from the water, hunched over in the fog. He was surrounded.

Palius charged the river, the grasping mud hampering every step. As he neared, he realized his foes to be ghouls. Anywhere else and their stench of decay would have alerted him to their presence. As it was, the bog allowed them to approach unnoticed and gain the advantage. Sores oozing black liquid stained their bluish skin, and their pointed yellow teeth matched the corneas of their eyes—their soulless eyes. They hissed, allowing their dark tongues freedom to lash out from between their pale lips.

More rustling came, and additional ghouls arrived—there were at least thirty! Palius danced about as best he could atop the muck, swinging his blade and decapitating the nearest foe. He then spun, dropping a second ghoul. Another lunged for him, and he jumped back, narrowly evading its clawed hand. His counter impaled the creature and drove it into its mates. Withdrawing his sword, he swung a wide arc, slicing open the chests of two others attempting to flank him.

The undead rushed in a concerted effort to break through his defenses. Palius gutted one while another's claw scratched his cheek—the wound burned, as ghoul rot invaded his skin. He dodged a couple more attacks, swinging his blade left and right to drop two enemies.

With his next lunge, Palius's balance faltered as his boot slipped in the mud. A ghoul jumped onto his back and sank its teeth into his shoulder while another raked his leg. Palius grabbed the head of the creature behind him and flipped it into three of its friends.

A crouching ghoul leaped, slamming Palius in the chest, and the fiend rode him to the ground, its fetid breath hot in his throat. Palius lost his grip on his sword and hastily drew his dagger. As he plunged it beneath his attacker's chin, dark blood sprayed into his mouth, and he gagged. He spat the foul ichor, his stomach heaving but finding nothing to add, and threw the corpse aside.

A ghoul grabbed his foot and pulled him several yards, where two others seized his arms. Palius struggled, freeing his weapon arm, but a pair of ghouls pounced on him, one biting his thigh and the other his neck. Through blurry eyes, yellow fangs descended.

Palius saw no more.

Chapter 1

Vecnor

Vecnor eyed the young man before him. The sword in the warrior's hand was nice enough, although a bit too long. The lad was unbalanced. Vecnor's own swords were even larger, but they posed him no problems. He often wielded both at the same time. On this occasion, however, they remained sheathed upon his back.

This was Vecnor's fourth challenger over the past few weeks. Being the largest man in all of Kalmaar, as well as the greatest swordsman, he was accustomed to the petty contests. But lately, the frequency of the events had grown to an annoying level. This was the third straight confrontation in which he refused to draw his weapons—he didn't even pull his knife. Instead, he utilized various items within reach. In the last duel, he pummeled a ruffian with a clay mug until it broke, and finished the contest with a dart from the tavern's dartboard, poking the thug between the eyes. At least that man had lived, unlike three scraps ago, when Vecnor had been fishing. He defeated a warrior with his fishing pole, which saw the challenger knocked into the Great East River, never to be seen again unless a sailor discovered the corpse floating in the Batorn Gulf.

Presently, Vecnor stood in the street holding a rusty horseshoe. He had already placed a mark on his opponent's cheek and broken one of the lad's fingers. Vecnor, meanwhile, remained untouched. He preferred to allow this challenger to live, but it was an unlikely outcome while the young man held that fancy sword.

The warrior advanced, releasing what must have been a battle cry. The cracking of the voice couldn't have intimidated a child lost in the wilderness on a moonless night. Vecnor deflected the blow with the horseshoe and countered with his elbow, breaking the braggart's nose. He then hooked the expensive sword with the shoe and twisted, pulling the weapon free and dropping it to the street. The challenger attempted to reclaim the blade, and Vecnor stomped his heel, snapping the lad's forearm.

The warrior fell to his knees. "You fight dirty!"

"No such thing." Vecnor stood above his downed foe, hoping the young man's good arm didn't move toward the sword.

"My father shall see you in irons!" The upstart's eyes darted between Vecnor's boot and the weapon's handle.

"This was *your* challenge," Vecnor said. "Baron's son or not, I will draw my blade if you reach for that."

The would-be-swordsman scowled as he rose, holding his arm close and slowly backing away.

Vecnor sighed in relief. Too many villages and cities discouraged his visits these days, and this would add one more to the growing list. It was hard enough avoiding the king's men. After refusing to join the Royal Guard, a bounty for Vecnor's capture kept him in southern Kalmaar and far from Burmagaard. He loved Kalmaar, but he did not agree with the king's ways. And he never would.

The baron's son tossed a pouch of coins onto the street with his good hand before his servants retrieved his sword and assisted him from the area.

Vecnor eyed the onlookers while scooping his prize. None of them appeared disappointed by the outcome. A few women leered, one winked, and a couple of men offered to buy him a drink. Vecnor couldn't remember the last time he paid for his own beer.

That evening, Vecnor stood at the bar of a thriving tavern; the baron's soldiers wouldn't likely spoil the party until morning. Plenty of praises came his way, as well as drinks and food, and he was propositioned by a couple of painted women. It was the same as the previous night, and the night before that—life had become too predictable. Behind Vecnor's smile was a sigh dying to escape.

His attention moved to the door when a man entered. The newcomer wore dark clothing, and a distinctive scar ran from the corner of his mouth to his ear. It was Mahlor. The warrior traveled with Vecnor from time to time — with the life Vecnor led, friends were scarce. He watched Mahlor worm through the admirers to the bar and signal the barkeep for a draft.

"What brings you to Barraday?" Vecnor downed a few gulps.

Mahlor grinned. "War."

Vecnor raised a brow. "I'll not fight for him. He already has dominion over Marcove, Nira, and Selt. What more does he want?"

"You misunderstand." Mahlor took a deep drink. "Radaam is dead."

Vecnor paused with his mug halfway to his lips, a grin overtaking him. Perhaps the line of evil kings had ended. Gazing over his shoulder, he spotted a suitable table in the corner, where a couple of men carried a conversation. He led the way to it. As he arrived, the patrons' attention slowly turned to meet his glare, and the chairs became available.

"How?" Vecnor asked after he and Mahlor seated themselves.

"Magic." Mahlor gave Vecnor a told-you-so look. "At his own hands. Something went wrong, and now he's dead. And he has no sons to follow him, not after he killed them. The throne is open and war is upon us. There are many that will vie for it."

"And now I can roam Kalmaar more freely."

Mahlor frowned. "Roam? You need to take the throne."

Vecnor raised his hand. "Nay! I cannot sit still for more than an hour, let alone on an oversized chair for years." He eyed his friend while running his index finger and thumb along his well-trimmed mustache and short, pointed beard. "I am my own warrior and swear fealty to no king, and I shall remain so for the rest of my days."

Mahlor shrugged. "It was worth a try." After another gulp, he said, "Yuris plans to make a claim. Are you two not friends?"

"More or less," Vecnor replied. "Yuris is definitely better than what Kalmirans have suffered. But I have no desire to get involved."

"I, for one, can get behind Yuris." Mahlor narrowed his eyes. "You must as well. He will see it as a slight if you do not. Do you wish to live on the outskirts forever?"

Vecnor released a slow breath, his attention wandering to the table. The word TUX was carved into the wood. He had seen it before, in other taverns throughout the realm. Someone had too much time on their hands. "You know I don't like collaborating with kings." He looked at Mahlor. "Even kings with good intentions. Power corrupts. And in another few decades, there will be another war and another king."

"But Yuris should last at least the rest of *our* lifetimes," said Mahlor. "What care have we beyond that?"

Vecnor sighed. "I'll give it some thought."

"Good." Mahlor drained his mug. "I'm heading north. Yuris's forces gather at the Serpent's Mouth. I'll look for you there."

Vecnor stood as Mahlor rose, and they clasped arms. Mahlor nodded and exited the tavern.

Staring at the letters carved into the table, Vecnor sat and pondered the situation. Yuris was likely the best man for the throne, as most lords were already corrupt. And though Vecnor wished to remain uninvolved, his friend was right. His absence would be construed as unsupportive. The thought of traveling freely appealed to Vecnor, and he made up his mind. But first he needed to do something about those damned letters. He pulled his knife and sank the tip into the wood to scratch them out.

"Why would you do that?"

Vecnor looked up. An elf sat across from him. How had the stranger approached unnoticed? Life had honed Vecnor's senses to be wary of his surroundings. The elf was an odd-looking fellow, possessing the gray skin and white irises upon black eyes Orlenfel elves were known for. But he was awfully short for one of that forest. In fact, he was the shortest elf Vecnor had ever seen. "What business is it of yours?"

"It has taken time to place my name in so many taverns," the elf replied, his voice deeper than Vecnor would have thought. "And I never leave it in the same city twice. It would be a shame to be unknown in Barraday."

Vecnor held a level gaze. "There are better ways to spread one's name."

Tux shrugged. "I could leave hundreds of dead challengers in my wake, I suppose."

A twinge of annoyance lowered Vecnor's brow. It wasn't his fault so many people fancied to make a name for themselves by battling him. "Speak your piece!"

Tux revealed the slightest of smiles. "I have someone that wishes to meet with you."

"Will he be a full-sized elf?"

Tux's grin faded. "He is impressed by your skills."

"Another duel," Vecnor grumbled. "I have had my fill for the week."

"Not a duel," Tux said. "He offers a job."

"I am my own warrior." Vecnor stared hard at the elf. "I swear fealty to no man."

"Good." Tux leaned back. "Because he is no man. He is an elf, and he is known as Elgarroth Sandanari."

It was a familiar name; a wizard living in Vermallon Forest for the past couple of centuries, as rumor held. Rumors also claimed Elgarroth's house to be impossible to find, even by Vermallon elves. But why would the mage wish to meet with Vecnor? He didn't care for magic.

"Tell your wizard I'm busy," he said. "There's war in Kalmaar, and I intend to make sure the right man gains control of Darmhorng."

Tux smirked. "Elgarroth thought you might say that. He wishes me to inform you that the war is in good hands. You have nothing to fear, and your aid in the matter is unnecessary."

Vecnor frowned.

"You are your own warrior, and swear fealty to no man," the elf added. "And if you accept this offer, you shall remain so for the rest of your days."

Vecnor glared across the table. Tux was mocking him! Still, the elf only repeated his words. He did not wish to tie himself to any king. Not even a friend. Whether or not the quest for the throne succeeded, the friendship would likely not survive.

"Good," Tux said, as if Vecnor had given an answer. "Travel west on Vermallon Road for two days and turn south. You will find Elgarroth's house."

The door to the tavern opened, and Tux turned to look. Vecnor looked as well. It was only a local. When Vecnor turned back, Tux was gone.

Chapter 2
Training

"What am I doing?"

Vecnor's question floated into the canopy of leaves. No one answered. Apparently, the birds didn't care. The only people he encountered since setting foot on Vermallon Road were bandits. The misguided fools momentarily barred his way just after he entered the largest forest in all of Vaeldor, demanding a toll. Little did they know they would limp back to their campsite, wherever that was, with less than half their muster. It wasn't until Vecnor beat a thief to death with the thug's own bow that the outlaws realized their mistake in pursuing the confrontation. Vecnor received an arrow in the side of his left thigh and a sword had nicked his right arm, but the pain was minimal. He would deal with the wounds once he found the wizard's house. But why seek the elf's home? Scores of men had offered jobs over the years; wealthy nobles with promises of a king's bounty. Vecnor never considered any of them. He enjoyed his freedom for the most part, so why entertain Elgarroth's invitation?

He had come this far. Might as well continue.

As Vecnor turned south the morning of the second day since setting foot on Vermallon Road, he wondered how accurate the elf's vague instructions would prove. Were they based on Tux's gait? Did the short messenger take into account that Vecnor's strides were twice as long? Was he supposed to have ridden a horse? These days, he traveled by covered wagon to conceal his presence, but the driver refused to enter the forest. Why hadn't Tux been more specific?

Before the last question fully exited Vecnor's thoughts, he stepped into a clearing. A quaint cottage rested in the middle of the glade, surrounded by well-kept flower beds, and before the cabin was a small fire enclosed by logs set into a square. Sitting to one side of the fire was Tux, staring along the shaft of an arrow, and on an adjacent log was another short elf with green eyes and white hair falling to his upper back. The white-haired elf wore a green robe, and he pulled a long pipe from his lips to release a billowing cloud.

Why did rumors claim the house to be hard to find?

"Welcome, Vecnor," the robed elf said. "Please have a seat, and we will care for your wounds."

Vecnor sat on the log across from the white-haired elf, and he winced while removing the arrow and unstrapping parts of his armor to access the injuries. Tux was then next to him, holding a sweet-smelling elixir. The elf poured a trace amount on the arrow-hole and a bit more on the cut. The wounds closed, and the pain faded. Vecnor had heard of healing waters made in Palidur. Had the short gray elf stolen it from the Holy City?

Tux capped the bottle and returned to his log.

"I am Elgarroth," the robed elf said. "And I am in need of a warrior."

❄ ❄ ❄

Six months passed, and Vecnor wondered why he ever agreed to work for the wizard. Sometimes he doubted he *had* agreed. Who needed to live for a thousand years? It seemed an exciting prospect at the time, but now Vecnor suspected Elgarroth of placing a spell on him to make the venture sound more appealing.

Elgarroth claimed to be a seer. Vecnor had heard of seers before, but they were always humans. To prove the declaration, the wizard spoke of several things from Vecnor's past—moments in his life not even his closest friends could have known. Maybe the information came from Tux, spying on Vecnor to gain such knowledge. But why?

Back then, Vecnor was an upstart young warrior, still unused to his height. It was all very strange.

To complete the pact, Vecnor had journeyed from the cabin with the mage, who sat atop an odd horse. The animal was small in stature, perfectly scaled to Elgarroth's size, but it wasn't a colt, for its eyes possessed a strong awareness and it had certainly seen many years. Vecnor rode a normal horse. He and Elgarroth passed through Sendorum, avoiding civilizations and camping beneath the stars. They spoke only while resting, and Elgarroth did most of the talking, either commenting on the weather or mentioning how the shape of the terrain had changed over the centuries. In truth, Vecnor heard very little of the elf's words. The decision to join the wizard burdened his thoughts, as well as the fear that he had made a grave error.

On the second morning after crossing Palidur Bridge, Vecnor awoke to see a large forest to the south and west. Had it been there when they set up camp? To the northwest, the trees butted against a massive lake. Or was it a sea? Vecnor and Elgarroth had been following the King Arman shoreline, but there was no way they could have reached the lake's southern edge already.

"Where are we?" Vecnor asked.

"Arman Forest," replied Elgarroth. The wizard was getting the horses ready for the day's travel.

Arman Forest? Vecnor wasn't well traveled this side of the Varlimor Mountains, but the woodland should have been another couple of days away. Where had the time gone?

The trees appeared as ordinary maples, cedars, oaks, elms, and several others Vecnor didn't recognize. But he knew better. It was a forest immersed in rumor and feared by non-mages. The most widely known stories were that it served as the final resting place of Vou's mortal remains, the wizard who ascended into the heavens to become God of Magic, and that any who entered became hopelessly lost. Vecnor had only ever heard about the woodland. Gazing at it now, the tales were hard to believe. All the same, this was as close as he cared to tread.

"We better get moving," said Elgarroth. "Time passes differently within the forest."

Vecnor's heart skipped a beat and his mouth went dry. What had he gotten himself into? He should mount his horse and ride away. Return to Kalmaar.

With a long exhale through puffed-out cheeks, Vecnor followed the elf.

The rest of the details were muddled. Vecnor recalled being surrounded by trees and Elgarroth standing before him. He was on bended knee with his head bowed.

"Do you swear to serve and obey me until your last breath escapes?" Elgarroth asked. "And in return, receive long life and the favor of Vou?"

Vecnor's chest tightened. The air was thin. He responded, but a strained whisper was all that escaped. "I so swear."

His eyes darted left and right. Every tree appeared the same; every bush, berry, and protruding root alike. There was no debris on the forest floor—not a stick or leaf. No paths existed.

His heart rate increased.

"There is no turning back," Elgarroth said, "unless death claim you. I ask again, upon the Sacred Ground of Vou, do you pledge your loyalty?"

Vecnor's throat constricted, and he drew in as deep a breath as his lungs allowed. "I am your loyal servant."

Elgarroth touched Vecnor's forehead, and everything went dark.

He awoke in a small room, lying in a bed just large enough to accommodate his size. How had he gotten there? Had he really been in Arman Forest? Was he there still? Lost among the magical trees?

He swung his feet to the side of the bed and rose. The chamber's only other furnishing was a table holding a washbasin and a fresh set of clothing. He cleaned and donned the perfectly tailored garments before opening the room's only door. It led to the front yard of the House of Elgarroth, where the wizard and Tux sat near the fire. Vecnor looked back. The room still bore no other doors, and there were no other entrances into the cabin. Strange. He walked to the fireside and sat on a log.

"I trust you rested well," said Elgarroth. "And now your training begins."

Had Vecnor made the right choice? Tux's sly grin did nothing to convince him that was the case.

Tux… The elf's full name was Eslimil Tuxendora. He claimed his father had been a gray elf of Orlenfel, while his mother was from a woodland called Salenti — a forest on the other side of the world, beyond any land Vecnor had visited. Tux showed exceptional skills in stealth, an uncommon trait among gray elves, yet he possessed the magical abilities the tall clan was infamous for, which enhanced those talents. He took charge of Vecnor's training, and while they journeyed together, Vecnor witnessed the elf leap much higher than what was normal, succeed in impossible shots where his arrow had surely changed paths, and disappear into shadows. But Tux didn't merely blend with the darkness like other experienced thieves. He literally vanished into shadow! The elf became part of the darkness, moving as smoke through windows, up to rooftops, or simply hovering, unseen and unknown to those around him until he materialized again.

Vecnor held no trust for Tux early on, but he soon considered himself fortunate to have the elf's companionship.

Presently, Vecnor panted while looking about the trees of Vermallon. Scanning their surroundings from atop a boulder was Tux, endless in energy. Since Vecnor's training began, they had journeyed from the southern end of the forest to the northern reaches near the Coranthiar Mountains and back again, with very little rest and almost no food. Upon returning to Elgarroth's house, Vecnor always received a few days to recuperate while he studied the elfish language. He and Tux would then complete the trek again. Other than facing aggressive animals and occasional bands of hobgoblins, Vecnor saw little combat in all that time.

"This is pointless." He gained Tux's attention. "I thought you said your master needed a warrior."

"*Our* master." Tux's smirk revealed him to enjoy Vecnor's exasperation. "And there is definitely a point. In the beginning, it took you two weeks to make this journey. A month ago, we did it in nine days." The elf's grin widened. "This time I aim for six."

Six days? Was Tux mad? Vecnor's lungs burned as if on fire! Eight days would be quite a feat, but six? Before all this began, Vecnor thought himself as durable as any dwarf. Now, he could surely work a dwarfish mine three times longer than the stout folk.

"Is it really as Elgarroth says?" Vecnor changed the subject. "Can he see through our eyes?"

Tux closed his eyes. "If you quiet your mind, you can feel his presence."

Vecnor did the same. Elgarroth was there. He couldn't see the wizard, but somehow he knew the elf was present, inside the darkness of his thoughts like a parasite. He opened his eyes and shook his head, as if to expel the mage.

Tux laughed. "He is not there all the time. Only when he wishes to see what you see. Hear what you hear."

"Can we prevent his intrusions?"

The Salenti-gray elf turned away and mumbled. "Of course."

Tux spoke in such a way every so often. Vecnor realized it was so Elgarroth didn't hear. It was another reason he liked the elf—Tux wasn't just an extension of the wizard.

Tux frowned, suddenly alert. "Hobgoblins." Cocking his head to the side, he added, "Half a score." He grabbed his bow, an exquisite piece of smooth gray wood, and turned to Vecnor. "Think you will draw a sword this time?"

Vecnor winked. "Only if I need it."

They had encountered hobgoblins on half a dozen occasions in the past, and Vecnor was yet to use his weapons. He wasn't showing off—easy confrontations bored him. Perhaps that was the reason he agreed to serve Elgarroth in the first place. He scanned the forest floor. A few long sticks lay about, but they would snap on contact. A couple of decent-sized rocks were available, but he had done that already. He could always use his bare hands. But should he punch or grapple? What about kicking? He knew better than to ask Tux for an arrow—the elf was protective of his *special* stock. Maybe he could grab a hobgoblin and swing the scoundrel like a club.

"These will be armored foes," said Tux. "Their steps are heavy."

It wasn't long before Vecnor detected the plodding footfalls, and mail jingled with every step as the hobgoblins rushed through the forest. Vecnor then spied the warriors. They wore blood-red cloaks over dark armor, and upon their heads were skull-like helmets. They were Zurkans; Soldiers of Blood; elite fighters of Benasti Forest. Half-hobgoblins, or krukari, made up the Zurkan ranks, and they were the strongest of their race. What were they doing in Vermallon? Vecnor reconsidered, and he pulled one of his blades.

The Benasti denizens held their weapons ready as they fanned out to flank Vecnor and Tux. Vecnor charged left to deny the attempt. He met up with the lead figure, knocking aside the krukari's axe and countering with a slash across the throat. The half-hobgoblin clutched the wound in vain as it fell.

Two Zurkans attacked, and Vecnor danced around, parrying a sword and a mace. With his free hand, he grabbed a thick branch overhead and lifted himself to kick the evil warriors into another pair of krukari. He released the limb and swung his blade, inflicting deep wounds across the first two Zurkans' chests as their comrades caught their bodies; and he followed with a bullrush, driving all four into trees and thickets.

The gashed Soldiers of Blood collapsed, and the other two scrambled to regain their feet. Vecnor smashed one in the side of the head with his hilt, cracking the skull-helmet, and head-butted the other, knocking the Zurkan prone. He then lifted the fallen mace and put forth a flurry with both weapons to dispatch the Benasti warriors.

The remaining Zurkans were dead. A single arrow protruded from each: one through the eye, one the heart, one the throat, and one the stomach. The last krukari had surely suffered before bleeding out — very unlike Tux.

Vecnor raised a brow at his companion. "Did you miss your mark on that one?" The half-gray elf was the most efficient archer he had ever met. Of course, he didn't know many elves.

Tux shrugged. "He threw an axe at me. He deserved to experience pain."

Vecnor grinned. He was well aware of Tux's hatred for Benasti residents.

"Let us get back to it, then." Tux slung the bow over his shoulder. "Time is wasting."

They headed north.

❋ ❋ ❋

Two years passed, and Vecnor was glad to be finished with the hikes through Vermallon Forest. Unfortunately, the next stage of training involved Elgarroth transforming him into an elf. At least he was a strong elf, he supposed. With the transformation, Vecnor's hearing improved and he could see in the dark. As well, his balance, though always an asset in his normal body, was enhanced all the more. He enjoyed these abilities, even if he didn't like being two feet shorter. Why not make him resemble an elf from Vermallon or Orlenfel? What was with these Salenti elves?

Worse still, Elgarroth had Vecnor travel through the forest under this guise to mingle with Vermallon elves and see if he could fool them. Although his ability to speak their language had grown immensely, he failed in that task time and time again. More than once, Vecnor wished to pummel some of the elves when their reactions were crass, but Tux was always present to remind him that fighting was not part of the exercise. Of course not. Why would the wizard want his warrior to fight? It took ten grueling years before Vecnor fit in with the elves, and though spending so much time in his elfish body was maddening, he found his enhanced hearing, vision, and balance did not leave him when he was himself again—a pleasing side effect.

Over the next five years, Vecnor visited the Varlimor mountains… in dwarf form. He already had a partial understanding of the dwarfish dialect from his days in Kalmaar, so it did not take as long this time to fit in. Upon completion of the task, he thought his language lessons to be concluded.

They were not.

He spent the next fifteen years traversing the realms of eastern Vaeldor, learning to speak Marc, Sard, Harbanian, Andrian, and Vircan. It pleased him to find that most dominions across the King Arman Lake spoke Moclen, and three additional years was all he needed to cover the western regions—only Philen had a dialect of its own.

The journey was not without strife, and everywhere Vecnor went, lords desired to acquire his sword into their army. He turned down their many generous offers. He avoided confrontations when he could, but often bandits attempted to waylay him in the wilderness, and stories of a roving knight spread as he slaughtered these outlaws. Soon, no one opposed Vecnor, save for the challengers he could never seem to be rid of—young men wishing to make names for themselves.

After fifty years of training, Vecnor had learned a lot. There wasn't as much combat as he would have liked, but one thing was sure: he had not aged a day. Regrettably, he also laid down no ties and his friendships were fleeting. It was similar to the lonely existence he led in Kalmaar before receiving Elgarroth's invitation. The only true friend he possessed was Tux, and it was a stronger bond than he had ever shared with anyone. Unfortunately, they saw each other less and less, as Tux was often on missions of stealth. This left Vecnor alone, with only his studies and exercises to fill his time. The isolation was almost enough to drive him mad.

Another twenty years passed before Vecnor finally had some fun. The Andrians and Eklanders were infamous for feuding over their border north of the Coranthiar Mountains, and a war between the barbarians to settle the dispute broke out at last. Elgarroth sent Vecnor and Tux to aid the Andrians in any way they could.

Vecnor was glad to be on the side of Andria; he found the Andrians more agreeable when journeying through the two realms. Though both were vicious at times, he was never comfortable with the Eklander ways, and he especially detested their acceptance of cannibalism. In Ekland, if a hunter did not return with an acceptable haul, they often became part of the main course. It was disgusting. Vecnor reported to an Andrian chieftain with whom he had built rapport, and the barbarian accepted his enlistment. Tux remained in the shadows, unknown to the Andrians—they would never take an elf into their ranks.

The war lasted nearly six years. Vecnor enjoyed the many battles, but after three years the cold and snow wore upon him, as well as the savagery. He received more wounds than he was accustomed to, and on several occasions, a timely black-shafted arrow pierced a flanking enemy, sparing him additional pain. To his relief, the Andrians drove the Eklanders back at last, and the skirmish ended. Over ten thousand barbarians lost their lives, all to resolve a disagreement over hunting boundaries.

As a reward for his part, Vecnor received a prized steed named Umbarc from the chieftain. Andrian mounts were the largest of all horses in Vaeldor, and while not as swift or well-balanced as the Batorn breed, Umbarc was keen of mind and skilled in combat. It was a grand gift.

Upon returning to Vermallon Forest, Elgarroth tied Umbarc's fate to Vecnor, and it pleased Vecnor to learn this. He had already owned three horses, and he could only imagine how many more he would need to train over a thousand years. As time passed, it seemed the sole reason Elgarroth had sent Vecnor into Andria had been to procure the animal, and not to help the barbarians at all. Tux did not confirm this suspicion, nor did the elf deny it.

"Is my training over?" Vecnor asked Elgarroth one night, after two uneventful weeks at the small house.

"Training is never over." The wizard puffed on his long pipe. "Life *is* training. And training is life. If we fail to learn, we fail to grow."

Vecnor looked at Tux, whose smirk was obvious. "When do I learn to speak *that* language?"

Tux chuckled. "It has been three hundred years now for myself, and I often have no idea what Elgarroth is saying."

Vecnor turned to the wizard. "Then what's next?"

Elgarroth furrowed his brow in thought. "Travel."

"Travel?"

The mage considered Vecnor. "Yes. Travel. Take some time to wander. Not in secret, mind you. Allow your presence to be known. Make friends, if you wish. Help those in need. Enjoy a festival or two. Show Vaeldor just how strong you are."

Vecnor eyed Tux. The Salenti-gray elf lifted a brow.

"I only have a few instructions," Elgarroth added. "Do not get into trouble or imprisoned, and do not die."

Vecnor smiled. A holiday at last! Of course, he doubted anyone he knew in his former life still lived. Perhaps that was on purpose.

Chapter 3

Tuxendora

Eslimil Tuxendora sat on a thick branch, staring at the castle a hundred yards away. It was dusk, and a change of the guard was at hand. Chaluck would give greetings to Faylun, the former arriving and the latter departing, as the two did every evening. The guards had obviously known each other for years, and they never conversed for less than a few minutes. It was all the time Eslimil needed.

"Evening, Faylun," Chaluck said. "Your son get over that cough?"

Eslimil closed his eyes and inhaled a steady breath. When he opened them, the world was slightly darker and the soldiers' conversation a bit distorted, as if the two spoke from the other side of a door. Eslimil could understand the words if he concentrated, but he cared not for the guards' mundane lives. He had a job to do.

Holding his breath, he floated from the branch and approached the castle. The torchlight was brightest near the towers, so he kept a safe distance. Entering the glow not only made his passing more noticeable, but it inflicted pain, as shadow and light were not meant to occupy the same space.

"At least the night's warm," Faylun's distorted voice continued the pleasantries, and the guards shared a chuckle.

Eslimil glided over the castle wall and past the sentries. Torches illuminated the walking paths in the courtyard while the windows of the keep danced with firelight forty yards ahead. He circled to the right until spying a darkened window on the third level around the back and made for it. Shutters barred entry, but that posed no problem. He seeped through the cracks and into an unlit room, and there he exhaled, as if breathing life back into the world. He was solid again.

Though all gray elves enjoyed special talents, some common and others rare, Eslimil did not believe any of them shared in his ability to blend with shadows. The few gray elves aware of this gift speculated it had something to do with the Salenti blood contaminating his veins. Eslimil's mother had indeed been a Salenti elf, as well as a mage. His father was a gray elf scout. The two met quite by accident over seven hundred years ago; there was likely no one alive that remembered them anymore. Several clans of elves existed, each remarkable and interesting, and the differences were usually obvious by height, from the shorter Salenti clan to the taller Vermallon elves. Gray elves were the most distinctive. They stood the tallest, over a foot higher than their Salenti cousins, and possessed grayish skin and extraordinary eyes. Eslimil often caught people staring, unused to white irises upon black eyes. Within Orlenfel Forest they were normal, but for the rest of Vaeldor, a sign of ill omen. For a time, it was the chief reason he concealed his visage beneath his hood.

Estranged from both Orlenfel and Salenti elves, Eslimil's family resided in Vermallon Forest. They were not necessarily free from the scorn of Vermallon elves, but the immenseness of the woodland often left them ignored and allowed for a peaceful existence. While Eslimil inherited his mother's height, his skills reflected those of his father's. Just as most gray elves, he leaped higher than what Vaeldor considered normal, and he could raise the temperature of his sword to a searing heat, making it truly lethal. Eslimil discovered his ability to blend with shadows when he was young. During a game of hide-and-seek with his mother, he held his breath when she neared, so as not to make a sound. The fact he had become shadow escaped him until she looked right through him. His knack for correcting the flight of arrows after they left his bowstring surfaced while hunting with his father. In the beginning, he could nudge their paths if ever he was off target, but the shift was subtle and unnoticeable. As time passed, he perfected the skill and took complete control, steering the arrows around obstacles to find targets hidden from view. His father gazed in disbelief.

"This is a rare gift," his father had told him after he repeated the procedure. "I would not share this with others. It is more than they need to know."

Eslimil better understood the advice once he began exploring the realms of Vaeldor. Among both elves and non-elves, archery was a serious affair, and most would consider his talent to be cheating. But was it cheating to do what came naturally? Eslimil proceeded to earn many coins in contests of skill, careful never to compete in the same region twice.

He enjoyed life both within and beyond the borders of the forest for a time. Boredom and curiosity, however, led him to establish a less-than-respectable reputation. He loved a good challenge, but with his abilities, challenges were hard to find. So he took to thievery. He honed his skills over decades, and his favorite pastime included taking that which could not be taken. As a result, he became extremely wealthy. But gold was never his objective.

He traveled throughout Vaeldor, carving TUX into a table within one tavern of every village or city he visited. The name often went unnoticed until after he committed some grand theft, and city officials eventually connected the carvings to the deeds. He became infamous, and bounties followed him, but no one knew whom he was and there existed no one that could catch him — even when he gave clues where he would strike next. It was great fun!

Then came the day Elgarroth appeared.

Eslimil had roamed for two centuries, unknowing of a place to call home since the untimely passing of his parents at the hands of hobgoblins out of Benasti Forest. But the wizard changed that. Through Elgarroth, Eslimil discovered the shallowness of his existence. Thievery was no longer as exciting as it once was, and he had no friends to speak of. He was alone. With Elgarroth, Eslimil found balance. The mage knew of his abilities and offered creative ways to use them. Eslimil's world was reborn.

Presently, life before Elgarroth seemed far away, yet Eslimil remembered it with fondness. But working for the wizard brought fresh challenges. Over three hundred years had passed since their alliance, and there was still much to learn. Eslimil only wished there were more missions like the current one. Most times, he played the scout, using his abilities to spy and gather knowledge. But tonight his special talents were necessary. Tonight, Elgarroth permitted him to do what he had always done best.

Eslimil stood in a darkened room of Castle Lambrak's third floor. The despicable king of Marcove had come across an item now secured within the royal treasury; an item in the monarch's possession because of his order to slaughter elves living in Mentrial Forest. An evil command, but not a surprising occurrence within the realm. Though infiltrating a woodland to war against elves was no simple task, the Marcove king sent an army of ten thousand against a clan boasting no more than seven hundred elves. Eslimil looked forward to completing this mission.

As his vision adjusted to the darkness, he saw a lavish bedroom. A hearth held no fire—Marcove was warm for eight months of the year—and a four-poster bed cradled a single person breathing a steady pace.

Eslimil crept to the bed. The sleeping figure was the prince of Marcove, heir to a malevolent throne that would grow more so with the passing of the king. How easy it would be to slit this horrible human's throat. But that was not the job at hand, and Eslimil was no assassin.

He moved to the door to listen. A single pair of boots walked the corridor outside—a guard by the sound of it. Down an adjoining hallway, three maidens skipped and giggled, but they headed farther away.

A loud snort and a shuffling sounded behind Eslimil, followed by a shout.

"I wish for my birthday gift now!"

Eslimil inhaled as he turned to the bed, taking on the form of shadowy vapors.

The prince sat, pointing his finger with his eyes shut. He slowly retreated to his plush pillows and smacked his lips. "I want it now…" He resumed his rhythmic breathing.

Eslimil reformed as he released his breath. He shook his head and returned his attention to the hallway. The footsteps had faded. He opened the door a crack. The corridor was empty and all sounds distant. He slipped through, closing the door behind him.

Before leaving Vermallon, Eslimil had committed a map of the castle to memory. He needed to ascend to the next level. A tower to the right would gain him access, but guards would be numerous. To the left, a large hall possessed two staircases — a route likely to be less secure.

He headed left.

The corridor stretched ten yards before reaching an intersection. The left passage led to servants' quarters, and to the right were a few doors, the final one leading to the hall Eslimil sought. He walked toward the door, hesitating only when the slightest swoosh of a robe reached his ears. Someone had entered the corridor behind him.

"Excuse me," a woman said. "Are you supposed to be here?"

Eslimil proceeded without looking back.

"Excuse me!"

He opened the door.

Beyond was a large hall. Over a dozen servants scurried about, preparing for a feast to celebrate the prince's birthday and too occupied to notice Eslimil's arrival. Several candles and two fireplaces provided illumination, and shadows danced along the edges of the room, including where Eslimil stood. Closing the door, he took in a breath, and weightlessness returned. He drifted to the rafters supporting the ceiling thirty feet overhead.

A woman burst into the hall. Her angry eyes searched the chamber, and her face reddened as she moved to a young man nearby. The man seemed confused and shook his head several times while she conducted her interrogation. She was obviously a servant of rank. After another glance around the room, she stormed out.

The young servant stuck out his tongue.

A fourth-story balcony surrounded three sides of the room's perimeter. Eslimil floated over the nearest railing, but as he was about to exhale, a soldier emerged from a hallway. Eslimil drifted back among the rafters, and the guard stopped. The man looked down at the hall, scratched his crotch, and began digging between a couple of teeth with the same finger.

Humans were disgusting.

The pressure mounted in Eslimil's lungs. He needed to breathe. But he could not return to the chamber below or the balcony—the oaf was still working on his teeth. Eslimil materialized atop a rafter, controlling his breathing so he did not pant. The soldier started chewing on something and moved on—he had evidently found what he sought.

Eslimil waited a few seconds. The echoes of the clatter below made it difficult to pinpoint any noises, but he believed the path to be clear and sucked in another breath. After returning to the balcony, he checked to make sure he was alone before exhaling and hastening into a nearby corridor.

Focusing on his surroundings, Eslimil heard nothing close enough to cause concern. He ran over the map in his mind until discovering his location and moved swiftly down the hallway to an intersection branching left and right. The king's treasure chamber lay to the left; the corridor to the right was vacant.

Eslimil dashed to the left.

Being in the middle of the fourth floor, there would be no windows to make the job quick and easy. Eslimil preferred it that way. Quick and easy meant simple and boring. Around the next bend, he reached the door guarding his destination. Muffled voices were obvious beyond, the loudest giving instructions for the procession to deliver the prince's gift, and several others responding with words of acceptance. Through the entryway, light from a nearby source evenly seeped through the cracks. Great. This was going to hurt.

Inhaling deeply, Eslimil passed through the seam along the bottom of the door. Searing pain greeted him, almost causing him to lose his breath. Torches burned to either side, and seven guards failed to notice his small cloud of darkness while focusing on the man giving orders. Eslimil quickly floated to the edge of the ceiling, where shadows were aplenty, and the burning eased. But his need for air did not diminish.

He drifted across the chamber until hovering above the far door, an iron portal secured by a few interesting locks. One was a heavy padlock with a single keyhole. Another had five switches, each possessing four positions—it would take days to figure out its combination. The third lock was obviously magical. It appeared the easiest to undo—simply pull a pin from a hole. But that was the bait. Surely it delivered a lethal consequence. Quite an array of protections.

Eslimil slipped through the crack at the top of the door and into the room beyond.

The treasury was dark and empty of occupants. Eslimil settled on the floor to gain much needed oxygen, and he slowed his breathing while his vision adjusted. There were chests, wine bottles, a suit of armor, several coffers, and a pearl necklace adorning a bust resembling the queen. Also present was a magnificent sword within an equally magnificent scabbard. The exquisite golden handle bore the likeness of an oak tree branch, and a pair of leaves made up the hilt. Jewels ran along the sheath, alternating between rubies, emeralds, and sapphires, and a golden filigree created a pattern of winds traveling its length.

Eslimil scrutinized the floor, noting a tripwire rigged to a crossbow. Scanning the walls, he spotted holes that likely propelled darts—probably poisonous. So pressure plates existed as well. He held his breath and floated past the traps.

Becoming solid next to the sword, Eslimil carefully grabbed hold. Just as he anticipated, the weapon was free of traps—the king would not dare risk harming the treasure. He eased the blade out halfway. It was beautiful. Mithkahr had belonged to the elfish hero of Mentrial Forest; a gifted relic forged in Orlenfel and bestowed upon the clan's bravest warriors for generations. Now, it waited to be given to a spoiled prince by an unscrupulous king.

Eslimil pulled a sword from his belt. The edges of the rusted blade showed chipping and the point was missing. He had mocked up the handle well enough to appear as Mithkahr's at a glance, and etched along the weapon's edge was the word TUX. He slid Mithkahr into the inferior scabbard at his side.

Leaving the grand sheath behind was unfortunate, but there was no choice. Still, Eslimil could do something more, even though no additional orders had been issued. Reaching into his pouch, he removed a beetle he had brought from deep within Vermallon. It was in a chrysalis state, and would remain so for another few days. Although a harmless insect, the juices within the cocoon bore an awful scent that would rapidly spread. As he sheathed the replacement blade into Mithkahr's majestic scabbard, he carefully inserted the pupa along the dull edge—drawing the sword would be enough to disturb the beetle's rest. It was a shame he could not stay to watch the show.

With a deep breath, Eslimil floated toward the iron door. It was time to return home.

CHAPTER 4
THE SILENT MARSH

Vecnor roamed the land for over two hundred years, making a name for himself. The most interesting stretch during that time was the Dragon Wars—an extremely dangerous period for much of Vaeldor, but exciting for Vecnor.

The conflict pushed him to his limits while he helped the realms of Sardina, Moclen, Fendora, and Philen battle the fire-breathing reptiles ranging from ten to fifty feet long. On more than one occasion, he thought he might not survive, especially when he found himself cornered in Philen by the largest dragon he had ever seen. He and a platoon of soldiers had tracked the giant lizard to its lair, where Vecnor inflicted several wounds to its body. But the injuries only infuriated the monster, and every soldier perished, burned beyond recognition. The dragon then waited patiently for Vecnor to come out of hiding, like a cat stalking its prey. If not for Tux's arrival, Vecnor would likely have met his end. Although the dragon's scales had turned away all arrows forthcoming from Vecnor's archers, it was not so for Tux's special stock. The long-shafted missiles penetrated deep, and Vecnor gained the opportunity he needed to escape.

The turning point of the war came after the dragons attacked Tenvale. Scores of mages responded by combining their efforts to unleash a spell more devastating than any Vecnor had ever seen. It was called Dragon's Fire, although it was not truly fire, and it decimated everything it touched. The wizards revealed its full strength when they assaulted the Ladal Mountains reaching out to meet the Varlimor range. Within the giant mounds lay a network of tunnels housing thousands of the reptiles. The majestic peaks were destroyed, and the dragons along with them, and left behind was rugged terrain bearing shiny stones that appeared to burn when reflecting the setting sun—a spectacular visage. The area was henceforth referred to as the Fire Hills.

Other than the Dragon Wars, the most noteworthy occurrence was a gathering of mages calling themselves the Council of Wizards. The group purchased land from the king of Moclen and erected a city independent of the monarch's rule. It lay across the King Arman Lake from Palidur, and was named Tikken City. From what Vecnor heard, the Council became home to the human seer, and their aim was to spread peace among the realms. As a part of this quest, sages rode forth to teach a common language within the human kingdoms. Not a bad idea, if it worked. Vecnor had viewed the city in its early stages, but was yet to visit since its completion over a hundred years ago.

Presently, Tikken City and its Council of Wizards were the least of Vecnor's concerns as he eyed the storm cloud hovering before him. The Silent Marsh, or Sistama, as Elgarroth and Tux called it; a swamp surrounded by a dark fog and emitting no sound. It had appeared thusly after the Battle of Balgorn ended, centuries before Vecnor's birth—he wished he had been there to fight Uustaag! No one venturing into the bog since its transformation was ever heard from again, including Elgarroth's first champion, an elf named Palius. And now it was Vecnor's turn. Thank Brondor Tux had accompanied him.

"I feel there to be something hidden," Elgarroth had said before Vecnor and Tux left Vermallon. *"Something to shape the world in the years to come. But I cannot penetrate its cloud."*

The wizard offered no other information or advice, for he had been unable to see through Palius's eyes once the elf entered, nor sense the warrior's thoughts. It was as if a powerful magic interfered. Elgarroth was certain the hero had fallen, but he knew not how.

"You ready?" Vecnor asked his companion.

Tux looked at Umbarc. "I cannot believe you brought him." The Salenti-gray elf had left his horse, Landolice, at home, and purchased his current mount from a reputable trainer in Harbnum.

Vecnor shrugged. He couldn't imagine going anywhere without Umbarc. The massive steed had taken to its responsibilities well. "Let's go," he said. They could stall no longer.

They entered the fog on horseback, and the world changed. Darkness surrounded Vecnor as the temperature plummeted, and for a moment he saw nothing. Then the swamp came into focus, shadowy as it was. He had stepped from summer into winter, but there was no snow, and the air was thin, as if he stood atop a mountain. The marsh floor comprised soft mud bearing a terrible odor of decay, and small lakes bordered by drooping black reeds abounded. Dark water filled the perfectly still ponds and streams; no breeze existed to encourage the tiniest of ripples. As for the trees, only a few pathetic saplings protruded from the muck, all of them bare of leaves, and there were no animals — at least none willing to show themselves or be heard.

"Do we come back later?" Tux shivered. "After we purchase more furs?"

Vecnor forced a chuckle. "The ones we used in Andria should suffice."

They donned the fur cloaks they had worn during the barbarian war and drew them tightly over their shoulders. Somehow, they had seemed warmer in Andria. Vecnor took a deep breath, and they rode forward.

The horses moved hesitantly through the muddy terrain, and with every step the odor grew stronger. After an hour, it smelled as if they traversed a battlefield where corpses had rotted beneath the summer sun. Worse still, the chill penetrated Vecnor's furs, and shivers invaded.

They reached a river of dark, stale water. Black lilies spotted the wide stream and a rancid stench wafted from its surface. A single tree stood near the bank, larger than the others and taller than Vecnor, and the same mud covering the ground dripped from its bare branches. The trunk looked as though it bore a twisted face frozen in a horrific scream, and its eyes followed Vecnor while he moved.

Vecnor averted his gaze. The fog was playing tricks on him.

They headed left in search of a place to ford across, but gardens of tall reeds extended from the riverside, pushing them beyond sight of the water. By the time they rounded the vegetation, the river was gone. Vecnor surmised it had shifted in another direction, but when they rediscovered it ten minutes later, the same tree issuing the silent scream greeted them.

Vecnor looked at Tux.

"This may be more difficult than I had hoped," said the elf.

Vecnor eyed the black water. "How deep can it be?"

Tux sneered.

"Not my first choice," Vecnor admitted. "But going around didn't work out so well."

Tux nodded. "I will await you on the other side."

The elf took in a breath and became shadow. His form blended perfectly within the swamp, and Vecnor lost sight of him until he materialized on the opposite bank.

Sometimes life wasn't fair.

"I suppose I'm to lead both horses?" Even as the words left Vecnor's mouth, the marsh swallowed them and they didn't travel far. He sighed and dismounted.

The river was like ice wrapping around Vecnor's greaves and cuisses as he trudged forward, and the disturbance of its surface released a pungent odor that stung his eyes and roiled his stomach. Though Umbarc waded dutifully behind him, Tux's mount fought Vecnor every step of the way—it lacked the experience of Umbarc and Landolice. The water rose to Vecnor's waist as he reached the midpoint, so it was probably a good thing Tux had floated across, and it receded while he continued. After several exhausting minutes, he and the animals exited onto the opposite bank.

"Let's hope I don't have to do that again," Vecnor grumbled.

Tux held the tiniest of smirks. "It did not look comfortable."

Vecnor found no humor. Slime covered his armor from the waist down, as well as the mounts' lower portions, and the chill of the swamp stung his legs. He handed Tux the reins to the smaller horse, and they mounted and moved on.

The ground softened further, and the horses sank several inches with every step. Vecnor and Tux dismounted to lead the animals, but after a mile, Tux's horse stepped into a hidden pool of deep muck. It was like quicksand, and carried an odor of festering rot; and when Vecnor and Tux pulled the mare's appendages from its sucking grasp, one of the legs snapped.

"What now?" Vecnor gazed at the poor beast lying in the filth. "Do we use herbs on a horse?"

The elf pursed his lips. "I will not leave her to die here."

Tux's attention darted left.

"What is it?" Vecnor reached over his shoulder to grab one of his swords.

"Something foul." Tux's voice was barely audible.

Vecnor pulled the weapon from his back and surveyed the fog. He saw and heard nothing. A form then appeared, fifteen yards in front of them. It was hard to see at first, but as it advanced, its bluish skin and yellow eyes became clear, and from its mouth lashed a black tongue over discolored teeth. Vecnor had learned about ghouls at the House of Elgarroth, but never had he encountered one. The undead fiend hissed with malice.

Vecnor met the creature's charge, bringing his sword about and slashing open its chest. Without a cry, it tumbled across the mud in a heap and ceased to move.

Another score of silhouettes emerged from the fog. Tux loosed arrows, dropping three ghouls, and Vecnor decapitated two others. A ghoul crouching on all fours moved like a crab, and when Vecnor lunged, it sprang onto him. One of its claws raked his neck while the other clutched the back of his breastplate, and with a hiss, its grossly sharpened teeth closed in on his face. An arrow pierced its skull, and it fell to the mud.

Thanking Tux would have to wait as another pair of ghouls approached Vecnor, one crawling behind the other. Vecnor sent the first creature tumbling with a hard kick, and as the second ghoul leaped, he skewered it with his blade and steered it aside.

The remaining ghouls retreated, disappearing into the fog, and the sloshing of their movements faded quickly.

Vecnor placed his hand over his neck and winced. It was as if a torch were only inches away from the scratches the undead creature inflicted.

"Let me see your wound," said Tux.

The elf opened his pouch and extracted healing herbs collected from one of Elgarroth's gardens. They were called Vermallon dusk. Vecnor thought the plants to be flowers for the first month he lived at the wizard's house, but as time passed, he realized they only looked that way to visitors. He knelt to allow Tux a better look—the burning had intensified. Times like this gave Vecnor an appreciation for the elf's skill in the art of healing. It wasn't a talent he felt important enough to learn himself... until now.

"Why does it burn?" Vecnor asked through clenched teeth.

"Ghoul venom," Tux replied. "Their claws are packed with a filth that spreads like a rash and decays the flesh. Most folks call it ghoul rot." He applied the herbs to the scratches. "It is not something you want to leave untreated."

The pain quickly eased; the burning faded. Vecnor sighed in relief as he stood, and he noticed the undead had enjoyed a few bites from Tux's horse. The animal no longer moved.

Tux followed Vecnor's gaze and shook his head. "Pity." The Salenti-gray elf had always shown an affinity for animals.

Umbarc was unharmed. A pair of ghouls lay at the mount's feet with crushed skulls and limbs bent at awkward angles. Vecnor grabbed the horse's reins, and he and Tux continued.

They traveled until the bog darkened, and as night fell and their vision dwindled, they halted. Vecnor attempted to light a torch, but he couldn't get his flint to spark. Strange, since his gear was dry.

Worse still, nearly all the food in his pack had spoiled, and from the look on Tux's face, the elf's had as well.

There was no point in sitting idle, so they closed ranks and walked on either side of Umbarc with weapons ready. Tux opted for his sword over his bow, for the swamp now revealed nothing beyond twenty feet.

"Apparently, the denizens of this place rely on senses other than sight," the elf commented.

Vecnor nodded, though he doubted Tux saw the gesture.

Several hours into the night, a pack of ghouls ambushed them. Vecnor destroyed more than a dozen, receiving a couple more wounds, and Tux defeated nearly as many while suffering a few scratches. Umbarc crushed four ghouls, and a bite mark marred his hind quarters. Again, the enemy fled before their numbers were exhausted. Vecnor pondered this while Tux readied more herbs. Why would the undead retreat?

"You really should learn to prepare these." Tux administered the healing concoction. "It can be difficult to apply to oneself."

"When we get out of this place," Vecnor eyed the darkness with his swords ready, "I'll learn anything you wish to teach me." He shook his head. "How is it the swamp has so many ghouls? From what I read, they're supposed to haunt graveyards and tombs."

"The marsh was not always as you see it." Tux moved on to treat Umbarc's wound—the horse had been snorting almost nonstop. "It was once called Gothnelli, and its inhabitants led prosperous lives. But I was very young when it transformed, and have never seen it other than it is today. It is, in essence, a giant graveyard."

"You were alive back then?"

Tux nodded. "My mother carried me during the Great War, and my father kept us safe in Vermallon, even after my birth. In the war's final days, a battle fought north of the swamp between the forces of Helmland and Virch left thousands of corpses from either side behind. A powerful necromancer questioned the dead to find answers about Uustaag and his strange minions, but the wizard vanished, and Gothnelli grew dark."

"Is there a connection between Uustaag's disappearance and this swamp?" Vecnor posed.

Tux shrugged. "Perhaps we shall learn that answer."

Another thought occurred, and Vecnor asked, "Are you older than Elgarroth?"

Tux looked up from treating his own wounds. "In age only. By about a century."

The elf finished, and they sat in the mud with their weapons on their laps. It was useless to travel any farther. They might walk in circles or disturb another nest of ghouls.

The next couple of days brought more of the same, as well as additional pitfalls. The quicksand-like muck appeared more frequently, and green-spotted puddles issuing a horrible, acrid stench drove Umbarc to give wide berths. At first, this proved a simple task, as the spots emitted a slight glow, but when the pools grew more numerous, they were not so easily avoided. Vecnor and Tux also battled three more packs of ghouls—it seemed the undead were the only inhabitants the swamp harbored. Umbarc's pace soon slowed and his ears twitched often, and Vecnor occasionally required Tux's help to move the horse along. For the first time, Vecnor feared for the animal. He should have followed his companion's example and left Umbarc at home.

An encouraging sign arrived when the marsh revealed a large body of water. It was hard to tell if it was a river or a lake, since the fog concealed its far end, and it stretched beyond sight to the left and right.

Tux frowned. "I will not attempt to cross this. There is no knowing how far it goes, or if I can hold my breath long enough. It is difficult enough to breathe in this place."

"At least it might guide us straight for a time," said Vecnor.

"Maybe," muttered Tux.

They put the water to their right and headed in what Vecnor hoped was a northerly direction. After two miles, a small river branched off, impeding further progress. To the left, it stretched into darkness.

Vecnor sighed. "We must cross. We've no food, and my water tastes like dead animals have been swimming in it." He looked at Tux. "I doubt we'll ever find what Elgarroth seeks. We have to get out of here."

Shivering beneath a layer of muck, Tux nodded. Evidence of ghoul wounds packed with the herb mixture adorned various parts of his anatomy—he had never appeared so haggard. "The fog grows darker." He scanned the marsh. "Let us cross before full night arrives."

Thankfully, Tux didn't become shadow and float across. Vecnor needed the elf's assistance in leading Umbarc, as it took all of his strength just getting the horse into the water. After ten feet, the river clutched at Vecnor's boots, like ghoul hands attempting to trip him, but it was surely weeds. The determination in Tux's movements showed the elf to be hindered as well, and Umbarc whinnied and reared. Vecnor swung his legs harder to tear through the vegetation, which appeared to ease the crossing for his companion and mount. Nearing the midpoint, Tux climbed atop Umbarc as the river crept to Vecnor's chest. The horse no longer required urging—it seemed the animal wished to reach the other side without delay—and the pace quickened.

Upon exiting the water, Tux dismounted, and they moved on without a break, suppressing their shivers as best they could. They needed to put some distance between the riverbank and themselves before darkness captured them. Less than a mile away, a hill appeared, and Vecnor's spirits lifted slightly to find firmer ground as they ascended.

Atop the mound stood a few trees, much taller than the pitiful ones they had seen thus far. The towering plants rose into the cloud, and no leaves were present—at least, not on the visible branches. The fog below the hill seemed to thin, allowing Vecnor to see a bit farther. A pond lay ahead and to the left, and to the right, the water they had been following continued. It was definitely a river.

"There are no useful sticks." Tux crouched beneath the trees, searching the mud. "How are we to have a fire?"

Vecnor sighed and pulled a blanket from one of Umbarc's packs. Although it had avoided submergence into the rivers, it was damp. He laid it down, wondering if there was a point. Sitting on the muck would likely make no difference. But having some semblance of a camp was preferable.

Tux held his breath and floated higher up the tree. The muffled sound of snapping branches followed, and several rotted sticks fell to the ground. Vecnor gathered them into a pile.

Tux materialized nearby, panting. "It is difficult to breathe up there." He vomited.

For half an hour, Vecnor and Tux alternated rubbing sticks and striking flint and steel, but the wood resisted all attempts to ignite. They resigned themselves to shiver in the darkness, sitting side by side against a tree to wait out the night.

Morning arrived. No ghouls had attacked, but Vecnor still found no sleep. From the circles beneath Tux's eyes, neither had the elf. There was nothing to eat, so they lifted their weary bodies from the filth and prepared to move on. Muck covered the blanket, as if it had crept onto the cloth throughout the dark hours, and Vecnor neglected to pack it.

They descended the hill.

Over the next two days, they crossed three rivers and suffered four more ghoul attacks. Tux exhausted his herb supply before the fourth battle, and the burning of the untreated wounds grew stronger with each passing hour. Bleeding, soaked, and shivering, Vecnor and Tux pressed on; and as hunger combined with their ailments, Vecnor wondered how much longer they would last. Just as he thought the swamp would be the death of them, the fog abruptly ended and they stepped beneath the warm sun. To the right was the river that guided them, over twenty yards in width, and a hill rose before them.

Umbarc practically dragged Vecnor as they rushed up the hill with energy they should not have possessed. Upon reaching the top, rocky terrain lay ahead and to the left. A forest of pine trees formed a wall extending from the swamp and into the southwest, and beyond the river that had strangely developed a current, fields of grass and wild flowers reached the eastern horizon.

"We are in Neja," said Tux. "The best way out is through Tall Pines Forest." The elf gazed at the mass of firs. "Palidur guards the only other exit," he added, "north of here, where the water is fordable. But they will not grant us passage. And we need to get our wounds taken care of before too long. Some of the forests' trees yield a healing agent called peak sap. It is uncommon, but I will recognize the trees on sight, and I know how to extract it."

Vecnor gazed north. He recalled stories of Warden Tower. Palidurians considered themselves enforcers of law and order across the realms, and many criminals evaded capture by hiding in the wasteland south of the Stone Eagle Mountains. Rather than pursue and risk falling victim to traps and ambushes, Palidurians erected the tower to guard the only traversable section of the Stony River, and they named the land Neja, or "prison" in their original language, before Tikken City's common tongue gained popularity. Through all his travels, Vecnor had never been on this side of the waterway.

Tall Pines was not a route without its own dangers. Packs of wolves and ogres roamed the woodland, sometimes working together. Before the Dragon Wars, the forest was also home to a fierce dragon, and its memory continued to ward off most hunters. For Vecnor and Tux, traversing the conifers shouldn't prove too difficult, and Vecnor would rather not tarnish his reputation with the Holy City by forcing his way across the Stony.

"Tall Pines it is," he said.

Tux's head snapped westward, and Vecnor's ears detected hoofbeats. A group of six riders approached.

"Nejans." Tux narrowed his gaze. "I doubt they come to welcome us."

Vecnor reached deep into his final pool of strength. He was in no mood to find creative ways to defend himself. If malice was the bandits' intent, they picked the wrong pair to accost.

Chapter 5

Tikken City Market

appy Birthday!"

Vecnor opened his eyes to see Tux staring at him. He had locked the door the previous night, but there was no keeping the half-gray elf out. Was it his birthday already? He rose, his muscles stiff. Inn rooms never provided beds long enough.

"I believe I owe Elgarroth some gold," Tux said. "I never imagined you would endure *two* hundred years. But six hundred fifty?"

Vecnor sat up, raising a brow. "No?"

"Well..." The elf shrugged. "Palius did not survive the first century."

"I am Vecnor!"

Tux rolled his eyes.

Indeed, Vecnor had served the wizard for over six hundred years. After the unsuccessful journey through Sistama, which Elgarroth insisted had not been a waste of time, missions were few, and Vecnor filled his days with training or traveling. He typically spent a year within most kingdoms, making his presence known while helping those in need. His legend grew, and wherever he roamed, people feared or revered him—sometimes both. He was careful not to become attached to those he associated with, for human lives were fleeting, and he never cultivated a lasting friendship outside the House of Elgarroth. At times the lonely existence saddened him, but Tux always arrived before his moods became too dark.

"Why are we going to Tikken City?" Vecnor asked. It was the first task he and Tux had worked together in some time.

"We are to observe a pair of young elves. Elgarroth is very interested in them."

"Recruits?" Vecnor grinned. "Are we being replaced?"

Tux held a wry smile. "Hardly."

Vecnor gathered his gear, and they departed from Rivercross, a thriving city north of the Squire River. Vecnor recalled when the settlement was not so large, back when he first began working for Elgarroth. Though the Korban Bridge had been around for a few centuries already, news of its existence had yet to spread, and trade was limited to folks living in eastern Virch and northern Moclen. Before the bridge's construction, the only route between the southwestern lands and the rest of Vaeldor passed through Tenvale, the Wizard Kingdom. This deterred merchants from making the journey in either direction. Rumors of the bridge then reached other kingdoms, and the population of Rivercross expanded as traffic through the region increased a hundredfold.

Vecnor and Tux rode over the Korban. The craftsmanship of the arching white stone was exquisite, and the images of dwarfish warriors on the sides looked so real that Vecnor often stared, waiting to see if their eyes moved. Thus far, they had not. How was it the bridge appeared as it did six hundred years ago? Like Vecnor, it didn't seem to age. Had Elgarroth assisted in its construction?

They traveled a good pace throughout the day, and as the sun began its descent, Tikken City was before them. The city had flourished over the centuries as trust and respect for the Council of Wizards spread, and the reach of their influence stretched from Philen to Kalmaar. With the Seer's visions to guide them, the Council's wisdom helped to quash many conflicts between kingdoms. As well, most realms accepted the common tongue the Council offered, and not even those from Moclen spoke the dialect that once reigned in the west—the years Vecnor spent learning the human languages now seemed frivolous. Of course, none of the barbarian regions adopted the language, and neither did Selt nor Beit, the latter two refusing to show such unity.

The wide-open gates of Tikken City revealed streets alive with activity. People from several walks of life wandered about, including humans, elves, dwarves, marteese, and even a handful of krukari.

"What's happening?" asked Vecnor.

"A festival," Tux replied. "The new Seer has arrived."

Vecnor frowned. "I thought human seers lived two or three centuries. Hasn't this one only presided for one and a half?"

"Yes." Tux turned to Vecnor. "But they spend at least fifty years training the next Seer before they retire." He returned his attention to the mass of buildings ahead. "Elgarroth is hopeful young Seac will build better relationships with other races than the current Seer. Council interests have always focused on humans."

"Why don't they know there's an elf seer?" Vecnor had posed the question several times in the past, but was yet to receive an acceptable response.

"It would disrupt the balance of things," Tux replied.

Vecnor would ask again later.

Tux pulled up his hood to conceal his face before they entered the city. Gray elves outside of Orlenfel were rare these days, and west of the King Arman they were nonexistent. Beyond that, Tux preferred to go unnoticed.

As for Vecnor, people immediately recognized him, and they marveled at him sitting atop Umbarc.

"It's the Rogue Knight!" gasped an onlooker.

"Black Death is more fitting," said another.

"I have a bed all ready for you, Master Rogue Knight," drawled a woman dressed in suggestive garments.

Gatherings of Salenti elves roamed the streets, more likely due to the increased traffic the festival brought than for the festival itself. They were similar to Tux and Elgarroth in size, but their pale skin was more in likeness to the wizard's. Vecnor had spent time with the Salenti denizens over the past century, and he found it hard to believe they shared blood with the warrior elves of Vermallon. These smaller cousins did not take life seriously, and found humor in just about everything, especially when it involved another's misery. And now, Tikken City was host to more Salenti inhabitants than Vecnor had ever seen in one place outside of their forest. The constant giggling was enough to drive him mad. How was it Tux and Elgarroth shared in their ancestry?

"Don't tell me we're here for Salenti folk," grumbled Vecnor.

"I will not know our targets until someone claims this." Tux patted a sword hanging on his belt. The ratty scabbard had been strapped next to his own fine blade since leaving the House of Elgarroth. "It should not take long."

They stabled their horses before heading to the market square. The Tikken City Market was always bustling, and the festival had the area completely packed. Besides the usual merchants, there were games to test one's strength, coordination, or memory, and performers juggled, played instruments, or danced. Though Vecnor stood tall above the crowd, his admirers dwindled as everyone focused on the entertainment or sifted through the goods.

Tux made his way around the perimeter, a task easy for one of his size. Vecnor gave up trying to follow after the first twenty yards, opting to observe. The half-gray elf halted near a merchant's cart possessing a score of well-polished swords, axes, hammers, and daggers. Looking over the wares were a couple of humans, three marteese, and a young girl. Tux pretended to inspect a dagger with one hand while pulling the filthy scabbard from beneath his cloak with the other. When he returned the dagger to the table, the sword accompanied it.

A Vermallon elf walked by the cart, his eyes wandering over the weapons, and he continued on his way. A marteese moved a hand over the blade, only to lift a sword next to it. The girl then reached for the dagger Tux had feigned interest in, but she hesitated. She grabbed the dirty handle instead.

Why was a child browsing a weapon cart?

The girl ran her fingers through her long, dark hair, exposing a pointed ear. She wasn't a child, but a Salenti elf, short even for one of her kind. Vecnor narrowed his eyes. She was quite fetching.

The tiny elf sneered at the scabbard. She then slid the blade out a few inches, and her jaw dropped. Sheathing the sword, she looked around, as if fearing someone watched her—Vecnor averted his gaze when she glanced his way. When he chanced a peek, the elf maiden was speaking to the merchant, who scratched his head and frowned at the merchandise. He evidently named a price, for she pulled a handful of coins from her pouch and placed them in his awaiting hand.

With her newly gained treasure, she skipped from the table—she actually skipped—to join a blonde-haired Salenti elf standing half a foot taller. This second elf was dressed as one experienced in the art of magic, and she was equally stunning in appearance. But when she wiggled her fingers, causing a man's trousers to drop to his ankles and send him stumbling into several shoppers, she no longer seemed so fair.

Vecnor hated pranks.

The dark-haired elf showed the dirty scabbard to the blonde elf, who laughed. But when the smaller elf pulled the blade halfway out, the taller one gasped.

Vecnor frowned as Tux joined him. "These can't be them."

Tux shrugged.

Vecnor sighed.

"They are leaving," Tux said.

The maidens scurried through the crowd. The dark-haired elf led the way, seemingly in a hurry to exit the square.

"Do we follow?" Vecnor asked.

"No." Tux scanned the area. "Wait here. I will return."

The half-gray elf moved swiftly through the shoppers, almost as if the market was empty. He stopped near a group of Salenti elves and exchanged words before dropping a couple of coins into one of their hands. He returned.

"Their names are Eraim and Selanna," Tux said. "That is all we need to know for now."

Vecnor raised his brow. "Now we go home?"

Tux nodded.

Why had Elgarroth sent both of them on this journey? It hardly seemed worth the trip.

※ ※ ※

Decades passed while Vecnor and Tux alternated keeping a distant watch on Eraim and Selanna. Elgarroth did not divulge what importance the maidens held. The elves lived in Dominelli, the largest settlement within Salenti Forest, and led ordinary Salenti-elf lives. They liked to jest and play pranks, especially upon humans when outside their woodland, and conversations between them were generally light and pleasant. Eraim was a bit older, though the years meant little to their race, and while Selanna proved herself a competent spell caster, Eraim's talents were widespread.

The smaller elf's ability to remain unseen and her deft hands surprised even Tux. But Eraim seemed to abhor thievery, and rarely did she keep things she liberated from others. Most times, she relieved wealthy braggarts of particular items, only to immediately spend them or redistribute them to those less fortunate. Eraim's combative prowess was far more interesting. An accomplished archer, she released arrows as quickly as Tux—the half-gray elf scoffed at the notion—and wielded her sword better than most seasoned warriors. On the occasions Vecnor witnessed her swordplay, she was truly impressive, and she maneuvered as gracefully as any gray elf, without the benefits of their natural skills— again, Eslimil disagreed. The only compliments forthcoming from Tux were for the exquisite scabbard she provided the sword she purchased in Tikken City, and her choice of gemstones to adorn it. Eraim enjoyed laughing as much as her kin, but her common sense often appeared to overrule her urges to play pranks. Perhaps there was hope for her.

Spying on the elves was boring work, but there was little else to do. Beneath the watchful eye of Palidur and through the wisdom of the Council of Wizards, peace reigned over Vaeldor.

Chapter 6

Kalmaar

Vecnor's travels dwindled, as they did every so often, and it was especially true after Elgarroth charged Tux with the sole responsibility of watching Eraim and Selanna. But he wasn't completely idle. He still toured the realms, but under his elfish or dwarfish guises. Elgarroth explained that Vecnor's legend would grow in his absence, and the wizard was correct. Once Vecnor returned as himself, eight decades after he and Tux first spied on the Salenti elves, he found stories about him to be inflated beyond reality. As for those that had known him when they were younger, they asked surprisingly few questions about his timeless appearance. In the end, they seemed grateful just to see him.

Presently, Vecnor was in his own body, and his task involved journeying across Vaeldor on another holiday, more or less. He was to drink in taverns, humble challengers wishing to match combative skills, and help lords, knights, and commoners overcome their plights. But also he was to make friends—specific friends chosen by Elgarroth—and do whatever was necessary to gain their trust.

His excursion began in Kalmaar, much to his liking. The reign of evil over the kingdom was a thing of the distant past, and it pleased him to see the worship of Brondor, God of Battle, restored. As Elgarroth anticipated, Vecnor barely spent a year within the realm before the king learned of his presence, and he was invited to Darmhorng Castle to train young Prince Karrak in the ways of combat. He accepted.

Vecnor and the prince bonded immediately. Despite Karrak's age, he had a mind for commanding and the reflexes of a seasoned warrior, and his eagerness to excel at every aspect of the life that lay before him was commendable. He grinned often in Vecnor's presence, and a gleam of respect constantly shone in his eyes.

"Will I get as big as you?" the lad asked after a couple of months, during a break in his lessons.

"No one gets as big as me." Vecnor winked. "But you will be prepared for anything. Be it sword, axe, or spear, you'll master them all."

"What about the bow?"

Vecnor sneered. "Bows are for elves! Have you ever seen an elf rule a nation? You shall reign through strength! As Brondor commands."

Karrak smiled. "And you'll be my champion!"

Vecnor held half a grin. In a way, the prince reminded him of Lord Yuris from over seven centuries ago. Vecnor had been ready to back Yuris's quest to capture the Kalmiran throne before Tux appeared with Elgarroth's invitation. A trace amount of regret still gnawed at him for having missed out on the fun, but just as Elgarroth predicted, Yuris was victorious. Unfortunately, Yuris's son never sat on the throne, as civil wars became a tradition, and the ruling seat switched from family to family. That custom ended when Karrak's ancestors seized control. It was a respectable lineage that grew more so with each generation, and Karrak would be the eighth to wear the crown when his turn arrived.

The thought of remaining as Karrak's champion tempted Vecnor; the lad was the exception to his rule about never serving a king. Unfortunately, the choice was not Vecnor's to make. He lifted his sword. "Back to your exercises."

The bond between Vecnor and Prince Karrak continued to grow as the future king became a young man. Regardless of the prince's mounting responsibilities, he always found time to train, and when tasked with sending a force to oust a tribe of ogres, he chose Vecnor to lead the mission.

A lord in the north had requested aid in defending his citizens from the giant raiders. For two months, ogres razed farms and stole livestock and farmers to appease their appetites. Vecnor arrived with two hundred Kalmiran soldiers to the region outside Orlenfel Forest, and when fifteen of the monstrous beings rumbled from the woodland, he and his men were ready. The archers rained arrows to weaken the approaching force, and Vecnor led the charge; and though the ogres crushed or maimed five Kalmirans for every one of theirs to fall, they retreated after losing only half their muster. A strange tactic for the brutes to employ. Vecnor and his soldiers thwarted two more raids over the next week before the attacks ceased. But the enemy was far from defeat, and Vecnor took his surviving warriors into the forest.

Beneath the high treetops of Orlenfel, the ogres had plenty of room to maneuver, and bows were less effective with the scattered trunks of various sizes—obstacles only elves seemed to possess the skills to overcome. So Vecnor lured the giants into ambushes. As the monsters grew weary of the traps, they began traveling in groups of four or more, and victories grew more costly.

Relief came with the arrival of the gray elves. The Orlenfel denizens bounded to unbelievable heights as they combined magic with their bows and swords. But their attacks didn't have the impact Vecnor had hoped for—the large enemies shrugged off most of the heated blades and exploding arrows. Though reluctant to do so, the elves joined forces with the humans in hopes of defeating the foe. But the ogres' numbers seemed inexhaustible.

"You are impressive," said a gray elf to Vecnor during a lull in the fighting. The warrior's voice was deeper than Tux's.

Vecnor gazed at the tall, slender elf. How could folks appearing so lithe fight with such strength? The white irises upon black eyes might have filled him with the same uneasiness apparent in his soldiers' expressions had he not spent centuries with Tux already. Unlike Tux, this elf stood only a head shorter than Vecnor.

Vecnor grinned. "Yes, I am. I am Vecnor!"

"Indeed," the elf said. "And I am Xorlunder." He viewed the ailing Kalmirans and gray elves segregated to either side of the shared encampment. "We have been battling this foe for nearly fifty years." He turned to Vecnor. "Never have humans offered help."

Vecnor raised a brow. "Would you have accepted such an offer?"

Xorlunder held a crooked smile. "I suppose not. But here we are, and I am grateful. Unfortunately, it will not be enough. The enemy will soon storm us with all they have." He glanced at his kin. "My father has no intentions of retreating. Tomorrow, this will end."

"Can you get me to their leader?" Vecnor asked.

Xorlunder considered him. "When do we leave?"

"Immediately."

❋❋❋

Vecnor and Xorlunder departed from the encampment unnoticed. The tall elf moved easily through the underbrush, often stopping for Vecnor to catch up. Still, Xorlunder appeared impressed not only with how well Vecnor traversed the terrain, but with his ability to do so without making too much noise. After less than five miles, the gray elf stopped to peer around a wide oak tree.

"There," the elf whispered. "Arubit. He is young, but larger than any ogre I have seen."

Vecnor craned his neck to have a look. Though the ogre sat, the creature was surely twice his height and ten times his girth. Blotches of pink and purple spotted its light gray skin, and a thick unibrow jutted above its beady eyes. Another thirty ogres—all huge, but none so much as Arubit—occupied the clearing obviously made by the snapping of trees or the ripping of their trunks from the ground. The monsters were eating dinner, comprising fallen soldiers from either side of the day's battle. It was no mystery why the gray elves did not launch a sneak attack. As efficiently as the Orlenfel warriors operated, this many ogres would wipe out any invasion after the initial strike.

"What is your plan?" asked Xorlunder.

Vecnor studied the clearing, noting each hole, stump, and bush. "Have your bow ready and remain unseen. Assist *only* if I ask."

The elf did not question the order or pry for more information. Xorlunder nodded once while taking a sleek bow from his shoulder and nocking an arrow.

Vecnor pulled his full helm from his belt and placed it on his head. It would limit his peripheral vision, but the terrain remained etched in his mind. He entered the clearing, gaining the attention of every ogre. Most kept chewing, but no one took any additional bites.

"Arubit!" Vecnor called out. "I challenge you!"

The enormous brute snarled. His eyes were young, maybe sixteen years in this world, but they revealed cunning and arrogance. He was their leader for a reason.

"Take dis rubbish from me sight!" Raw meat and flesh escaped Arubit's mouth while he spoke.

"I understand your fear." Vecnor paused as several ogres reach for their tree-like clubs. "To be bested by a human… That would be embarrassing."

Arubit's brow scrunched together as a growl rolled in his throat. "You puny weapons not scare any of us! One man not worthy of me time."

"Then choose one from your following," Vecnor said. "You have nothing to lose. And maybe you'll enjoy the show."

Arubit scanned the treetops, his mouth twisted in thought. His lips then thinned as they formed a grin. "Kodahn!"

An ogre lifted his club and stepped forward. He was not so large as Arubit, but still bigger than the average ogre. Kodahn smiled, revealing several missing hand-sized teeth, and he wore the smirk with obvious pride. The ground shook with each step as he moved to the center of the clearing.

"Me gets first bite when me wins," Kodahn said. "No puny arm for me!"

"Agreed," Arubit grumbled.

"Me wants a leg," said an ogre Vecnor believed to be female. Her chest sagged to her waist.

The rest of the crowd began speaking at once, and Vecnor caught a few of their queries and statements.

"Who gets the head? Arubit or Kodahn?"

"Kodahn, you bumbler! He the one kill puny man!"

"I want intestines."

"There not enough to go around! Me want piece too!"

"Eyes are tasty. Me want eyes!"

Vecnor drew his swords and twirled them, gaining the ogres' attention. "This is all quite fascinating. But I'm still alive."

"Not for long!" Kodahn growled.

The ogre took two steps, reducing the twenty-foot gap separating them to ten, and swung the club down with surprising speed. Vecnor dodged to the side and charged, bringing his left sword in an arc and slicing the ogre's calf. He followed with a spin, and thrust his right blade into Kodahn's lower back, careful not to penetrate too deeply — he dared not cripple the oaf. He danced away, displaying his blood-covered weapons for all to see.

Kodahn roared, charging with a distinct limp, and the club fell twice. Vecnor dodged both strikes. He leaped onto a wide stump, forcing the ogre to turn, and received the attack he had hoped for. Kodahn was unbalanced, and Vecnor allowed the weapon to strike his left pauldron. But even an unbalanced attack from an ogre was enough to maim most warriors, and Vecnor tumbled across the clearing. His shoulder remained whole, but it was an injury he would not soon forget.

The ogres erupted with excitement.

Vecnor rose, acting as if he had lost his senses, and stumbled to a tree. Kodahn charged and swung, and Vecnor ducked behind the maple, allowing it to absorb most of the blow. He accepted the remainder of the strike on his right hip and went sprawling again.

The ogres laughed.

Vecnor stood, lowering his swords as a man whose strength was failing. It hurt to move, but he made his way to a wide stump he had eyed before entering the encampment. Kodahn followed, lifting the club high, and gravity added to its force as the ogre brought it down. Vecnor dropped, and the ground quaked when the enormous weapon struck the stump, halting an inch from his head. He pushed his helmet free, as if Kodahn had knocked it loose, and scraped the studs of his gauntlet across his lip, nose, and cheek to make them bleed. Vecnor then rolled to his feet, panting.

"Stop!" commanded Arubit.

Kodahn squeezed his club, his eyes filled with ire while glaring at Vecnor. "Puny man is mine!"

Arubit lifted his chin. "Me the one who is challenged. Me the one who makes the kill."

Vecnor almost smiled.

Kodahn's grayish-purple face turned multiple shades of red, and he stomped away while Arubit strode forward. The ogre leader carried a club similar to the others, except it bore spikes, as if the weapon alone couldn't pulverize most foes.

"After me eats you," Arubit said, "me eats the elf hiding in the tree."

The ogres scanned the maple where Xorlunder was cleverly hidden.

Not cleverly enough.

Vecnor raised his swords, twirling the right blade twice.

Arubit charged.

Vecnor side stepped the first blow, and the club split the stump that had been his refuge moments ago. The weapon came again, and Vecnor steered it above his head with his left sword—his shoulder screamed out for the pain. He advanced, thrusting a blade into his opponent's stomach and causing the brute to roar, and followed with an upward slash to Arubit's elbow.

The ogre's right hand released the club, leaving one hand to make the next attack. Vecnor drove the weapon's spikes into a stump. He countered with both swords, issuing a pair of gashes across Arubit's chest. The ogre kicked at Vecnor while jerking the club free, and Vecnor ducked beneath the enormous leg and thrust a blade into the filthy barefoot, inciting another bellow. Arubit collapsed with a ground-shaking crash.

Vecnor leaped onto the monstrous body, dragging a sword along the torso as he raced toward Arubit's head. He then pushed the other sword partway into the ogre's throat.

"You will take your folk and leave this forest." Vecnor leaned over so Arubit could hear his next words clearly. "And if I ever see you again, I will kill you!"

The clearing fell silent. Arubit, the strongest of his clan, lay beneath Vecnor, breathing heavily while his reddish eyes on yellow orbs darted left and right. The ogres appeared hesitant to move.

"Benasti Forest not bad place to live," Arubit mumbled at last. "Orlenfel stink of elfs anyway."

"I best not discover a trail of carnage in your wake," Vecnor warned. "And remember my promise. You leave today."

He looked at the gawking ogres as he stepped from Arubit's chest, adding a cut from the monster's throat to the side of its neck — enough to make the chieftain cringe. After lifting his helmet from the ground, he exited the clearing, and no one attempted to stop him.

Xorlunder dropped from the tree to join Vecnor. "I cannot believe what I just saw. There is no equal to your strength or skill, regardless of race."

"I am Vecnor." He smiled, tasting the blood seeping from his lip. He wiped his blades clean and sheathed the weapons, grunting as his shoulder and hip reminded him of their conditions.

"We should tend to your injuries," Xorlunder said.

Vecnor shook his head. "Not until we're safely away. I can bear it until then."

And so, the ogres abandoned Orlenfel Forest. The gray elves thanked Vecnor and the Kalmirans for their assistance, but Vecnor refused all offers of reward. Before departing with his soldiers, he shared one last conversation with Xorlunder.

"I want you to remember this day," Vecnor said. "A time will come when others need your help."

"We do not trust outsiders." Xorlunder shrugged. "As impressive as your display was, my telling of the story may not be enough to move those that did not witness it."

"I meant *you*." Vecnor eyed the gray elf. "I cannot say how I know, but a day will arrive when help is sought. *You* must answer that call."

Xorlunder held a measuring gaze. "You are strange, even for a human. But I believe your words. How shall I know when this help is the assistance you speak of?"

"If ever the Council of Wizards reaches out," Vecnor said, "I beg you to listen. Even if their request seems trivial."

"Were you sent by the Seer?"

Vecnor smirked. "More or less."

The surviving Kalmiran soldiers, a score in all, returned to Burmagaard as heroes. They knew nothing of Vecnor's visit to the ogres' camp, and Vecnor made no mention of it when reporting to Castle Darmhorng.

A decade later, Prince Karrak became king at last. Vecnor was not present for the coronation. He had said his goodbyes a week prior, much to Karrak's dismay.

Vecnor's road led him northward to Peltagarr. There, he enjoyed a festival to celebrate the ascension of the new king, and no event involving Brondor was complete without tournaments of combat; contests of swords, axes, hammers, bows, and knives, as well as fist fights and tests of strength. Vecnor entered the tournament of swords. None of the competitors presented a challenge, but he was not there for the prize—a gold ring set with a single amethyst. He dazzled the crowds, utilizing both of his blades, and took care not to kill anyone willing to yield, which included all but one arrogant fool.

Once the contests were over, Vecnor visited a Brondor church to pay his respects, just as Elgarroth's instructions commanded. In the building's courtyard, several children fought with wooden weapons while training to represent their god. Vecnor smiled. To the opposite side was a lone girl holding a pair of wooden swords. She attempted to twirl the blades, but her left hand was lacking in coordination.

Vecnor approached.

"You!" The girl's excitement stretched her smile from ear to ear. "You're the one from the tournament! I watched every match."

"I am Vecnor!" He kneeled to look at her eye to eye.

"My name's Elloria." Her grin remained. "You must tell me how you swing both swords so well."

Vecnor chuckled. "First, it's in your stance."

He instructed Elloria on proper form for an hour. Upon completion—rather, once the children were called inside for spiritual guidance—he proceeded to the worship hall to pray.

Over the next decade, Vecnor performed heroic deeds across the western realms. Elgarroth insisted he enter Neja as well—a place he always avoided—for a line of kings had emerged among the outlaws a few centuries prior. Vecnor complied. He didn't enjoy the year he roamed the wasteland, but he discovered not all Nejans were criminals, and many of them were deserving of respect. Still, he spent more days battling bandits there than within any other dominion.

After leaving Neja, Vecnor headed home, as he did every five to ten years. His list of friends was not yet complete, but the road had grown weary and he craved solid rest. And though he had plenty of gold for inn rooms, there was something special about the clearing where he lived. There, he recovered twice as fast as anywhere else. But as he reached the edge of the hidden glade in Vermallon Forest, elfish voices that were not Elgarroth's or Tux's brought him to a halt. Guests? His body transformed into its elfish guise and Umbarc shrank before they set foot on the cabin grounds, confirming his suspicion. It was Selanna and Eraim… again.

Selanna first visited four decades ago, insisting Elgarroth mentor her. The wizard surprisingly agreed. Eraim accompanied the golden-haired elf most times, and the two had randomly showed up ever since. Presently, the Salenti elves sat around the fire with Elgarroth, enjoying a laugh. Eraim was the only one to acknowledge elf-Vecnor's arrival, offering a nod while Selanna asked Elgarroth a seemingly innocent question, attempting to discover a part of the wizard's past. Elgarroth dodged the query with masterful skill. Tux was nowhere to be seen, as was usual when the maidens were in attendance.

Please see to the wood, Elgarroth said in Vecnor's head.

So much for rest and relaxation.

Chapter 7

Ironside Keep

After a week of chopping wood and serving food and drinks, Vecnor headed west from the House of Elgarroth to complete the next task on his list. Selanna and Eraim were still present, as Elgarroth was instructing the former on incantations while the smaller elf wandered among the trees. Because of these wanderings, Vecnor remained in his elfish guise until exiting Vermallon Forest. He and Umbarc then reclaimed their true forms and turned north.

A week later, Vecnor rode past Bouldertown, arriving at the southern edge of the Coranthiar Mountains the following day. There, a mountain ranger and his family made a life in the wild. Vecnor posed as a traveler headed to Andria, and the family was hospitable and boarded him in their barn. The next morning, he paid his way clear to stay a fortnight by working around the house. He performed arduous tasks that Wistin, the owner, could not handle alone or with the help of his petite wife nor his young daughter, Arrikan.

Arrikan was a delightful child. She seemed advanced for her age and exuded a passion for mountain living, but also she enjoyed games and caring for Umbarc. She almost made Vecnor wish he had children of his own.

Once his stay ended, Vecnor left, but he visited four other times over the next eight years. The family always welcomed him.

After his initial visit to the ranger's house, Vecnor journeyed for a decade between Kalmaar and Moclen. While in Kalmaar he roamed the land, doing good for Kalmirans, and occasionally offered his sword to King Karrak, who attempted more than once to retain his services permanently. But he never remained for more than a couple of months. In Tikken City, Vecnor became well known to the Council of Wizards, taking on tasks too dangerous for their personal guards to handle alone. Rarely did the wizards allocate their military for matters other than protecting Council members visiting foreign realms, but occasionally they assisted Urell Coast in combating monsters from Tall Pines Forest or dispatched soldiers to help keep the growing number of bandits in check. During the last mission Vecnor attended, he made friends with a young guard named Dellen. The red-headed soldier showed lots of potential, and Vecnor did what he could to encourage the man.

Vecnor spent the next few years in Sardina, passing from the north to the south and back again… and again. While in the south, he frequented Ironside Keep in the Varlimor Mountains. Vecnor remembered when Grellmor Ironside first built the pass between Sardina and Marcove. It was a costly venture, and had unintentionally provided access for Marc and Nomish raiders into the west. But construction of the stronghold carved into the mountainside restored the peace, and the road eventually became a profitable route for trade.

Seven generations later, Grellmor's descendant ruled Ironside Keep. Lord Vikur performed the duties of his father and his father's father—and so on—along with his brother, Arkor. Vikur stood tall and wiry with unkempt brown hair, while Arkor was muscular with dark hair and a face to catch a lady's eye. And their personalities proved just as contrary. Vikur was boisterous and fun loving. Arkor was a man of few words.

When Vecnor first arrived at the keep, it surprised him to find a tavern within, as well as several bedrooms for rent. Apparently, two centuries of peace had led Vikur's father to add guestrooms to house weary travelers, and Vikur added the barroom to complete the transformation to an inn. The stronghold remained a military outpost, however, and the hands of its soldiers never strayed far from their weapons with the approach of strangers. Even Arkor appeared uneasy during Vecnor's original visit. It was not so for Vikur.

"Hello, friend!" The Lord of the Keep spoke louder than was necessary for the few feet separating him and Vecnor. "First-time visitors get a drink on the house!"

Vecnor tilted his head. "That's very generous."

"As long as they're not here to stir up trouble, that is." Vikur eyed the swords on Vecnor's back.

Vecnor chuckled and extended his arm. "Name's Vecnor."

Vikur accepted the locking of arms, giving a hard squeeze. "Pleasure to meet you, Vector!"

"It's Vecnor." He emphasized the syllables.

In truth, Vecnor knew Vikur pretty well at that point. He first saw the Lord of the Keep competing in Brondor Tournaments in Kalmaar. Vecnor did not participate in those particular events— Elgarroth forbade it. Instead, he remained in the background to observe. Vikur had employed an older fighting style that confused his opponents, and easily claimed one of the coveted champion rings.

In a matter of hours, Vecnor and Vikur became good friends, and the Lord of the Keep recruited Vecnor to take part in missions for Ironside. During these outings, Vecnor complemented Vikur's battle techniques, making them a formidable duo. Together, they defeated bandits and goblins causing trouble on and around the mountain pass. Though Vikur proved an abled warrior, he talked too much during combat for Vecnor's liking. This often led the lord to receive minor wounds, as well as scars to brag about upon returning to his stronghold.

After a few years, the attacks on the pass ceased. Vikur's only occupation was then sitting in the Ironside tavern on a large chair atop a dais, where he regaled visitors with exaggerated tales about his forays of the recent past. Many accounts were told again and again, each retelling increasing Vikur's heroics until they exceeded Vecnor's contributions. Vecnor hated that chair.

"You should keep a permanent room here," suggested Vikur while he and Vecnor enjoyed a couple of tankards. "It's better than coming and going all the time."

"I have matters elsewhere." Vecnor signaled the barkeep for another beer. "But I'll be around."

Vikur grinned. "It's the competition, isn't it?" He took a long drink and slammed the mug before nodding at the bartender. "I'm used to it. Not everyone can keep up with me."

Vecnor released a chuckle.

"Take my little brother, Arkor." Vikur nodded toward a corner table. "*There's* a man given to jealousy." He shook his head, his smirk prominently displayed.

Vecnor gazed at Arkor. The solemn warrior dined alone. A wooden shaft extended from Arkor's left elbow in place of his arm, and at the end was a hook. That was new. Just a year ago, Arkor had been whole, and he proved himself a solid fighter during one of Vecnor and Vikur's excursions. Hopefully, the change did not hinder the warrior's future too much.

Turning back to Vikur, Vecnor asked, "What happened to his arm?"

"Last year, we met a pair of short elves." Vikur glanced at his brother. "Salenti elves, they called themselves. I've never heard of them. Only ever seen elves from Vermallon, and they're much taller. Stronger too, I'll wager. I once hunted in Vermallon —"

"Your brother's arm?" Vecnor raised a brow.

"Oh! That!" Vikur laughed. "It all started with a pair of —"

"Salenti elves…"

"Yeah." Vikur furrowed his brow. "Did I already tell you this one?"

Vecnor slowly shook his head.

"Right." Vikur's smirk returned. "So this mage, Selanna, comes to the keep."

Vecnor rolled his eyes. Of course it had been Selanna.

"She was playing with magic," Vikur continued, "and a storm starts raining hail." He chuckled. "Never even seen snow on the pass, let alone balls of ice."

Vecnor frowned. "Why did she summon hail?"

The Lord of the Keep waved off the question. "Oh, there were Sardina soldiers following her and her friend, Erane. "

"Eraim," Vecnor said.

"What?"

"Nothing. Please continue."

"Right." Vikur took a swig. "So, Selanna claimed soldiers were unjustly following her and Erade, and she created a small group of clouds to drop ice and scare them off. And I have to say, they left the pass faster than you can imagine!"

"So how did Arkor lose his arm?"

"What?" Vikur's frown turned into realization. "Oh. That came the next day."

Vecnor sighed.

"Sometimes animals wander onto the pass," Vikur said. "And that morning, we awoke to find an enormous lizard outside the keep." He spread his hands all the way apart. "Thing was ten feet long! Selanna, the mage, she says it must have come from underground and died on the road. Emray says she thought it moved, but Selanna says she's positive it's dead." He took another drink. "So Arkor gets impatient, like he always does, and decides to push it into the chasm." Vikur shook his head, his grin spreading. "The thing bites his arm off!"

Vecnor glanced at the corner while the Lord of the Keep bellowed a laugh. Arkor obviously heard the retelling, and wasn't amused. But the one-armed warrior seldom found humor in any of his brother's stories.

Vecnor ordered another beer.

Chapter 8

The Holy City

In between Vecnor's visits to Ironside Keep, he continued building his reputation across Sardina. He helped Charndova defend their walls against raiding barbarians from the south, tracked bandits terrorizing hamlets along King Arman Lake, and battled hobgoblins from Vermallon Forest looking to purloin livestock and gain slaves. As usual, the king of the land made an attractive offer in hopes of gaining Vecnor's services on a permanent basis. Vecnor declined.

During the hobgoblin skirmish, Vecnor happened upon a band of holy warriors out of Palidur. They fought with the discipline of elite soldiers, swinging maces and hammers beneath the command of a paladin standing a foot shorter than most of them. The young woman wielded a golden mace, striking harder than one her size should be able to, and Vecnor sensed divine strength fueling her. Of all the people on his list, Elgarroth was most interested in this woman. She was the one Vecnor must protect at all costs.

The Palidurians were holding their own when Vecnor arrived. But another wave of hobgoblins advanced from the forest, and several krukari were among them. Vecnor then spied a pair of large raiders in dark armor and red cloaks, and upon their heads were skull-like helmets. Zurkan warriors from Benasti Forest. The battle could easily get out of hand.

He charged Umbarc into the melee, slashing his sword from side to side and dropping a handful of hobgoblins. As the evil reinforcements arrived, he dismounted, pulling his other blade while his monstrous steed trampled the enemy. Twenty yards away, a Zurkan with a large axe cleaved a holy soldier. The Benasti warrior then decapitated another. Vecnor advanced, catching the krukari's attention, and they squared off.

Though tall and muscular, as were all Soldiers of Blood, the krukari stood a head shorter than Vecnor. Still, the half-hobgoblin showed no fear. It brought its battleaxe down with brutal force, and Vecnor knocked the weapon aside with his right sword and slashed the Zurkan's thigh with his left. The krukari roared in defiance of the deep gash, swinging its long axe. Vecnor cut through the weapon's haft with one blade before plunging the other into the Zurkan's chest. The raider collapsed.

Vecnor pulled his sword free as the short paladin used her golden mace to snap the leg of the other Zurkan. In the Benasti warrior's wake lay slain holy soldiers, but it added no more kills to its tally as it fell to its knees and the woman bashed its head.

Impressive.

Vecnor returned his attention to the enemy, flailing his swords and killing another score of hobgoblins and krukari. As their numbers dropped to a dozen, they fled for the trees. But the paladin wasn't satisfied. Upon her orders, her contingent gave chase, allowing none to escape justice.

"Who are you?" the woman asked Vecnor as the last hobgoblin fell. "The outlander's champion?"

He smiled. "I am Vecnor."

The paladin removed her helmet and looked him up and down. She was ordinary in appearance, with a face one could easily lose in a crowd, and couldn't be much older than twenty. But she bore an intensity unusual for a warrior her size. "I've heard of you. You've quite the reputation among commoners."

Vecnor bowed.

"But you had no business interfering in this battle." Her eyes narrowed. "You do not fight in harmony with others, and your reckless flailing nearly struck a few of my men."

"I was hardly reckless," he said. "And I defeated as many as your men combined."

The paladin's unwavering glare conveyed her indifference. Her gaze moved to his swords, the blades still dripping with proof of his claim. "And you spoiled the land with evil blood."

"Would you prefer I use a mace next time?" He winked. "Or a hammer or table leg? Maybe I'll rip a limb from one of the enemy and use that."

"You jest?" She placed her mace through a loop on her belt. "I have no time for jests."

"And whom do I have the privilege of speaking with?"

"Merssa Goldmace." She stood half an inch taller with the announcement. "Paladin Knight of Cafior." Merssa eyed her returning soldiers. "And now I must go. Feel free to stay out of our way in the future."

This woman was going to be a treat.

Vecnor interrupted several more of Merssa's operations, and received several more reprimands. It seemed there was nothing he could do to appease the paladin. When vicious creatures from the Fire Hills attempted to expand their hunting grounds, Vecnor joined Merssa's quest to drive them back, using the flat of his blades and issuing as few cuts as necessary. It was still too much. He showed up with a massive hammer while she battled bandits. He bashed the enemy's heads too hard and scattered their brains across the grass. When he tried a pair of maces while Merssa settled a dispute between neighboring lords feuding over farmland, he rent too much flesh from soldiers attempting to ambush her holy entourage. Upon finding her and her platoon battling goblins near the Varlimor Mountains, he used a wooden ladle to thump the small foes while punching with his gauntlet. Once the conflict ended, he smiled at the paladin's approach.

"Do you mock me?" she asked.

Vecnor tossed the ladle over his shoulder, maintaining his grin.

"And why are you following me?" She lowered her brow. "Who sent you?"

"What can I say?" Vecnor shrugged. "I love battle. And it seems to follow you wherever you go."

"I broker peace and put down evil," Merssa said. "I am the Voice of Palidur when outside its walls." She held a measuring gaze. "And I do not need you joining us like a fool to show off your skills with an array of weapons."

Merssa turned and walked away.

"Next time, bring your blasted swords," she added without looking back.

Vecnor smirked.

Afterward, he felt more welcomed in Merssa's company, though her attitude warmed only slightly. But he cared not. Her demeanor was endearing, and her ability to lead others second only to King Karrak. There was something special about Merssa Vecnor couldn't quite place. Her dedication? Determination? Bravery? All paladins possessed those traits. But paladins also tended to be twice her size. The only thing certain was that Vecnor enjoyed traveling with her. She had a knack for rooting out evil, which meant plenty of fighting.

Merssa also performed several tasks outside Sardina's borders, and Vecnor joined her when he could. While in Moclen to combat a budding cult of Demoligius, the evil deity of fire, Vecnor recruited the help of Dellen. The Tikken City guardsman continued to impress, and had progressed from a typical sword to a larger blade, reminiscent of one of Vecnor's, though visibly smaller. Dellen took an instant shine to Merssa, and asked Vecnor about her when they were alone.

"I think you're overreaching," said Vecnor. "She's a paladin."

Dellen lifted his brow. "She's also a woman."

Vecnor chuckled. "Are you sure she's aware of that?"

"Love conquers all, my friend." The guardsman winked. "It conquers all."

During another assignment into Moclen, it surprised Vecnor to learn Merssa was familiar with Selanna and Eraim. Apparently, the mischievous duo had accompanied her on a couple of excursions, when Vecnor was occupied elsewhere. Until that moment, Vecnor had only seen the elves from afar. The relationship between the paladin and Salenti maidens was confusing, for Selanna perpetually irritated Merssa, and on more than one occasion, Merssa threatened to charge Eraim with crimes if the elf didn't abandon all shady activities. Still, the Salenti tricksters likely helped Merssa complete her tasks quicker than was usual and with fewer losses to her squadron. All the same, Vecnor hoped the paladin didn't put too much faith in the pair.

Eraim and Selanna took an instant liking to Vecnor, meaning they enjoyed searching for ways to tease him. He wore a stoic expression when the two were around, hoping to avoid their shenanigans, but comments were unavoidable—especially from Selanna. The only consolation was fighting beside Eraim. Though Vecnor had seen her abilities already, she was much quicker when up close. As well, she was capable of pleasant conversations when Selanna was busy with other matters.

Vecnor also joined Merssa when she traveled to Ironside Keep on business. Palidur learned of Denvale denying access to Marcove unless travelers paid a toll, and the High Order of the Holy City sent the paladin to express their disapproval. Vikur accompanied Merssa and Vecnor, insisting he related with Marcs better than most. During the meeting with the lord of Denvale, however, Vikur's constant interruptions, jests, and outrageous suggestions led the paladin to expel him from the room. Merssa then resolved the issue with threats of allocating holy soldiers to "assist" in keeping the town safe. The Marc lord relented, offering a sarcastic apology, but a sincere one swiftly replaced it beneath Merssa's ensuing glare.

On the return trip to Ironside Keep, Vikur was not at a loss for words, and he spoke of how he and Merssa made a great team.

"It was a good idea asking me to leave the room." Vikur chuckled. "The fool would have agreed to anything to keep *me* from coming back in!"

Vecnor expected Merssa to shove Vikur into the chasm north of the pass. Instead, she expressed her desire for him to cease speaking several times. Vikur always laughed.

"I didn't realize how funny paladins could be," he said after they reached his home.

Though the hour was late, Merssa declined Vikur's invitation to stay until morning, opting to brave the dark road ahead rather than a night in the keep.

Vecnor took in a deep breath. He now possessed more friends than he had ever known. But to what end? He would soon disappear, and they would likely not see him again until they were much older. A depressing thought. He pushed it down deep, as he always did. It was better to live in the moment.

CHAPTER 9

COUNCIL OF THREE

The time came at last when Elgarroth called Vecnor home. Vecnor had just finished traveling with Selanna and Eraim while the two visited Kalmaar to "absorb culture" in the far east. Elgarroth had encouraged him to do so, and the elves happily accepted his company. Most days, Vecnor felt like a parent keeping his children from finding too much trouble—especially in Selanna's case. The whole affair made him grateful to receive the mental summons.

As they entered Vermallon, Selanna expressed a desire to visit Rivercross and pester merchants. While the mage and Eraim discussed their route, Vecnor slipped away from Vermallon Road and into the trees.

Tux was sitting on a log when Vecnor arrived at the clearing. Vecnor had seen little of the half-gray elf over the past five decades. It wasn't uncommon for them to spend years apart, but they were busier than usual, from seemingly random investigations to supervising the elf maidens. Elgarroth was not present.

Vecnor took a seat by the fire. Tux nodded with his typical lack of emotion. The elf seldom revealed expressions of happiness, surprise, or anger—or any other, for that matter. After spending time in Orlenfel Forest, Vecnor realized this to be a gray elf trait.

"What have you been up to?" Vecnor asked.

Tux poked the flames with a long stick. "Nothing fun, I promise you." He looked at Vecnor. "I have spent my days beyond the Shield River. Some of it working with the Guardians, but also I had to familiarize myself with Beit." He sneered at the campfire. "Such a despicable realm."

Vecnor lifted a brow at the elf's strong words.

"But it was not as bad as Helmland." Tux shook his head. "Horrible place. Nothing lives there. Just a few reminders of the Enemy."

Vecnor found it odd that Tux occasionally referred to Uustaag that way. Though the Great War was before Vecnor's time, most folks during his childhood called Uustaag the Face of Evil, while others said warlord or similar such words. It was Vermallon elves that began the Ancient Enemy of the North label, and it spread quickly. Elgarroth always used Uustaag's name when referring to the krukari.

Vecnor proceeded to share his travels with Tux. The elf seemed more interested in playing with the fire.

"Quite a pair, Selanna and Eraim," Tux said once Vecnor finished his story. "Eraim, especially. She is a tricky one."

Vecnor nodded. "A very skilled warrior with that sword you provided."

"I pray she deserves it." Tux eyed Vecnor. "It is very special. And very old. A legendary artifact, forged by my people."

"She calls it Mithkahr," mentioned Vecnor.

Tux came close to smiling. "She is educated to know that name."

Elgarroth stepped from the house. The wizard's expression was calm, but something was amiss.

Had the lighting dimmed?

Elgarroth looked from Tux to Vecnor as he joined them. "Darkness approaches."

A chill coursed down Vecnor's spine.

"Something to do with Helmland or Beit?" asked Tux. "Perhaps Selanna and Eraim?"

"Or Merssa?" added Vecnor. "Or one of the many strange acquaintances I've made over the last twenty years?"

Elgarroth shook his head. "It is all of them. They all play a part, of that I am certain. It is not exactly clear… It seldom is. You both know Selanna is important to me, but I will tell you this: Merssa is another matter. It is vital she survives. In my visions, succeeding without her…" He shook his head again. "Let me just say that she is instrumental in overcoming what lies ahead."

"What is it?" Vecnor leaned forward, awaiting the answer.

"I am not sure. I only know that a storm is coming. It will cover Vaeldor with an evil power that should not be possible." Elgarroth stared into the flames. "And it will test us all."

Vecnor released a slow exhale. For centuries, he had traveled Vaeldor on errands for his master—tasks proving enjoyable for the most part. In all that time, Elgarroth had never appeared so grim. So concerned.

"Everything we have done has led to this," Elgarroth said. "I know not where this evil comes from, but it will begin shortly. Perhaps a couple of weeks. Maybe sooner."

"What are we to do?" asked Vecnor.

"We guide," Elgarroth replied, "through counsel and actions." He looked pointedly at Vecnor. "We do not lead or try to solve this on our own. That is not our purpose in this world."

It seemed to Vecnor he was being picked on. Of course, he was more likely to take control of a situation than was Tux. Elgarroth's point was probably warranted.

"Do you have any insight into what it is we are to face?" asked Tux. "Monsters? Wizards? War?"

Elgarroth gave a slight shake of his head. "All of that and more. I hesitate to share too much, for the path has many intersections. But I will keep you informed as the directions of Vaeldor become clearer." He looked at Tux. "For now, you need to observe activities in and around Palidur." He turned to Vecnor. "You will go to Tikken City."

Vecnor raised a brow. "Observe?"

"No." Elgarroth narrowed his eyes. "There will be fighting there. I am not sure what they will face, exactly. But in this particular instance, you have permission to take charge and resolve whatever comes your way."

Vecnor grinned. "I can do that."

"Once Merssa arrives," Elgarroth added, "you will play your part. You will be at her disposal until I tell you otherwise."

Vecnor nodded.

❊ ❊ ❊

Vecnor readied Umbarc while Tux brought Landolice into the clearing. The elf's mount was a Batorn steed, sleek black in color, and the fastest horse Vecnor had ever seen. And like Umbarc, it was more intelligent than others of its breed—a positive side effect when the animals were accepted into their roles and granted long lives.

"Elgarroth has never behaved this way." Tux looked at Vecnor. "I wish you well on your part. Be safe."

"Don't worry about me." Vecnor winked. "I am Vecnor."

Tux revealed a rare smile, and they clasped arms.

"Watch yourself," Vecnor said.

He led Umbarc to the northern edge of the clearing. With a deep breath, he began the journey to Tikken City.

Chapter 10
Wind of the Dead

Vecnor reached Tikken City after eight days on the road. Many recognized him upon his arrival, and it wasn't long before Dellen found him in a tavern.

"Well, look what crawled into my fair city." The guardsman smiled as he approached.

Dellen was larger now, having come into full manhood, and he sported a short, curly beard to match his dark red hair. As usual, he wore a Tikken City tabard over his chain shirt, a night-blue surcoat with a circle of eleven stars. But this one differed slightly from those of the past. The topmost star was gold and not white. Dellen was Captain of the Guard.

Vecnor grinned. "Does the captain have time for a drink?"

"Perhaps later." Dellen glanced over his shoulder and back. "I'm on duty at the moment."

"And what does your duty demand… at the moment?"

"As you can imagine," Dellen scratched his beard, "the Council is aware of your arrival. Has them a bit nervous, wondering if there's any particular reason for your visit."

Vecnor chuckled. Over the past decade, Seac the Seer viewed his presence as a bad omen. He couldn't blame the wizard. And on this occasion, the Seer was right to be concerned.

"I'm on a holiday." Vecnor lifted his mug to his lips.

"So… no Merssa?" Dellen scanned the barroom with hopeful eyes.

"Sorry. I'm traveling alone."

"Good." Dellen put his hand on Vecnor's shoulder. "Very good." He headed for the exit, saying, "I'll catch up with you later."

Over the next couple of days, Vecnor visited merchants and hung out in taverns, playing the part of a man on vacation. Everywhere he went, citizens paid for his drinks and food. It was rather boring. On the third day, things changed.

Vecnor was browsing the goods of a weapons merchant in the market square when an icy breeze came out of the northwest. The wind grew in strength with each passing moment, lifting loose dirt, rattling signs, and flapping cloaks like banners, and the stronger it blew, the colder it became.

The storm has arrived, Elgarroth said in Vecnor's mind.

Vecnor made his way to his inn room to don his armor and strap on his swords. He then returned to the street, where screams of terror greeted him. Racing toward the nearest calls for help, he spotted a raggedy skeleton raking its bony fingers across a fleeing man's back. Cowering nearby were a woman and two young boys. Vecnor advanced, pulling one of his blades and slicing through the skeleton's ribcage and spine. It collapsed to the cobblestones.

"Thank you, Black Rogue!" the wounded man said.

Vecnor gazed up and down the street. "Get your family inside."

Without making sure they carried out his order, Vecnor hurried north until a scream sounded from a house on the right. He kicked open the door to find another family terrorized by the undead. Two skeletons and a zombie, all dressed in formal garb, advanced on a mother huddled with her child in a corner. A man lay bleeding on the floor.

Vecnor decapitated the zombie without delay. He then drove his sword through both skeletons with a single swing, reducing them to piles of bones.

"Where did these things come from?" he asked the petrified woman.

"The... The..." She swallowed, pointing at an open door. "The family crypt."

Beyond the door, stairs descended into darkness. Vecnor followed the steps into a small, dank room bare of furnishings. The light from above revealed six empty niches, like bunks carved into the walls, and each was large enough to house an adult. Three appeared unused, while broken panels of wood littered the floor beneath the others, as if the corpses had busted their way out.

Vecnor returned upstairs, where the woman was dabbing the man's wounds. Without a word, he exited back onto the street.

Several zombies and skeletons now infested the city. Did all the houses possess crypts? Guards fought the sudden enemy, but the watchmen were scattered and unorganized.

"Dellen!" Vecnor said to himself.

He pressed deeper into the city, slaying undead while barking orders for guardsmen to follow. The soldiers made no objections and fell in line.

"Where's your captain?" Vecnor demanded every time another soldier joined his ranks.

None of them knew.

They battled east toward the Council Building. Before reaching the walled structure where the wizards resided, Vecnor spotted Dellen at last. The captain swung an enormous hammer, and three dozen guards fought beside him — half the size of Vecnor's following. With their forces united, they quickly cleared the area.

"Vecnor!" Relief filled Dellen's eyes.

"Where's your army?" Vecnor asked.

"Half will have been in the barracks. The others have their own homes." Dellen shook his head. "They're spread across the city."

"We'll start at the barracks," Vecnor said, "and work our way from there."

Dellen nodded.

They headed south, opposed by walking corpses at every turn, and the farther they pressed, the larger their force became. By the time they reached the barracks, their number had tripled. Assembled outside the building were another hundred warriors, and several more exited while fastening their weapon belts.

"Strange how this block is free of the undead," commented Vecnor.

"Very few family crypts in the area," Dellen said.

"How many houses have them?"

Dellen shook his head. "They were a custom when Tikken City was young. Perhaps two-thirds of the homes. There must be thousands buried below."

"Not anymore," Vecnor mumbled. "We'll have to check all residences."

They battled throughout the day, defeating the undead until the number of corpses dwindled at last. The size of their force had grown to over six hundred, and some showed signs of fatigue, but there was no rest to be had as a high-pitched tone blared across the sky.

"That's the west tower," said Dellen. "We're under attack."

The captain led the way, blowing his horn every so often to rally his troops. Upon reaching the gate, Vecnor and Dellen found several watchmen already gathered, and their combined muster provided the army Vecnor had hoped for.

A constant thumping sounded against the large doors, but it wasn't a battering ram. It was like hundreds of fists pounding on the wood without rhythm. Atop the walls, archers loosed arrows at those attempting to gain access.

"Captain Dellen!" a guard called down. "We've skeletons and zombies. A horde of them! And more approach."

Dellen turned to Vecnor. "What do we do?"

Vecnor eyed the bowmen on the ramparts. "Arrows are of little use. They might drop some of the zombies, but skeletons… They're worthless against that foe." He grinned at the captain. "You ready?"

Dellen frowned. "Are you sure? They'll never break in. I mean, I know we can't have them infesting the fields outside, but… Are you sure?"

"I'm Vecnor!" He winked. "Have them open the gates."

The battle beyond the city wall lasted a few hours. The day was won, and a picturesque sunset captured the sky as if to mark the victory. Tikken City lost over three hundred soldiers, but they defeated ten times that number.

After returning through the gates, the large doors were closed tight and celebrations began. But Vecnor and Dellen did not join in the many rounds of toasting Tikken City's achievement. The captain separated his finest warriors into squads, and they searched throughout the night for undead still roaming about. The rest of the watch, he tasked with carting dead bodies from the city, as well as removing the corpses from outside the west gate.

Unease weighed heavily upon Vecnor's mind. Never had he experienced undead in such numbers. And this was only the beginning.

CHAPTER 11

A DREADED RETURN

The Council of Wizards summoned Vecnor the next morning. He and Dellen were still searching homes when the messenger tracked him down. The hunt uncovered very few undead through the night, mainly a smattering of zombies feasting on victims in alleyways, and Vecnor discovered a zombie-child locked in a bedroom by its parents for safekeeping.

The meeting with the Council was short. Seac and the wizards wished to express their appreciation for Vecnor's part in protecting the city—a waste of time. Upon exiting the building, Vecnor spied a Palidurian ship along the Tikken City docks. Merssa had arrived.

That evening, a messenger addressed Dellen while Vecnor and the captain enjoyed a well-earned dinner in a tavern.

"A note from the Council, sir." The man presented a sealed parchment.

Dellen accepted the scroll with a nod, and the courier departed. After breaking the wax seal, the captain's lips moved while he read the letter, and a smile crept to one side.

"The Council summons me." He rolled the parchment and looked at Vecnor. "It seems the dead rose across the lake as well. And Merssa has arrived to investigate."

Vecnor lifted his brow. "I see."

"I have orders to journey with her to Neja." Dellen struggled to conceal his grin while his eyes sought the door.

"She's not here on holiday," Vecnor said. "Last night was disturbing, to say the least."

Dellen nodded. "I know. But I can't help feeling we are constantly brought together for a reason." He eyed his weapon leaning against the table. "Did you notice I use a hammer now?"

"I once used a ladle."

Dellen ignored the statement. "I vacationed near Palidur last summer. The Holy City's an intimidating place, but I dined with Merssa a couple times. We talked at length about my use of the sword and the harm it brings to the soil."

Vecnor held his laughter in check.

The captain lifted the hammer. "You think she'll like it?"

Vecnor changed the subject. "If it's Neja you aim for, I'll join you."

"I haven't been there in years." Dellen frowned. "Despicable place. I welcome your company."

The next morning, Vecnor waited with the captain in the empty audience chamber of the Council Building. Dellen insisted on reporting before sunrise, so they didn't keep Merssa waiting—he knew her well. While the captain made small talk, Vecnor half listened. His eyes returned time and time again to the door. How had Merssa gotten on without him over the past year? As strange as it seemed, he missed her commanding presence. But more than that, he realized the danger that lay before her. How badly he wished to divulge everything Elgarroth had shared.

Merssa arrived shortly after Dellen began reminiscing about the prior day's battles. Her expression was business-like, as usual. During their pleasantries, and Dellen making a love-struck fool of himself, Vecnor learned Selanna and Eraim would be joining them.

The room suddenly seemed darker. It wasn't Eraim so much; he enjoyed fighting beside her. But she never traveled without her annoying companion. Though Vecnor had only journeyed with the pair on a handful of occasions, he had witnessed enough of the mage's pranks to last a lifetime, including the additional nine centuries Elgarroth added to his normal years. That made ten lifetimes. Why someone as talented as Selanna used her abilities to spill drinks,

summon indoor rain, and cause peoples' limbs to seem to disappear —
among several other infuriating tricks — was beyond Vecnor. Merssa
was cognizant of his feelings about Salenti elves, and he was sure she
found humor with the situation — as much as was possible for the
paladin. In the end, there was nothing he could do, and he cringed
when Selanna passed through the door.

They set out on the northern road. The day was interrupted by
the icy wind's return, and not long after, the company destroyed a
few zombies, two of them older and the third one a fresh corpse. Later
that day, they encountered a dwarf named Poluran on Korban
Bridge. Poluran was large for his race, being from the Stone Eagle
Mountains, and he fought skeletons with a magnificent battleaxe.
The weapon seemed familiar to Vecnor, as if he had heard stories
about it many centuries ago, but he couldn't recall from where.
Elgarroth saw it as well, for Vecnor sensed the wizard in his mind,
but offered no hints as to its origin. Poluran joined the company once
the skeletons were defeated.

The following night, they faced ghouls while camping within a
small woodland, and Vecnor grimaced when one of the fiends
scratched Merssa's neck. It reminded him of his time in Sistama. The
undead were no match for the company's strength, and the battle
ended in victory. Other than Merssa, only Dellen received injuries.

"Is it not odd for ghouls to travel about the wild?" Selanna asked
Vecnor while Merssa tended to the ghoul wounds. "I thought they
inhabited crypts and ruins and such."

She was right to question the creatures prowling like animals on
the hunt. Before Vecnor could respond, Elgarroth entered his mind.

We must learn more. Do not mention Sistama.

The command suited Vecnor just fine. The expedition through
the swamp haunted him still, and he desperately wished to avoid
reliving it.

"In most places," he answered Selanna. "But it is strange, I
agree."

"Perhaps the Wind has drawn them from their lairs," suggested Eraim.

A horrid thought. Probably close to the truth.

The journey led them to Ellaville. Ghouls had decimated the village in northwestern Virch, and the only survivors were an innkeeper named Larman and his family. Vecnor, Merssa, and Dellen found them tucked away in the tavern cellar. Merssa offered to take them elsewhere, and although she could've been more hospitable with her proposal, Larman accepted without reacting to her icy demeanor. Like Vecnor, the man seemed to sense the goodness in her soul.

In Eastgate, things worsened. The conversation with Baron Karlsum bore no fruit. It only brought to light the lord's cowardice. Merssa's apprehension grew when the wind blew yet again, and the company raced from the Baron's stronghold.

Vecnor stood in the doorway while the others searched the sky. The wind had ceased.

"It comes from Sistama." Selanna's focus remained southward, as if the buildings of Eastgate didn't exist.

"You're sure?" Merssa's voice was dry, and uneasiness haunted her eyes.

Selanna nodded. "I thought it came from Helmland, but it is not so. The wind came from the south; from Sistama. I have no doubt."

"I hear a great dragon lives there," said Dellen.

"Nonsense." Poluran shook his head. "Those creatures are long gone. It's ghosts that haunt that land."

"*Something* haunts it." Eraim lowered her brow. "I have lived in Salenti for nearly one and a half centuries, and Sistama has been draped in darkness since before even my days. Something lurks there, that is certain, but I hesitate to guess as to what."

"I have gazed upon it on occasion," Selanna said, "though I never dared to enter. There exists no book in any library to explain how it has come to such darkness. It is an impenetrable black cloud, emitting no sound, and the trees of the Tall Pines that feed on its waters grow in grossly twisted shapes. All who have dared to enter have never been seen again."

Not Sistama. Elgarroth's concern was obvious. *You are not ready for the swamp. I do not wish for harm to come to Selanna, and Merssa* must *survive.*

"I have been there." Vecnor ignored the wizard's warning. The company's discussion was surely leading Merssa to enter the bog, and he needed to make sure they were prepared—as prepared as was possible. He'd deal with the consequences later. "It has been ten and two years since my path led me so," he lied about the time, "but I have seen the desolate marshland from within."

The paladin shot him a look both quizzical and annoyed.

"That is where I first fought the likes of ghouls." He shook his head. "It is infested with them."

Elgarroth said nothing.

As expected, Merssa announced her intention to enter the marsh, and they rode south.

Before reaching the swamp, they encountered a strange village called Cafdella. It was an oasis in the middle of the wasteland, and a humble priest of Cafior resided there with his loyal following. The lanky man went by the name Borse, and though Merssa failed to see it, he radiated a gentle soul. Borse treated Merssa with respect, even in the face of her doubt and sarcasm, and everyone enjoyed a meal within the village's Feast Hall.

The journey to the swamp continued, and the company camped outside its dark border. During the night, a marteese in dirty, tattered clothing emerged from its cloud. It was Olinin, a mage from Neja who had dedicated his life to helping those of mixed races. As well, he had spent the past two centuries studying the Silent Marsh. His skin was blue and freezing to the touch, and his agony plain for all to see. He didn't live much longer, but before his demise, he presented Selanna with his map of the bog and a piece of parchment bearing a single name written in Ancient Moclen: Trannum.

Come morning, Vecnor led the way into the dark haze. His heart pounded in protest as the freezing air stung his lungs and the evil essence turned his stomach. But none of the swamp's elements were shocking during the arduous trek—how could anyone forget the murky plants, unmoving water, sludge, green-spotted pools, and wading through rivers? Ghouls were present as well, but they kept their distance. Strange.

As evening arrived, they reached the hill where Vecnor and Tux had camped long ago, and Poluran discovered the tattered remains of the blanket Vecnor discarded. How had the material survived? It was as if time crawled within the marshland. Just as before, the soil atop the mound was not so saturated and Vecnor could see farther into the haze. As well, Sistama had tainted all food, rotting everyone's meat and wilting their vegetables, and starting a fire was impossible, even with Selanna's magical assistance. The company settled in for a miserable night.

The next morning, Selanna and Merssa neglected to seek Vecnor's input while discussing a new course of action. Worse still, the mage persuaded Merssa to cut across the swamp to make for a quicker route. Did they believe Vecnor enjoyed the vile bog? That he preferred being covered in freezing muck and smelling like a corpse? Perhaps lack of sleep and edible food affected their minds. Not only had Vecnor braved the quagmire before, but with Olinin's map, he could certainly lead them to the house the marteese discovered. Unfortunately, Selanna had no more patience for following rivers, regardless of Vecnor's warnings about getting lost, and convinced Merssa to alter the plan. Vecnor's disdain for the elf turned to anger. But it wasn't his place to decide. He obeyed Merssa's order.

They got lost. And despite Vecnor's attempts to return to the original path, Merssa was unrelenting in her resolve to cut through the swamp, even after Twisted Wood attempted to dump them into Flesh Pond and ghouls attacked in the night. It was as if she bore a need to defeat the Silent Marsh. Or perhaps to *not* be defeated by the marsh. They battled more ghouls while crossing the Slime River, and

Merssa nearly perished. Vecnor needed to be more careful. It was time to abandon his anger and focus on the mission.

A fallen tree bridging a channel was the final obstacle before reaching the cabin. A mysterious river filled the canal, seemingly alive as its calmness transformed into a raging current intent on toppling those crossing over. Merssa refused to acknowledge the occurrence. Vecnor was the last to go, and he leaped to safety a moment before the river swept away the tree-bridge to destinations unknown.

They arrived at the stone house, but its only door could not be opened from the outside. So Eraim climbed down the smokestack to gain access for the company. Anxiety filled the haze while everyone waited, and silence rang in Vecnor's ears. A minute seemed like an eternity, but the door opened at last, revealing Eraim's filth-ridden expressions of horror and then relief.

Vecnor took in a deep breath, realizing he had deprived his lungs the entire time Eraim was absent. He released the tension from his muscles with a steady exhale. The small elf was not his charge, yet he wouldn't have forgiven himself had something happened to her. Perhaps it was the conversations they shared on their way to this horrid place. Since leaving Tikken City, they had fought side by side and held intimate discussions, and Eraim treated Vecnor with respect and compassion. He was suddenly aware of a hollow space in his chest; the presence of an emotion abandoned centuries ago. It would have to be buried again. He turned his focus to the mission.

The cabin was more than it appeared, and Selanna discovered a secret library larger than the house itself. The chamber lacked the odor and moisture of the swamp—it was as if the company had been transported elsewhere. Within were thousands of books, most bearing Trannum's name written in the Ancient Moclen script. The titles mainly dealt with the undead.

Poluran discovered a trapdoor leading to an underground chamber. The room contained only a pedestal upon which rested a large orb. A blue fog swirled inside the orb, shedding an eerie glow, and cold mist drifted from the item to the floor. The spinning vapors captured Vecnor's attention, holding him motionless until Selanna yelled.

"Do not touch it!"

It was too late. Poluran had placed his gauntlet on the sphere, and the fog reversed its direction, rotating faster as it rose from the orb and took the shape of a skull with its right eye shining brightly.

"Who dares to disturb my house?" the skull asked in a hoarse whisper. "All trespassers have forfeit their lives!"

The image dissolved into billowing red smoke that worked its way toward the stairs. Vecnor retreated a few paces with Eraim and Selanna, and the cloud increased in mass until forming a pillar from floor to ceiling. From within came a low growl, and the fog returned to the orb, reclaiming its blue hue and leaving a horrific demon behind.

The monster's red scales defied the room's blue light. Its dark, forked tongue licked the scaly lips of its elongated snout as black smoke seeping from its flaring nostrils obscured its beady eyes. The demon's massive arms ended in three-fingered claws, and it hunched over on thick legs while its short tail swayed back and forth. The fiend's jaws opened, revealing multiple rows of sharp teeth and issuing steam as it roared to announce its presence.

The air thinned as Vecnor's heart pounded in his chest. Never had he faced anything so dreadful.

"Hezeb!" Selanna yelled. "From the pits of Hell!"

Vecnor attacked, but his sword barely penetrated Hezeb's scales. His reflexes took over when Selanna's magical green spheres unbalanced the demon, and he drove it several steps with his shoulder to move it away from his companions. He had never felt so small, not even when battling Arubit. The warmth of the monster's scales penetrated his armor while its sulfuric breath was hot on his face, and searing pain nearly overwhelmed him when its claw tore into his side. Its teeth were sure to follow, but the demon roared at the ceiling instead. Eraim had flanked the creature and buried Mithkahr into its back. The infernal beast cast Vecnor into Dellen, and he and the captain crashed to the side of the stairs.

Dellen rose, but intense pain prevented Vecnor from doing the same. Hezeb, meanwhile, had knocked Mithkahr from Eraim's hand. Selanna released another green ball onto the demon, allowing Eraim to escape its deadly teeth, and Hezeb spun to face the mage. It then balked before the golden glow surrounding Merssa.

"By the Might of Cafior," the paladin called out. "I will smite thee! Back to Hell with you!"

Vecnor struggled to his knee. He couldn't allow Merssa to fall victim to the demon. She struck Hezeb again and again, driving the fiend several steps, and the monster gouged her shoulder with its claw. Selanna launched green spheres to assist the paladin, but Hezeb shrugged them off, its fierce hatred affixed upon its prey. It exhaled fire, forcing Merssa to retreat, and lunged with its gnashing teeth. Vecnor forced himself to his feet and rushed to intercept, but he was too far away.

Dellen was not.

On the previous day, the captain threw himself into harm's way to save Merssa from ghouls in the Slime River. And now he shouldered the paladin from the demon's path. He received the full fury of the beast as Hezeb lifted him from the floor with its jaws and tossed him aside.

Vecnor rammed Hezeb as the creature returned its attention to Merssa — her golden glow had faded. He drove the monster into the pedestal, and the orb created haunting shadows as it rolled across the room.

"Taste Clanghorr!" called out Poluran.

Hezeb roared louder than before, knocking Vecnor prone as it spun to face the dwarf. It then moved with a severe limp toward the stout warrior, leaving a trail of steaming blood.

"Cafior!"

Merssa returned with her mace, her golden glow alive. Half of her body showed charring, and blisters covered most of her exposed skin, but she revealed no pain as she hit Hezeb again and again, driving the monster to the floor. She did not relent until the demon vanished within a cloud of red fog and a flash of light.

The room calmed, but only for a moment. From the corner where the orb had settled, the illumination intensified. A bitter wind then swirled about the chamber, colder than any before it, and the glow evolved from blue to white. Poluran brought down Clanghorr, shattering the sphere and showering everyone with razor-like shards. The light vanished, and the room calmed again.

Hezeb was defeated. The orb was destroyed. Dellen lost his life, and Vecnor and Merssa bore vicious wounds. Merssa was in a horrible state and should have used her healing water on herself, but she forced Vecnor to drink it—additional proof of the caring soul buried beneath her aloof exterior. Vecnor would have to take extra care to protect her while they exited the bog.

Escaping the house was another matter, for the swamp had summoned every ghoul residing within its borders to the area. But Poluran discovered a path of escape, and after Selanna blew out the back wall of a fireplace, they won the race to the river. There, Olinin's boat sat on the shore. Once everyone was aboard, Selanna used magic to steer the craft from the marsh and into Tall Pines Forest. She was resourceful, and her show of power impressed Vecnor. For a moment, he saw her in a different light.

After setting a cairn upon Dellen's body, they struggled through the woodland and to the Trapper's Inn in Sikilaville, a village near the border of Urell Coast and Moclen. The innkeeper was most helpful, providing food, rest, and healing herbs, and he assisted them in procuring horses to transport them back to Tikken City.

Though time was pressing, they rode at a normal pace to accommodate Merssa—her wounds were beyond what the herbs could accomplish. They reached the city at last, and upon entering the Council Building, servants escorted them to private rooms to clean from the road. It was then that Vecnor sensed Elgarroth's presence in his mind.

"Where have you been?" Vecnor's annoyance led him to speak aloud. Had the wizard withheld guidance because he disobeyed?

My attention was needed elsewhere. And you forget I cannot see or hear anything in the swamp.

Vecnor nodded to himself. He should have remembered that. He proceeded to report all that transpired within the bog.

You did well, Elgarroth said. *Go to our usual meeting place at once. No goodbyes.*

Leaving without a word would not sit well with the others. But Vecnor had already defied Elgarroth once. He dared not do so again so soon. He grabbed his gear and departed.

Chapter 12

The High Order

Eslimil spent countless days watching Palidur. It was not easy spying on paladins; they were constantly aware of their surroundings. How was it the Holy Knights did not suffer deaths at young ages from stress alone? Most of the time, Eslimil concealed himself within shadowy alleyways, disappearing whenever someone thought they saw him. At night, when darkness was abundant, he moved closer to his targets. But other than conversations about rising dead and the mysterious wind, there was nothing to learn from the Holy City or its High Order.

A week after Merssa's departure for Tikken City to gather information, a messenger from the Council of Wizards arrived from across the lake with news that she had proceeded to Neja. A couple of the High Priests were visibly upset and questioned having tasked her with the mission.

"She was to speak with the Seer and return!" snapped Garren, the High Priest of Arronaus.

"Merssa is a paladin," said Soren, the High Paladin of Soleran. "And a paladin does not ignore the path of evil."

"But we did not authorize her to journey to Neja," Jerove pointed out. He was the High Priest of Cafior—Merssa's order. "We have more experienced paladins for such a task."

Nilborg, the High Priest of Soleran, cleared his throat to gain the Order's attention. He was the eldest of the group. "Divine favor knows no age. A paladin's connection is not determined by how long they have served Him or Her."

"I agree with Soren and Nilborg," said Arduer, the High Paladin of Cafior. "We should allow Merssa some room in this matter."

The meeting continued, but there was nothing more to draw Eslimil's interest.

A week later, when he thought boredom might claim him, Elgarroth spoke.

Vecnor returns to Tikken City soon. I will meet you both in the usual place. But first you must deliver an elixir to Merssa.

Eslimil sighed. He did not enjoy pilfering from the Holy City—it was like stealing from the poor box in a church. They were the only occasions he chose not to leave his name behind.

Later that night, he passed unseen into the Grand Cathedral's High Temple and floated beyond the altar to the Font of Life, a stone basin seeming to rise from the floor and decorated by a dozen holy runes etched around the rim. It was not particularly eye catching, appearing as if a novice stonemason had completed its construction, but it was unique. Twice a year, servants filled the receptacle with ordinary lake water, and priests performed blessings every morning until the water took on special healing properties. The High Order distributed this elixir to paladins before sending the knights out on assignments, each typically receiving one or two—it depended on how much there was to share. The bowl was nearly empty.

Eslimil looked around the massive domed chamber. He was alone. Below the font were several vials upon a small shelf, some gold, some silver, and others copper. Grabbing a silver vial, Eslimil filled it, leaving enough water for perhaps a couple more.

He moved to the nearest door—the one leading to the Cafior chambers. Holding his breath, he blended with the darkness to pass through the cracks of the door, float along the ceiling of the empty hall beyond, and exit the cathedral.

The silver cobblestones surrounding the building were alive with Palidurians. Moving to a darkened area near the wall, Eslimil landed to take in a few breaths. A warrior peered into the shadows and frowned, unsure if someone was there, and Eslimil quickly inhaled. The man shook his head and walked away.

Eslimil drifted over the wall and around the buildings of the Cafior Sector, alighting on rooftops when the need to breathe arose. He continued until passing over the outer wall to the north, and glided beyond detection of the sentries before exhaling. After a few deep breaths, he gave a low whistle, and Landolice joined him shortly after.

The Batorn steed carried Eslimil almost nonstop around King Arman Lake. They arrived at Tikken City after less than a week and halted just within view of its northern and western gates. There, Eslimil waited until Vecnor and his company appeared along the road out of the north. Umbarc was not with them. The sight of Vecnor atop an ordinary horse was comical—it had been centuries since Eslimil viewed him so—and Selanna and Eraim were strangely dressed. The mage wore a tunic, while the smaller elf looked like a young boy with her hair tucked into a hat. By Merssa's slumped posture, the paladin was surely in dire need of the potion Eslimil carried.

Leaving Landolice behind, Eslimil followed the company unnoticed into the city. It was not hard to sneak into the Council Building—he had performed the task enough to do it in his sleep— and he remained hidden, listening to servants until learning the location of Merssa's guest chamber. He moved swiftly, taking the shortest route to the bedroom, and arrived ahead of the paladin and her escort. The door was unlocked. After depositing the silver vial onto Merssa's night table, Eslimil departed through the window and returned to Landolice. There, he started a small fire.

It was not long before the sun set, and Eslimil detected the approach of his companion. But his eyes never left the wavering flames.

Vecnor dismounted. "You leave the elixir for Merssa?"

Eslimil nodded once.

"Good." Vecnor sat down. "She needs it."

"She will want to be healthy before returning to Palidur." Eslimil looked at the warrior. "It would not be wise to face what awaits her otherwise."

Vecnor raised a brow. "The High Order?"

"Precisely."

Vecnor shrugged. "She's a strong one. She can handle them."

A small silhouette on horseback rode toward Tikken City from the north.

"He has arrived," Eslimil said, offering a piece of sweetbread while watching Elgarroth pass through the city gate.

Vecnor accepted the food. "I'll tell you about my return to Sistama while we wait."

❋ ❋ ❋

The fire was hardly necessary, for the night was warm, but Vecnor knew Elgarroth preferred it. He stood as the wizard approached, an hour after the elf had entered Tikken City. Tux remained seated, staring at the flames.

"Merssa plans to enter the Stone Eagles." Elgarroth sat on the ground.

Vecnor did the same.

"She hopes Trannum's lair is among the white stones known as rorbak," the wizard added. "I suspect she is correct." He turned to Vecnor. "You will join her come morning."

Vecnor nodded.

"I know not what they will encounter," Elgarroth's brow lowered, "so be on your guard. I fear they are not ready to face the necromancer if he is there." He stared intently at Vecnor. "And you are not to confront him."

Vecnor sighed. "Understood." Even after eight centuries, the wizard felt it necessary to remind him of his place.

"What would you have me do?" asked Tux.

100

Elgarroth turned to the Salenti-gray elf. "You will find the house where Olinin dwelt. I want everything he recorded about his journeys into Sistama."

Tux nodded.

Elgarroth rose. "Until next we meet."

Vecnor and Tux watched as the wizard mounted and disappeared into the night. Vecnor had expected a scolding about disobeying an order.

"Do you think he's angry with me?" Vecnor asked. "For entering the swamp against his wishes?"

Tux shrugged. "Maybe. But it is more likely he foresaw and understood your decision. I would not be too concerned."

Vecnor hoped the elf was right.

Without another word, they settled in to get some rest.

CHAPTER 13
TRANNUM

Vecnor rejoined Merssa in Tikken City shortly after sunrise. The paladin was at the Council stables with Eraim, Selanna, and Poluran.

"Where have you been?" Merssa demanded before turning to glare at Vecnor.

"Tending to affairs," he replied.

Eraim gave Vecnor a heartwarming smile. Poluran offered a nod.

"Well, you were almost left behind," Merssa said as she mounted.

They exited Tikken City on horses provided by the Council—the animals that transported them from Sikilaville were unfit for the journey ahead. Following the northern road, they reached Rivercross by dusk, and while Merssa and the elves retired to inn rooms for the night, Vecnor and Poluran headed to the tavern to enjoy a drink. Vecnor had just begun a third tankard when Vikur appeared, pushing his way through the crowd.

"Vecnor!" the Lord of Ironside bellowed. "Is that you, you *dog?*"

Vecnor hadn't seen Vikur in months. Arkor was present as well. The two joined Vecnor and Poluran, and the Lord of the Keep revealed that he and his brother were investigating the undead. There was then no stopping them from joining the mission into Neja. Merssa wouldn't be happy, but another couple of swords might prove handy on the road ahead.

"We leave early tomorrow," Vecnor said, regardless of Poluran's glares—the dwarf didn't care for Vikur. "If you wish to join us, I suggest you get some sleep. That's what I'm going to do." Vecnor stood. "Until tomorrow."

He left the tavern.

The next day, Merssa's disdain for Vikur's presence was obvious. But she did not turn the Ironside brothers away.

The group proceeded north, again passing through Ellaville. A gang of thugs now occupied the desolate village, and Eraim employed her talents to disrupt their attempts to extort a toll for safe passage. The company then made their way to Eastgate and stopped at Larman's Haven.

Larman's family had their hands full with the inn they had purchased—its popularity had grown significantly. When Vecnor and his companions last visited the Nejan city, ruffians hassled Larman, naming the innkeeper a "Palidur lover" to stir up trouble. Vecnor had chosen that moment to announce his presence, declaring himself a friend of Larman's in hopes of warding off future events from bringing the barman further distress. It was obvious Vecnor's reputation preceded him within the city, and he was pleased to see the establishment in good order.

Larman was excited to see Merssa, and the innkeeper set the company up in a private dining room. They weren't there long when they were interrupted by Bayn and Gruzim, a marteese mage and a hideous krukari warrior they had met the last time they visited Eastmarch. The pair had been underlings to Olinin, and Bayn claimed they wished to avenge their master's death. Though the marteese appeared sincere, Gruzim was another matter. There was something in the half-hobgoblin's eyes Vecnor didn't trust, but he couldn't prevent Merssa from accepting the pair's enlistment. He would need to keep an eye on the krukari.

A more pleasant reunion came when Pallit arrived. Borse, the priest of Cafdella, was indeed intuitive, and saw fit to send the warrior to Eastgate with the horses the company left behind before entering Sistama. Pallit also committed his sword to joining the mission. Being an ex-King's Ranger, as well as one who had seen the area of the rorbak before—the Forbidden Area, as the dwarves of Rornibur referred to it—Vecnor welcomed Pallit's assistance.

They spent the next several days riding across Neja to Vol Maren. There, they stayed a night at the Ogre's Breath, where it was readily apparent that Pallit was on good terms with the King's Rangers. Pallit took charge of the arrangements from that point, and guided them into the Stone Eagle Mountains the following morning. It was an arduous trek, but they made it to the rorbak, and it wasn't long before they discovered the secret entrance to the tomb.

The panel constructed of rorbak opened to reveal a large octagonal chamber carrying the odor of old bandages. Each wall possessed a single door, and Merssa split the company to search them. Vecnor remained with the paladin, as did the rest of those that set out from Tikken City with her, and all was quiet until Eraim called out an alarm.

"Battle!"

The small elf darted from the abandoned laboratory where they stood, and Vecnor wasn't far behind.

Across the enormous hall, a mass of ghouls issued from an open door, and Vikur, Arkor, Pallit, Gruzim, and Bayn had their hands full. Vecnor strode past Eraim to arrive first, wielding one of his swords, and stepped between Vikur and Arkor to hack down several of the fiends. Eraim and the others joined the fray, and the undead bodies piled up as the battle came to an end. Everyone survived, although Pallit and Bayn took nasty wounds.

In the middle of the octagonal room, Poluran discovered a secret shaft descending into a cavern. A chasm occupied most of the massive cavity, and the company followed a narrow ledge ending at an archway decorated by demonic skulls. Merssa led the way through, and they entered a chamber of endless skeletons.

The enemy emerged from small archways to surround the group. Vecnor guarded Merssa's flank, but this became difficult when the paladin attempted to cross the room to help Bayn. Vecnor scooped a fallen shield and charged, shattering dozens of the undead as he plowed past Merssa. A couple of rusty swords struck his armor, but he received only a minor cut. Selanna then released impressive magic, shaking the floor and halting the skeletons' advance on one side, and the company focused their efforts on the opposite side. This allowed Vecnor to lift Bayn over his shoulder and race through the far arch, and Poluran, Pallit, and Gruzim followed.

After setting the wounded marteese in the adjoining corridor, Vecnor assessed the situation. Merssa stood just inside the archway, keeping the path clear. Beyond the paladin, Eraim, Vikur, and Arkor protected Selanna's back while the mage continued making the skeletons dance.

"I cannot hold them forever!" Selanna warned.

Arkor raced from the room while Vikur remained to assist Eraim. Though blood flowed from a gash on the small elf's leg, she crumbled a skeleton with every swing of Mithkahr. It was obvious she had no plans to abandon her friend.

Vecnor ran to battle beside Vikur. "Eraim! Get out!"

The elf glanced at Selanna with worried eyes before limping to the exit.

Selanna stomped her foot, shouting an unintelligible word, and the floor before her cracked, tossing the undead into the air. Upon landing, the skeletons shattered, but more immediately issued from the dozens of alcoves.

"Go!" Selanna commanded, racing past Merssa and from the room.

"Move!" Vecnor ordered Vikur.

The Lord of Ironside obeyed, and Vecnor dislodged multiple enemies with every swing as he followed. Merssa now split her attention to either side of the exit, and Vecnor scooped her into his arm as he passed into the hallway.

"How dare you!" the paladin scolded.

Vecnor set Merssa down as Selanna raised a magical force to keep the skeletons from pursuing. Merssa and Pallit then tended to all wounds as best they could, and they moved on.

The next room was ominous. A pentagram bearing a ram-like skull dominated the circular chamber, leaving a narrow path around the perimeter to the door at the opposite end. Try as they might, the company could not traverse the room before a pillar of flame arose in the center of the star, summoning the demon Ragab. The lanky fiend stood taller than Vecnor, and dozens of bony protrusions ending in points adorned its reddish-brown, leather-like skin, the longest a two-foot spike extending from its forehead between ram-like horns. And though the pentagram kept Ragab contained, the horrific monster was no less lethal. It killed Bayn with fiery breath, pierced Vikur's shoulder with the spike atop its head, and repeatedly battered Merssa by casting her into the wall with an unseen force. They defeated the demon when Selanna issued a stream of lightning from her fingertips. Ragab vanished, leaving behind the fading sound of its mocking gurgle.

Wounded and worn, the company continued to the next room to find Trannum. The skeletal wizard stood at a podium of black stone, reading from a large tome with its one glowing eye. Only Merssa stepped forward to confront the necromancer, even after strange undead warriors arrived through a magical gate on the far wall. Yellow skin was pulled tightly about the newcomers' bones, and the same blue light emitting from Trannum burned in their eye sockets. Selanna called them dunarchins. Vecnor respected Merssa's courage, but his orders were clear: the paladin must survive. And in their present condition, defeating the enemy was impossible.

"Vecnor?" Selanna's eyes begged him to deter Merssa from her actions.

Vecnor put his hand on the paladin's shoulder. "He has not attacked," he said. "He must wish to speak."

Merssa looked at Vecnor, her expression one of disbelief.

"And there's no harm in listening," Vecnor added.

The paladin scanned the others, and her shoulders slumped as the state of the company registered in her eyes.

Trannum chuckled. "Very perceptive, Vecnor."

Vecnor stiffened. How did Trannum know his name?

A fog entered his mind, but it was not a spell cast by the skeletal wizard. Elgarroth protected Vecnor from something, and not for the first time. Merssa spoke heated words at the enemy, but he heard nothing. Trannum gestured, so the necromancer responded. Poluran added a statement. The conversation continued, but then Vecnor's companions ceased moving as their eyes glazed over. He stared blankly forward to hide his awareness. Trannum's bony hands moved in a strange pattern, and Vecnor's pains eased. Had the undead wizard healed his injuries? Was that not a divine power granted only to priests of the highest devotion?

The dunarchins marched through the gate from where they had come, disappearing into the darkness filling the arch, and Trannum followed. The shifting mist within the portal then vanished, and the chamber rotated until the furnishings became a blur. When the spinning ceased, Vecnor stood with the company outside the tomb, and the rorbak door slammed shut. The fog in his mind faded.

The others gazed about, finally released from their trances. But their expressions were forlorn and they didn't speak. The necromancer had enchanted them—even Selanna. All at once, they headed down the mountainside, back the way they had come.

Neither Pallit nor Poluran cared to lead, so Vecnor took charge, lest someone reach a terrible end at the hands of the Stone Eagles. Thankfully, his companions weren't mindless and followed most instructions, but occasional shoves and forceful commands were necessary during the steeper declines. It was tedious, but they reached Vol Maren and returned to the Ogre's Breath.

Borse is the answer, said Elgarroth. *He will know what to do.*

Vecnor put each of his companions to bed before approaching the innkeeper.

"They are not to be disturbed." He handed a small pouch to the man. "And breakfast *will* be provided." His glare left no room for misunderstandings.

The street was dark and empty while Vecnor walked to the stables. Though the barn was closed for the night, his pounding on the door summoned a young groom to allow access.

Vecnor pointed out the horses belonging to his companions. "I want these animals prepped and ready to ride come morning." He placed two gold coins in the lad's hand.

Taking Umbarc, Vecnor rode across the city to the southern exit. The gate was shut. He dismounted and reported to the gatehouse, where a guard looked him up and down with nervous eyes.

"I need to leave," Vecnor said.

"Sorry, sir," the soldier responded. "The gate opens for no one during dark hours, save by order of the king."

"I am Black Death," Vecnor growled. "You will open this door, or I'll tear apart your tower and kill everyone in it." It was an empty threat, but he had no time or patience for friendly requests.

The large doors opened.

Vecnor headed east, pushing Umbarc hard across Neja for days until arriving in Cafdella. It was an hour past noon, and the citizens of the lush village were exiting Feast Hall. The people parted before Vecnor and his giant horse, some of their jaws hanging and many eyes seeking potential hiding places. As he neared the building, he dismounted.

Within the hall, a handful of servants cleaned tables while Borse spoke to a man and woman whose smiles appeared frozen in place. The tall priest spotted Vecnor, and he issued a few more words before the couple departed.

"Young love." Borse turned to Vecnor. "You missed a most wonderful ceremony." His smile persisted, but his eyes revealed him to sense something was amiss. "I trust your fine horse was returned to you?"

"I thank you for that," Vecnor said. "But I need your help."

The priest frowned. "Merssa?"

"Yes. And the others. Their minds have been poisoned."

"I see." Borse watched the servants work. "I shall gather my things." He turned to Vecnor. "I must leave instructions, but I will be ready in an hour."

Vecnor waited in the street. The fear in the citizens' eyes faded, but no one drew to within fifty feet of him and his mount. Once Borse joined him with a couple of packs, Vecnor lifted the priest onto Umbarc, and they rode north into Eastgate.

Larman beamed when they entered Larman's Haven. "Ah! Master Vecnor! But where's Merssa and the others?"

"They will be here shortly." Vecnor eyed the dozen customers in the tavern. "This evening, in fact." Elgarroth had assured him that was the case.

Larman's smile faltered. "Is… Merssa…?"

"She'll be here," Vecnor said. "But I'll need to rent your entire tavern for the night."

"I see." Larman rubbed his neck. "More of that undead business, no doubt." He glanced at his patrons and turned back. "It shall be done. No worries."

"And, Master Larman?" Vecnor caught the barman's attention before the man scuttled off. "I need this affair to remain quiet. Nothing is to be said to anyone once it's over. Including Merssa and her companions."

"You can count on me." The innkeeper gave a half-hearted smile. "Truly." He turned to the barroom. "Last call! Early night for everyone!"

Vecnor prepared bedrooms for each of the company—even Gruzim. Larman would not hear of him paying, and he did not argue, for his funds were running low. He arranged a few tables to accommodate the entire party once the tavern was empty, and Fellna placed a mug of beer before each chair. As Merssa's group wandered aimlessly into the room, Larman's boys rushed out the door to stable their horses.

Vecnor stood at the head of the table, next to where Borse sat. The priest rose.

"Welcome all." Borse gestured at the vacant chairs. "Please, come and sit."

Merssa and the others complied.

Borse addressed the company, but his words didn't seem to matter. His voice was calming even to Vecnor, who did not suffer like his companions. Vecnor watched the priest circle the table, speaking to each member while placing his hand upon their shoulder, and one by one, their faces brightened and they sat a little taller—had darkness lifted from their eyes and drifted into nothingness? Borse then took his seat and posed a question.

"So what do we do next?"

The vacant expressions stirred. The priest repeated the inquiry, and the company looked about, as if seeing the tavern for the first time, and found their voices.

Vecnor released a sigh of relief. Then it struck him: fatigue far worse than trekking across Vermallon Forest during his training. He moved quietly from the chamber to gain much needed rest, but there was no avoiding Eraim and Selanna. The elves did not tease him, however—not even the mage. They thanked him. They then permitted him to enter his room, and he collapsed onto the oversized cot Larman kept at the ready for him. He had barely shut his eyes when Elgarroth's voice entered his mind.

You must come home. Make haste.

Vecnor groaned.

Chapter 14

Benasti Forest

Vecnor arrived at the House of Elgarroth after nine days on the road. He was exhausted. Umbarc was exhausted. But there was no rest to be found upon entering the clearing, where the wizard and Tux sat near the fire.

"Join us, Vecnor." Elgarroth gestured to the open logs.

Vecnor sat to Tux's left, across from Elgarroth. Eslimil stared into the flames, as usual.

"I have looked over Olinin's maps and notes." Elgarroth's brow lowered. "And when I take into consideration Welmirth's journals and what we have witnessed, I have ascertained much." He took in a slow breath. "The cabin in the swamp was the abode of the necromancer Trannum while he researched Uustaag the Dark, after the Great War ended. He questioned dead soldiers at Palidur's behest, attempting to uncover the source of Uustaag's power."

"He must have found it," said Tux.

Elgarroth sighed. "Perhaps. Everything he has accomplished since is beyond the means of a single mage." He looked from Vecnor to Tux. "Dark days lie ahead."

"What are we to do?" Vecnor asked.

"For the moment," the wizard lifted his pipe, "you will both journey to Benasti Forest."

Tux sneered.

Vecnor frowned. "Benasti?"

"Yes." Elgarroth narrowed his eyes at nothing. "There are elements of Olinin's notes that have me curious about Gruzim."

"He is shady, to say the least," Vecnor grumbled.

Elgarroth gave Vecnor a knowing look. "I agree. Have either of you heard of *Brazan*?"

Vecnor shook his head.

Tux looked up from the fire, his expression suggesting he had tasted something foul. "It is the journey of ascension for the ruling power of the evil woodland."

"Close," said Elgarroth. "It is the path by which those in line for the throne can challenge the current ruler; one taken by the sons of the Lord of Benasti. They enter the world to live among the outsiders. It teaches them to survive amid their enemies, and they are not to return for three years, or until they have attained sufficient skill to best their father in combat. If they fail, they are killed. If successful, they take his title."

"Why is this important?" asked Vecnor.

"We need to know if Gruzim is on this journey," Elgarroth replied. "Everything Olinin mentions about the krukari points at Brazan. He did not trust Gruzim, but he mentored the warrior regardless, hoping to be a positive influence."

Vecnor raised a brow. "Will Benasti reveal this information to us?"

Elgarroth shook his head. "They will need some persuading."

Tux let go a sly grin.

Vecnor gave a nod. "Understood."

❖ ❖ ❖

Vecnor journeyed east with Tux. Being familiar with the terrain, they did not follow Vermallon Road, and they exited the woodland faster than the path would have granted them. After crossing the nearest bridge over the Great East River, they headed due south.

Benasti came into view the next day. From the outside, it appeared as a normal forest. But evil lay within. All Kalmirans were aware of the vicious tribes of hobgoblins and krukari making the trees their home and shunning all outsiders. They were bandits and

114

murderers. Vecnor often wondered if Benasti villages housed any merchants or craftsmen. Why purchase or make what you can take from others?

They entered the woodland, and the first mile revealed only small animals and conversations between birds. But the peace would not last. Sure enough, they happened upon a band of hobgoblins hiding among the underbrush.

"Ahead, to the right and left," Eslimil whispered. "In the thickets."

They dismounted. Vecnor did not pull his swords. He stepped away from the horses and took a drink from his flask while Tux walked around a tree to feign urinating. Once within a shady spot, the elf vanished. Vecnor put away his waterskin and turned to the tall bushes.

"I know you're there." He used the hobgoblin tongue. "And none of you will leave this place alive."

With the slightest twitch of the foliage, Vecnor pulled one of his swords and prepared for the attack. Four arrows streaked toward him, and he dodged three while the fourth caromed off his armor. A dozen Benasti warriors charged.

Vecnor smiled at the hobgoblins and krukari, swinging his sword with ease and slaying half of them without taking a wound. As the archers released additional missiles, he pulled his second blade and made an easy time of the rest. One arrow pierced his left shoulder, but his pauldron allowed only a minor injury. Tux, meanwhile, loosed arrows from above. Three long shafts entered the bushes, each inciting a brief scream, and a hobgoblin ran, disappearing into the forest.

As the woodland silenced, Tux dropped from a branch.

"Why did you let him get away?" asked Vecnor.

"We need one of higher rank to find what we seek," the elf said. "That hobgoblin will bring such a creature to us."

Vecnor pulled the arrow from his shoulder and tossed it aside. The wound would have to wait.

They continued on foot, Tux leading the way, and the horses followed. As dusk arrived, they halted. The forest was darkening fast.

"They have been here." Eslimil spoke in elfish. "And they have wolves."

"Benasti wolves…" Vecnor mumbled. He detested the beasts. They seldom ventured outside their woodland, but he had faced them during a few Benasti raids into northern Kalmaar in the distant past. The animals grew nearly as high as a Batorn horse's shoulder. They were cunning and cruel, and preferred to keep their victims alive as long as possible while they feasted. It was as if the screaming improved the taste of the flesh. "How many?"

"There are tracks to suggest four," the elf replied. "Could be more." He inspected the ground, as if the darkness presented no hindrance. "And a score of warriors."

"From what I've heard," said Vecnor, "they'll strike when the night is darkest."

Tux nodded. "We have an hour. Might as well face them here."

Vecnor sat against a tree with one of his swords on his lap. They didn't bother lighting a fire; it wouldn't help. Besides, Vecnor's vision at night continued to improve with each century, and he was sure he saw almost as well as Tux.

The hour passed. Nothing approached. Another half hour nearly expired when Vecnor detected the distant rattle of a chain, and he opened his eyes. The area remained still, the shifting feet of the horses the only movements. It was not fear that unsettled the animals; they were warriors and readied themselves for battle. Another chain rattled, closer and to the north. Likely intentional; a distraction while the Benasti denizens surrounded their prey.

Vecnor stood. The wound in his shoulder presented a stinging sensation, but it wouldn't interfere. He pulled his second sword and wandered to a spot where he could swing both freely. There, he closed his eyes and allowed his ears to take over. A branch snapped to the left—a large opponent was fifty feet away. To the right, at least a dozen assailants approached cautiously. They would not arrive too soon. Behind him were the galloping strides of a Benasti wolf, and before him were two more. The latter would come first.

Vecnor opened his eyes as the pair of wolves rounded a tree twenty feet ahead, one trailing the other. Though the darkness allowed humans to see only glowing red eyes approaching in haste, he viewed the mongrels as they were. Matted yellow fur covered their bodies, and long fangs protruded from their upper jaws. Vecnor had experienced their tactics before, and he raised a blade high while keeping the second one low. The lead animal pulled up short—an attempt to lure Vecnor in. He played its game and lunged, surprising the hound with his reach and piercing it between the eyes. The trailing mongrel leaped over the first, and Vecnor kneeled, slashing overhead and gutting the beast with his second sword.

He rose and spun in time to kick the wolf approaching from the rear. Though it was a strike to send most animals reeling, it only knocked the creature's jaws aside and veered it from its path by a couple of feet. That was all Vecnor needed, and he decapitated the monster.

From beyond the trees charged four hobgoblins and a krukari. Vecnor twirled his right blade while the soldiers closed, and in less than ten seconds, he dispatched all five.

Three krukari approached from the side. Vecnor gutted one, head-butted another, and pummeled the final half-hobgoblin with an elbow, a kick, and a crushing fist to the nose. As the second krukari regained its senses, Vecnor skewered it.

Next came a pair of Zurkans, one carrying a large axe while the other wielded a maul. Vecnor released his left blade and allowed the krukari with the hammer the first swing. He caught the haft of the weapon in his gauntlet, and stunned the Soldier of Blood with the hilt of his sword. In the same motion, he wrenched the maul free and used it to parry the battleaxe. He then dropped his remaining sword and drove the second Zurkan into a tree as he wrested the axe from its grasp.

Four hobgoblins entered the area, hesitating while Vecnor twirled the axe in his right hand and clutched the maul in the other. The Soldier of Blood against the tree rushed him, and he crushed the krukari's shoulder with the hammer before bringing the axe across the warrior's throat. Meanwhile, the first Zurkan lifted one of Vecnor's swords with both hands.

"You best put that down," said Vecnor.

"Come get it!" the half-hobgoblin hissed.

Vecnor shrugged, and he twirled the weapons with ease and grace. The axe buried into the krukari's head, and the hammer followed, splitting the warrior's skull like a piece of firewood.

Vecnor turned to face the hobgoblins. They were gone.

The forest quieted. Three additional wolves and a dozen Benasti warriors littered the perimeter with arrows protruding from their corpses. Umbarc and Landolice had claimed six victims of their own. Among the carnage, Tux knelt above a Zurkan with his smoking sword at the krukari's throat.

Vecnor released the Benasti weapons and gathered his swords, taking a moment to wipe the blades upon a Zurkan's red cloak before approaching Eslimil.

"I'm glad you took him alive," Vecnor said. "I guess I got carried away."

Tux grinned to one side without looking from his captive. The krukari was missing its left hand, and its right arm and leg bore vicious wounds. Blood covered its lips as it snarled at the elf.

"Rumors of a little gray elf are true," the Zurkan growled.

"You never know which rumors to believe." Tux's demeanor was calm. "*I* once heard Soldiers of Blood were formidable warriors." He sniffed. "I guess they cannot all be true."

"You attack from above like a coward!" The krukari spat on Tux's sword, and the bloody spittle sizzled.

"Consider us the vanguard of Gruzim." Tux pushed the blade against the Zurkan's throat, issuing smoke and the stench of burning hair and flesh.

The half-hobgoblin clenched his jaw, but he did not scream. "I know not of what you speak!" The krukari winced when the sword pulled away.

"I say we let him live," said Vecnor. "Let Gruzim kill him slow with his spear."

The Zurkan's eyes widened.

"Knowing Gruzim," Vecnor added, "he might want to first shave off the rest of that arm. Maybe a leg."

The krukari revealed a touch of fear. "I have always been loyal to Gruzim!"

Vecnor held up a finger to silence the lout. "That's all I needed to hear."

The Zurkan frowned, its confused eyes darting between Vecnor and Tux.

"Shall we go?" Vecnor asked his companion.

"What about this *thing*?" Tux moved the glowing sword close enough to make the half-hobgoblin cringe.

Vecnor chuckled. "Leave him. He'll get no aid from the Benasti scum. More likely they'll slit his throat when they discover him."

Tux smirked while rising and sheathing his smoking blade.

They mounted and returned to the House of Elgarroth. Upon arrival, the wizard sat at the fire puffing on his long pipe. Vecnor and Tux took their places on the logs and waited. There was no need to give a report.

"Olinin's suspicions were correct," Elgarroth said after a moment.

"Do we go after Gruzim?" asked Vecnor.

"No." Elgarroth sighed. "There is no time. Merssa and the others prepare to seek the orbs. I see many paths, and not all of them end well." He looked at Vecnor. "You will head to Bouldertown to join Merssa in her quest. She must survive the encounter with the Andrians."

Vecnor nodded.

Elgarroth turned to Tux. "Of the other quests, Vikur's carries the most risk. A dark dilemma lies before him, and every path shows him stealing away the orb in the night to take to Tikken City. He will be wounded and alone, with many miles to traverse, and bandits will likely seize the item. This cannot come to pass."

"Do you wish for me to join him?" asked Tux.

Elgarroth shook his head. "He must not know you are there."

The half-gray elf maintained a steady gaze. "It shall be done."

Vecnor lifted a brow. "And Gruzim?"

Elgarroth stared at the fire. "There are several paths of possibility there as well. We will leave it to hope that Poluran finds a desirable road."

CHAPTER 15

ANDRIA

Vecnor entered Bouldertown as dusk settled over northern Harbnum. Being isolated from the rest of the kingdom, the large village was a self-sufficient community, most known for its hunting and quarries. Merchants frequented Bouldertown only once or twice a year, as the society boasted many skilled blacksmiths, fletchers, millers, masons, bakers, and the like, and their needs were few. The Vermallon forest to the east was rife with game, the hills were fertile, and the quarries at its northeastern edge were rich in granite, slate, and marble. Enormous rocks were common, some a couple of feet in diameter while others were ten feet and larger, and a wall ran from boulder to boulder around the village's perimeter to hold off roaming beasts. Good folks lived in Bouldertown, and Vecnor enjoyed his visits. Unfortunately, those occasions came only once or twice a decade, if he had the time.

"Aren't you Vecnor?" asked the town stableman.

"That I am." He handed over the reins. Umbarc preferred to remain unrestrained, but an animal of that size was better off corralled in a stall than wandering the narrow pathways serving as streets.

"I remember you and your fine steed from eight years ago," the man said. "In fact, there are several that still talk about you chasing off those griffons."

Vecnor smirked. "Yes. How could I forget?"

He recalled that day fondly. The griffons roaming the Coranthiar Mountains rarely traveled so far south, preferring to hunt closer to their nests among the high peaks, but a dozen of the creatures grew adventurous and came in search of easy prey. Vecnor had been in town, and he slew a few before they retreated to their usual territory.

He headed to the Griffon's Roost near the middle of the village. Upon entering the tavern, several heads turned his way.

A patron standing at the bar squinted. "Vecnor?"

"Vecnor!" the room called out, and they returned to their plates, mugs, and conversations.

Vecnor walked to the patron. The man was a local, but Vecnor couldn't recall his name. His cheeks were scruffy, equal parts black and white stubble, and the wrinkles about his eyes ran deep. He studied Vecnor and smiled. "If I didn't know better, I'd swear you were Vecnor's son."

Vecnor grinned. "Alas, it is I."

"So it is." The man chuckled. "Let me buy you a beer."

"Very good!"

Vecnor remained at the Griffon's Roost throughout the evening, but Merssa did not arrive. So he secured a room for the night. The following day, the paladin entered the tavern, and her attention snapped his way.

"Vecnor?" Her tone seemed to ask, "*Where have you been?*"

"Vecnor!" the patrons resounded.

Seeing Merssa lifted Vecnor's spirits, and finding Borse in her company was a pleasant surprise. But something else caught Vecnor's eye: she was happy. Despite the evil looming over Vaeldor, Merssa Goldmace glowed, and it wasn't due to any divine connection or protective aura.

The rest of her party arrived, including Pallit and Wezlok, the latter a Lorian wizard. It was a small group, and Vecnor understood why Elgarroth had sent him. If problems arose with the Andrians, they would need his help.

Vecnor spent most of the following day with Pallit, wandering the streets of Bouldertown. They discussed life in Neja, and the ranger seemed surprised by Vecnor's knowledge of the realm's history. Of course, Pallit didn't realize Vecnor drew from personal experiences. For the ranger's sake, he spoke only of good memories concerning Neja, omitting the occasions he had entered the region as an enforcer to break up gatherings of evil men before they threatened surrounding territories.

Later that day, Merssa introduced Vecnor to Arrikan, who was to be their guide into Andria. Vecnor supposed he should have suspected that eventuality. It had been a few years since he last saw Arrikan, yet she had changed so much. She was a lovely woman beneath the dust and dirt she wore with pride, and carried with her a reputation as an accomplished ranger among the Coranthiar slopes. Arrikan recognized Vecnor at once, and in her smile was the little girl that followed him around the ranch and played with Umbarc. Her embrace melted his heart. The realization then set in: she marched into the clutches of evil. The dread of imagining Arrikan's corpse erased all joy, reminding Vecnor of the reason he didn't make friends. He would do what he could to make sure she returned home safely.

The journey led them into the lower peaks of the mountains to the north. Though the path was trying, the bickering between Arrikan and Pallit was entertaining and kept Vecnor's mind from dwelling on the dangers ahead. Once the competition between the rangers subsided, the pace quickened, and the company emerged into Andria in good time.

Shortly after, they happened upon a barbarian hunter in the wild. The Andrian bore a mortal wound, and spoke of his chief, Dimarr, and the chieftain's treasured blue ice. Trannum's orb. It had to be. According to the hunter, Dimarr was obsessed with the blue ice. The Andrian then expired, and moments later transformed into a zombie, confirming Dimarr's treasure was the item the company sought.

Upon reaching Dimarr's hill, they found a simple village comprising a dozen wooden structures with straw roofs. An unkempt garden to the side nurtured more weeds than edible plants, and fire pits and large cooking spits sat unused in the center. To the northern edge, the hill butted against a cliff wall, and a small waterfall spilled over a ledge to feed a pond emitting a blue glow —the same hue shining from Trannum's eye socket. Dimarr's hunting party was absent, and less than a score of women of various ages were visible. A few of the women bathed within the pond, sending a shiver down Vecnor's spine. What ill effects would soaking in an orb's essence impose?

Glares greeted the company's arrival, suggesting the orb would need to be taken by force. Vecnor was loath to kill the barbarian women — it wasn't their fault Dimarr subjected them to the necromancer's power. But try as she might, Arrikan could not achieve a peaceful solution with words. The Andrians were resolute in defending their chieftain's treasure.

The battle began, and Vecnor did his best to incapacitate the women. Still, some had to be slain, and their corpses became zombies within minutes. Once the skirmish ended and the hill had calmed, Vecnor retrieved the orb from the water while his companions debated how to accomplish the task — there was no time to spare. As he lifted the item from the pond, the glow retreated into the glass ball. But also Dimarr and the hunters returned, and malice shone in their eyes.

The battle began anew.

This was likely the event Elgarroth feared, and Vecnor put forth his full effort, striking down barbarian warriors and their Andrian steeds. One horse struck his shoulder with its hoof, and the pain was intense, but he couldn't let up. Not with Merssa rolling on the ground, trying to avoid being trampled. He slew the offending animal, only to see the paladin regain her feet and run toward Dimarr.

Vecnor pursued Merssa until spying four horsemen aiming for her. He roared, flailing his swords and gaining their attention, and the barbarians sped up to overrun him. Spinning from the lead figure's path, he slashed the animal's neck, and the mount tumbled into the next horse. The third and fourth riders bore down, a sword striking Vecnor's wounded shoulder while he parried the other aside, and one horse swung its head, nearly knocking him to the ground.

Vecnor hacked the attacking steed's leg, causing it to rear and fall, and thrust his second blade through the other hunter's thigh and into the horse's abdomen. He released the weapon as the Andrian mount reeled.

Vecnor turned to face the second rider, as well as the first barbarian, who was now on foot. He flashed his sword with speed, dropping the two and the mount in little time. He then lifted a small axe from one of the fallen and threw it at the final unhorsed enemy, striking the Andrian between the eyes.

That left the hunter Vecnor had pinned to the horse. The steed lay unmoving, and the barbarian struggled, unable to break free. Vecnor ran past, decapitating the warrior while retrieving his second blade.

Thirty yards away, Merssa pushed Dimarr's corpse from atop Borse. She checked on the wounded priest, failing to notice the chieftain's transformation to the undead. As the zombie rose, Vecnor severed its head.

Wezlok, Arrikan, and Pallit dispatched the remaining zombies, the Lorian releasing magic and the rangers using swords, and the hill quieted again. The women that had retreated into their homes earlier then exited to glower at the invaders. Vecnor swallowed the excruciating pain radiating from his shoulder, and he bared his teeth while lifting his swords, converting several of the glares into expressions of fear. But how long would that hold them?

Nearby, Merssa destroyed the orb with her mace. Good riddance. Vecnor didn't understand the need for the Council of Wizards to study the evil items.

"What of the remaining villagers?" asked Pallit as he limped to join Vecnor, Merssa, and Borse. Arrikan was with him, and Wezlok followed at a distance of ten feet.

"We must cleanse this place," said the Lorian. The elf bore not a scratch and his clothing was spotless. Yet, he likely killed more barbarians and zombies than did Vecnor.

"We will not decide their fate." Merssa scanned the Andrians. "For good or evil, they will be spared. We have done what we came to do. Now let us leave this place while we still live."

It was an admirable decision. But Wezlok had a point. What ill had the orb already wrought? Still, it was Merssa's choice to make. Hopefully, she had made the right one.

Once they left the hill behind, Borse summoned divine power to mend everyone's wounds. The company then returned to Harbnum and headed south. As they neared Vermallon Road, Vecnor slipped into the trees to return to the House of Elgarroth. It wasn't the way he preferred to separate from the group, disappearing without a word. Hopefully, his companions were used to it by now.

Chapter 16

Bandits

Eslimil rode amid the plains of southern Kalmaar, and it was not long before he discovered a group of bandits roaming the area. The collection of no less than twenty criminals lived off the hard work of others, pillaging farmhouses on the outskirts of villages and pestering travelers. But never did they hassle noblemen. That was the surest way to gain the attention of local lords. Eslimil kept watch over the cowards for two weeks, and it sickened him to witness their despicable actions, including a couple of murders. But he was there for other reasons and could not give away his presence. Not yet.

After a mental urging from Elgarroth, Eslimil headed east until discovering a large encampment manned by Barraday soldiers outside the Serpent's Range. Vikur and his orb seekers entered the camp from the mountains just after noon, their mission to retrieve the item a success, and the Lord of the Keep moved as if he bore many injuries.

That evening, Tarm took the evil sphere from its guarded tent and crept among large rocks to gaze upon it. From Eslimil's position, it appeared as if the duke spoke with the glowing ball. But it was a brief conversation, and Tarm fell silent while staring into its blue light. Vikur then arrived. The Lord of the Keep had moved gingerly from his quarters to interrupt Tarm. Any words between the two were beyond Eslimil's hearing, but Vikur's wary expression was unmistakable. The discussion ended, and the duke returned the item to its secured resting place before retiring to the largest tent.

Vikur meandered around the campsite, glancing at the stars and scratching his head as if consumed by conflict. Several minutes later, he made his way to the horses and led one of the animals outside the watch's perimeter. He then approached the shelter housing the orb, where he incapacitated all but one of three guards, and the soldier ran, sounding an alarm while Vikur entered. After cutting through the side of the tent, the Lord of the Keep exited with the box containing the item and raced toward his horse. He slowed upon encountering a pair of watchmen, just close enough for Eslimil to hear their shouts.

"What's happening, Lord Vikur?" asked one.

Vikur slid the box behind his back. "We're under attack! All hands to the duke!"

The guards ran for the tents.

Vikur continued to his mount, and he struggled to lift himself onto the saddle. With a kick, the horse bolted into the darkness.

The animal was of the Batorn breed, exceptional specimens known for speed and balance. It could travel deep into the night, and though Vikur would likely miss much in the darkness, the horse would not lead him astray. Vikur surely depended on this. But Eslimil knew where they headed, and Landolice could outrun the swiftest steed the Batorn region had to offer.

Eslimil raced alongside his charge, beyond the human's detection. After a couple of miles, the Lord of the Keep neared a group of bandit sentries. Eslimil skirted the four thugs while Vikur captured their attention, and they mounted their horses to follow. Though they rode inferior animals, Vikur's exhausted steed eventually slowed, and Eslimil halted as the bandits veered toward their quarry. In choosing to impede the Lord of the Keep, the outlaws provided sufficient reason to act at last.

Eslimil pulled his bow and plucked an arrow from his quiver. The rogues were a hundred yards away, riding in single file, but the distance and lack of lighting were of no concern. Eslimil raised his weapon and released the string. His mind melded with the arrow as it sped across the night sky, altering its path slightly to strike the lead rider in the back of the skull. The other bandits halted to look around while Eslimil rapidly launched three more. Guiding multiple shots involved greater concentration, but only one required a nudge, and all three pierced the hearts of their targets.

The threat now eliminated, Eslimil hastened to catch up to Vikur. The lord's pace had slowed to a trot. After another mile, the human stopped, unaware of the failed attempt to hinder him. Vikur struggled in the darkness, nearly falling from the saddle while dismounting, and staggered fifteen feet before dropping to his knees. Without any blankets, he collapsed and fell asleep.

Eslimil rode around the perimeter. There was nothing to disturb Vikur's rest. He dismounted and approached the Lord of the Keep on foot, halting fifty yards away—even wounded, Vikur was a seasoned warrior and would sleep lightly. Taking in a breath, Eslimil became one with the shadows and flew to Vikur's horse, exhaling upon the opposite side. He hummed a calming tune to keep the animal from spooking, and the shifting of its feet eased. Vikur's midsection raised and lowered, keeping a steady rhythm.

Eslimil moved around the mount until reaching Vikur's waterskin, and he extracted a gray flower from his pack. It was a toxic herb found in Orlenfel Forest, but ironically, its roots bore special healing properties. He pinched where the roots attached to the stem and snapped the plant in two—leaving it intact had preserved its healing qualities long enough for the journey. Having no immediate need for the flowers, Eslimil tucked them back into his pouch. He dropped the roots into Vikur's flask and gave it several swirls before returning it to the saddle. It was not the most efficient way to use the herb, but it should suffice to get the Lord of the Keep to Tikken City. After making sure Vikur still slept and no bandits or wild beasts neared, Eslimil held his breath and returned to Landolice.

Vikur arose with the morning, stretching his arms overhead until his injuries forced them to retreat. He then took notice of Eslimil sitting atop Landolice a hundred yards to the east. Vikur mounted before taking a drink from his skin, and he wiped the sleep from his eyes and squinted at Eslimil. Without further hesitation, he kicked his horse into action and rode westward in haste.

The ploy had worked. Whether Vikur believed Eslimil to be a bandit or a mere traveler was irrelevant. With the package the lord possessed, he would not chance any encounters in the wild.

Eslimil proceeded at an easy pace, allowing Vikur to gain ground until he was sure the human no longer detected him. He then picked up speed, veering to the south and pushing his mount to make certain the way ahead remained safe. As luck had it, Vikur steered clear of any further bandits throughout the day, and though diluted, the gray flower roots enabled the lord to travel deep into the night without wavering.

The following evening, Barraday drew near, an event sure to increase the chances of undesirable encounters. Bandits could not resist monitoring roads outside larger settlements for easy prey. Eslimil continued forward while Vikur settled in for some sleep, and sure enough, an encampment of seventeen brigands lay two hundred yards west of a road passing north and south, less than a mile from the slumbering lord. Vikur would likely veer west around the city to avoid notice, remaining north of the outlaws, but once the thieves were alert, there were no guarantees the lord would evade detection in the daylight. It was a risk Eslimil could not take.

Within the campsite, three men guarded the night. One stood near a group of horses, taking too much pleasure in striking a mount to keep it from wandering. The poor animal obviously wished to eat from a patch of grass not far away.

Returning to the road, Eslimil crossed to its eastern side and searched the terrain. Tracking at night was no easy task, but it was not long before he located discarded bones next to the remains of a campfire. Closer examination revealed the bones to have belonged to rabbits. Nearby, tracks of at least a dozen horses led farther east.

He followed the trail a few hundred yards and discovered another encampment. This one housed fourteen bandits, and two were on guard while the others slept around a fire. One guard stood near the horses at the eastern edge.

Eslimil inhaled deeply and lifted from Landolice. Drifting around the reach of the firelight, he descended amid the horses. They were of a breed from Marcove, so the bandits were foreigners. As Eslimil materialized, the animals shifted, and he patted the surrounding mounts and offered soothing whispers until they calmed. The whinnies caused no alarm; the guard had not moved. Closer scrutiny revealed the man to be sleeping while standing. How many years of practice had that taken to perfect?

From a nearby saddle hung a quiver of arrows. After lifting the worn leather case, as well as a random saddlebag, Eslimil took in a breath and returned to Landolice to inspect his prizes. Protruding from the quiver were several notched shafts, some with mangled or missing fletching. The pack contained a whetstone, flint and steel, a flask of what was surely oil, half a dozen arrowheads, and a small knife. Perfect.

Returning to the first camp, Eslimil halted beyond the brigands' detection. Nothing had changed. He cut the pilfered saddlebag along its seam and slit one of its straps before ripping it the rest of the way. Placing the ragged pack onto his saddle before him, Eslimil grabbed his bow while eying the bandits. No one stirred. He lifted an inferior arrow to his bowstring, and the warmth radiating from the gray wood retreated — the weapon recognized poor craftsmanship.

Eslimil sighed. He did not like disappointing his treasured bow. He received it after making his vow to Elgarroth nearly a thousand years ago in Arman Forest. Once the oath was completed, he spotted a five-foot-high yew sapling illuminated by a ray of sunshine. Elgarroth called it a *Gift of Vou*, for the trees of the woodland were ancient, and saplings were a rare sight — the forest did not grow or spread; it simply *was*. The wizard instructed Eslimil to prick his finger and allow a drop of blood to follow the grooves of the young tree until penetrating the ground. The sapling then fell over and took on a dark gray color. When Eslimil lifted the small tree, its branches detached, and it became a single piece of smooth wood. It was weightless in his hand, radiating a calming warmth and forming an immediate bond. After adding a bowstring, Eslimil found the weapon extended his control of arrows over greater distances while providing the power of a crossbow, and drawing the string was effortless, bringing no fatigue, no matter how many arrows he loosed. The bow would be with him forever. It was a part of his being.

Eslimil eyed a guard sitting by the fire and readied the substandard arrow. There was no need to aim, but old habits were hard to break, and he measured the distance and soft breeze. Once satisfied, he freed the projectile into the night sky. The mangled fletching steered it a few inches off target, but Eslimil reached out, making the necessary correction. It impaled the bandit's thigh, and the man's scream alerted the entire camp.

Eslimil released three additional arrows. The first, he guided into the shoulder of a rising bandit; the second, he allowed to strike the ground; and he steered the third into the throat of the man near the horses. Shouts erupted, and the outlaws scrambled to don their gear. Eslimil launched two more, permitting another arrow to miss and piercing the forearm of a thug who had mounted. Other bandits climbed onto their saddles, and they peered in Eslimil's direction.

Turning Landolice eastward, Eslimil dropped the whetstone to the ground. He rode twenty yards and tossed the tinderbox, and picked up speed, discarding the remaining items from the saddlebag one at a time. Upon reaching the rabbit bones, he threw down the bag. Those giving chase should have no problem following the rest of the trail, but Eslimil released the quiver of lesser arrows after ten yards, just in case. He halted north of the eastern bandit camp, and there he waited.

A half hour passed, and it seemed the first group of bandits would never arrive. But then torches appeared in the west. Eslimil trained his bow on the resting brigands and launched two of his own arrows, striking the shoulder of a sleeping raider and piercing another's leg. He then fastened his bow to Landolice. Too much care went into crafting his fine shafts, and he refused to waste any more. Of course, the pair were beyond enough to rouse the bandits.

Eslimil smiled as the groups became aware of each other. He would have enjoyed watching the chaos unfold, but the fading shouts would have to suffice as he bolted Landolice northward. Twilight had captured the sky, and he needed to return to Vikur before the lord awakened.

A couple days sped by, and Vikur remained unhindered while continuing his journey. As well, the healing herb in his flask kept him healthy, and he soon followed the only road traversing the Border Hills. The trail was created by Kalmirans too many centuries ago to count, and they had erected watchtowers along its length to keep travelers safe from goblins, hobgoblins, and bandits.

Satisfied with Vikur's safety for the moment, Eslimil veered west to traverse the wilder regions of the hills, as he had done hundreds of times before. It was faster, and he preferred his passing to go unnoticed by the tower sentries. Besides that, he could not recall the last time he encountered thieves within the rolling terrain, and avoiding roaming beasts posed no problems.

Upon entering Marcove, Eslimil took a direct path toward Denvale, anticipating Vikur's route through the untamed fields—the Lord of the Keep was surely aware that bandits watched the roads and Mentrial Forest night and day. Not far to the west was a small group of brigands. Eslimil moved about, imitating a pack of wolves growling in the night, and easily scared them off. A different tactic was necessary when he happened upon a band of hobgoblins a couple miles farther. Their eyesight in the dark nearly rivaled that of elves, but Eslimil was not an ordinary elf, and he saw twice as far as the fiends. There were eight of them. One carried a crate, another held a large sack from which protruded a bloody hand, and at the rear, a hobgoblin led a couple of cows.

Eslimil sneered. His hatred for hobgoblins ran deep, and he would have liked nothing more than to slay them all. But that was not his mission. Still, there was no better way to chase them off than by dropping a few from their ranks. He fitted an arrow to his bowstring and aimed high and to the left. After releasing the projectile, he quickly launched another to the right and a third one straight toward the creatures. The last arrow arrived first, needing no correction as it sank between the eyes of the hobgoblin toting the bloody-hand bag. Eslimil guided the first arrow, arcing it to strike the one leading the animals at the rear, and he steered the second arrow to approach from the opposite direction and plunge into the heart of the thug holding the crate. All three victims fell.

The group of raiders drew their blades and searched the night with wide eyes. Eslimil released another arrow into the dark sky, and it descended onto one of the rogues, adding a fourth to the tally.

"Back to the forest!" barked a hobgoblin in its disgusting language, and the survivors abandoned their haul as they ran south.

Eslimil scowled. It was a shame the creatures gave up so easily.

Vikur's trip to Denvale was then without interruption, and once he entered the city nestled against the mountains, Eslimil ceased to follow. The Lord of the Keep was well known within the settlement, and would soon reach his home. From there, the journey through Sardina should prove easy enough.

Turning Landolice, Eslimil headed east.

CHAPTER 17

WORNOVIR

Upon returning to the House of Elgarroth, Vecnor found Tux sitting before the fire. Elgarroth wasn't present.

"He left for Tikken City," Tux said without a glance, as if reading Vecnor's mind.

Vecnor took a seat. "What about Vikur?"

Tux looked up. "He escaped with the orb. Though I am not certain handing it to the Council of Wizards is best."

"We should just be rid of them." Vecnor shook his head. "What it did to those Andrians… The orbs should be destroyed."

"If only that were our decision to make," muttered Tux. He stood. "I am off to gain some rest."

Vecnor nodded. "I'll do the same."

He followed Tux to the single door of the cabin. Eslimil opened it to reveal a bedroom with lavish furnishings of exquisite craftsmanship. The bedposts resembled trees, and the canopy appeared to be made of living branches. Beside the bed, a steady stream of water fed a washbasin, issuing from a hole in the wall and providing a comforting sound. Vecnor thought he even heard a bird chirp. At the opposite end of the room was a worktable, and next to it was a stock of slender wooden shafts—arrows in the making.

"I will see you soon," Tux said, and he closed the door behind him.

Vecnor reopened the door. It now led to his bedroom. A few furnishings had been added over the centuries, and the space had grown in size. His bed lay to the right, just as Tux's, and his washbasin held clean water—it never seemed to gather filth. To the opposite side stood a wooden dummy for sword exercises, and against the far wall was a desk holding a journal, a quill, and a jar of ink.

Vecnor walked to the desk and sat. Opening the book to his last entry, he briefly read about his excursion into Benasti Forest. He dipped the quill into the ink and wrote on the following page about his time in Andria. It was calming to write, a hobby Vecnor picked up five hundred years ago. Too many memories had diminished, and he didn't wish for any more of his accomplishments to drift into nothingness. Though no one would ever read the book, simply writing the words helped him to remember. Once he completed his account, he laid down to gain some rest.

The room went dark.

※ ※ ※

Vecnor awoke to a knock on his door. Elgarroth must have come home. He swung his feet from the bed and looked around as the light returned. A fresh set of clothing lay on his desk. Stepping to the washbasin, he rubbed cool water on his face to chase away the last traces of sleep. He then donned the clothes and exited the cabin.

Elgarroth sat near the fire with a troubled expression, and Tux was just taking a seat. Vecnor joined them.

"I assume the path Vaeldor has taken is not a favorable one," Tux said to the wizard.

Elgarroth gave a wry smile. "It could have been better."

"Is Merssa all right?" Vecnor asked, suddenly concerned.

"Quite." The wizard grabbed his pipe. "She is very healthy." He hesitated, as if reluctant to utter his next words. "Gruzim has obtained an orb."

Vecnor pursed his lips. That was no surprise. "Is Poluran all right?"

"He is unharmed... physically," Elgarroth answered. "But this failure has left him doubting himself."

Vecnor gazed at the treetops, searching for nothing. Elgarroth had said they needed to "leave it to hope" that Poluran found a way. But the dwarf's wit was no match for the krukari's, regardless of the stout warrior's good intentions. Elgarroth could have sent Vecnor or Tux into Garthglen Swamp, but what would have become of Merssa or Vikur? Moments like this made Vecnor appreciate not having to make such decisions.

"What will Gruzim do with the orb?" inquired Tux.

Elgarroth took in a slow, deep breath. "He has given it to one called Malgabi." The mage furrowed his brow. "Malgabi is a strange being. He is a creation of Trannum's meant to blend with the living. He is mostly undead, but possesses a spark of life. Though he will not age or succumb to poisons or diseases, he is dependent on an elixir to keep his body from decaying."

"Do we go after him?" asked Vecnor.

Elgarroth shook his head. "It is too late for that. It would bring unwanted attention from Trannum. Unfortunately, we must allow this to play out. I have glimpsed this road, and it is not a pleasant one. Tens of thousands will lose their lives, but there is no stopping that now."

So many deaths, and they could do nothing? Vecnor frowned. "What then? Do I return to Merssa?"

"No." Elgarroth gazed into the fire. "Both of you need to disappear." He turned to Vecnor. "Well, at least *you* need to disappear. For a while." He glanced at Tux. "Eslimil has remained unnoticed through it all."

"For how long?" Vecnor asked.

"Years," replied Elgarroth. He returned his attention to Vecnor. "You shall have to travel in disguise."

Great. Vecnor was going to live in either his elf form or dwarf form. Maybe both.

"Both of you will keep watch," Elgarroth added. "But you are not to interfere. Observe and report."

Vecnor looked at Tux. This was a task better suited for the half-gray elf than for himself. It had been years since he was last ordered to be a spy. Such boring work.

"When do we start?" Eslimil asked.

"Right away." Elgarroth turned to Tux. "You shall track down Malgabi and see what he is up to. He has just traversed Vermallon Road and is in Nira. I believe he is heading south."

Tux raised a brow. "Benasti?"

"I think not," Elgarroth answered. "Farther south. Where exactly, I am uncertain."

Tux gave a nod.

The wizard studied Vecnor a moment. "You will return to Andria," he said at last.

Vecnor nodded, though he didn't understand what they could possibly learn from the barbarians.

"Keep a distant watch on the women from Dimarr's hill," Elgarroth explained, as if seeing Vecnor's thoughts. "I know not what lingering effects the orb may have placed upon them, but I sense there to be something amiss."

Definitely boring work.

⁂

It took a couple of weeks for Vecnor to reach Dimarr's hill. Well, not Vecnor, exactly. In his elf form, he went by Tewlon, though it was seldom uttered aloud. Tux gave the name to him, claiming it meant "wrought in muscle" among the gray elves. Tewlon did not ride Umbarc, but a smaller horse appearing similar to a Batorn steed. Vecnor wasn't good at giving names, so he called this version of his Andrian mount Barcum. He was sure Umbarc disliked the transformation as much as he disliked being an elf.

Dimarr's village was abandoned. It appeared as if the survivors had packed everything and left. From the mess, they weren't coming back.

Though not as skilled a tracker as Tux, Vecnor had learned a lot over the years, and Tewlon found the path by which the barbarians departed. He followed it north, then west, and then southwest, and after a week, he discovered them. They had relocated to a village called Wornduir, a decent sized town amid a woodland north of the Coranthiar Mountains. A muscular Andrian named Zutok was its chief, and from the way he carried himself, the man was an accomplished hunter. A local shaman lived just outside the village, as it was customary to keep their clerics secluded unless summoned.

Tewlon set up camp half a mile away in a rocky area practically clear of animal life. There were no rivers or streams, and the surrounding trees comprised mostly pines. Besides Umbarc—rather Barcum—Tewlon's only company were thousands of insects that delighted in his presence. Barcum disliked the location, but they needed to remain out of sight, and Tewlon could not fathom a hunting party drawing anywhere near. Luckily, Elgarroth had supplied him with a flask able to hold ten times the amount of water one would assume. Likewise, he possessed a pouch containing enough dried meats, bread, apples, and oats to keep him and Barcum fed for a year.

On the first day of spying, Tewlon recognized a few of the women from Dimarr's hill—barbarians he had fought personally. It took months before he confirmed the rest. It should have been obvious, for they clung together like a civilization within a civilization, but he had to be sure. By the time he made a mental note of each of Dimarr's followers, thirty-four in all, most had taken lovers and a few had given birth. Nothing appeared out of place, other than the shaman's seeming distrust of the newcomers, but Zutok would not hear it.

Another couple of months crept by with little to report, and the food supply was running low. But Tewlon dared not hunt for fear of discovery. As his rations neared depletion, Elgarroth paid him a visit. Unfortunately, the wizard brought six more pouches. Tewlon and Barcum were going to live there for a while yet.

Several years passed, and beyond having to endure rugged winters, boredom threatened to drive Tewlon mad. What he wouldn't give for a beer! Dimarr's women carried out their mundane lives, and besides spending more time with each other than with Wornduir citizens—their male companions didn't seem to mind them isolating themselves—there was nothing to pique Tewlon's interest. Most had borne children, and many gave multiple births. It was as if they needed to reproduce. Including the offspring, their population was no less than three times its original count.

Though Vecnor often spoke to Umbarc as if the horse were a person, Tewlon began conversing with other animals during his fifth year outside Wornduir. He even scolded a tree for dropping needles on his bedding while he was gone for the day. The evergreen did not dare to argue, nor did it complain when he scooped the needles and threw them in the tree's face. He desperately needed companionship.

Nearing the midpoint of that year, something curious took place within the village. It began with a heated conversation between Zutok, the shaman, and a hunter. It appeared the hunter was in agreement with the shaman that Dimarr's women and their children should leave. Zutok stood firm, and the complaint was abandoned. The disgruntled hunter climbed aboard his large steed and started down the road at a hard pace, where one of the boys in question walked across the packed dirt. Tewlon was sure the Andrian saw the lad, but the man didn't pull up on the reins. He pressed the mount to speed up.

Tewlon gasped as women screamed. The horse reared upon striking the child, and after taking control of the animal, the hunter continued forward, mangling the small body further and disappearing beyond the trees. Villagers flocked to the boy while the one Tewlon supposed to be the mother remained eerily calm, as if awaiting something.

The child stirred. His eyes opened and he rose. Though dirt and blood covered much of his body and tattered clothing, he moved casually to his mother and grabbed her hand. The two walked away while the villagers stared with mouths agape—all but Zutok. Shortly after, the village chief stormed to the area where the women and their children dwelt, and Tewlon heard him order them to leave at once and never return.

Dumbfounded, Tewlon watched the women gather their belongings. What had he just witnessed?

It is time to come home.

Time to come home? Now? Surely Elgarroth had not seen the incident.

What you observed is most disturbing. But you are needed.

Perhaps the wizard *had* seen it.

Though Tewlon disagreed with the order, he headed back to his campsite to retrieve his gear and Barcum.

Tewlon rode with little rest until reaching the House of Elgarroth, and Vecnor was relieved when he and Umbarc reverted to their true forms upon entering the clearing. Elgarroth sat near the fire alone, but as Vecnor dismounted, Tux exited the cabin. Vecnor joined the wizard as the Salenti-gray elf did the same, and he noticed a large mug of beer sitting next to his usual spot. Had Tux placed it there? Not likely. Eslimil never served the drinks!

Vecnor drained the tankard in seconds. It had been so long since he enjoyed a drink that it made the forest spin. He shook his head to steady his vision.

"It is good to see you both." Elgarroth's smile held no joy. He picked up his pipe from the log next to him, and smoke issued from its bowl as it came to life. "Before we begin, I have some pleasant news." He turned to Vecnor. "Merssa and Borse have wedded."

Vecnor raised a brow. "Is that so?"

"It is." The wizard's countenance warmed. "Twice, as it was. Once in Palidur, and again in Dellabville, so non-Palidurians could join in the celebration."

"She has grown so much." Vecnor gazed at the fire, a twinge of regret crossing his mind that he had missed the occasion while sitting outside Wornduir.

"That she has." Elgarroth smirked. "Borse has been an exceptional influence on her." He drew from his pipe. "She has also been named High Paladin."

That bit of news shocked Vecnor. "The Order allowed it?"

"They did not have a choice," the wizard replied. "More than just the Cafior Sector supports her." His eyes drifted to the fire. "But her road remains difficult. She will face resistance, and things will worsen." He looked at Vecnor. "But I sense joy in her life. For a time, at least."

"She deserves it," Vecnor said.

Surprisingly, Tux nodded in agreement.

"And now, to business," Elgarroth announced, prodding Vecnor with a raised brow.

The wizard certainly knew most, if not all, of what Vecnor had seen. But when the three of them met to discuss matters, Elgarroth occasionally allowed them to relay their journeys and everything they had learned.

"You were correct in your assumption," Vecnor said to Elgarroth. "The orb Dimarr possessed had a lingering effect on the women that survived." He gazed at Tux, knowing this to be news to the elf. "They have birthed several children. Abnormal children. I saw one of them trampled by an Andrian steed, and the boy walked away unscathed. He should have been dead, and I think he might have been for a short time." Vecnor shook his head at the memory. "Perhaps they are undead."

"That remains to be seen," said Elgarroth. "It is enough to know something is amiss. And we shall check in on the Andrians to learn more. For now, their existence is clouded in contradiction. But I sense the children are not undead. At least, not completely."

The wizard's attention shifted to Tux.

Eslimil seemed hesitant to respond. "Trannum is in Nomedd."

Vecnor frowned. Why would the necromancer inhabit the sweltering barbarian realm?

"I picked up Malgabi's trail in Kalmaar, and followed him from there," the half-gray elf continued. "It was not hard tracking him, for he is an arrogant dog that cannot help making his presence known." Tux glared at nothing. "He enjoys sewing chaos wherever he goes."

"The Nomish didn't object to Trannum's company?" posed Vecnor.

"There were none to oppose him." Tux's expression became grave. "The realm was quiet. After following Malgabi west, I learned why. The barbarians are zombies."

Vecnor sat up. "How can this be?"

"From what I gathered," Tux said, "Trannum invaded Nomedd with an army of the undead, including hundreds of dunarchins. And as they conquered the Nomish, the evil force expanded to encompass the entire population." He turned to the fire. "But the necromancer did not kill *all* the barbarians. Thousands were taken alive."

"For what purpose?" Vecnor asked.

"Dunarchins," Elgarroth replied. "Undead firstborns possessing many abilities zombies and ghouls do not. They walk beneath the sun, wield weapons, hold conversations… They are Trannum's elite. The creatures sense other firstborns, and they yearn to increase their ranks to please their master. But dunarchins are not created from corpses." Elgarroth glanced from Tux to Vecnor. "The procedure requires living subjects."

A chill raced along Vecnor's spine. It was no doubt an excruciatingly painful experience.

Elgarroth looked at Tux. "Please, continue."

"I know not how," said Eslimil, "but a dark stronghold exists south of the Varlimor Mountains at the base of the hills. I have only ever seen open fields there in the past, and Nomish do not erect castles. That is where Malgabi went. And though I did not see Trannum, I am positive the necromancer was there. But Malgabi did not stay long. He returned to Kalmaar to meet with Duke Tarm."

Vecnor's chest tightened; his breathing was strained and his head grew hot. Why would Tarm hold council with Malgabi?

"I could not hear the entire conversation," Tux said. "But it is treason the duke intends."

"Not if I have something to say about it!" Vecnor growled.

"Alas, that is not our purpose." Elgarroth's expression held sympathy. "You know this. We interfere only when the fate of Vaeldor is concerned. Otherwise, we are to guide."

Vecnor detested this part of his oath. He was a man of action, and King Karrak was a friend. "I'll guide my swords through Tarm's neck!"

Tux sneered. "I share in your anguish. I cannot express how difficult it was not to place an arrow through Malgabi's heart."

"King Karrak is a mighty warrior and great leader," Elgarroth said. "It is uncertain whether Tarm will succeed. And I cannot imagine the duke gaining the support of Kalmirans in this affair." The wizard sighed. "Of course, with Trannum involved…"

This did nothing to ease the anger welling inside Vecnor. With a controlled exhale, he pushed his mounting explosion into the sky. "Then what *are* we to do?"

"We observe and report," Elgarroth replied. To Tux, he said, "Keep track of the spreading evil in the east." He turned to Vecnor. "You shall journey the realms west of the Varlimor Mountains. Trannum is patient, and he will allow the kingdoms to assume he has disappeared. Humans will be content to believe it is so."

Vecnor nodded. Over the centuries, he learned how easily humans swept unwanted history from their doors, like a day's filth from a shop floor. His mind then returned to King Karrak. Hopefully, the urge to pass east of the mountains and enter Kalmaar didn't get the better of him.

"Neither of you are to intervene," Elgarroth reminded them. "Observe and report."

CHAPTER 18

·OBSERVE AND REPORT

Eslimil journeyed south from the House of Elgarroth, and it was not long before he reached the hidden raft to cross the Great East River. It was a contraption he installed a few centuries prior, when passing between Vermallon and Kalmaar unseen became difficult due to expanding human settlements in the Batorn region. He had dropped hints to its location to a few Vermallon elves, trusting them to keep it secret and maintain it as if it were their own. At one point, Elgarroth insisted he make sure Eraim learned of its existence. It was a strange request, considering the small elf would eventually find it on her own.

After crossing the rapid waterway, Eslimil rode up the mountainside of Varlimor's northern reaches near the Candermane Falls. He then located the hidden entrance to the Candermane Tunnel. Dwarves had carved the passage centuries ago as a shortcut between the east and west, allowing them to conduct trade while avoiding human settlements and Vermallon Road. From the waterfall, they simply followed the Great East River into Sardina. After Grellmor Ironside opened the pass between Marcove and Sardina, usage of the subterranean path dwindled until ceasing altogether. Though a longer trek, the dwarves preferred the mountain pass to the forest travel the northerly route required. Presently, the Candermane Tunnel saw little traffic other than random animals seeking shelter.

Eslimil squeezed through the entrance with Landolice close behind. The opening was too narrow for the horse, but Elgarroth had enchanted the animal long ago, and Landolice's bones became extremely flexible to make entry possible. The corridor then widened, and the horse's form stabilized.

They followed the passage until reaching a small square window. Mist sprayed intermittently from the cascading water outside, and the walls and floor glistened with saturation. The window was Eslimil's own addition to the underground construction. Besides offering a bit of light, it worked as an escape route, though he had only used it once. Several decades ago, a band of Vermallon elves spotted him when he let down his guard, and he sought refuge within the tunnel. Unfortunately, the scouts were aware of its location. Rather than race along the miles between the eastern and western exits, Eslimil held his breath and drifted through the opening. The sunlight was painful, but a recess above the window provided a ledge, and there he sat until the elves abandoned their search.

Eslimil watched the spray, waiting for the right moment, and he and Landolice rushed past, remaining dry for the most part. They then spent the next couple of days following the passage until emerging from its eastern exit. There, Eslimil utilized the long-forgotten path left by the dwarves, moving south through the mountains for two more days to the Morimont River. The water was swift but shallow, and he crossed on horseback without hindrance.

Riding across Kalmaar was not difficult, and Eslimil traveled night and day, avoiding villages and wandering bandits. Upon reaching Barraday, a sour taste invaded as he pictured Duke Tarm sitting on a throne and scheming against the crown. King Karrak's line had brought peace to the realm, and now a greedy duke that sold his soul to a great evil would challenge that peace. Humans could be despicable.

Eslimil continued south through the Border Hills until an encampment of mercenaries blocked his usual path. That was how Tarm planned to boost his force—foreigners were going to fight in the war. And then what? How did Tarm expect to keep their loyalty if they succeeded? The duke was playing a dangerous game.

Giving the soldiers a wide berth, Eslimil made his way into Marcove. Guards loosely watched the repugnant kingdom, and it was not long before he passed into Nomedd.

The barbarian country was unchanged since Eslimil's last visit; the land was bare of inhabitants, and herds of wandering animals and birds were all that greeted him. He turned west and skirted the foothills of Varlimor, and a day and a half later, the dark stronghold came into view. Smooth, seamless stone made up the small castle, and the surrounding territory was reminiscent of Helmland—nothing grew.

Eslimil rarely suffered fear, but his skin crawled while he gazed at the scene. Turning Landolice, he entered the rolling terrain and worked his way to a spot a half mile north of the stronghold, beyond sight of the structure. From tracks scattered about, the area had seen nothing outside small animals for some time. He unsaddled his steed and set up camp.

Days led to weeks, weeks to months, and months to years. Eslimil observed the fortress from the cover of the hills, knowing Elgarroth witnessed much of what he saw. For the most part, nothing. Nothing entered and nothing exited, save for Malgabi. Eslimil occasionally followed the despicable worm, but the half-undead being revealed little. The evil messenger usually traveled into Marcove and southern Kalmaar, where he made friends with lords and ladies. Eslimil did not need to get close to know Malgabi was spreading lies and offering wealth to gain favor, making sure King Karrak received no help when the time came.

Malgabi's most interesting journey led Eslimil farther north and into Benasti Forest, where the strange being met with Gruzim—the krukari had defeated his father years prior to claim dominance over the woodland. No one detected Eslimil's presence among the high branches, and he witnessed a pact between Malgabi and the Lord of Benasti. Apparently, the forest's denizens were to be the final piece of Tarm's army.

Eslimil's blood boiled, and he put an arrow to his bowstring. His aim alternated between Trannum's lackey and the krukari lord.

Stay your hand. Elgarroth's words were clear.

Eslimil pushed the wizard's eyes from his mind—years of practice had perfected this talent. But he could not shut out the voice.

Remember your place. This action could have dire consequences.

Eslimil relaxed the tension on the string and returned the arrow to his quiver, his hand shaking for the ire coursing through his veins. This was the hardest part of working for the seer. He allowed Elgarroth to resume watching.

A Zurkan entered the clearing and addressed Gruzim. "My liege."

The Lord of Benasti glared at the Soldier of Blood, saying nothing.

"Lord Gruelenor is prepared for Brazan," the Zurkan said. "He needs only your leave to begin."

"Bring him," grumbled Gruzim.

A young krukari dressed in dark leather armor stepped into the opening. He was almost as hideous as Gruzim—could anyone truly match the Benasti lord? A sword hung at his side and a bow was slung over his shoulder.

"So..." Gruzim sniffed. "You think you're ready for Brazan?"

Gruelenor looked up with an expression falling short of respect. He appeared thirteen years in age, and a hint of resentment radiated toward his father. He said nothing.

"So be it." Gruzim waved off his son. "Get from my sight!"

Gruelenor left, followed by the Zurkan.

"How are your other sons?" asked Malgabi once they were alone.

"That's no concern of yours," replied Gruzim.

The half-undead creature grinned. "I hear Gruelenor is the favorite to replace you."

Gruzim held a level gaze. "The whelp has strength and a mind." He looked in the direction his son had departed. "Maybe too much of a mind. And that will be his downfall." He turned to Malgabi.

"None of my sons are worthy. I need a woman capable of producing something greater."

"That day may yet come." Malgabi smirked. "Perhaps soon." He bowed and walked away.

Gruzim sneered.

Eslimil took in a breath and drifted higher into the trees before materializing. He then leaped from branch to branch, his passing nothing more than a traveling squirrel, until reaching the eastern edge of the woodland. After letting go a whistle, Landolice came running, and Eslimil mounted. They waited until Malgabi exited the forest, and the puppet led them back into the deep south and to the dark castle. There, Malgabi remained for several weeks.

A month later, activity in the middle of the night roused Eslimil from sleep. Hundreds of ghouls toting numerous logs arrived at the stronghold. A crowd of dunarchins emerged from the structure and began cutting the wood with axes and saws.

Undead working with tools?

Come morning, a squad of fifty dunarchins bearing picks and shovels headed west while the woodworking dunarchins continued in their labors. Malgabi then exited and rode into the east.

Follow Malgabi.

"What about the dunarchins?" Eslimil asked, not meaning to have spoken aloud.

Concentrate on Malgabi.

Eslimil returned to his camp to gather a few supplies and his horse before heading eastward in haste.

❈ ❈ ❈

Tewlon and Barcum traveled south through Sendorum and Sardina—Vecnor should have known they wouldn't retain their own bodies. He visited nearly every city, village, and hamlet in his path, and frequented taverns to drink with locals. He was generous with his coins and took part in contests of skill and strength—many were curious about a muscular elf. Also, he found ways to bring up the undead in conversations, and it was readily apparent most folks did not wish to think about the Wind of the Dead. Though the walking corpses had been destroyed or disappeared into the wild years ago, the subject remained an uneasy one.

Months later, Tewlon headed north into Harbnum, and then toured Virch and Neja. After a few months in the wasteland south of the Stone Eagle Mountains, he journeyed into Moclen and Urell Coast, and braved the wilds west of Salenti Forest to reach Fendora and Philen. Everywhere he went, the reactions of civilians were the same.

For nearly eight years, Tewlon trekked back and forth across Vaeldor. But never did he encroach on Tenvale's borders, for powerful wizards might detect the magic concealing his true identity, nor did he pass west of the Varlimor Mountains, in accordance with Elgarroth's wishes. When returning to smaller towns, many recognized him, and backs turned before Tewlon could speak. No one wished to relive the undead nightmares any longer. It was as if his efforts were for naught.

Occasionally, Tewlon saw familiar faces: Eraim and Selanna in Tikken City, Merssa and Borse outside Palidur, and Arrikan and Pallit in Harbnum. But most of them did not know him. Only Eraim and Selanna had ever seen his elfish guise before, so he stayed clear of the two. Seeing Merssa play the parts of wife and High Paladin made Tewlon's time on the road seem more worthwhile, and he forced himself to turn away before anyone thought him a gawking fool. Witnessing Eraim ruin a couple of Selanna's pranks on unwary travelers in Tikken City was pleasing as well. Once, in the city's market, his gaze rested too long on the small elf, and she glanced his way. Tewlon quickly ducked into a crowd exiting the square, and didn't look back until he was three blocks away. There was no time to play the ogling buffoon.

While sitting in a tavern in Harbnum, on the verge of going insane from boredom, Elgarroth contacted Tewlon.

Dunarchins travel west through Dright Swamp. I believe they aim for the Fire Hills. Find them and see what they are up to. I will track them as long as I can.

Tewlon headed south, glad to have a new task, and he neared the Fire Hills after nine days. The closer he drew to the rolling terrain, the faster the blood flowed through his veins—maybe he'd get to destroy a few dunarchins.

They approach the eastern reaches. Look for them there.

Tewlon nodded, appreciative of Elgarroth's assistance—the hills were too vast to search. Was Tux monitoring the undead firstborns?

He followed the rising terrain westward until the Ladal Mountains rose above all else. It was evening, and the low sun reflected off the smooth surfaces of the Fire Hills, shining through the gathering haze and making it appear as though the hills were burning. The spectacle attracted sightseers from near and far, but it had come at a terrible cost. Vecnor recalled when the hills were part of the mountain chain to the west, before Tenvale brought the Dragon Wars to an end. Hundreds of the enormous serpents dwelt within those mountains until the wizards' devastating attack scarred Vaeldor forever, and the miles of high peaks were lost. Left behind were thousands of grottos—remnants of the network that once pierced deep into the ground. As plant life sprouted, animals returned to inhabit those caves, including bears, badgers, and snakes, but also tigers, lions, and other monstrous creatures crept up from the south, now that the terrain was not so impassable. The growing dangers of the region discouraged lords from erecting villages, and visitors traveled to witness the "fire" only when accompanied by experienced scouts charging a healthy fee.

"Well," Tewlon said to Barcum as he dismounted, "I suppose it's time to begin searching." He faced the horse. "Signal if you see anything."

The animal nodded with a snort, and while it headed south, Tewlon ascended the rising land to the southwest. The rolling hills soon exhibited dozens of openings at various elevations, some of them small, a foot or so in diameter, while others were as large as ten feet. All was quiet.

Tewlon drew his sword—in elf form he used a single blade. Though it wasn't alarming for animals to remain unseen amid the hills, he expected an occasional growl warning him to stay away, or the sound of paws scrambling up or down the slopes. There was only silence. He whistled a high pitch, and a neighing answered to the east. Barcum had seen nothing. Moments later, Tewlon detected three stomps followed by a snort. He made his way toward the noises to find Barcum near the corpse of a tiger with extra-long fangs. A severed arm housed within a protective greave lay beside the body.

"Good boy," Tewlon said to his mount.

He squatted to inspect the tiger. It had been a powerful creature; a descendant of an animal from Tarn Arum Jungle in the deep south. Probably born in the Fire Hills. Slash marks from several blades marred its hide—or the same blade at least a dozen times. Glancing at the disembodied arm, Tewlon saw no blood. The skin of the appendage was yellowish and wrapped tightly around the bone. It had belonged to a dunarchin.

Tewlon scanned the countryside. Nothing moved, and now he knew why. Animals would not willingly challenge the undead, so why had the tiger done so? Many sets of footprints surrounding the corpse disappeared into the west. Perhaps a small army of Trannum's elite warriors.

"I believe you found what we're looking for, Barcum."

The horse stomped its displeasure with the name.

Tewlon grinned. "I don't enjoy being this way any more than you."

The dunarchins' route was obvious; they made no efforts to conceal their passing. Tewlon led Barcum, following the tracks until dusk. As night captured the hills, he stopped, fearing he'd lose the trail in the dark. He guarded halfway to morning and Barcum the other half, and come twilight, they returned to the hunt.

The Ladal Mountains drew nearer as the day came and went, and the next day, Tewlon spotted his quarry at last. There were no less than fifty dunarchins wielding picks and shovels. The creatures looked to have been excavating among the eastern region of the Fire Hills, as well as the western reaches of the neighboring mountains, and more than a dozen large holes lay in their wake.

"What are they doing?" Tewlon asked.

Barcum didn't reply.

"We had better get comfortable." Tewlon turned to his horse. "This could take a while."

He rubbed his smooth chin while scanning the immediate area. Moving too close to the undead was risky; ghouls had an uncanny way of smelling the blood that pumps through the veins of the living, and dunarchins might be no different. Higher up was a cave offering cover, and hopefully a better view of the enemy.

They ascended the slope until reaching the shelter. Tewlon made a quick inspection to find the cave had been vacant for weeks, and he led his mount inside. He then spread out his blanket and removed Barcum's saddle to make the horse more comfortable.

"Stay," he ordered Barcum once he finished.

Tewlon exited the grotto and crept to the edge of a cliff overlooking the dunarchins. Though their cold bodies were difficult to see, even with elfish sight, their glowing eyes and the motions of their silhouettes beneath the moonlight were obvious. They excavated in three groups across an area of two hundred yards without breaks for food or water, and once a hole reached twenty feet in depth, they moved to another location to begin a new one. The work was tedious, but the diggers didn't seem to mind. After a few hours, Tewlon turned in for a short rest while Barcum guarded. The dunarchins weren't going anywhere soon.

And so it went. The undead firstborns continued in their efforts day after day, night after night, and week after week. Tewlon feared he might call the Fire Hills home for years, like the woodland in Andria while spying on Wornduir, but after five months, the purpose of the digging became clear. Tewlon exited his cave one morning to spy large bones within a nearby pit. Closer to the mountains was another ditch laden with ancient remains. Dragon bones. How had the skeletons remained undisturbed after the Wind of the Dead swept across Vaeldor? Perhaps the burials were too deep. Maybe the Wind hadn't blown this far south.

"This cannot bode well," Tewlon said to no one.

The dunarchins uncovered several more skeletons throughout the day. It was as if they discovered an old nest of the majestic reptiles.

A noise to the east captured Tewlon's attention. Another fifty dunarchins approached, pulling wagons as if they were draft horses. He slinked into the cave to stand in the shadows of its opening and keep watch. The carts proceeded to the excavation sites, and while the diggers continued working, the new arrivals loaded bones onto the wagons.

Come home, said Elgarroth. *Remain unseen.*

Tewlon took in a much needed breath—how long had he been holding it? Below, the dunarchins carried on with their tasks. What could this mean? It was a riddle he would not soon figure out. He entered the cave to pack.

Leading Barcum on foot, Tewlon descended the Fire Hills into the northeast, careful to avoid making noise. Once they were half a mile from the dunarchins, he mounted and headed north at a quicker pace.

They reached the House of Elgarroth ten days later. No one was home, and Vecnor and Umbarc did not transform back into their true forms. Evidently, his mission was not yet complete.

Head into Selt, said Elgarroth. *Keep watch on the eastern edge of the mountains surrounding the Echo Valley Rapids.*

Tewlon dismounted and opened the cabin door to see the kitchen. It possessed three tables, a cooking pit, and several pots and knives. Vecnor had never seen the equipment in use, and he wondered who prepared the food. Perhaps Tux was the cook. It was only fair, since

Vecnor chopped the wood and served the drinks. On the counter he found a magical pouch filled with rations. Great. The journey would take some time to complete.

Tewlon and Barcum passed through Vermallon Forest, crossing Vermallon Road and heading northeast until reaching the edge of the woodland. Nira was then before them. They saved a day—maybe two—by making a direct line through the trees instead of traversing the forest road. As well, they avoided several villages—Nirans tended to be boring, concerned more with farming than all else. As Tewlon stopped within a settlement the following evening, however, he found the conversations of locals not as dull as expected. There was war in Kalmaar, and the Nirans were growing nervous.

The urge to turn south crept into Tewlon's bones. But Karrak was intelligent, as well as skilled in many forms of combat—Vecnor saw to the latter. The king was surely up to the task. Right? Granted, Karrak had aged a bit, but he came from good stock. His fathers lived long, robust years before him. He was prepared.

Having convinced himself, Tewlon continued north. But the farther he traveled, the worse the news became. Benasti Forest had marched into Kalmaar. Did they fight for Tarm? There was no way they aided Karrak—the king would never hear of it. Perhaps they were taking advantage of the fighting to sew chaos. Tewlon drew in a deep breath and prayed for Brondor to give King Karrak strength.

Upon reaching the Nira-Selt border, Tewlon traveled under the darkness of night. Centuries of strife between the realms had inspired a constant watch from either side to deny access. Demoligius priests ruled over Selt, a nation devoted to the evil fire god and the battalion of demons serving the deity, and the only reason Nira had not fallen to the northern realm was due to the line of Karrak thwarting every attempt of Selt to spread its reach. And with threats of dealing with the Kalmiran army if they pressed the issue, the fire dominion had stayed its hand for several decades.

Evading notice wasn't difficult for a single rider—especially an elf—and Tewlon arrived at the western edge of Lake Charal. He rounded the southern end of the water until reaching the Echo Valley Rapids, and headed east through the fields toward the distant mountains. The tall mounds forced him south, and he skirted them for half a day until they allowed a northward trek. The air then cooled as Tewlon followed the rising terrain another day, now a week since leaving the House of Elgarroth, and he halted at last. Fatigue was heavy upon him and Barcum, but it was a crowd of people that caused him to balk. Gathered near the base of the mountains were Seltans and dunarchins.

Tewlon left Barcum behind and out of sight, and he moved to higher ground and carefully worked his way to a better vantage point. A dunarchin dressed in robes, perhaps an undead wizard, conversed with a group of five Seltan priests. Segregated to either side were at least six hundred dunarchins and Seltan warriors. The priests and the dunarchin mage seemed to come to an agreement, and a decorated Seltan, probably a general, approached a nearby wall of rock where the outline of a large door was barely discernable from the surrounding stone. A servant followed, carrying a black box about a foot in length. The general removed a necklace holding a key and unlocked the box, and from within he pulled a larger key appearing to be made of onyx. He inserted the dark implement into the rock and stood back, and a priest stepped forward to perform a strange ceremony, moving about in the manner of a dancing flame. Upon completion, the cleric turned the key, and the door opened.

A dozen Seltan soldiers and a few of the priests entered the mountain. Minutes later, they exited carrying a mummified body—another corpse that had not risen with the Wind of the Dead. They gave the mummy to the dunarchins, and after the robed dunarchin clasped arms with the lead priest—Tewlon sneered at the sight—the undead firstborns headed south with their prize. The Seltans closed the door and marched east.

Tewlon and Barcum trailed the dunarchins. The creatures walked a steady pace, passing into Nira in the night without lights and slaying a squadron of watchmen near the border—the Nirans were unprepared for the encounter. There were no breaks, so Tewlon received no rest, but the gait was not too taxing. He gritted his teeth when the undead killed farmers in their path, the urge to interfere nearly overwhelming. But he could not take on an army. Fortunately, the force mainly traversed unpopulated areas, minimizing those murders. They veered west to skirt Vermallon Forest into southern Nira, and turned away from the trees to follow the Great East River toward the bridges. Tewlon was relieved to see them round a large village along the way. They reached the first bridge after dusk, and the dunarchins surprised a score of Niran sentries. The soldiers quickly fell. The undead firstborns then crossed the river and traveled southeast until entering Benasti Forest.

Tewlon followed, regardless of the dangers of navigating the evil woodland alone. As luck had it, the watch of the hobgoblins and krukari seemed nonexistent. As well, the dunarchins no longer appeared concerned with keeping their passing unnoticed, and they trampled the underbrush, focused on the way ahead and never looking back to notice Tewlon and Barcum in their wake. After a mile, they stopped before a company of Zurkans bearing a skeleton on a stretcher. It was an old corpse, most of it laying in pieces, and quite unremarkable. The undead accepted the offering and proceeded south beneath the trees.

Return home.

Elgarroth's summons arrived just in time. Pressing deeper into the forest without Tux was too risky. Tewlon and Barcum headed north.

CHAPTER 19
CASTLE GUARD

Vecnor and Umbarc returned to their natural forms when they arrived at the cabin. Elgarroth was alone at the fire, smoking a pipe, and Vecnor dismounted and sat across from the wizard.

"Will Tux be arriving soon?" Vecnor asked.

Elgarroth lowered his pipe. "Alas, Eslimil must remain in the south to keep watch on the enemy."

"What news is there?"

"Nothing that is good." The mage stared at Vecnor. "King Karrak has surrendered the crown to Tarm."

Vecnor's lips parted, but words were impossible with the thoughts racing through his head. Why hadn't Elgarroth allowed him to intervene? The overthrowing of Kalmaar's throne could only lead to greater suffering. Why subject Kalmirans to such a fate? How was the feat even accomplished? The duke could *never* best the king in combat. Vecnor closed his eyes to calm his mind. Upon opening them, he asked, "What has become of him?"

"Karrak resides in Darmhorng's dungeon," Elgarroth replied. "Malgabi ordered that he is to live."

Malgabi! Who was the actual leader behind the revolt, Tarm or Trannum's puppet?

"Tarm raised a foreign army," Elgarroth said. "And he received help from Benasti."

Vecnor released a frustrated breath. The rumors in Nira were true.

"As we speak," Elgarroth added, "the enemy prepares to march on Nira. But we will touch more on that later. For now, I wish to discuss that which you witnessed."

Thoughts of Karrak had nearly driven all thoughts of corpses and dragon bones from Vecnor's mind.

"The dunarchins have taken the dragon remains to Trannum's stronghold," Elgarroth said. "I fear to learn what the necromancer has planned."

"You don't know?"

"I have my suspicions. But we will have to wait and see." The wizard hesitated. "Then there are the dead kings."

"Kings?"

Elgarroth nodded. "The corpse in Selt was Dunuthar the Wicked."

Vecnor frowned. "The priest-king from before my time?"

Elgarroth nodded again. "And in Benasti you saw Anduiff."

That was a name Vecnor had nearly forgotten. The evil krukari was lord over the forest longer than any other. Vecnor was a normal human then, and it was the last time Kalmaar openly associated with the dark woodland… until Tarm. "Why didn't their corpses rise years ago? When the Wind blew?"

Elgarroth peered into the campfire as if he had not heard the question. His eyes then returned to Vecnor. "The intent for these corpses is not clear, but one of the tomes Selanna procured touches upon dead kings." He shook his head. "Trannum has uncovered power greater than any since Uustaag. How he has accomplished all we have seen should be impossible. I do not believe he draws strength from Vou alone. And everything he has done… It has been methodical, as if he has planned for every contingency. For each possible action I see Vaeldor employ against him, his response is immediate and harsh."

"Perhaps we need to alter our approach," said Vecnor.

Elgarroth let go a chuckle. "You may be correct. Warriors, kings, and the High Order have been dictating every move. It is time we steer them back toward Seac's prophecy." He glanced at a tome lying at his feet. Had it been there all along? "It is also time to see what else Trannum has recorded in that library of his. I must discover from where he obtained his power."

"You're not sending me to Sistama... are you?"

Elgarroth held a brief smirk. "No. I need you elsewhere." He turned to the fire. "I will make that journey myself."

Himself? Elgarroth never left the clearing, other than occasional visits to the Council of Wizards. That was why he had Vecnor and Tux. Things must be dire indeed.

"Is that wise?" Vecnor posed.

"It is necessary," replied Elgarroth. "But it is not an expedition I can take just yet. I shall first travel to Darmhorng to speak with Karrak." In response to Vecnor's narrowing gaze, he added, "You will be far too busy for such a task." The wizard set down his pipe. "And it is time I get to it. Selanna and Eraim depart from Palidur soon to visit me. I must return before they arrive."

"What am I to do?" asked Vecnor.

Elgarroth balked, as if unsure of his answer. "You need to keep watch on Tarm. You will pose as a castle guard and perform duties for the throne, regardless of who sits on it." The wizard emphasized the last part. "Do not stand out. Do not recruit or sway the opinions of others. You are not to interfere. Just observe."

Vecnor pursed his lips. Elgarroth must be desperate to send him to Darmhorng. He needed to leave his anger behind for the sake of Vaeldor. "It shall be done."

"Good." Elgarroth scanned Vecnor from head to feet. "You will need a new form."

❈❈❈

Norvec rode Barcum through Vermallon Forest. Elgarroth had nothing to worry about—Norvec could never stir things up in Darmhorng. He was of regular height and build, with a face that could easily blend into a crowd. And without Tux around, Vecnor had to come up with the name on his own. Elgarroth completed the disguise with a royal uniform and a sword typical of a Kalmiran soldier. Vecnor hoped his new body was up to the task.

War consumed the road into Kalmaar, and Vermallon elves protected their eastern border while Nirans patrolled the area north of the Great East River. So there was no passing into the south by normal means. With that in mind, Norvec journeyed to Tux's ford — Vecnor had used it many times, and was well aware of its location. After crossing the river, Norvec scaled the mountain alongside Candermane Falls and entered Candermane Tunnel.

Elgarroth's enchantment allowing Umbarc to squeeze through the narrow opening was both confusing and disturbing, so Norvec focused on the way ahead while Barcum entered behind him. It was better than riding the extra miles necessary to go around the mountains' northern reaches. Upon exiting the tunnel two days later, Norvec headed south, following the faded dwarfish path Eslimil revealed to Vecnor centuries prior. The trail skirted Benasti Forest to a fordable section of the Morimont River, and after riding across the waterway, Norvec turned east. He followed the water to Lake Garaard, and Darmhorng Castle and Burmagaard appeared in the distance.

Norvec dismounted near a copse of trees concealing a secret entrance into the castle's dungeon. Elgarroth instructed him not to use the underground passage, as the wizard didn't wish to risk its discovery, so he'd have to walk the remaining three hundred yards.

"You're on your own," he said to Barcum. "But don't wander too far. And be safe."

The horse nodded and whinnied.

Norvec patted Barcum's neck, and the animal trotted back along the river. Taking in a deep breath, Norvec headed east.

A road connected the northern entrance of Burmagaard to Darmhorng Castle. The rear of the stronghold butted against Lake Garaard, and a twenty-foot wall encompassed the rest. The castle gate was open. Many people wandered the fields surrounding the city, some returning from hunting trips, some working in gardens, and others enjoying a walk or a ride, and a couple of wagons carried miners on their way home from the Varlimor Mountains. Norvec mingled with the hunters, nodding to a few. When they veered toward the city's north gate, he proceeded to Darmhorng.

He strode past the guards at the gatehouse, maintaining a look of confidence, and no one questioned him. Within the courtyard, soldiers and lackeys rushed about on errands, blacksmiths pounded horseshoes, and young squires trained with wooden swords. Norvec continued to the stronghold's entrance. A pair of guards stood to either side of the open doors, holding a conversation and paying little attention as he walked by without a word.

Knowing the interior of Darmhorng well, Norvec reported to the dungeon guardroom. It possessed a sturdy table and a couple of benches, and half a dozen crossbows hung from the wall. Four guards sat at the table, one apparently sleeping, one doing nothing to stifle a yawn, and the other two looking as bored as Tewlon felt while spying on Wornduir. The latter two stared at Norvec as he took a seat, their brows furrowing.

Norvec pulled out a deck of cards. "Anyone fancy a game of Slay the Dragon?"

"Cards aren't allowed," said a guard as he elbowed the dozing soldier into waking.

Norvec winked and dealt everyone a hand.

The warriors looked at one another and grinned, and that was that. They accepted Norvec.

A few hours later, four soldiers arrived to relieve the group. Norvec left the cards on the table and exited with the others, all of them speaking as if they were old friends, and they headed for the dining hall.

Two weeks passed, and no one questioned Norvec's presence. Ralspen, the lieutenant in charge of his squad, frowned upon first noticing him, but after seeing how well he executed orders with skill and discipline, the officer said nothing. Every few days, Norvec produced another deck of cards from one of Elgarroth's magic pouches, and he always left it behind. Unfortunately, he could not access the dungeon—Ralspen didn't supply those particular soldiers. But he made sure a deck found its way down the stairwell. Perhaps the cards might occupy the guards when Selanna and Eraim sneaked in to visit King Karrak—Norvec was certain that was the plan.

A couple of months later, Malgabi arrived to meet with Tarm. The two entered the library to be alone, but Vecnor knew the castle better than most, and Norvec utilized a secret passage to gain access. He squatted among the bookshelves, unknown to the room's occupants.

"You are to take Marcove," said Malgabi, "and add it to the growing empire."

"For what purpose?" asked Tarm. "It's a pitiful kingdom with little to offer."

"Because it is the master's wish." Malgabi's tone was insistent. "Do you question his wisdom?"

"No." Tarm was quick to reply. "Of course not."

"You could very easily—"

"I need no assistance in the matter!" Tarm's voice grew hot. "I can take care of Marcove without your help."

"Very good," said Malgabi. "But I caution you, do not allow your men to cross the border into Nomedd."

"Why?" Tarm's suspicion was obvious.

"Let's just say they will not like what they find."

While the two spoke, a thought occurred to Norvec, and he glanced at the rafters. Barely visible within the shadows upon a support beam was a figure cloaked in black. Darkness filled the hood, and it turned slightly to face Norvec. Norvec nodded once, and the figure returned the gesture. Of course Tux was present! And the elf always saw through Vecnor's disguises.

"What about Gruzim?" posed Tarm. "How much longer before I can slay the creature?"

"Don't be a fool!" Malgabi's voice contained laughter. "You know you are to leave him be. He will rule over the Batorn region so you can concentrate on things here."

"I have capable men to handle such tasks," the false king spat. "I don't need the likes of Benasti scum working beside me. And especially not their *lord*."

"This is the way it shall be." Malgabi's tone was icy.

Silence followed. Then footsteps of one pacing.

"What about the crypts of Radaam and Cadorn?" Tarm asked. "Word has reached me they were pillaged last year and the kings' bodies taken. Was that *your* doing?"

"Do not concern yourself with the deceased." Malgabi's voice was smug again. "They belong to the master now."

"To what end?"

"He'll reveal that in good time," Malgabi replied. "And I assure you, it will be glorious!"

More kings. And Radaam among them. If dunarchins were made from firstborns, what evil might the corpses of monarchs release? A chill raced along Norvec's spine. He began to creep back through the secret entrance when Tarm's words brought him to a halt.

"What about Karrak? Dare I say I still hold respect for the man? And why do I keep his Royal Guard imprisoned? Why not just be done with them?"

"Other than keeping him alive," Malgabi said, "Karrak is not your concern. Master will send for him soon enough."

"What will happen to him?"

There was a pause. When Malgabi spoke at last, it was obvious the question would go unanswered.

"Do not be hasty to dispose of Karrak's soldiers. They may become useful."

Norvec crawled from the room and pulled the secret door closed behind him. He couldn't bear to hear anymore.

Thoughts flooded his mind while he made his way along the passage. Tarm didn't seem as evil as he first believed. But the man remained a puppet for the necromancer and needed to be overthrown. Hopefully, Eraim and Selanna would be of some help in that matter, though Norvec was unsure what they might accomplish. The two had surely visited the dungeon by now, but Karrak would never allow them to execute a rescue. It would shame the king in the eyes of Brondor.

When Norvec exited the secret tunnel into the pantry, he detected movement. Someone was rummaging among the shelves. He peeked around the crates concealing him to spy a scullery maiden collecting items for the kitchen. Pulling a coin from his pouch, he cast it into the far corner, away from the only door. The maiden's attention snapped toward the noise as she gasped, and Norvec scrambled through the exit.

"Norvec!" said a soldier named Paknal. "There you are. Lieutenant Ralspen issued our orders an hour ago." He glanced at the pantry door. "What were you doing in there?"

The door opened, and the maiden exited. She bowed to Norvec and Paknal before moving on to perform her duties.

"You dog!" Paknal chuckled. "We'd best report. The queen's pregnancy has expanded her usual list of demands. We've quite the day ahead."

They left the kitchen.

Queen Mayry was a demanding woman, and she treated everyone as lowly servants—even the soldiers protecting her. A week ago, she made Norvec fetch her fresh water. After that, he had to rub her feet. The queen's midwife received the worst of the treatment. Mayry had struck the poor woman several times in Norvec's presence—every discomfort was the fault of the midwife. What would the queen require today? Pillow fluffing? Being spoon fed? It was neither of those. On this occasion, Norvec and his unit did not tend to Mayry personally. It seemed there was a popular baker in Barraday whose pastries had taken priority over all other cravings. And now Norvec's squadron had the pleasure of traveling to the opposite end of the kingdom to escort the man and his family north, so they could settle into their new lives.

The order took two weeks to accomplish.

Norvec saw little of Tarm over the next several months. It was probably for the best. As well, his time with Mayry whittled away, as she had grown picky about those allowed in her presence, and it seemed Norvec wasn't attractive enough—not particularly displeasing news. But all of that changed when the royal child was born.

It was a festive day, and the arrival of baby Durl was celebrated throughout Burmagaard and Darmhorng. The mood surrounding the castle darkened, however, when Durl went missing not long after. A search of the royal grounds ensued, followed by the invasion of every house and building in and around Burmagaard. Durl could not be found. Darmhorng was in such an uproar that news about Karrak's death nearly went unnoticed. The king had escaped his cell and attacked the guards. It seemed no one cared, save for Norvec and a handful of soldiers that still respected the fallen monarch.

Norvec learned of Karrak's fate from guards who had witnessed the aftermath. It appeared to have occurred right around the time Durl disappeared. Karrak was over seventy years old, yet he defeated five jailers before expiring—some rumors held him to have overwhelmed twenty! Though the news rekindled Norvec's ire, he found solace in that Karrak had earned his way into Brondor's Halls. Unfortunately, the king's escape led to the imprisoned Royal Guards being removed, and wagons took them south, never to be seen again.

It was not long before Mayry was with her second child. And this time, the list of those allowed to assist her shrank even further. Her security tripled as the pregnancy reached its end, and for several months after the infant's arrival. Solinin was the name given to the boy, and Mayry rarely left the baby's side. It seemed she held a suspicious eye even for her husband.

The next year, Darmhorng received news of Kalmaar's victory over Marcove. The southern kingdom collapsed under the pressure of the Kalmiran army with minimal casualties. No one appeared happier than Mayry. Most of the following years were relatively peaceful. The illusion of peace faded, however, whenever Gruzim visited the castle. It wasn't a frequent occurrence, but it happened often enough to drive Norvec sick for the wanting to strike down the krukari. Fortunately, he never dealt with the Lord of Benasti, or rather, Lord of Peltagarr, as that was where Gruzim reigned, and the visits rarely lasted more than a few days.

As for Solinin, Norvec saw little of the boy, as the protective watch of Mayry remained firm. But once Solinin turned six, his sword training with Tarm began. It was the only time Mayry was not with her son, though a few of her loyal servants always meandered, pretending to clean. The queen obviously did not trust her husband with the child.

Tarm employed his best soldiers to spar with the prince, and although Elgarroth instructed Vecnor to remain in the background, Norvec exhibited combative skills to lift him into the ranks of the elite. So naturally, he was present for most of the lessons. Perhaps he might hear something said between father and son; something useful about Trannum's plans.

Additional years passed, and Mayry's watch over Solinin waned. It was likely due to the queen's vanity and constant need for servants to attend to her desires. In the absence of her spies, Solinin's training altered. The sessions no longer comprised only swordplay and archery. Tarm and his son spent hours in the library, speaking of strategies in battle, holding philosophical discussions, and debating right and wrong; good versus evil. Solinin proved an excellent student with an inquisitive mind.

"On which side of good and evil will history place us?" asked the lad, now a dozen years in age. "And the fact that we associate with Lord Gruzim? Or the Death Lord that visited last year?"

Norvec flinched at the mention of the Death Lord, recalling the chilling fear that encompassed the castle while the monster and its skeletal dragon were present. It was Trannum's newest creation, made from the corpse of an evil king. Tarm named the visitor Cadorn, a great and evil ruler of Kalmaar before Vecnor's time. Norvec never saw the dark warrior up close; the creature met with Tarm and Malgabi behind closed doors for several hours. All of Darmhorng was on edge until Cadorn and the undead mount departed that night.

Tarm frowned while considering his son's question. "Sometimes the line between good and evil is not so easily judged. Is a man evil for slaying guards, taking husbands from their wives and fathers from their children, if the deed is done to free those wrongfully imprisoned? Some folks consider that man a hero. But to the families of the guards…"

"Did you free such persons?" Solinin posed.

Tarm didn't smile, but he appeared pleased with the question all the same. "Then there are those whose minds are corrupted by dark magic. Though their actions might be considered criminal, what if it was not of their free will? Should they be branded evil?"

Solinin scrunched his face in thought. "I suppose it depends on what the man does after the spell has passed."

Tarm grinned to one side. "You are a smart boy. And you're correct. But sometimes it's not so easy to right those wrongs. Sometimes it takes years to achieve."

Norvec pondered the false king's words while remaining at the door to guard against intrusions. Did Tarm speak the truth? Had Trannum possessed his mind? Was he attempting to repent? Back in the Stone Eagles, the necromancer placed a spell on Merssa, Eraim, and Selanna, forcing them to abandon all hope. Unlike those three, Tarm didn't have Borse to free him. It was a path the duke had to travel on his own. Norvec's ire for Tarm shifted to Trannum.

Solinin's training continued over the next few years, and although kingly duties often kept Tarm away, the false king did not relent in raising the prince to be a thinking man. Norvec did his best to aid in that endeavor during his sessions with the lad. As well, he pushed Solinin, in hopes the young warrior would exceed the puppet ruler in swordplay, and Solinin seemed appreciative of the special attention.

"Can there be good among the undead?" Solinin asked Norvec one day.

Did the young man refer to the dunarchins that visited the castle last year? Or the Death Lord that led them? Norvec wasn't sure he was the right person to ask, so he provided information given to him by Elgarroth years ago.

"After one dies, their soul escapes this world to reside within the realm of their deity. But when their corpse is risen by dark magic, their soul is ripped from that paradise and trapped between worlds. Their body wanders, trying to satisfy a hunger that cannot be quelled. What's left of their mind is driven mad. Do you believe such a madness can lead to good?"

"I like you, Norvec." Solinin smirked. "I'm going to request more lessons with you. I don't think Father will object."

Norvec searched for Elgarroth, fearing he had gone too far. He was alone in his head. "Nah." He raised a hand. "Your father is the greatest swordsman in the land." The words left an ill taste on his tongue. "I am only here to help, as the king requires."

On the eve of Solinin's fifteenth birthday, Norvec found the prince sitting near Lake Garaard. The lad was unaccompanied, staring across the water at the distant trees of Benasti Forest.

"Hello, Norvec," Solinin said as Norvec approached.

"Prince Solinin." Norvec bowed. "Is something wrong?"

The young man stared at the horizon. "That depends." He turned to Norvec. "Are you the type of soldier that believes in what he teaches? Or are you a lackey of Kalmaar?"

Norvec frowned. "I don't understand. Did I displease you?"

Solinin chuckled. "Nonsense. Other than my father, you're the only one worth speaking to." He stood. "I'm leaving."

"But…" Norvec's mind raced. Leaving? Part of him feared for the prince. Another part was relieved. "To where? How?"

"The 'how' is easy enough." Solinin glanced about. No one would overhear. "I believe I can trust you, and I hope my judgement is not misplaced. But I cannot leave without you knowing. I hold too much respect for you."

Norvec raised a brow. "You said the 'how' is easy?"

"I received Father's birthday gift early." The prince grinned, pulling a large pouch from his belt. He opened it to reveal exquisite jewels. "I was told not to mention it to anyone. Not even Mother."

Norvec stared at the collection of earrings, necklaces, rings, and gemstones. He had seen them before, in the queen's chambers. "But surely the guards will see you leaving."

"It's not uncommon for me to ride around the lake." Solinin half smiled. "If I can reach Benasti," he looked across the water, "I believe I can exit the kingdom unnoticed. From what I hear, the forest holds less than a third of its normal population of hobgoblins and krukari."

"What about the wolves?" asked Norvec.

Solinin shrugged. "I cannot remain any longer. The undead… The Death Lords… The Benasti cowards… Father is growing bitter, and Mother rarely speaks to him. The only time Father smiles is when we speak of traveling." He sniffed. "Of course, that is something a king cannot do. Even so, we have studied maps of the realms, traced roads, and he has taught me the names of several cities he insists I would love. Like Tikken City."

"A fair city indeed," said Norvec.

Solinin furrowed his brow. "You've been there?"

Norvec grinned. "Once or twice."

"How would *you* get there," the prince narrowed his eyes, "if you took a holiday and didn't want anyone to know?"

Norvec sighed. Elgarroth might disapprove, but his affection for the lad had grown over the years. He couldn't leave Solinin to face the monsters of Benasti Forest. Not when another option existed.

"There's a section of the Morimont River shallow enough to cross near the southwestern border of Benasti," he said. "That's where I'd go. But I would stay clear of the forest. The dwarves made a path long ago, so ancient that even they have forgotten it, and it leads to a secret tunnel. If I follow that tunnel, I'll find myself south of Vermallon Forest, among the northern reaches of the Varlimor Mountains. From there, I'd descend into the valley and follow the old dwarf trail into Sardina."

Solinin held a wry smile. "You're making this up."

"But I'd want a horse," Norvec added, "even though I'd have to set it free at the secret tunnel's entrance. And I'd leave before winter. The mountains can be tricky once snow arrives."

"You speak the truth?" Solinin's eyes portrayed more hope than conviction.

"If you show me your map," Norvec winked, "I'll mark it down for you. But only if you swear to share it with no one."

The prince held a measuring gaze. "Who are you?"

"Just a Kalmiran that has led an interesting life," Norvec replied. "That is, until I got stuck babysitting *you*."

Solinin grinned. "If you ever do get out for a holiday, you must come find me."

"For me, holidays are rare." Norvec placed his hand on the prince's shoulder. "I wish you luck."

They returned to the castle and entered Solinin's chamber to view the maps. Norvec grew nervous that Tarm or Mayry might discover their meeting, but he took the necessary time to mark the secret ways and explain how to traverse the trails and Candermane Tunnel safely. Once they finished, Solinin gathered a few items from his room, including his sword and winter cloak, and readied to leave. He and Norvec then clasped arms, followed by an embrace, and Norvec fought back a tear. Solinin was a flower growing among a field of weeds, starving for nutrients. Perhaps now the lad would find a better life.

Norvec traversed the castle with Solinin several paces behind, making sure they didn't run into Mayry. They made it to the courtyard, and Solinin proceeded to the royal stables to obtain his Batorn steed.

Norvec sighed. He was going to miss the young man.

Peering over his shoulder, Norvec spied Mayry and three handmaidens exiting the castle. The queen scanned the courtyard, surely seeking her son. There wasn't much time, and when the women neared, Norvec placed his boot on a water trough and put forth all his strength to topple it. Its contents raced across the dirt and over the ladies' lovely shoes.

"What in the name of…?" Mayry's face grew red, and she spun on Norvec.

"A thousand pardons, Your Majesty!"

"You insolent fool! I shall see you hanged!" She turned toward the castle. "Guards! Guards!"

Seconds later, a squadron arrived. Weblar led the soldiers, a lieutenant Norvec was familiar with from the training grounds. Norvec had defeated several of the lieutenant's men in mock combat to earn a place among Solinin's trainers.

"Your Highness?" said Weblar.

"Throw this *oaf* in the dungeon!" she shrieked. "Immediately! I do not want to see him again until his head is no longer atop his shoulders!"

"Yes, my queen." Weblar bowed. "It shall be done."

The lieutenant nodded to his men, and they seized Norvec's arms.

Norvec glanced over his shoulder. Solinin was gone.

"Blasted peasants!" Mayry and her maidens trudged back into the castle.

"Well, Norvec…" Weblar grinned. "You best hide in the barracks for a while. Maybe grow some facial hair."

"Yes, sir!" Norvec smirked as the soldiers released him. "I shall make myself invisible."

It was a good thing none of the guards cared for the queen.

Norvec entered Darmhorng, careful to avoid Mayry, and approached the barracks. As he arrived, he found Tarm awaiting him outside the door.

"Follow me," the false king ordered before heading farther down the hallway.

What now? There were too many reasons Tarm might want to speak to Norvec, none of them good. He had no choice, and he followed the man into a tidy study. He had never seen Tarm use it before.

"Close the door," Tarm said.

Norvec did as instructed and turned back. "Sire —"

Tarm held up a hand. "I have watched you for some time. Your skills are beyond that of a mercenary or soldier." He sat on the desk. "And I saw you speaking with Solinin by the lake."

"I only made sure the prince has all he requires."

Tarm waved off the statement. "I also witnessed your little show while Solinin rode off."

"Um..." Norvec was at a loss.

Tarm stood. "Please, tell me he has gone for good." The man's expression combined desperation and hope.

Norvec slowly nodded.

"Good." Tarm's eyes welled with sadness, but then they narrowed on Norvec. "Who are you?"

Norvec didn't answer. He lifted his chin as high as his body allowed and maintained a level gaze.

"Never mind." Tarm walked to the door. "It doesn't matter." He turned back. "But I thank you for your part. If this is Selanna's doing, I am indebted to her twice."

Selanna? What had she done? Norvec still did not speak.

Tarm opened the door. "Well, it's time we return to our duties. Malgabi arrives this week." His face soured. "And Gruzim." He shook his head and focused on Norvec. "You should remain clear of the queen."

"Yes, sire."

Tarm nodded once and left.

It is time to come home, said Elgarroth. *Wait until nightfall, and let no one witness your departure.*

The world lifted from Norvec's shoulders; the castle suddenly seemed brighter. The wizard's message arrived not a moment too soon. Norvec dreaded what the guards would have to endure once Mayry discovered her son's absence. But it was no longer his concern. He headed for the barracks.

Chapter 20

A Moment's Rest

Umbarc, not Barcum, came running from the fields of northwestern Kalmaar in response to Vecnor's call. Great relief had swept over Vecnor when he transformed into his true self once he was a mile from Darmhorng. He did not wish to fight as Norvec if faced with opposition while returning to the House of Elgarroth.

After crossing the Morimont River, Vecnor and Umbarc made their way north into the mountains. By morning, snow drifted from the sky, and a half hour later, the flakes painted the region white. Strange, since winter was yet a month away. Hopefully the weather had not hindered Solinin. Vecnor had prepared the prince for that contingency, and the young warrior rode one of the finest steeds Darmhorng had to offer. Still, Vecnor occasionally glanced down the slopes to make sure Solinin's body wasn't lying in a valley. A morbid thought.

Vecnor pulled his heavy cloak from a saddlebag and strapped it over his shoulders. But little did it protect him from the wind whipping out of the east. He urged Umbarc, and the massive horse pushed through the snow with ease—being from Andria, the animal was used to such weather. They slept in caves through the nights and continued north while the light lasted, reaching the Candermane Tunnel at last. To the northeast, a thick white blanket covered southern Nira. The land likely had not seen spring in some time.

The subterranean passage was frigid, though free of snow, and Vecnor discovered evidence that someone had camped within the first chamber. It must have been Solinin—Tux never left any signs of passing. Vecnor released a breath of relief and slowed his pace to make sure he didn't catch up with the young warrior. He exited near the falls two days later to see that winter had not followed him. To the contrary, it was a mild autumn day. He put away his cloak and headed north.

Riding nonstop, Vecnor reached the cabin in good time. Elgarroth and Tux sat around the fire in silence, their expressions grim. Vecnor unsaddled Umbarc and joined them.

"Trannum made his move while both of you were away," Elgarroth said once Vecnor took a seat. "More than a decade ago, in fact. Though it is old news to most of Vaeldor, Ironside Keep and Palidur have fallen. Sardina is under Trannum's control."

Vecnor's heart skipped a beat. He had sent Solinin into Sardina. Perhaps the prince's training and familiarity with the undead would help the young warrior find a path. The full weight of the wizard's words then struck. "What about Merssa and Vikur?"

"They are alive," Elgarroth replied. "Ballrik rescued his father through a secret tunnel after a Death Lord arrived with an army of undead. Poluran is with Vikur now, and the former Lord of the Keep is not well. His spirit is weak, and I fear for him.

"As for Palidur," Elgarroth added, "Merssa, Soren, and Nilborg are the only surviving members of the High Order. Merssa has claimed the land north of Palidur Bridge, and she is raising a force to challenge the necromancer."

"Other than Death Lords and dunarchins coming and going," said Tux, "I saw nothing at Trannum's stronghold to suggest a war had begun."

Vecnor stared at the fire. Vaeldor suffered while he squandered years in Kalmaar, spying on Tarm and enjoying time with Solinin. Why hadn't Elgarroth sent for him sooner? He looked at Tux, and the elf's expression matched his outrage.

Elgarroth turned to Vecnor. "It might interest you to know that Tarm will soon be dead. Gruzim will slay the king and take the throne, and Mayry will be at the krukari's side."

Though disturbing, the last part wasn't surprising.

The wizard puffed on his pipe and gazed into the smoke, as if reading text. "This union will produce a son, and that child will be strong. I see him aging quickly. Trannum's doing, no doubt. But for what purpose, I cannot tell."

Vecnor shifted on the log, wishing to speak, but frustration didn't allow for the words to form. Elgarroth answered his unasked question.

"As I have told you, things will worsen before they can improve. I placed both of you where you could do the most good. Had you interfered, the outcome would likely be very different. But I assure you, Vaeldor would not be better for it. And we shall leave it at that."

Vecnor took in a calming breath. The elf seer wouldn't sit by and allow thousands of pointless deaths. He had to believe that. "What about Solinin?" he asked the wizard.

Elgarroth studied the fire. "I see Solinin crossing Palidur Bridge. He will be mistaken for a survivor that was trapped behind enemy lines. Soldiers will question him and set him free."

At least that part would end well. Vecnor's heart lightened, if only slightly. "What about Sistama? Did you make the trip?"

Tux looked up, obviously unaware of the conversation Vecnor and Elgarroth shared years ago.

Elgarroth nodded. "I visited the last home Trannum knew in his living days. The swamp remains a lair for ghouls, though I doubt there are as many as when you two ventured there."

"What did you find?" Vecnor asked.

Elgarroth's brows drew together. "The books Trannum wrote are cryptic. But I found the tome Selanna was missing; the one referencing Death Lords." He looked from Tux to Vecnor. "As I am sure you both realize, the spirits of these evil kings are far more powerful than dunarchins. They retain the skills and knowledge they possessed while alive, as well as additional abilities granted to them by Trannum. The necromancer enchanted them with the magic that once powered the orb taken from Garthglen Swamp. They are the reason for the fall of both Ironside Keep and the Holy City."

Vecnor shook his head. "I'll admit, when Cadorn visited Darmhorng, fear gripped at my heart."

"It is an unnatural fear," said Elgarroth. "And the icy aura they radiate bears the same effect as the Wind of the Dead. Simply flying across a battlefield on their bone dragons can raise the fallen and change the course of a war."

Vecnor's stomach soured. "I heard mention of Radaam."

Elgarroth nodded. "Seven evil kings of old were taken to Trannum, to be exact. There are also over twenty thousand dunarchins, and they continue to hunt for more."

"With the necromancer's ability to grow his forces," said Tux, "I fail to see how Vaeldor can win."

Elgarroth drew from his pipe. "Indeed. There are no easy roads. The best path is Seac's Prophecy of Trannum. The *companies four* must be formed, and I believe I have set Merssa on this course of action."

"We'll be involved, right?" Vecnor posed.

"That goes without saying. But as to where you offer the greatest chance of success," Elgarroth shrugged, "I have yet to determine. Troubling images have haunted me, the most disturbing involving Vikur, Poluran, and Ballrik."

Vecnor frowned. "They wouldn't return to the keep, would they?"

Elgarroth stared at Vecnor for several seconds. "Not Ballrik. He has no desire to see its walls again." He sighed. "As for Vikur, he has lost his keep, and he cannot live with that failure. I'm afraid he will try to rectify the situation."

"And Poluran will be there to help him," added Vecnor.

Elgarroth nodded. "Poluran is old. His days are numbered. And before he goes, he craves the chance to right his perceived wrongs. It will not end well."

Vecnor turned back to the fire. Elgarroth would never allow him to steer Vikur to a better path. The elf would say something about it affecting the war, or that it provided no benefit to Vaeldor. So there was no point in pursuing the topic. This was part of Vecnor's occupation he could do without. Perhaps the wizard should have withheld the information.

Elgarroth gave Vecnor a knowing look. "It is for the best. Though misguided, their expedition will advance the prophecy."

Exactly as Vecnor expected.

"I am also concerned with the offspring of the women from Dimarr's village," Elgarroth said. "The Andrians call them zhomians, or black hearts. As I thought, they are neither wholly alive nor undead." He looked at Vecnor. "And they do not die unless their hearts are destroyed."

"Another one of Trannum's blasted experiments," grumbled Vecnor.

Elgarroth lifted his brow. "An accidental creation. I believe Trannum realized their existence only recently."

"Should we not destroy them?" posed Tux.

Elgarroth shook his head. "There are too many, and they are spread wide. A Brondor paladin named Sullis hunts them, and he will inform Merssa of all she needs to know. But they remain clouded in contradiction. While some flock to Trannum's call, others resist the necromancer. We will have to allow their part to run its course."

Tux shook his head. "What are we to do for now?"

"Get some rest," Elgarroth replied. "You shall need all of your strength very soon. I, on the other hand, must depart. There is an intriguing soul named Nidor I wish to visit. A barbarian paladin out of Holindale."

"Barbarian paladin?" Vecnor furrowed his brow. "I've never heard of such a thing."

"No." Elgarroth returned his attention to the campfire. "It is quite the anomaly. And a paladin of Silcor... Another mystery. I have not seen such a being in all my years." He looked at Vecnor and Tux. "I believe the gods are intervening."

"If that is so," said Tux, "then an evil deity has certainly involved itself."

Elgarroth inspected his pipe. "That is my fear."

"With all the undead," Vecnor searched the surrounding trees, "it must be Shadia. Her priests often deal in necromancy."

The wizard puffed a couple of times and released the smoke. "I am not so sure. This feels darker."

Tux eyed the mage. "There is only one darker than Shadia."

"Thard'Dun," Vecnor muttered.

Elgarroth shook his head. "The very deity Uustaag worshipped."

"Should I visit the Guardians?" asked Tux.

"No." The wizard gazed at the sky. "There is a more pressing matter on the horizon. So rest. I will let you know when the time comes to act." He regarded them both. "You must then employ all of your abilities. Hold nothing back."

Vecnor didn't like the sound of that. The road ahead was surely grim for Elgarroth to issue such an order.

CHAPTER 21
RESCUE MISSION

Sitting before the fire, Vecnor took another bite from the freshly prepared turkey leg he found in the kitchen. Tux was not around, but he knew the elf must be home because of the smoke issuing from the chimney. It always smoked when Vecnor or the elves were present, and its steady stream revealed Tux to be inside.

Vecnor had just finished a two-hour workout with his swords, preparing for whatever lay ahead. Elgarroth did not divulge the next mission before departing a week prior. The wizard rarely did. It had something to do with the shifting roads of the future, and Elgarroth preferred to keep those paths secret until they became clearer.

Elgarroth journeyed east to speak with Nidor. Vecnor couldn't help wondering about the paladin out of Holindale. What did such a being look like? Act like? How could a barbarian harness the discipline necessary to follow the code steering a paladin's life? Vecnor had known hundreds of Andrians over the years, and not one of them possessed such a drive.

Tux exited the house, and the chimney smoke eased to a trickle. The elf appeared well rested. He reopened the door and entered, and moments later emerged with a piece of sweetbread, an apple, and a handful of boiled acorns. He nodded at Vecnor and took a seat at the fire, and the two ate their lunches in silence. Shortly after they finished, Elgarroth's voice sounded in Vecnor's head.

Gather your gear. The time is at hand.

Tux looked at Vecnor. The elf received the command as well.

Without a word, they walked to the door. Tux entered first, and Vecnor waited for the door to shut before doing the same. Laid out on a large table opposite his bed was his equipment. He donned his armor and strapped on his belts, and checked his pouches to make sure he had everything he needed. All was in order.

Vecnor exited to find Tux waiting. The elf wore his dark gray leather with a sword at his side, and slung over his shoulder was his special bow.

Elgarroth spoke again.

Enter the house.

Vecnor opened the door to a small room. To the left, a table held three crystal vials. To the right, an archway was etched into the wall. Runes adorned the arch, and from the sawdust on the floor, they were carved recently.

Each of you drink from a vial. This will provide some protection.

Vecnor raised a brow at Tux, who shrugged. They had never been required to imbibe an elixir before. Each of them removed a stopper and downed the contents. The flavor reminded Vecnor of burning wood, and the aftertaste was like ash on his tongue.

"Fire?" Tux asked the room, his expression a combination of perplexion and concern.

Yes. The elixirs will protect you from the heat. And my enchantments should resist the demons' attacks.

"Demons?" Vecnor's heart rate increased as he recalled Hezeb and Ragab. "We're entering Hell?" he posed, hoping he had misunderstood.

It is necessary. Ballrik, son of Vikur, will sacrifice himself to save thousands of lives.

Vecnor frowned. "I thought we didn't serve individuals."

This is an exception. Though his life beyond this sacrifice has no bearing on the upcoming war, we cannot allow his fate to end in such torment. He deserves better. The last vial is for him.

Vecnor and Tux shared a determined glance. They couldn't help Vikur. The least they could do was rescue Vikur's son. Still, it wasn't like Elgarroth to ignore the rules. It was proof a heart existed in the wizard's chest.

The portal came to life as the arch filled with a swirling orange light, like billowing flames. Tux grabbed the third vial.

Once you enter, our link will be severed. You are to journey forward half a mile to reach the portal where Ballrik will appear. Return him through this gate.

Vecnor and Tux nodded in unison. With deep breaths, they stepped through the archway.

A strange world replaced the room. It was searing hot, though it didn't bother Vecnor in the slightest, and a haze limited his sight to a hundred yards. Thirty feet overhead, a layer of gray smoke hung like a ceiling over the bizarre terrain. Random wisps of darkness swirled within the giant cloud while flashes of lightning that did not descend illuminated silhouettes, like deformed whales swimming through an ocean of smog. Behind Vecnor was a freestanding arch of stone filled with green light, and scattered ahead were rock formations, appearing as stacks of flat round stones. Most stood eight to fifteen feet high while others pierced the canopy of fog. There was no breeze of any kind—the air tasted stale and bore the scent of old, open wounds. In the distance, Vecnor detected a moan. It rose and fell, like the call of an insect, and another began as it faded, sounding from a different distant location.

Vecnor drew his swords while Tux nocked an arrow, and without a word, they walked forward on the rock-hard soil. As they neared the tree-like pillars, Vecnor took a closer look. Were they indeed piles of flat stones? Or solid formations? Some bore streaks of what appeared to be thick blood, and one possessed a small hole oozing the same red fluid. Vecnor put a sword between himself and the column when an enormous centipede scuttled around its surface. The many-legged worm was five feet long and a foot wide, and in place of its mandibles were teeth reminiscent of a cat's. The creature clamped its mouth over the opening and began sucking.

Vecnor glanced at Tux. The elf watched the centipede, his face twisted in disgust.

They moved forward.

After a hundred yards, the pillars dwindled and spouts of fire sprang from the landscape ahead. The jets did not seem to come from any source; they simply issued from the ground, rising to heights of ten feet and leaving scorch marks on the cracked soil. Thousands of the dark spots were visible. Vecnor and Tux proceeded with caution, and one such flame erupted beneath Vecnor's foot. Though he didn't feel its burn, he reflexively pulled away. He expelled a relieved breath, and he and Tux continued at a quickened pace.

Thirty yards farther, the spouts ended, and a rise sat at the edge of Vecnor's vision. Nothing changed while they approached, and its slope led them to within a few feet of the ceiling. Vecnor then froze. The land fell before them, and he saw across the resulting valley to mountainous formations of the rock trees half a mile away. The pillars stood against each other, appearing more like a wall, and missing columns created tunnels leading into darkness. The wall stretched beyond sight to the left and right, and at least a hundred openings were visible.

Tux nudged Vecnor and nodded at the valley. A forest of stone pillars covered much of the low ground to the right, and within was a clearing roughly thirty yards in diameter. A lone rock formation stood in its center, bent over to form a freestanding arch filled with blue light. Vecnor then noticed the "trees" differed from the ones he had seen thus far. They ended in points, and each impaled the back of a motionless body, suspending them at various heights. The corpses appeared human, though Vecnor couldn't be sure. A moan emitted from one of them.

"Tormented Souls," said Tux. "Do not look at them."

Vecnor frowned. "Have you been here before?"

Tux shook his head. "Something I read."

Vecnor returned his gaze to the blue light. "That must be the gate we seek."

Tux nodded.

They descended the slope. Though it looked steep, it was not as difficult as Vecnor would have thought. The moaning picked up in frequency once they reached the bottom, as if in response to their presence, and the impaled bodies were twitching.

After stepping among the spires, Vecnor couldn't help glancing at a Tormented Soul. It was a man in tattered clothing stained with what must be his own blood. One eye lay on the ground while the other pale orb gazed longingly at Vecnor, and his cracked lips parted to show decaying teeth coated by a black substance.

"Save me!" The man's voice was hoarse, as if years of wailing had dried out his throat. "It wasn't my fault. I don't belong here. Have mercy!"

"Do not look at them!" Tux snapped.

Vecnor faced forward, and the Tormented Soul's tone became a venomous hiss.

"It was you! *You* killed my wife! You bastard! I shall haunt your dreams 'til you go mad!"

Vecnor glanced back. The man's eye was now black and his teeth pointed, and a dark, forked tongue lashed in and out between his lips. Vecnor quickly turned away.

The moaning increased as they moved on, and try as he might, Vecnor couldn't resist looking at another victim. A woman. Other than her singed hair and ragged clothing, she was intact, and makeup adorned her face. She smiled and winked.

"My, aren't you a large man," she drawled. "I could use a large man like you. Do you fancy a good time?"

Vecnor focused on the way ahead, and the woman spoke harshly.

"You will die a thousand deaths! You will join my lovers from the ages and beg for mercy! I will have you!"

Again, Vecnor glanced back. Just as with the other Tormented Soul, her eyes were black, her teeth pointed, and a forked tongue danced with her words. But also her skin was shriveled and charred, as if she had been burned alive.

"Should I lead you by the hand?" asked Tux.

Vecnor cleared his throat. "We're almost there."

He kept his eyes forward, and he and Tux soon entered the clearing. The arch stood fifteen yards away, covered in runes that were likely written in blood. Less than a hundred yards to the left, the tunnels in the wall-like rocks towered above the stone forest, and from them, a steady stream of smoke fed the fog overhead. Vecnor's muscles tensed, and he gripped his swords tighter.

The portal grew bright, almost white, and a human warrior clutching a jewel-encrusted scepter tumbled through. The brilliant glow surrounded the man while the archway dulled to dark gray, and the ceiling took on a red tint. All at once, the Tormented Souls ceased moaning and began shouting a mixture of obscenities and pleas for help.

"You! You sent me here!"

"I smell your blood!"

"Please! Take me from this place!"

"The light! The light! It burns!"

"I hunger for your flesh!"

"Have you seen my little boy?"

The warrior rolled to his knee. His scabbard was empty, and strapped to his shoulder was a quiver holding a dozen arrows, but he possessed no bow. Beneath his grimace was a handsome face, and he dropped the scepter as he clapped his hands over his ears and pressed his eyes closed, as if to shut out the screams and strange surroundings.

"Ballrik!" Vecnor called. Though he had never met the young man, the resemblances to Vikur and Arkor were undeniable.

Ballrik's eyes opened, and he reached for his empty sheath while backing away. The Tormented Souls then stole his attention. His bottom lip quivered as his face paled, and it appeared he might faint, but when his skin started to smoke, he crumpled and began screaming.

Tux rushed forward, pulling the vial he took from the House of Elgarroth and removing the stopper. He forced it into Ballrik's mouth and upended it.

Ballrik ceased smoking; the aura surrounding him winked out. Above, the ceiling's red tint faded, and the Tormented Souls returned to their moaning. The young warrior momentarily calmed, but as his eyes focused on Tux, he scrambled from the elf's reach.

"Who are you? How do you know my name?"

The light filling the arch swirled, pulsating a brighter shade of gray as it emitted a blast of wind.

"I'm Vecnor. Now get behind me!"

Ballrik's jaw dropped while he viewed Vecnor, and he slowly nodded. He obeyed the command, accepting a dagger offered by Tux as a demon emerged from the archway. Ragab.

Vecnor controlled his breathing while eying the demon. It appeared just as it had in Trannum's tomb. Bony spurs protruded from its leathery brown skin, and a two-foot spike extended from its forehead between ram-like horns. As the creature rose to its full height to tower overhead, Vecnor spied multiple gashes covering much of its hide in green blood. The demon was fresh from battle.

Ragab snarled as its attention snapped Vecnor's way—not the gurgle of delight the fiend emitted in Trannum's tomb—and its red, cat-like eyes glowed with malice. The demon swung its oversized, six-fingered claw, and Vecnor danced safely back. Countering with his blade, he slashed through its lanky wrist, and the monster shrieked as its giant hand fell to the ground. Ragab belched fire in retaliation, and Vecnor braced himself, but like the fire spout earlier, the flames brought him no harm. He lunged, piercing Ragab through the chest. The creature's eyes darkened as it collapsed.

Several more shapes spilled from the arch, tumbling from the gray mist like an avalanche, and the wind ceased as the light vanished. Monsters then filled the clearing, including beastly insects, reptilian creatures, and human-like demons. Some had horns, some wings, a few possessed scorpion tails, and several bore combinations of those features. Most walked, while others crawled, slithered, or flew, and a dozen were wreathed in flames. Many had claws and bared pointed teeth while more than half wielded tridents, wicked swords, halberds, or barbed chains—some weapons were on fire. Although most of the demons were as tall as Ballrik, others reached only half his height or less, while several stood twice as high. The smallest were one-foot-tall imps that carried tiny, two-tined spears and giggled at Vecnor and his companions. The largest comprised a pair of monsters rising over twenty feet and appearing as scaly centaurs with flaming hair and bat wings. Hezeb was among the denizens of Hell, standing greater than twelve-feet tall, and smoke issued from the enlarged nostrils upon its jutting maw, just beneath its beady eyes. It roared, exposing multiple rows of vicious fangs.

Vecnor suddenly felt small. Beside him, Tux held an arrow ready. Ballrik stood nearby, wide-eyed and shaking while holding the dagger. The way back to the spires was now blocked by a dozen enemies, and every evil head turned toward Vecnor and his companions.

"Clear a path!" Vecnor commanded Tux, and he twirled his swords as he faced the clearing.

The first demon to approach was a beetle-like creature with a jagged shell and smoking mandibles. As it rose onto its hind legs, Vecnor saw that its four "arms" ended in spear-like appendages. The fiend thrust its arms in succession, and Vecnor knocked aside three attacks; the fourth penetrated his thigh. He grimaced and countered, slicing off two arms, and the monster's gray blood sprayed as it retreated with a shriek.

Five tiny demons leaped high into the air, and Vecnor spun his blades overhead while kicking a deformed, human-like creature possessing claws, one large and one small. His boot crushed the latter's nose, and his spinning weapons shredded the descending imps. He then brought a blade down to gash the clawed demon from chin to stomach.

Vecnor retreated slowly and without looking back. A reptilian beast lay to his right with arrows buried deep in its eye sockets, and a dog-like being with crab claws was to his left with a dark shaft protruding from its throat and two more from its chest. A ball of fire struck Vecnor, and then another, cast from flying demons that held additional burning orbs ready. The flames washed over him as nothing more than a hot breeze, and the attackers frowned.

A giant snake lunged, its teeth as long as daggers. Vecnor stopped its advance by placing a gash across its mouth. A second snake bit into his shoulder—the opposite end of the same creature. He cut deep into the attacker's neck and added another slash to the first head's jaw. The reptilian demon retreated.

Vecnor's hands shook as the shoulder wound grew hot. Unfortunately, Elgarroth's elixir didn't protect him from the poison now coursing through his body. His time was limited.

The ground trembled beneath a charging centaur demon, and Vecnor's arms lowered, his morale fading. He then noticed the moaning was louder than before—the forest of spires was close. He resumed the retreat with urgency, fending off a green monster with needles for teeth while passing additional creatures pierced by multiple arrows, including two man-like demons with horns, a female with bat wings and fangs, and three dwarf-sized fiends made of rolling flesh. As the centaur neared to within ten yards, Vecnor decapitated the green demon and dashed for the spires.

Tux stood at the edge of the rock trees, using his sword to slay a goat-headed man with claws—the fancy bow was slung over the elf's shoulder. Though his blade had often become red hot in the past, it was now white and left a trail of ice wherever it struck. Tux possessed injuries to his cheek, ear, arm, and stomach, but he remained nimble as he leaped to meet the dive of a vulture-like demon twice his size. The frosty weapon pierced the creature's flesh, and it cried out; and Tux slashed two more times before he alit, dropping his foe to the hard ground.

Ballrik was without the dagger as he hobbled among the spires. Blood issued from the young warrior's scalp, chest, and leg. He disappeared amid the rocks, where calls, hisses, begging, and curses now accompanied the moaning.

As Vecnor entered the stony forest, a stabbing sensation penetrated his armor between the shoulder blades. The pain was intense, and he stumbled. He gritted his teeth and pushed on, glancing back, but nothing was close enough to have struck him.

"Please!" said a Tormented Soul. "One sip of your blood is all I need. Then I'll be whole again! *Please*! You have more than you need!"

Vecnor ignored the utterances and continued.

Ballrik came into view. A woman impaled on a spire beckoned the young warrior with flattering words, and he limped toward her, as if in a daze. The Tormented Soul grinned when Ballrik neared, her teeth growing longer, but then Tux arrived, defying gravity while leaping onto the side of the spire above her. The elf sliced her head from her body, and Ballrik snapped from the trance.

Tux jumped to the ground, panting, while Vecnor caught up. Blood trickled from the elf's forehead and along his nose. "There are too many to overcome!"

Vecnor looked back. The Tormented Souls continued their chorus of insults and pleas, but no demons gave chase. "Why don't they pursue?"

"Perhaps it is these wretched creatures." Tux glanced at the decapitated body. It was limp, and she moaned no more.

"They'll surely try to block our path," Vecnor said. "We must move."

"Leave me!" Ballrik fell to his knees as tears streamed down his cheeks. "I can't make it."

"You're not dying here!" Vecnor growled.

He sheathed one of his blades and lifted the young man over his shoulder, aggravating the burning sensation of the snake bite. As well, the stabbing pain in his back felt as though it had penetrated deeper. He followed Tux as best he could around the spires until reaching the forest's border, where six flying demons awaited them. But the creatures didn't attack. They ascended into the cloud with grins on their hideous faces.

Tux led the way up the rise as if there were no slope. Vecnor stumbled a few times, but he refused to sheathe his blade. As he made it halfway up, he spotted the enemy circumventing the Tormented Souls by paths he had not noticed before. From the nearest route, Hezeb emerged, running with speed Vecnor would not have thought possible on its massive, short legs.

Tux arrived at the top of the ridge, and Vecnor accepted the elf's outstretched hand when he neared. Eslimil pulled with surprising strength, making the final steps less taxing. Below, Hezeb advanced effortlessly up the slope. Ballrik continued to whimper.

The field of erupting fire was next, and Vecnor and Tux ran a straight line without fear of the flames. As they reached its end, Hezeb roared from ten yards away. The demon belched fire, and though it brought no pain, the heat filled Vecnor's heart with dread.

Vecnor tossed Ballrik forward, and the warrior tumbled several feet while Tux entered the area of stone trees. Ballrik sat up, but he did not rise. The warrior's eyes were downcast, his expression one of hopelessness.

"Through the rocks!" Vecnor commanded, adding enough emphasis to scare Ballrik into obeying.

Vecnor turned to face Hezeb. His shoulder hung low and the stabbing pain in his back entered his lungs, causing him to wheeze. The demon's scales glistened in the hazy atmosphere, sparkling between shades of red and silver, and it glared with its tiny eyes. Its dark, forked tongue slid in and out between scaly lips, and its three-fingered claws clenched and opened while it sized up its foe. A pair of demons flanked Hezeb by twenty yards, one a reptilian fiend with horns and the other a walking panther with tentacles for arms. The creatures seemed to smile as they advanced.

Three arrows struck the panther in rapid succession, piercing its chest, throat, and one of its eyes. The monster fell. Additional arrows impaled the reptile in its forehead and mouth, and two more sank into its stomach, but it kept coming, although at a slower pace.

Vecnor drew his second sword. Though his blade had failed to penetrate Hezeb's scales when they battled in the basement of Trannum's cabin in Sistama, this time would be different. Elgarroth placed enchantments on his weapons, so he would never again be powerless in the face of evil. He lunged, and Hezeb did not dodge — the demon likely believed the attack could not bring it harm. Its eyes widened when the sword pierced its hide, and smoking blood escaped as Vecnor pulled the blade free.

Hezeb countered with its fiery breath. Vecnor ignored the feeble attack and brought his swords from right to left, one after the other. The first carved into the demon's chest, and the second sliced near its throat, cutting its breath short. The monster gnashed, biting one of Vecnor's blades with its rows of teeth and snapping the weapon in two. Vecnor retreated a step, casting the hilt aside.

To the left, Tux finished the reptile demon with his frozen sword — the elf's quiver was empty. Farther on, another dozen fiends entered the plain of spouting flames.

Hezeb's jaws clamped shut inches from Vecnor's head. Vecnor danced back and slashed upward, cutting through its maw as the demon advanced. The beast knocked him to the hard soil, and he thrust his blade as he was trampled, penetrating deep into Hezeb's stomach. The massive body fell, pinning Vecnor to the ground.

Try as he might, Vecnor couldn't push the corpse aside — his left shoulder was nearly useless. Tux arrived, and together they slid the mammoth demon enough to allow Vecnor to stand. He jerked his blade from Hezeb's carcass as the pursuing demons approached to within thirty yards, and he and Tux dashed into the stone forest with all the speed they could muster.

The arch to the House of Elgarroth drew to within a hundred feet. Ballrik was halfway there, leaning against a rock formation as if exhausted. Above him, a demon with reddish skin and the lower body of a goat descended from the cloud, twirling a barbed chain.

Vecnor's spirits sank. His breathing was shallow, and he would never reach Ballrik in time with the wounds he bore. Tux appeared hampered as well, but the elf found strength enough to leap atop one of the stone trees and jump from pillar to pillar to close the distance quickly.

Ballrik dodged the creature's initial attack; the chain wrapped around a nearby column and cut through, showering pebbles in every direction. The demon regained its twirling motion and struck again, wrapping Ballrik's leg within the barbs, and the young warrior cried out.

Tux pulled his bow as he halted atop a column twenty feet away, and he fitted his sword to the string—Vecnor had never seen Eslimil perform such an action before. The elf drew back the slender blade, and upon releasing the bowstring, his eyes narrowed in concentration. The frosty weapon maneuvered around rock pillars and passed completely through the demon. The fiend collapsed.

Tux raced to Ballrik, and Vecnor joined them as Eslimil finished unwrapping the chain. The barbs left nasty wounds on Ballrik's leg, and the blood seeping through small holes in Tux's leather gloves for the effort didn't escape Vecnor's notice.

They hurried toward the arch, and roars, hisses, and curses hurtled their way as the demons closed the gap. Vecnor and his companions neared to within ten feet when one of the giant, deformed fishes descended from the cloud. It was like an enormous crocodile wearing its skeleton on the outside, and in place of its front legs were pincers. The demon's tail was scorpion-like, and wings that should have been too small for flight waggled atop its shoulders.

Vecnor dropped his sword to heave Ballrik through the arch. He then pulled Tux close with his weakening arm just before a giant pincer snapped where the elf had been, and ducked as the monster's enormous teeth clamped together. Two of the fangs tore through his armor and raked his back, and the force pushed him and Tux through the portal.

They were back in the small room in the House of Elgarroth. The archway went dark. Ballrik lay on the floor, bleeding from many wounds, and Tux landed next to the warrior. Vecnor collapsed nearby, experiencing pain unlike any he had known.

The door opened, and Elgarroth entered. Vecnor's vision blurred and his lungs burned with every attempted breath. He no longer felt his left arm. Was it still there? He closed his eyes in hopes the action would ease his agony, and all sounds faded.

Chapter 22

A Time of Healing

Vecnor wasn't sure how much time had elapsed. Weeks? Months? He had remained in his room, confined to his bed. Elgarroth came often to apply healing concoctions and change bandages, as well as administer elixirs for the poison. At first, Vecnor ran a high fever and could not eat or drink, but after what felt like a few weeks, he could sit up and consume small amounts. Even so, he needed assistance, as his shaky hands made holding utensils difficult. Once Vecnor could feed himself, Tux continued with the treatments, and Elgarroth did not enter his bedroom again.

"It was a month," said Tux, offering a mug of beer.

It was Vecnor's third day under the Salenti-gray elf's care, and he had begged for the drink a couple of hours earlier. He accepted the mug.

"I've been in here a month?" He frowned. "It feels longer."

"No." Tux held a wry smile. "We were in Hell for a month."

Vecnor furrowed his brow. "It was less than a day. An hour at most."

"Time does not pass equally on the other side of the gate." Tux lifted a tray of food from the table and brought it to the bed. "And yes, you have been in here for a month and a half since our return. It is nearly spring."

Vecnor drank deeply from the mug, allowing the information to sink in, and wiped his upper lip with his sleeve. "What about Ballrik?"

"The human survived," Tux replied. "He is resting in a guestroom."

"How badly was he hurt?"

Tux shrugged. "No worse than yourself. Although he was not poisoned."

"That blasted snake!"

"And the crocodile," said Tux. "You did not tell me one stabbed you in the back with its tail."

Vecnor shook his head. *That* was what pierced him before he entered the spires. "Is Ballrik up and about?"

"Elgarroth is bringing him along slowly. Or rather, *I* am doing so now."

"How is it you always escape the worst of things?" Vecnor mumbled, touched by jealousy.

Tux held a mocking grin. "I am Eslimil." He chuckled. "There is your way of fighting, and there is mine. But I assure you, I received my share of injuries. Of course, I also recover more quickly than you."

Vecnor flashed a sarcastic smile before returning to his queries. "What have you told Ballrik?"

"Nothing." Tux sat on Vecnor's only chair, appearing comical on the large seat. "Elgarroth has chosen to keep him asleep until he is fully mended. His mind is fragile, and Elgarroth does not wish to risk him going mad."

Vecnor nodded. "I'll be getting out of bed today." He bit into a biscuit. "My body craves activity."

"I figured as much." Tux dropped from the chair. "The woodpile is depleting, so it is for the best." He smirked as he exited the room.

Vecnor sighed.

❈ ❈ ❈

For the next several days, Vecnor chopped wood and practiced with the new swords he found in his closet. His reflexes were sloppy from all the bedrest, and the wounds to his shoulder and back persisted, presenting discomfort. But every passing day brought improvement.

He checked on Ballrik often. The warrior slept peacefully, except for when Vecnor or Tux administered the elixir. Though Ballrik didn't wake, the young man frowned and twitched. The potion was obviously not a healing draft, but Tux reported Elgarroth to have given instructions to use every last drop, and every day a new one appeared in Ballrik's room. Vecnor thought it odd, but it seemed Ballrik had aged from the time spent in Hell, and continued to do so. Several gray hairs had sprouted and a full beard was coming in, and wrinkles had formed around Ballrik's eyes. At least the wounds were nearly gone.

Elgarroth returned at last, and Vecnor and Tux joined the wizard at the fire as he brought his pipe to life.

"It is good to see you both recovered," Elgarroth said.

"What about Ballrik?" asked Vecnor. "Why does he still sleep?"

"Ballrik is a story for another time." Elgarroth looked into the flames. "But he is where he needs to be at the moment."

A vague answer.

"There is no easy way to say this," Elgarroth's expression was grim. "Solinin is dead."

Vecnor's mouth was suddenly dry. "What?"

"He died defying Gruzim." The wizard shook his head. "The krukari is Trannum's newest Death Lord. I am sorry."

Gruzim! Vecnor saw red. Why hadn't Elgarroth allowed him to kill the creature?

"But for now," Elgarroth added, "it is the war you must both be concerned with."

Tux sat up straight. "Is it time?"

Elgarroth nodded. "The armies prepare to march. It all begins tomorrow, when the *companies four* set out."

Vecnor's head swam with emotions. For eight hundred years, he had served Elgarroth. But never were the missions so dire. He met Trannum, encountered a Death Lord, and battled demons in Hell. Every step was harder than the last. "What are we to do?"

"For the time being, nothing." Elgarroth looked from Tux to Vecnor. "There are too many possibilities. I must wait until some paths are chosen before we can hope to guide. It will be a couple of weeks at least before that day comes." The wizard forced a cheerful expression. "So gather your patience." Glancing at the woodpile, he added, "I see you have replenished our stock. Very good."

Vecnor held a wry smile.

"And since we have the time," said Elgarroth, "I shall relate to you the instructions Merssa has given the *companies four*."

❖ ❖ ❖

Over two weeks passed. Vecnor spent most of that time pacing or staring into the campfire. He desperately wished to join the war to do what he could to help, and finding patience grew harder by the day.

His visits with Ballrik continued, and although the warrior appeared fully healed, Vecnor and Tux administered the elixirs and Ballrik remained asleep. The aging was not Vecnor's imagination; the wrinkles about the eyes had spread to the forehead and the gray hairs had tripled. He thought of asking Elgarroth for an explanation, but he sensed the wizard was not willing to discuss it.

After yet another day of waiting, Vecnor spent time grooming Umbarc. The horse wasn't in need, but it kept him busy.

"I smell hobgoblins." Tux approached, his expression lethal. "The air reeks of them."

Vecnor frowned. "Hobgoblins? In Vermallon?" It had been more than a decade since the creatures befouled the southern region of the woodland.

"Yes." Elgarroth was suddenly nearby. "They have invaded the forest. But they are not our concern. The elves will see to them."

"The war has surely begun," said Tux.

Elgarroth scanned the trees to the northwest. "Indeed it has. And the company of Sullis nears, pursued by Benasti soldiers."

Vecnor tightened his fists. "Shall I aid them?"

"They will come to us." The wizard walked to sit by the fire. "And we must prepare." As Vecnor and Tux followed to do the same, he added, "The roads are becoming clearer, but I do not dare send either of you out too soon. You will remain in your rooms until you are called."

Vecnor sighed. Though his chamber bore every comfort he required, his blood yearned to act.

He and Tux entered the house.

CHAPTER 23
THE GREAT EAST RIVER

Vecnor lay on his bed, watching the ceiling. Waiting was the hardest part for a warrior. At least his room now had a window, though he doubted it was visible from the outside, and he had a good view of Elgarroth sitting near the fire. After losing interest in the slow-moving shadows above, he swung his feet to the floor and gazed at the front yard.

A gray elf raced into the clearing, followed by several other folks, all of them bewildered by the sudden break in the trees. Vecnor recognized the elf as Xorlunder, and the robed individual trailing after was the wizard Melac. A bearded man was next, surely Magneer by his resemblance to Pallit, and then a krukari that must be Gruelenor, the one Tux mentioned after visiting Benasti Forest. A large man with a dark complexion came last, carrying a warrior. The tall figure was obviously from Holindale, making him Nidor, and the form over the barbarian's shoulder was definitely Sullis, the Brondor paladin from Harbnum Elgarroth described when discussing the *companies four*. It seemed everyone but Xorlunder and Melac bore injuries, and a Benasti arrow protruded from Nidor's shoulder while another was buried in Sullis's side.

Nidor and Sullis tumbled to the ground as the Dale attempted to halt. Xorlunder spoke, though Vecnor heard nothing, and Elgarroth responded. The two exchanged words again, and Sullis struggled to a knee to add to the conversation. Nidor then helped the injured paladin to one of the logs.

Vecnor cringed as Nidor pulled the arrow from Sullis. The Brondor paladin wavered on the edge of consciousness, but before he could pass out, fire engulfed Nidor's hand, and Sullis winced when the flame lowered to touch the wound. The injury vanished, and Sullis's jaw hung while he stared at Nidor in awe.

Vecnor closed his mouth, realizing his actions mimicked the Brondor paladin's. Elgarroth had declared divine intervention when explaining Nidor's existence. What other hidden talents did the young barbarian possess?

Finished with Sullis, Nidor extracted the wooden shaft from his own shoulder and healed the wound before tending to Magneer.

Away from the fire, Gruelenor stood alone. The krukari's resemblance to Gruzim was sickening. But Gruelenor was not his father, and Vecnor needed to keep that in mind. Gruelenor possessed a couple of injuries, but shook off Nidor when the barbarian approached to offer aid.

Please heat some water. Elgarroth's request came while the wizard's attention remained on the visitors.

Vecnor walked to the cabinet in his room. Within was a large iron kettle, and he filled the pot with water from his basin and headed for the exit. It wasn't surprising when he transformed into Tewlon as he opened the door. The conversation outside the cabin halted as all eyes followed him while he placed the kettle on a hook and swung it over the fire. He looked at no one and said nothing and returned to the house.

Tewlon went back to the cabinet and pulled six clay mugs. He set them on a silver tray and opened a drawer to add a folded rag and a pouch. After waiting an ample amount of time for the water to heat, he lifted the tray and exited.

Everyone fell silent again as Tewlon returned to the campfire. Using the rag, he swiveled the iron pot from over the flames and poured steaming water into the mugs. He then opened the pouch and added a healthy pinch of herbs to each cup. Pulling the drawstrings, Tewlon set the bag on the tray, and lifting the tray from the log, he distributed a mug to those around the fire. He walked to Gruelenor last. The krukari seemed hesitant to make eye contact. Tewlon extended the final cup, holding it a few seconds until Gruelenor accepted the offer, and at that moment their eyes met. The krukari's focus quickly shifted away, but there was no malice, no hatred, and no treachery. Gruelenor was definitely not his father.

Tewlon returned to the house, reclaiming his true form as he closed the door.

An hour elapsed with no instructions from Elgarroth. Vecnor passed the time writing in his journal. Finally, the wizard's voice came to him.

We need a tent for our visitors. They will be staying a while.

Vecnor opened the cabinet. A neatly folded tent occupied a whole shelf. He grabbed the material and exited the room.

Three days crawled by, and Vecnor watched the company through his window. They stayed in the large tent Tewlon erected and lingered about, sharing conversations, sitting by the fire, sharpening weapons, and checking their gear. The nobility displayed by Nidor was surprising. The barbarian was born in the Desert of Fire to a life of competing with neighboring tribes and fighting for survival. Yet the Dale carried himself as a gentle soul eager to bring out the good in everyone. Sullis, on the other hand, took his worship of Brondor to extremes, as was the way of many paladins. Vecnor found Magneer to be similar to Pallit in personality, and Gruelenor was tight-lipped. Xorlunder and Melac were just as Vecnor remembered them.

Tewlon chopped wood every day, but also he was responsible for serving food, and it was during these times that he saw Tux. The elf worked in the kitchen, baking bread, gutting fish, and preparing meals.

"I hope this does not last much longer," Tux muttered while mixing ingredients into a sauce. It was nearing dinnertime on the third evening. "A war is being fought. This is not how I believed I would serve Vaeldor."

"From what I've heard," said Vecnor, "there hasn't been much of a war just yet." He tossed a piece of fish into his mouth, earning a frown from Tux. "They're still mobilizing for the most part. The battles have been small and few."

"Regardless…" Tux shook his head.

"I agree."

Vecnor lifted the tray of food and exited the kitchen, and Tewlon carried it to the tent.

On the fifth evening, after it was dark, Tewlon was about to turn in for the night when he spied Nidor speaking with Elgarroth near the fire. Elgarroth had not allowed Vecnor or Tux to hear most of the conversations with the others, as if knowing too much might alter something he or the half-gray elf did in the future, but on this occasion, Tewlon wandered toward the logs until their words were clear.

"No. That does not matter," Nidor said. "But if I may, what of Ballrik? Where is he?"

"Of where he is and where he had gone," Elgarroth replied, "you need not concern yourself. His act was one of great valor, but unfortunately, it will be known only to a few. Of his fate, he was spared the gruesome end that surely awaited him. Though his actions brought certain death unto him, he was not lost to the world of demons. Worry not of him or his whereabouts. Realize only that he has played an important role in making success in this war possible."

So that was it. Ballrik would not be returning to his life. Would he awaken at all? Tewlon crept toward the cabin, but he was sure Elgarroth glanced his way.

A few days later, Elgarroth informed the visitors it was safe for them to leave. It was still an hour before dinner, so Vecnor would not have to serve the meal—thank Brondor! The company immediately prepared to depart, their spirits high, and after another half hour, they were gone.

Tux helped Vecnor take down the tent. They folded it up as best they could, but somehow it seemed bigger than when Vecnor removed it from the cabinet. Once finished, they joined Elgarroth around the fire. The wizard sipped from a glass of wine, and a second glass rested on the ground near Tux's log while a mug of beer awaited Vecnor.

"That took longer than I had hoped," Elgarroth said while Vecnor drank deeply.

Vecnor pulled the mug from his lips. "They left a bit of a mess."

"Not the tent." Elgarroth gave Vecnor a sidelong glance. "The visit itself. The armies have made it farther than I planned." He sighed. "But we have time yet to do what we must."

"And what is that?" asked Tux.

"You will come with me," Elgarroth said to the Salenti-gray elf before turning to Vecnor. "And *you* will follow those who just left."

"Why did I not just accompany them?" Vecnor posed.

"I want you to follow," the wizard replied, "for others are tracking them. It will be advantageous if you are not with them when they meet. I shall provide more information as it becomes available."

Vecnor nodded. It made little sense, but it would likely work out for the best.

"We all depart first thing tomorrow morning," Elgarroth added.

They rose from the logs, and each of them entered the house.

Once in his room, Vecnor checked his armor and weapons. He knew they were ready, but the action steadied his mind. Once satisfied, he went to bed.

❄ ❄ ❄

Vecnor awoke. The hour was early. He changed into his traveling clothes, donned his armor, and strapped his swords to his back. He then opened the cabinet, where three pouches bulged with contents, and added them to his belt. As he handled each, it was obvious one held rations, one healing herbs, and the final pouch contained various tools that might come in handy. Also present was a waterskin, and Vecnor took that too.

He exited the cabin to see Elgarroth and Tux atop their horses. Umbarc stood ready, and the animal's saddlebags bulged with

207

supplies—likely ropes, spikes, warm gear, torches, extra blankets, and such. Vecnor mounted.

"Where are you two headed?" he asked.

"South," Elgarroth answered.

From Tux's expression, the half-gray elf knew no more than that. And from Elgarroth's eyes, Vecnor wondered if this was the last he'd see of either of them.

"It has been a pleasure," he said.

Tux nodded. "Galenfial guide your steps."

"And Brondor guide your arrows swift and true," Vecnor responded.

Tux smirked. "I shall take care of that myself."

"It is time," said Elgarroth.

Vecnor took in a deep breath and released it. "Onward, Umbarc."

The Andrian horse followed the southern trail beyond the cabin, and Vecnor glanced back before the trees concealed the clearing. The elves were gone. He rode at a quickened pace toward the ford, knowing the head start the company held. But he and Umbarc had made the trip enough to know the way, and they took a path more direct than the map Eraim had drawn—a route dependent on landmarks. The morning sun rose high, and nearing an hour past noon, the roar of the Great East River was evident.

Vecnor slowed Umbarc and gazed about the underbrush. It was obvious others had moved through the region on foot—many more than the six he followed. Dismounting, he put on his helmet.

"Stay," he said to Umbarc, and he drew his swords and proceeded.

After thirty yards, the river came into view. The company was three quarters of the way across, and in an awful state. Scorching marred the raft, Melac lay unmoving, Nidor and Gruelenor were down, and arrows had pierced everyone but Xorlunder. To Vecnor's right upon the shore, Kalmiran and Benasti archers paused in their efforts to look his direction, their eyes widening and grins spreading—did they take him for a Death Lord? A group of dunarchins to the left snarled, obviously recognizing him for what he was. Ahead of Vecnor, a dunarchin mage paid him no heed as it eyed the craft with lightning crackling at its fingertips.

Vecnor strode forward and slashed through the mage's neck before the spell was unleashed. He then turned on the dunarchins, and the undead pulled their swords.

Though skilled with the blade, the dunarchins were like novices before Vecnor, and he carved into their ranks. Arrows caromed from his backplate, launched by the living bowmen, but his focus remained on the undead firstborns as he reduced them to piles of body parts.

A couple of missiles penetrated Vecnor's armor as he spun, issuing minor wounds at best, and the Kalmirans pulled blades and charged. But they were no more of a challenge than the dunarchins, and Vecnor took pleasure in slaying humans siding with the necromancer. As the last one fell, he advanced on the hobgoblins and krukari. The Benasti warriors opted to use their bows while he butchered several, and arrows he knew to have come from Xorlunder pierced a few more. The final three hobgoblins fled into the forest.

Vecnor panted as he turned to see the raft had reached the other side, where Sullis secured it to the shore. The Brondor paladin lifted Melac's body while the others made their way onto the bank, and Xorlunder, Nidor, and Magneer looked Vecnor's direction. Their mouths moved, holding a brief conversation, but the words failed to penetrate the roar of the water.

Let them go, said Elgarroth.

Vecnor stared across the river. He dared not remove his helmet; such an action might cause them to balk. He would wait for them to move on before retrieving the raft to follow. Sullis then cut the rope and kicked the craft into the water's current. Terrific. That would complicate things. The company headed south toward the Candermane Falls, and Xorlunder offered a nod and wave of thanks before joining them.

Vecnor gazed to the east. Without the ford, crossing the Great East River was no small task.

"Umbarc!" he called.

CHAPTER 24
MOUNTAIN DUEL

No roads existed to cross the Great East River outside the bridges in Nira and the Palidur Bridge connecting Sendorum and Sardina. But Palidur Bridge was not an option. Southern Nira, meanwhile, was under the necromancer's control. Yet it was the only viable path, and Vecnor drove Umbarc hard to make up time.

Within Vermallon Forest, Vecnor encountered a few Benasti and Kalmiran patrols, but slew only as many as were necessary in his haste. Occasionally, the enemy was engaged in combat with elves, and the forest folk welcomed his assistance, brief as it was. He rode through most of the night, and just before dusk of the following day, he reached the woodland's end.

Vecnor dismounted and crept through the remaining foliage to spy the field beyond. A large encampment lay three hundred yards to the east, but nothing stirred. It was as if an army had departed in a hurry—surely due to the presence of the North Army. Luck was on his side.

He settled among the trees for the night, not wishing to arrive at the bridge too soon. Umbarc helped to guard, but no one disturbed them. Come sunrise, Vecnor mounted, and they left the cover of the forest.

The plains of Nira remained quiet, and it wasn't long before the air cooled. Ten minutes later, a layer of snow covered the ground. Vecnor slowed to secure a heavy cloak over his shoulders. A few miles farther, he skirted a village next to the river to keep his passing unnoticed. Smoke issued from every chimney, but the streets were barren. To the northwest, a distant group of soldiers sat on horseback. They made no attempts to hail or impede Vecnor's eastward progress—apparently, a single rider was no cause for alarm.

As evening arrived, the first bridge over the Great East River appeared. Red snow adorned the northern end of the construction—a massive battle was fought there—but there were no corpses. Perhaps more zombies for Trannum's horde. Near the bridge was movement, but it was too distant to make out details.

Though clouds covered the sky, to the west it was not so, and Vecnor halted until the sun was at his back. The orb would confound even an elf's view of his approach. Once his shadow stretched before him, he urged Umbarc into a charge.

Before the bridge were a dozen figures dressed in furs. The southern side was unmanned. The sentries shielded their eyes as they tried to spy Vecnor, but the best they could hope for was a silhouette surrounded by orange light. They were Kalmirans. Vecnor unsheathed his swords as he drew to within forty feet, and the enemy pulled their weapons as well. Umbarc was then upon the first pair of soldiers and did not slow. As the steed crushed the men underfoot, the others raised hammers and axes. Vecnor cut down two, using his knees to maintain balance, and Umbarc reared and stomped another.

The guards now saw Vecnor clearly, and three of them dropped everything to flee as fast as they could. Of the final four, Umbarc trampled two while Vecnor hacked down the others.

Vecnor turned Umbarc onto the bridge, and the horse bolted across the stones. It was a sturdy path, clear of snow and wide enough for five to ride abreast. Umbarc kept a hard pace even after reaching the opposite side, and Vecnor steered the mount due south.

The snow deepened while they proceeded, but it did not hinder the Andrian steed, and they continued well into the dark hours before stopping at last. Vecnor used dry branches from the saddlebags to build a fire—Umbarc carried enough wood for two more—but he didn't plan to stay long. If the soldiers pursued with larger numbers, or worse, the undead, his trail would be easy to follow. He laid on his blanket and closed his eyes to gain some sleep, but his ears remained alert to his surroundings. A couple of hours later, Vecnor packed his gear and left behind the smoldering ashes. There was no point trying to hide the campfire remnants without new snow to cover his tracks.

Vecnor and Umbarc continued south through the night. With the dawn, the clouds brightened, and Vermallon lay miles to the northwest while rolling fields of white stretched ahead. They paused briefly for a cold meal and moved on. Shortly after, the forest disappeared. Vecnor veered southwest.

The day passed without signs of pursuit, and Vecnor and Umbarc encountered nothing. As the clouds darkened with the setting sun, the Varlimor Mountains lined the western horizon. Vecnor continued through most of the night, again stopping for a few hours of rest, and before the morning sky arrived, he turned due west.

The Varlimor chain loomed ahead and to the left as noontime came and went. There were no breaks for food, and when the evening sun dropped beneath the clouds, Vecnor spied the region he knew to hide the eastern edge of Candermane Tunnel.

Racing Umbarc through the snow, he reached the mountains before dark. There, the tracks of those he pursued were obvious, heading higher into the slopes. Sullis must have determined it necessary to alter the plan. The company surely had a few days on Vecnor, but they were on foot. With any luck, he would overtake them soon. He pushed Umbarc to follow.

The sun set and the air cooled further. In most places, the tracks could still be discerned, but in others the growing darkness obscured them. Fearing he might lose the path altogether, Vecnor camped among a few trees and used the last of his wood to have a fire.

The night was restless as the wind picked up, and Vecnor passed the time cleaning his blades, eating from his pack, and adding sticks to Umbarc's saddlebags. In the end, he received only a few hours of sleep. The sky then brightened, and he returned to the hunt.

The air warmed slightly as the day progressed. Below, patches of green defied the extended winter over the fields of southern Nira. Within the mountains the snow remained, and though Umbarc was skilled in traversing the terrain, the path occasionally followed routes the horse could not go and Vecnor had to find another way. Luckily, he did not lose the trail, but it took longer than he had hoped. That evening, he found a cave the others had used, and he camped there for the night. The company had not made a fire, and from the looks of things, they were still a couple of days ahead.

The snow depleted over the next day and a half, but impressions in the mud and soiled footprints kept Vecnor on target. He figured he had closed the gap to only a few hours, and he declined to sleep that evening, wanting to gain more ground. But as night progressed, he heard the call of an undead dragon — a sound that hadn't pierced his soul since he played the part of Norvec.

The hollow screech ending in a hiss came out of the northeast. The air about Vecnor then took on an icy chill, and he detected the fear aura of a Death Lord. With Elgarroth's protections, the only effect was the rising of tiny bumps on his arms. A dark shape appeared in the sky, moving west, and four points of blue light shone against the clouds — the eyes of the dragon and its master. Its path headed toward Candermane, where the enemy might detect tracks in the snow. It was a possibility Vecnor must prevent.

He dismounted and pulled his swords with a flourish, and the motions did not escape the enemy's notice. The bone dragon turned. The monster swooped low, and though yellow vapors seeped from the corners of its mouth, it did not release its withering gas. Was a single target unworthy of such an attack? Perhaps dragon skeletons had only so much poisonous breath to expel.

"Umbarc! Move!" Vecnor ordered.

The horse bolted into the west.

Charging to gain momentum, Vecnor leaped as the dragon arrived. His timing was perfect, and he thrust his sword into the mount's left eye socket. The force of the dragon's speed wrenched the weapon from his grasp, and he bounced off its skull, a rib, and finally its hind leg before he landed. The skeletal monster screeched a higher pitch as it crashed into a mountainside, and several shorter calls followed while it struggled against the trees and boulders that collapsed onto it.

The Death Lord survived the impact. It approached, with only its eyes giving away its location. Vecnor's left elbow and right leg ached, and he had likely bruised a few ribs, but he retained possession of one of his swords. Lifting a thick branch with his free hand, he pushed himself from the ground as the undead king came into focus. Wisps of black smoke rose from the mace it carried while its other arm lay hidden behind a shield, and hanging about the Death Lord's neck was a silver necklace of a hissing snake with glowing orange eyes—a symbol of Demoligius. It was Dunuthar, ancient priest-king of Selt.

Vecnor advanced, and Dunuthar moved against him, swinging the dark mace as they met. Vecnor dodged the blow. He countered, and the Death Lord shielded his blade aside. Vecnor followed with the make-shift club, intentionally striking the shield and driving Dunuthar back a step.

Behind the evil king, the dragon continued fighting against its entanglement while Umbarc attacked. Vecnor prayed his mount fared well.

Dunuthar swung again and again, and Vecnor evaded the mace. The undead warrior then smashed its shield into him, knocking him prone. It was as if a block of ice had crashed into his body, and frost covered his armor where the dark metal made contact. Vecnor rolled when Dunuthar attempted to stomp on him, regaining his feet and swinging the stick upward into the shield. The tactic pushed the protective shell over the Death Lord's head, giving Vecnor an opening, and he cut through his enemy's arm at the shoulder. The limb and the shield fell.

Dunuthar's eyes grew bright, but the dark king revealed no pain while it swung the mace to either side. Vecnor gave ground, dodging the blows and parrying the final attack with the stick. The blackness exuding from the evil weapon crawled along his club, rotting everything it touched, and Vecnor released it before the mist reached his hand. The wood dissolved into smoldering ash.

To the right, Vecnor spied his second blade. He raced to retrieve it, and Dunuthar did not impede him. Instead, the Death Lord picked up its lost limb and reattached it. Vecnor stood with one sword high and the other low, his spirits sinking as the undead priest-king raised the shield.

Vecnor charged, flailing his weapons and putting Dunuthar on the defense. Though the Death Lord deflected most of the barrage with its shield, Vecnor slashed its chest, right leg, and helmet, each strike gashing the black steel. No blood flowed, and Dunuthar still showed no signs of pain, but the Death Lord fell back several steps.

Dunuthar countered, and Vecnor moved with all the grace he possessed, evading the dark mace and pulling his blades from its path. He then found the opening he sought. It was risky, but he needed to unbalance the undead king. Vecnor rammed the Death Lord with his pauldron, driving the evil warrior back. An icy torment invaded his shoulder as he and Dunuthar separated, but he shut out the ache and slashed twice. One blade cut into his enemy's leg and the other severed the hand holding the mace. Vecnor followed with a thrust, piercing the priest-king's helmet. As blue steam issued from the armor, Vecnor kicked Dunuthar in the chest, knocking the Death Lord to the ground.

Numbness claimed Vecnor's shoulder as icicles pierced his foot. He summoned all of his strength and swung his right sword through Dunuthar's neck, cutting the helmet free. The lights faded from the eye slit. The chilling fear dissipated.

Vecnor charged with a limp toward the undead dragon. The monster had escaped the debris, and it breathed its yellow cloud at Umbarc, but the horse evaded the attack as it bolted away. Vecnor roared, and the dragon's remaining eye turned to spy his approach. With a screech, it leaped into the sky and sped into the east.

Vecnor dropped to his knees. Though his shoulder was numb, pain raced along his arm and into his fingers. His body ached, and it was as if frozen daggers pressed deeper into his foot. Umbarc raced to him and lowered so he could reach the saddlebags, and he pulled a gray flower root and bit into it. The pain eased. After a few slow breaths, he retrieved Vermallon dusk and rubbed its leaves over his injuries. Though the potent herbs provided immediate relief, they could not overcome the exhaustion brought on by the Death Lord's touch. Once Vecnor treated the final wound, he crawled into a nearby grotto to gain some rest.

Chapter 25

Forest of Ill Repute

Vecnor awoke to Umbarc's nudging, the steed rescuing him from a sinister dream. Everywhere Vecnor had turned, the undead were assailing him, and he had no armor or weapons. Perhaps the contact with Dunuthar brought on the nightmare. Fortunately, the chill was now faded from his body and his injuries were well on the mend, thanks to the powerful herbs.

It was morning, and Vecnor and Umbarc continued east. The return of patchy snow revealed them to be on course, and six distinct footprints showed all members of the company were still alive—at least, they were yesterday. Nearing dinnertime, Vecnor discovered another cave that had housed Sullis and the others. Again, the group had lit no fire.

Vecnor exited the cave and moved on. He pushed Umbarc well past sunset, and the mountains declined while the number of trees increased. Below, the southernmost fields of Nira showed no traces of snow. *Was* it Nira? Or Kalmaar? It depended on where you lived as to your opinion. But what did it matter? No one inhabited the plains due to its proximity to Benasti Forest.

Vecnor dismounted and leaned against a tree on the soft, wet ground to have a bite. Umbarc sampled grass surrounding nearby maples and white birches. The air was cool but bearable, and after the meal, Vecnor pulled his blanket over his shoulders and sat to gain a moment's rest.

❈ ❈ ❈

Vecnor's eyes snapped open. It was dark. Umbarc stood motionless; the horse was sleeping. Hopefully, they hadn't dozed more than a couple of hours.

"Umbarc!" Vecnor stirred the mount. "Let's go."

He followed the trail as best he could in the darkness. A few members of the company were unskilled at passing in secret—likely Sullis, Nidor, and Melac—and their boot prints were obvious amid the scattered snow. Vecnor entered the foothills, following the path until the mountains fell behind. To the right, Varlimor stretched eastward, covered by trees and snow, and ahead, grassy fields and wildflowers lay beneath puffy white clouds under the early morning sky. Where was Sullis leading the others now?

Vecnor dismounted to inspect the ground. It was soft and easy to read, and the tracks continued east. A scrap of fur among boulders caught his eye, and he discovered the heavy cloaks the company had worn. He pressed on, skirting the mountains and stopping every so often to make sure he still followed the trail. The soil then hardened, and Vecnor thanked Tux for all the training over the centuries that allowed him to continue the chase. As dusk arrived, Benasti Forest replaced the mountains, and the footprints disappeared.

"It's not ideal, I know," Vecnor said to Umbarc, scanning the vast woodland. "But we'll have to stay here. Maybe I'll see something when the light returns."

Vecnor gazed westward when the setting sun found a window in the clouds. The moment was brief, and the opening closed to return the land into shadow.

Umbarc whinnied and snorted.

"The very *next* time the light returns," Vecnor amended his statement.

He lit no fire, but the night air was pleasant. Vecnor rested on and off, and nothing exited the woodland against him. Come morning, he inspected the grass. He had not lost the trail after all. It headed into the forest—an unexpected and alarming turn. Even with most of the woodland's inhabitants off fighting the war, Benasti remained a dangerous place.

Vecnor shook his head. "What are you boys up to?"

He sat atop Umbarc for the first hour after entering the forest. The path left by the company was more than obvious again, and he hoped no Benasti folks had stumbled upon it. As the tree limbs hung lower, Vecnor dismounted and walked. A few miles farther, he discovered a cold campsite where the others had surely slept. Signs of additional boot and wolf prints were present as well. Time was growing short.

Vecnor picked up the pace. The route grew difficult as the undergrowth became thicker, and thorns tugged at his armor and gear every chance they got. The extra tracks soon disappeared, leaving only the trail of the company, but the enemy was likely gathering its forces before striking. Vecnor moved faster, sometimes pushing through or hacking the foliage attempting to hinder him.

The forest darkened with the evening, and the air tasted like wet soil. Vecnor halted. Even with his exceptional sight, he might miss a crucial detail. A wolf howled, but it was too distant to cause concern. He sat against a tree and closed his eyes.

The morning was not as bright as the last, but Vecnor saw well enough and moved on. Five miles later, he discovered where the company had slept the previous night, and the additional tracks reappeared. But there were no signs of battle.

Vecnor pressed on with no breaks, and once darkness descended, he stopped, satisfied he had closed the gap to an hour. He took brief naps until the light returned, and he and Umbarc continued.

Shortly before noon, the forest opened up where the Batorn River had carved a path through the trees. The trail entered the water, and Vecnor's shoulders slumped when he realized the company had walked through the night, putting him several hours behind. Worse still, the pursuing footprints had doubled.

Vecnor mounted, and Umbarc carried him across the shallow waterway. Upon the far bank, he headed upstream until the Benasti denizens giving chase made the company's exit point obvious. As the tracks left the river and the trees closed in, Vecnor resumed walking ahead of his steed.

The forest grew darker, even before the arrival of night. Vecnor pulled a torch from his gear and brought it to life with flint and steel—he could afford no more stops. After a few miles, he discovered an area where the company had sat against trees, but they didn't stay long.

Vecnor walked through the night, and with the morning, he stumbled upon a battle scene. Hobgoblin and krukari corpses littered the forest, as well as several dead wolves. Arrows protruded from many bodies while others bore gashes, and charring suggested a fiery blade had inflicted a couple of the wounds. Beyond a tree to the right, a Zurkan's blood filled depressions in the soil obviously created by the krukari's large hammer. The Soldier of Blood's chest was split wide open. Above, a crossbow bolt jutted from a thick branch, and blood coated its entire shaft. No one from the party Vecnor followed was present.

He took in a slow, relieved breath. "We're close now," he said to Umbarc.

Umbarc snorted.

Several miles farther, Vecnor spotted tiny pools of blood near a couple of trees. The company had stopped to tend to their injuries, and the puddles were tacky.

He turned to Umbarc. "They were here an hour ago."

The horse stomped its hoof.

Vecnor peered at the sky. Though the sun hid behind white clouds barely visible through the branches, he knew it must be nearing noon. He inspected the vegetation. Enormous feet had trampled much of the underbrush.

"Ogres…" He pulled Umbarc's reins to look the animal in the eye. "The battle ahead is not for you."

No matter how well trained, Umbarc wouldn't survive a single blow from an ogre. The Andrian steed shook its head and snorted its protest, but Vecnor's glare was unwavering. The mount retreated a step in concession.

"We best pick up the pace," Vecnor said.

They headed southwest at a jog, arriving at the Batorn River an hour later. Thankfully, the company had walked straight through the water this time, and Vecnor continued his pursuit without delay.

The woodland opened up as they entered the southern region of Benasti, and the sounds of animals returned. But when a roar echoed across the forest, the chatter ceased. An ogre. And it wasn't far ahead.

"Stay!" Vecnor commanded Umbarc as he donned his helmet.

He drew one of his swords and sprinted around trees, through brush, and over logs until reaching the battle site. Gruelenor and Xorlunder stood near a bloodied ogre while Melac was to the side, seemingly unsure of what to do. Nidor and Sullis lay among the bushes, struggling to move, and Magneer was motionless at the base of a tree—hopefully unconscious. To the left was a dead ogre, and in the center, the largest of the enemy had its back to Vecnor. The enormous brute turned, and though the fiend was much older now, Vecnor recognized Arubit at once. The ogre's tiny intellect held no confusion as to whom Vecnor was, nor to the sincerity of his parting words in Orlenfel Forest, and its eyes widened. Vecnor advanced.

Arubit swung a tree-like weapon every bit as large as the club in Orlenfel, but it bore no spikes through its bole. Vecnor used all of his strength to steer the attack aside with his blade. He countered, inflicting several wounds while drawing his second sword to add a few more. Arubit sought a retreat, but Vecnor kept his word, and he thrust one blade into the ogre's chest and slashed the other across its massive neck. The collapse of Arubit felled a couple of trees as well.

Vecnor turned to the final ogre. It exhibited many cuts, none of them deep enough to slay it. The creature trembled beneath his gaze, and it bolted faster than he would have thought possible. From the thudding of its feet, the monster would not stop until it was far away.

Gruelenor held his sword, watching Vecnor. Xorlunder joined the krukari, the elf's blade lowered. To the left, Sullis leaned against a tree, and Melac's hands were poised, as if ready to cast a spell. Nidor approached with no weapon in hand.

"Thank you, stranger." The barbarian's voice was deep. He extended his arm. "We are indebted to you twice now."

Vecnor sheathed his swords and removed his helmet. "There is no debt." He clasped arms with Nidor. Turning, he called out, "Umbarc! Come!"

"Vecnor?" Xorlunder stared in awe. "Can this be?"

"Impossible." Nidor glanced at the gray elf.

"That is my name," Vecnor said.

"Nidor!" Gruelenor hollered. The krukari had moved to help Magneer sit against a tree.

Nidor rushed to the two, and his hand became alight. Magneer cringed at the paladin's touch, but the reaction quickly faded. While the Dale worked, Sullis walked with some effort to stand before Vecnor and frowned.

"Your name is Vecnor, you say?" Sullis posed. "I am a paladin of the Temple of Brondor, and that name is held high among my order in Harbnum, for he is the champion of my religion. But the warrior who used that name lived many years ago, so I would reconsider boasting such claims in my presence, whether in jest or otherwise."

"Regardless," Vecnor bowed his head, "Vecnor is my birth name. I do not claim to be the same Vecnor you speak of, but if you wish to address me, that is the name I answer to."

Sullis stared, as if dealing with inner turmoil. "Very well. And by whose authority do you act? Why have you trailed us?"

"I act on my own authority, as far as it concerns you," Vecnor replied. "As to why I have trailed you, I think you should be grateful that it is so. But if you must know, it was requested that I provide what help I can. I am aware of your mission, and I offer my sword."

Sullis held a measuring gaze.

Xorlunder broke the silence.

"This man is who he claims to be. It is he who came to Orlenfel, battling through hundreds of hobgoblins to convince me to part with my clan and give aid to this war. This is great news indeed, and it fills me with hope renewed!"

Vecnor recalled only the excursion against the ogres in Orlenfel many years earlier. Had Elgarroth used his likeness to visit the gray elves? With everything he was involved in over the past year, it was possible. He nodded. "Good to see you, Xorlunder."

Nidor arrived at Sullis's side, and the Dale administered his fiery healing to the Brondor paladin's wounds. Sullis didn't show the slightest discomfort at the burning touch.

At that moment, time slowed. It was Elgarroth. The wizard placed visions in Vecnor's head. He saw the North Army defeating the enemy to cross the Great East River. They then battled through undead, Kalmiran traitors, and Benasti warriors to arrive at Orlenfel Forest, but at a substantial cost. The gray elves now marched with them through northern Kalmaar, and Gruzim led a horde of dunarchins, ghouls, and zombies in their wake.

Vecnor's sight flew across the sky to hover above Burmagaard. Thousands of Zurkans, Benasti soldiers, mercenaries, and outlaws resided within the city, while Kalmirans and Marcs dwelt in hundreds of tents among the fields outside the walls. To make matters worse, a legion of undead stood eerily still a couple of miles to the south. The vision descended into Burmagaard, passing into the cellar of a home to spy on a secret meeting; a plot to overthrow the evil regime as soon as the "savior" broke free from her prison.

Vecnor withdrew from the basement gathering and exited Burmagaard. He entered Darmhorng and plunged into the dungeon to view a lone woman sitting in a cell, drained and broken. It was Elloria, priestess of Brondor; the "savior" Burmagaard awaited. Vecnor had not seen her since she was a smiling lass trying to teach herself to fight with two swords, and her condition was almost enough to still his heart. Soldiers bearing tabards with Karrak's coat-of-arms occupied the neighboring cells.

Vecnor's mind went dark. A blizzard engulfed the darkness. Within, a group of people struggled to survive: Rholmar, paladin of

Arronaus; Pallit, father of Magneer and husband of Arrikan; Soren, High Paladin of Soleran; Lorylla, daughter of Xorlunder; and Rybeal, a wizard from Philen.

The darkness momentarily returned, giving way to figures running through a mine: Greyor, a dwarf from Morimont; Millord, a dwarf from Rornibur and cousin to Poluran; Arrikan, mother of Magneer and wife of Pallit; and Selanna and Eraim.

Darkness again, interrupted by another snowstorm. The South Army was being devastated on the mountain pass while Merssa stood defiantly before a Death Lord. Jurak.

The visions faded. Vecnor faced Sullis while Nidor treated the paladin's wounds. For a moment, Vecnor found no words. How had it all gone so badly? Elgarroth claimed the plans were sound. There was no way Trannum could have been prepared for everything. Would Eraim escape the mines? And Merssa… Vecnor's body went numb. *All is lost*, he thought.

No, Elgarroth said. *Things have gone awry, but it was never going to be easy. The road is cracked, but the foundation remains sturdy. Think only on your part. Convince them to free Elloria. This is vital for our chances of success. Reveal only what is necessary. But also, someone must proceed to Morimont. We cannot win without the dwarves.*

I'll make them see, Vecnor thought in response. There was no other choice in the matter.

Chapter 26

A Simple Herb

Eslimil rode with Elgarroth along Vermallon Road into the west. The path was free of travelers, elves, and bandits, as the threat of the enemy drove almost everyone from the forest while the Vermallon elves gathered at its eastern border. Upon exiting the woodland, Elgarroth turned south, and they entered Sendorum.

The journey across the realm was swift. No one hindered them as they passed through villages and cities, and the Sendors they encountered appeared on edge, awaiting news of the war. Very few abled men were among them, as most were off fighting.

Upon reaching Palidur Bridge, they found Merssa's compound nearly deserted. The desolate scene sent a shiver along Eslimil's spine. The only ones present were soldiers wounded while taking Palidur, as well as the doctors and priests that tended to their injuries. Closer to the Great East River, five hundred sentries were alert. Snow no longer fell, but clouds remained overhead and a haze sat like a curtain, hiding the Holy City from view. The guards formed a wall before the bridge, and one eyed Eslimil and Elgarroth as they approached.

"Master Elgarroth?" The soldier frowned. He was older, and unfit to march for days across snowy realms in defense of Vaeldor. "I wasn't aware you were returning."

Elgarroth smiled. "My companion and I must cross."

"You sure?" The man glanced over his shoulder at Palidur Bridge. "I mean, you know your business, but you hardly have furs enough for the weather ahead."

Elgarroth lifted his brow.

The soldier shook his head, as if suddenly remembering to whom he spoke. "Let them pass!" he called out.

Elgarroth nodded his thanks, and Eslimil followed the wizard onto the bridge.

The temperature plummeted, and the wind picked up while they passed over the Great East River. Halfway across its breadth, the first signs of the battle to retake the Holy City defiled the wide path. There were no bodies, but splatters and streaks of blood remained and chipping marred the stone. Even the monuments of Vennimor and Bormungdaher showed scars. Farther on, scorching discolored the bridge.

Eslimil and Elgarroth continued into Sardina, and beyond a snowy field bathed in red stood Palidur. To the east, smoke issued from a mountain of burned corpses, its dark wisps swept away by the wind before rising even an inch. The city gates were closed, and sentries manned the walls.

"Do we stop?" asked Eslimil.

Elgarroth shook his head. "Time is pressing."

Pity. The thought of a blazing hearth was appealing.

The soldiers along the battlements watched Eslimil and Elgarroth ride by, their faces combining curiosity, nervousness, and fear. None of them called out.

The wind grew colder still as the Holy City faded into the north, and the snow deepened. But Elgarroth was a powerful wizard, and their horses stepped atop the snow as if it were solid ground. As well, the air about Eslimil warmed in defiance of the winter, and the winds parted, as if an invisible shell protected him. He exhaled a relieved breath.

They traveled for two days alongside the King Arman, resting only a few hours each night. The lake was frozen for nearly a mile out, and the villages and cities lining the shore were devoid of inhabitants. Hopefully, the people had fled to safer lands. Ahead, the eastern edge of Arman Forest appeared. The snow ended thirty yards from its border, as if unwilling to creep any closer, and the late sun highlighted its greenery while birds, butterflies, and squirrels happily went about their business without a care in the world. Jealousy tugged at Eslimil's soul.

Elgarroth headed southeast, and every landmark fell from sight. Three days later, the northernmost mountains of the Ladal chain came into view, and over the next day, the Fire Hills were visible. Dark clouds hovered above the hills, obscuring much of the terrain behind heavy snowfall. The hard pace continued, and early the following morning, the river feeding Starlight Lake appeared, as well as the Southwood beyond it. Elgarroth turned due south.

The mountains grew larger in the southwest, and to the east, the storm-covered hills stretched beyond Eslimil's sight. Elgarroth veered toward the region where the dunarchins had exhumed the dragon bones. The clouds were not so dark there, and the snowfall was light. As they arrived to within twenty yards of the rising terrain, they stopped.

"This is where we part," Elgarroth said.

Eslimil frowned. They were not remaining together?

"I have business in Holindale," the wizard added. "You, on the other hand, must journey to Tarn Arum."

"The jungle?" Eslimil had never been that far south. He knew of no one over his thousand-year existence that had.

"Yes." Elgarroth gazed southward, as if the hills did not exist. "Powerful healing herbs known as Arum vines grow there. I need you to collect one."

"A whole vine?" To Eslimil's recollection, the sinuous plants were typically several yards in length.

"Arum vines are not actual vines," Elgarroth explained. "They attach themselves to the vines. You will have a mental picture of them shortly."

Elgarroth closed his eyes, and Eslimil received a memory of the herb. Not only that, but he gained knowledge of a location where they flourished. They were single leaves bearing jagged edges, and grew along lengthy vines amid tall trees.

The wizard opened his eyes. "Take only one. Those that dwell in the jungle are wary of outsiders."

"What is it for?"

"Hopefully nothing." Elgarroth's focus shifted to the southeast. "But a serpent made its way north from Tarn Arum years ago and took up residence near the Varlimor Mountains. It is old and cunning. If the Dright company encounters it and one of them is bitten, the herb will be *very* necessary."

Eslimil nodded. "Understood."

"Once you obtain the Arum vine, head for Mud Lake. I shall meet you there."

"Why did you bring me to this spot?" Eslimil asked.

"There is a path over there."

Elgarroth pointed to where the mountains and Fire Hills converged. At first, Eslimil saw nothing. But then the path became clear. Would it have appeared if Elgarroth had not been with him?

"It is the quickest route through," the wizard said. "Beyond, you will find no snow."

"Why did the Dright company not go this way?"

"It would have added over a week to their journey," Elgarroth replied. "That would not have worked at all. Now make haste."

Eslimil nodded, and he rode toward the hidden path.

The worst part of separating from the wizard was the return of the frozen wind ripping through Eslimil's layers. Also, Landolice's hooves sank into the snow. But the darkest clouds remained in the east, and as luck had it, the snow was only an inch deep in most places. The frozen portion of the journey lasted just shy of two days, and by the second evening, Eslimil emerged onto a grassy plain bathed in sweltering heat.

From maps he had read—or perhaps information Elgarroth placed in his mind—the jungle lay six hard-days' ride to the south. Eslimil needed to accomplish the feat in half that time. With that in mind, he pushed Landolice, breaking only during the hottest parts of the next two days, and only for a few hours. Centuries of conditioning himself and his steed had made such travel possible. Throughout the journey, the mountains remained to his right, now the Borleen chain, and the West Twin River appeared on his left. Eslimil kept his distance from many herds, including bison, large cats, and antelopes. He also saw gorillas, brightly colored birds, monkeys, snakes, and enormous crocodiles. Through the nights, his keen sight steered him clear of coyotes and wolves. Most of the animals seemed curious about his presence, and only a close encounter with a pair of lions posed any threat. But Landolice was swift, and the predators' pursuit lasted only a minute.

The second evening provided less relief from the daytime's heat, and the following day, the blazing sun was almost unbearable. Perspiration saturated Eslimil's underclothes and created a sheen on Landolice, but they continued without complaint, even with the inexhaustible horde of insects buzzing about.

Nearing dusk that evening, the jungle stretched from the mountains and beyond the eastern horizon. Though the trees were yet distant, Eslimil saw them clearly. There were varieties he had never encountered, so he had no names for them, and the vegetation was a mess of tangled growths. Several animal calls emitted, but as the sun set with Eslimil's arrival, the communications ceased and the songs of insects began.

Eslimil continued in the dark, riding along the tree line until spotting an opening in the foliage. He then passed beneath the canopy of large leaves to find no easy trails existed through the mess of twisting vines and undergrowth. Several trees grew sideways, some towered overhead, and others stood no higher than twenty feet and bore colorful fruits.

He dismounted to inspect the nearby vines, eying the paths of each in search of the plants Elgarroth placed in his mind. Nothing. Using his sword to clear vegetation, Eslimil moved deeper into the jungle until spotting them at last: jagged leaves growing along a vine thirty feet overhead. Arum vines.

Taking in a deep breath, weightlessness took over, and Eslimil floated up through the branches. Upon reaching the herbs, he hovered over a thick branch and released his breath to sit atop the limb. He then carefully removed a single leaf and its stem from the vine. As he placed it into his pack, a rustling sounded below. A huge cat was stalking Landolice in the darkness. The horse stood perfectly still — probably sleeping.

Eslimil jumped down to the next branch with perfect balance. The tiger froze to peer up at him, revealing enormous fangs protruding from its upper jaw. He dropped to another tree limb, now more than halfway to the ground, and the tiger began to climb.

Now that Landolice was out of immediate danger, Eslimil took in a breath and vanished. But the tiger's head followed his shadowy form while he moved toward his mount — somehow it could see, smell, or sense him. He changed direction, so as not to lead the animal's attention back to its original target, and the cat's eyes remained affixed upon his position.

And now he needed to breathe.

As Eslimil's body took shape, he dropped to the jungle floor and pulled his sword. The tiger was nearly as big as Landolice, and its jaws opened to emit a roar and show off its two-foot fangs. It sprang with its giant claws extended.

Eslimil jumped straight up and landed on the tiger's back. He thrust his weapon a couple of inches into its hide, and as he did so, he willed the blade to grow hot. The beast roared louder, and Eslimil pulled his sword and bounded away before the massive body could crush him as it rolled.

The speed of the cat was nothing short of amazing, and it was on its feet and pouncing again in no time. Eslimil thought of leaping into a tree, but he feared the animal would catch him, so he sprung to the side instead. Unfortunately, a vine grabbed hold of his boot and he did not make it as far as he had planned. The tiger was then upon him.

Eslimil pulled in as much oxygen as he could in haste, and although he had become shadow, the displacement of air beneath the beast was like being crushed by a boulder. The force pushed him from under the cat and expelled his breath, and he tumbled across the moist ground.

Landolice was gone—the horse had retreated from the area. It was time for Eslimil to make his escape. He scrambled away as the tiger's long teeth gnashed, and the jaws clamped shut with terrifying power. It lunged, and Eslimil leaped twenty feet upward to land on a thick branch. He jumped to another as the monstrous feline pursued, narrowly evading its oversized paw, and hopped from tree to tree. The tiger was relentless, its size damaging branches in Eslimil's wake, and by the time he reached yet another tree, the monster was right behind him. He dropped toward the ground, and the cat followed. But after five feet, Eslimil held his breath. The tiger descended to the jungle floor while he ascended, rising to places the enormous beast could not follow.

After an upward glance, the predator abandoned the chase and slinked deeper into the wilderness. Good. Although scary, the tiger was not evil. And Eslimil detested bringing harm to animals.

He floated across the treetops as far as he could before descending onto a branch to catch his breath. Returning to shadow, Eslimil continued to the edge of the jungle.

Landolice stood in the darkness, waiting. Eslimil landed on the saddle and materialized. As he turned his steed to begin the northward journey, he sensed a presence nearby. It was Elgarroth, and the wizard's expression was grim.

"I will take that leaf," Elgarroth said.

Eslimil glanced at the jungle. The tiger did not emerge. He extracted the herb from his pouch and held it out. There was no point asking why he was sent to retrieve it when it seemed the wizard could have easily performed the chore. There would be no answer. And it was his job to do Elgarroth's bidding.

Elgarroth accepted the leaf and placed it into a pocket in his robe. "Head east into Nomedd," he instructed, "and remain in the southern region when passing through Dright Swamp. The area should be clear of the undead when you arrive." He gazed into the distant northeast. "Once through the bog, go to the hills north of Trannum's stronghold. You will see Selanna at some point. Follow without her knowledge, and do not interfere unless I tell you to do so." The wizard looked Eslimil in the eyes. "You are not to engage the enemy."

"I understand."

"I must hurry now." Elgarroth's attention shifted back to the northeast. "I pray I am not too late."

Too late for what? Eslimil would likely never know.

"Take care," Elgarroth said, and he sped off into the darkness.

Eslimil sat for a moment, watching the wizard. The shrinking figure wavered and disappeared. If only he could travel like that!

He sighed and spoke to Landolice. "Sorry, my friend. But there is no rest for us just yet."

They headed east.

Chapter 27

Battle for Kalmaar

It took some convincing from Vecnor before Sullis agreed to split up the group. In the end, Nidor, Xorlunder, Gruelenor, and Melac followed Vecnor to Darmhorng Castle while Sullis and Magneer continued to Morimont to reach the dwarves. Vecnor lent the Brondor paladin Umbarc to make the journey as swift as possible, and they parted ways after exiting Benasti Forest.

Vecnor's companions spoke very few words while walking east along the Morimont River toward Burmagaard. Some asked questions he would not or could not answer, and only Xorlunder seemed willing to press for more information. Vecnor's focus often fell upon Nidor. The barbarian exuded pure goodness, similar to the aura surrounding Merssa. But Nidor was different somehow, and not just in his humility. Where Merssa took charge as a stern enforcer, Nidor played the friendly guide. Yet, there was something more that Vecnor couldn't see. And he still could not comprehend the existence of a barbarian paladin of Silcor. Although most inhabitants of the Desert of Fire worshipped the fire god, there were few priests or shamans to speak of. So how had Nidor become so devout? So knowledgeable of Silcor's ways? And why was a paladin of his strength and skill born so far from civilization and proper training? It was a true mystery.

Vecnor halted within view of Darmhorng Castle and the city of Burmagaard, and they entered the copse of trees harboring the secret door Eraim and Selanna used to gain access into Darmhorng's dungeon. There, Vecnor instructed the company to get as comfortable as possible, which proved difficult when a couple of days pelted them with heavy rain and sleet. But they remained vigilant and kept watch on the enemy. When a Death Lord arrived at the castle, Vecnor knew the time to be drawing near, and Elgarroth spoke at last.

You may proceed. The wizard's voice seemed troubled, as if he wished to say more.

What is it? Vecnor asked.

I hesitate to mention… Merssa has passed.

Blood filled Vecnor's ears, and the beating of his heart was the only sound. It was as if he were in a dream. No. A nightmare. The words resonated in his mind until losing all meaning; losing all credibility. It was a lie. It couldn't be true. Yet, it was. Was it Jurak on the mountain pass? For years, Elgarroth insisted Merssa must survive. What changed? Why hadn't the wizard allowed Vecnor to help her, as he had so many times in the past? He could have been there for her. He *should* have been there for her!

I assure you, this is for the greater good, Elgarroth said. *And it was by her own choice. It is critical you succeed from this point. Do what you must. Do not allow Gruzim or Anduiff to aid their master.*

"Mees!" Xorlunder said, just above a whisper. The elf peered through the trees, keeping watch on Darmhorng and Burmagaard. "A legion of undead! A hundred yards to the southeast!"

Vecnor hurried to the edge of the grove. The abominations were on a path for Morimont, likely to contest the dwarves. "They aren't aiming for us. They're headed west."

The company uttered more words, but Vecnor hardly listened. Why would Merssa choose to die? Why would anyone…? He pictured Merssa, Tux, Elgarroth, and Eraim. He would die for any of them. The images transformed into Borse and Cavalor, and Vecnor understood. His focus returned to the surrounding trees, where his companions were nervous about the undead army marching against Sullis, Magneer, and the dwarves.

"We must trust it to the gods now." Vecnor sighed. "But do not fear. The dwarves of Morimont are the greatest warriors of their race, in my opinion. And they will know resistance awaits them."

"Shh!" Xorlunder hissed. "They are almost upon us."

Merssa reentered Vecnor's thoughts as the dunarchins, ghouls, zombies, and skeletons marched past. His mind shifted to Tux. The half-gray elf was surely alone and surrounded by evil. But Eslimil was accustomed to such a life. He thought again of Eraim. Other than Tux, the tiny elf was skilled beyond anyone Vecnor had known. But she didn't have Eslimil's centuries of experience. Would she be the next to perish in this horrid war? Vecnor clenched his fists, glaring at the undead. He was ready to fight them all! But there was a task to complete, and he remained quiet.

"Gather your gear," he said once the enemy had passed. "We move now."

The company did as instructed while Vecnor located the trapdoor concealed beneath dirt and leaves. Still numbed by the grim news, any words spoken by his companions went unheard, and he pounded his boot onto the wood with enough force to break it from its hinges. Xorlunder's eyes widened.

"It won't be much of a secret after today," Vecnor pointed out. Besides that, it wasn't Brondor's way to sneak into castle dungeons. Those missions were given to Tux.

Vecnor dropped through the opening to the flooded tunnel below, and the others followed. He led them along a narrow passage until it ended at a blank wall; the secret entrance into the dungeon. The hidden panel emitted a horrible grating sound as Vecnor forced it open, but he worried not. Nor did he fret when the chill of a Death Lord rushed into the hallway, though the looks of horror from his companions didn't escape his notice.

He walked briskly through a storage room and to the next door. It was locked. With a single kick, Vecnor launched it from its hinges and proceeded along the dimly lit corridor beyond. At the adjoining intersection, a pair of soldiers arrived to investigate, and Vecnor dispatched them without hesitation, thrusting his sword through one and snapping the other's neck with his gauntleted hand.

To the right was the first set of cells, marked by reinforced doors with barred windows. But Vecnor's vision depicted Elloria behind floor-to-ceiling bars — the cells reserved for important prisoners. He sent his companions right to look for the priestess, though he knew she wasn't there, and he proceeded alone to the left. For the moment, he preferred the solitude.

The hallway terminated at an iron-bound door. Vecnor cared not whether it was locked, nor did he check, and he forced it open with his shoulder. Beyond, a dark guardroom sat empty. A reinforced door stood to the right and a door of iron was across the chamber.

Get the keys from up the stairs, said Elgarroth. *They are necessary to free Elloria.*

Vecnor headed right.

Thoughts of Merssa standing alone before Jurak returned, and yet another door fell victim to Vecnor's rage. He climbed stone steps to an oaken door and kicked it down as well, surprising a dozen guards within the adjoining guardroom. He advanced.

The soldiers hesitated, and Vecnor slew half of them before they readied their weapons — more fools taking him for a Death Lord. He killed a few more before a mace struck his left arm, but there was no pain, and he defeated the rest. With the chill of the evil king permeating the castle, Vecnor knew what came next, and before the first zombie rose, he mutilated most of the corpses. The remaining undead guards presented little opposition before their heads rolled across the floor.

Vecnor grabbed a ring of keys from a hook on the wall and returned to the stairs. As he descended, a touch of nausea invaded. Wraiths were near.

He rushed down the steps to find his companions battling the dark spirits in the guardroom. Gruelenor slashed in vain at a wraith hovering over Melac, while another drove Xorlunder to the floor and pierced the elf's chest with its shadowy claw. Nidor's entire body was aflame, and the paladin ended a third wraith's existence with his fiery sword. As Vecnor cut through the evil ghost pinning Xorlunder, reducing the fiend to a cloud of black vapor, the final wraith disappeared through a hole in the ceiling.

Gruelenor turned to Nidor with concerned eyes. "One got away."

"To warn its master, no doubt," said Vecnor as the flames about Nidor vanished, leaving only the paladin's sword alight. "We need to keep moving," he added, pulling Xorlunder from the floor before tossing the ring of keys to the Dale.

Striding to the iron door, Vecnor shouldered it. The portal's resistance was the strongest he had faced since entering the dungeon, but it busted from its frame nonetheless, and he passed through. A single torch dimly illuminated five cells on either side of the corridor beyond, each possessing a door of bars, and most contained a pair of stone cots, a bucket of water, a couple of wooden plates, and two prisoners, their faces defeated and drained of color. The last cell on the right housed Elloria.

The priestess's chamber was bare of furnishings, and she sat against the far side with her wrists shackled to the wall. Her head remained bowed. A set of rafters were obviously a recent addition to the small room, and a strange mechanism connected them from the barred door to the ceiling, where numerous cracks marred the stone. It was rigged to collapse. That must be why Elgarroth insisted Vecnor grab the keys.

Satisfied he had caused enough of a ruckus to appease Brondor, Vecnor stood back and allowed the others to proceed. As expected, unlocking the cell door with the proper key disabled the trap, and Nidor and Xorlunder entered to exchange words with Elloria and unlock her restraints. When the priestess declined to be freed by acts of stealth, Vecnor stepped forward and spoke.

"If it's battle you wish, then that is what you shall have. We are not here to steal you away, Priestess, and there has been no secrecy in our approach once we arrived. Two armies will soon converge on

Burmagaard, and they need your faithful following to defeat the enemy!"

Elloria gazed at Vecnor, her youthful eyes no different from decades ago, apart from their sadness. "I do not know how many of my folk remain." She shook her head. "It has been longer than I can recall since my imprisonment. Any soldiers not captured may have indeed sought refuge to await my return. But whether they have escaped enemy eyes, I cannot say."

"Rise, Priestess!" Vecnor commanded. "It is time for battle! Time to put the enemy down and reclaim what was taken!"

Prisoners from the neighboring cells gathered in the hallway, freed by Gruelenor, and they stood taller as color returned to Elloria's face.

She rose to her full height and lifted her chin. "Yes." Her voice was stronger. "Yes! The time *has* come." She looked at her men. "We will take back what is ours! Or we will die in combat!"

The soldiers raised their fists into the air. "Brondor!"

Elloria turned to Vecnor. "Who are you, stranger?"

"He is Vecnor!" announced Xorlunder. "The ageless warrior, come to us in our time of need."

Elloria's eyes narrowed. "Vecnor?" A smile slowly formed. "It *is* you! I met you once, when I was but a child. My, how you have not changed. But it must be you. I can feel it."

"I remember." Vecnor couldn't stop the whisper from escaping. Normally, he never confirmed such utterances. "But first, some of my companions are in need of aid. Can you help them?"

"Already I feel my power growing." Elloria gazed at her soldiers, their state of fatigue registering in her eyes. "I have no herbs, but I'll do what I can."

Nidor pulled a handful of Vermallon dusk from his pack and handed them to the priestess. Had Elgarroth provided the barbarian with the herbs? It mattered not, and Vecnor surrendered his own stock as well.

Elloria immediately tended to the wounded and weary, and while she worked, Gruelenor arrived with the prisoners from the first set of cells. Nidor entered the corridor to assist the priestess in her efforts, and his hand became alive with fire. The soldiers balked, but as he touched them and their woes evaporated, their expressions eased and they bowed with appreciation.

Once everyone was ready, Vecnor donned his helmet and led the company back through the guardroom and up the stairs. Upon entering the chamber where he procured the keys, he viewed the bodies of those that had risen after being slain—a reminder of the chill oozing from the ceiling.

"Do not forget the evil effects of the Death Lord's presence," he said. "The living will need to be put down twice."

Elloria and her men picked up weapons from the fallen, and several of them donned the damaged chain shirts. Vecnor then guided them up another set of stairs to a reinforced door with a barred window. It was the guardroom where he had spent years playing the part of Norvec. Thoughts of Solinin invaded, and he lowered his shoulder to force his way into the chamber beyond.

Within the room, the castle guards hesitated to use their crossbows as fear captured their eyes. Vecnor flashed his swords about, hewing into their midst, and they released their bolts at last. The sting of a small arrow pierced Vecnor's side, but he did not slow, and Elloria's men overwhelmed the enemy, as well as the zombies that resulted. The rest of her soldiers then outfitted themselves, and the priestess lifted a second blade and waved it about with a grin.

Turning to her faithful, a youthful vigor replaced Elloria's aged appearance. "Let our enemies litter the ground beneath our feet! And may Brondor give us the strength to claim victory! Or the courage to carry on until the last of us has perished in combat!"

"Brondor!" Vecnor answered with her men. It had been too many years since he felt like a Brondor warrior!

They battled through the castle, slaying Kalmirans, Marcs, and hobgoblins. As they pressed deeper, the enemy included dunarchins and ghouls. They reached a grand staircase ascending to the second level, and Vecnor, Nidor, and Gruelenor split from the others so Elloria could make her presence known to her followers in Burmagaard.

Upon the upper floor, the odor of decay and death assailed Vecnor's senses, and he and his companions battled through dunarchins, ghouls, and wraiths until reaching the throne room. Within the large chamber was a score of Zurkans, as well as the source of the chilling fear. From the sword and axe the Death Lord possessed, Vecnor knew it to be Anduiff.

The Zurkans charged.

Vecnor welcomed the Soldiers of Blood, slashing his swords left and right with the skill of centuries and dropping an enemy with every blow. The krukari warriors swung axes and swords and thrust their spears, and he effortlessly knocked most of their attacks aside. Their corpses he ignored, counting on Nidor and Gruelenor to protect his flanks from the zombies they would become. Once the final Benasti warrior fell, he addressed the Death Lord.

"Anduiff!"

The undead fiend had watched the combat, as if it were a play constructed for the dark king's personal amusement. A distant screech echoed outside, and upon a balcony beyond an open doorway, a skeletal dragon answered the call.

"Another time," Anduiff said in a deep, hollow voice.

The Death Lord raced through the opening and leaped atop the undead mount, and the dragon launched into the sky.

Vecnor ran to the balcony. The morning sun illuminated widespread combat along the streets of Burmagaard, and a fog surrounded a massive battle in the east. Anduiff, meanwhile, flew westward beneath a gathering of dark clouds.

"He does not aid the battle for the city?" asked Nidor. "Or join the battle to the east?"

Vecnor frowned. "No. He flies to the dwarves." His gaze shifted to the streets below. "To Burmagaard!"

He led the way back through the stronghold and into the courtyard. Elloria and her men must have defeated all enemies, for nothing opposed them and mutilated corpses marked her passing like a trail of bread crumbs. Outside the castle grounds, the road to Burmagaard was barren and the city gate was open. Vecnor entered, and he and his companions assisted Kalmiran soldiers locked in combat with hobgoblins and krukari. The enemy was vanquished, and with Anduiff gone, the bodies did not rise.

Vecnor removed his helmet and hooked it to his belt before addressing the Kalmirans. "Where's Elloria?"

"To the south, I believe," replied a soldier. "But who are you?"

"I am her faithful servant." Vecnor bowed.

Rising spirits lit up the warriors' eyes, and grins stretched from ear to ear.

For two hours, Vecnor, Nidor, and Gruelenor led the soldiers across Burmagaard, slaying bandits, hobgoblins, krukari, and traitor-Kalmirans. Elloria was then in sight, along with hundreds of warriors that had joined her, and she acknowledged Vecnor's approach.

"The enemy's numbers are failing!" the priestess said. "I have two full squads clearing the streets to the east and west. We will win Burmagaard before the day is out!"

The sky darkened and the air chilled, and all eyes turned skyward. Anduiff returned, flying just above the buildings and raising the fallen to fight for Trannum. Elloria cursed the Death Lord as it circled, and the dragon sped away toward the battle in the east, where the North Army surely fought.

Utilizing both swords, Vecnor decapitated zombies with every swing. There was then a void on his right as Nidor and Gruelenor advanced into the growing enemy. Vecnor remained with Elloria—she was his priority at the moment. The priestess barked orders, and her captains split the force into three squadrons. She led the charge into hundreds of Benasti zombies approaching from the east, and Vecnor followed.

The undead seemed endless, and several minutes passed before Vecnor realized the contingent had battled a few blocks from where he last saw Nidor. A part of him feared for the paladin's safety. But Silcor was strong in the barbarian, and he had to trust the Dale was up to the task.

Once the area was cleared of zombies, traitor-Kalmirans issued from surrounding buildings. But they did not draw weapons. They knelt before Priestess Elloria with heads bowed, swearing their oaths, and she accepted them into her growing army.

Xorlunder and Melac approached Vecnor. He hadn't seen them since they left the castle with Elloria. Neither bore any visible wounds.

"Vecnor!" Xorlunder hailed. "I was hoping you would find us. But where are Nidor and Gruelenor?"

Vecnor shook his head. "We were separated after Anduiff flew over."

The smiles retreated from the gray elf and the mage.

"It couldn't be helped," Vecnor said. "We may see them again. But we must focus on capturing the city. A battle looms in the east, and they will need our help before long."

Xorlunder nodded. "I understand."

Elloria returned to Vecnor, her expression confident. "We head northeast. New recruits report mercenary soldiers to be gathering there."

Vecnor drew a sword and grinned. "Lead the way!"

The priestess's force was five hundred strong, and they marched for half a mile to find the enemy. The mercenaries had secured three blocks, and their host stood among a market square while dozens more lined the rooftops.

Elloria ordered the charge.

Vecnor engaged the opposition while Xorlunder loosed arrows and Melac released balls of fire. The mage then turned his attention to the rooftops, where crossbowmen picked off allies, and smaller globes of flame created lesser explosions and launched the snipers from their perches. Less than a half hour passed when the mercenaries routed to flee the city, but Elloria ordered her men to pursue, and none of them reached the eastern gate.

Night descended, and the soldiers secured the area while Vecnor, Elloria, Melac, Xorlunder, and a captain named Feddas gathered in a small shop covered in sawdust. Scattered wood-working tools and tables adorned the chamber, as well as several planks of cedar, oak, and pine.

"We lost two hundred men," Xorlunder said. "But we have gained another four hundred. Mostly Marcs and Nirans."

Elloria grinned. "Brondor smiles upon us this night."

"Do we continue in the dark?" asked Captain Feddas.

Elloria stared at nothing. "No. I think not. Though Brondor's Glory burns in my veins, the body needs rest. We break for three hours."

"It will be done." The captain bowed and departed.

Another man entered. His eyes were sharp and his expression confident.

"Ah, Captain Fremar," Elloria said.

He bowed. "You sent for me, Priestess?"

"Take your men and check on the other squadrons," she ordered. "Tell all survivors to gather at the southern gate at dawn."

"Yes, Priestess."

"Once you've finished," she added, "keep watch on the northern perimeter. I want nothing sneaking up on us."

"It will be done." Fremar bowed.

Elloria gave a firm nod, and the captain set out.

The priestess studied Vecnor with a furrowed brow. "I cannot get over you being here. It is surely Brondor's Will. I will not disappoint Him this time."

Vecnor tilted his head. "I'm at your disposal."

"I do not know if spirits of Brondor need rest," she said, "but do what you must to prepare."

Vecnor smirked as he exited, followed by Xorlunder and Melac.

The surrounding buildings served as make-shift barracks, and guards marched the streets and watched from rooftops. Vecnor found a house devoid of occupants, and he sat heavily on a chair too small to provide genuine comfort. Regardless, he would have a moment's rest.

"Is it truly Brondor that sent you?" asked Xorlunder.

Vecnor opened his eyes. "It's possible."

Xorlunder gave a wry smile. "You still have a bolt sticking from your armor."

Vecnor had forgotten about the arrow that pierced him back in the dungeon, its shaft now broken. The sting blended with other minor injuries he had sustained since then. And now he lacked healing herbs. "I shall deal with it in good time." He closed his eyes again, determined to sleep while the distant clash of steel and screams filled the night.

❈ ❈ ❈

An hour passed when a horn sounded outside. Vecnor awoke, and he, Xorlunder, and Melac reported to the street to find a score of wraiths attacking. Vecnor advanced, slaying four dark spirits, and Melac used magical fire to destroy a couple more. Elloria called upon Brondor's Might, and from her hand issued a blinding flash of holy light. Once Vecnor's sight returned, not even a wisp of smoke suggested that wraiths had existed.

Elloria addressed Vecnor. "And with the darkness, the undead slink from their hiding places. I suppose they will allow no more rest than what we have achieved."

Vecnor nodded. It was a pity.

Elloria instructed Captain Feddas to assemble the troops.

The contingent marched south at a cautious pace, battling ghouls at every turn. After half a mile, they headed southwest and confronted a large force of Benasti warriors, including fifty Zurkans. The Soldiers of Blood presented a challenge before expiring, and though more allies were lost, every street saw additional Kalmirans running to enlist.

As the sky brightened in anticipation of sunrise, Elloria's small army approached the southern gate to find the allied squadrons awaiting them. The combined force might have exceeded a few thousand, but when lightning splintered the large wooden doors, a legion of dunarchins stormed the breach before they could unite.

"Forward!" commanded Elloria.

A group of soldiers rushed into a nearby tower while Captain Feddas signaled the charge. Shortly after, the tower horn blared across the city—the battle would need every abled warrior. Hopefully, the remainder of the faithful would emerge from their hiding places to give aid.

Vecnor advanced, dispatching several enemies while the undead firstborns drove a wedge into Elloria's men. Xorlunder abandoned the bow and fought beside the priestess while Melac unleashed spells to incinerate dunarchin mages. As the fallen enemy piled up, Vecnor sheathed one of his weapons and lifted a dunarchin by the throat. He swung the wriggling body like a club, pummeling a few others before cleaving their heads, and tossed the creature into its comrades.

"Vecnor!" called Nidor from the north.

The barbarian hastened toward the battle with Gruelenor and Captain Fremar at his sides, and a group of scouts and a handful of Kalmiran soldiers ran in his wake. The paladin's sword and eyes were ablaze.

"Glad to see you two alive!" Vecnor said once the Dale joined the combat.

Nidor's expression showed no relief. "We are being flanked!" The paladin struck a dunarchin's shield, driving the undead warrior back.

Vecnor clenched his jaw. Another army? Was it the remnants of the force that marched on Morimont, returned to Burmagaard?

Storm clouds moved overhead, and the chill of a Death Lord followed. Overcome by urgency, Vecnor pulled his second blade and advanced, slashing with speed and precision. His display inspired those around him, and their weapons lifted higher. A few attacks struck Vecnor's armor, inflicting minor wounds, but he did not slow.

"They're here!" Gruelenor called out.

Several allied warriors followed the krukari and Nidor to oppose ghouls and dunarchins advancing from the north. The glowing eyes of the undead firstborns filled the wide streets, but beyond them charged the Morimont army, and the dwarves' roar was music to Vecnor's ears. Better still, Umbarc led the stout folk with Sullis upon the saddle, and behind the horse was Magneer.

The Death Lord remained high above, providing no help to its soldiers, and the dark clouds rolled into the east as it abandoned Burmagaard before the final dunarchin fell. The early sun then illuminated smiles across the dirty, blood-smeared faces of the victors as a cheer resounded into the sky.

Vecnor stood tall and cupped his hands to either side of his mouth. "It is not over!"

A hush captured the city.

"Feel good about this battle," he added. "But the war continues!"

Vecnor spied King Kolermane approaching. The dwarf clutched a mighty warhammer, and a jeweled crown sparkled atop the warrior's white hair. Vecnor had met the king on a few occasions in the past, but not as himself. The dwarf king knew him as just another dwarf, albeit a strong one.

"Where are the folk of Rornibur?" Kolermane asked. "I was informed that they march with the North Army."

Behind the king, a sea of grim dwarfish faces awaited the answer.

Vecnor bowed low, and Elloria's men followed his lead.

"King Kolermane, Lord of Varlimor," he said as he rose. "Your kin lie to the east with what remains of the North Army. Beside them stand citizens from nearly every realm of Vaeldor, human and elf, and they have been locked in combat for more than two days. How they've fared thus far, I do not know. The Death Lord, Gruzim, leads the enemy there, and Anduiff races to join the battle."

"Then let us waste no more time with words!" The king turned to his army. "To battle!"

The dwarves raised their weapons and cheered a single grunt, and they marched with unmatched discipline toward the east gate.

Kolermane eyed Vecnor. "You fight with the strength of many dwarves. It would honor me to have you and yours at my side."

"The honor is ours." Vecnor sheathed his swords and nodded at Elloria.

The priestess looked upon the Kalmirans, Marcs, and Nirans gathered before her, greater than two thousand in all. "We march!"

"Brondor!" shouted half of the soldiers.

The combined forces of Varlimor and Burmagaard proceeded east with determined expressions. Vecnor walked to Kolermane's right with Elloria beside him. Behind them were Xorlunder, Nidor, Gruelenor, and Sullis, and Melac rode atop Umbarc, for the mage was drained of power. Before long, the fog encompassing the battle appeared; a massive sight reminiscent of Sistama. Kolermane advanced into the cloud, and the army matched his pace.

A foul reek invaded Vecnor's lungs as he inhaled the surrounding vapors, and many soldiers vomited. He had eaten so little over the past day, there was nothing to regurgitate. The battle then came into view. A village lay half razed, and divided and exhausted was the North Army, comprising soldiers from nearly every race and realm. Scattered packs of zombies, skeletons, and ghouls savagely attacked, while dunarchins fought in disciplined ranks and wraiths ruled the sky. As the Morimont-Burmagaard force engaged, Anduiff descended from the cloud, as if having awaited the dwarves' arrival, and its dragon released withering gas onto the stout warriors.

Vecnor charged a crowd of ghouls. His blades sung, and all enemies before him perished. Beside him, Nidor reduced ghouls to ashes with every swing of the flaming sword. Vecnor also noticed flashes of fire protecting the barbarian any time the undead deigned to make physical contact—the Dale's connection to Silcor was truly strong! Gruelenor and Magneer fought nearby, but Vecnor paid them no mind. He pushed forward, downing foe after foe. But not all of Gruzim's soldiers were among the undead, and Vecnor took pleasure in slaying Benasti warriors and a few Benasti wolves—twice.

A horn sounded to the south, where a force of dunarchins approached with Anduiff at the lead—the Death Lord no longer rode its dragon of bone. The dark king signaled the undead firstborns, and the evil army advanced.

"We're cut off!" yelled Magneer.

Vecnor scanned the battlefield. Nidor, Gruelenor, and Magneer were with him, separated from all others by various forms of undead, and ghouls were coming. Their best chance for survival until help arrived was to stick together. But Nidor had other plans, and Vecnor hastened to catch up as the barbarian fearlessly charged into the dunarchins. The undead firstborns balked, as if afraid to confront the paladin—a strange occurrence—and the Dale showed no mercy, his flaming sword incinerating the enemy with every strike. Vecnor fought beside Nidor, and they slew dunarchins beyond count while Gruelenor and Magneer battled the ghouls to protect their flank.

Elloria and Sullis returned with hundreds of Kalmirans, carving a path to reunite with Vecnor and his companions. The immediate area was then cleared, allowing for a moment to regroup.

"This day will never end!" said Sullis, gazing at approaching zombies. Half of them were fresh corpses that fought for the allies not long ago. "We must defeat the Death Lords if we are to achieve victory!"

"Anduiff is to the south!" hollered Magneer. "I've not seen Gruzim!"

Sullis eyed the Death Lord. "I'm going after Anduiff! But I'll need a path!"

Vecnor heard no more as Gruzim stole his attention. The Death Lord descended on a skeletal dragon to land among the undead to the east. Visions of Merssa and Solinin plagued Vecnor's mind, and the fire in his veins burned hotter. The krukari had dealt enough evil onto Vaeldor!

Slaying all enemies in his path, Vecnor kept watch on Gruzim while forcing his way across the battlefield. The Death Lord turned to meet Anduiff's gaze, and they seemed to communicate; perhaps argue. An undead dragon then swooped from the clouds to take Anduiff away.

Vecnor's heart leaped into his throat. Elgarroth had said to keep the Death Lords from aiding Trannum. But there was no preventing Anduiff's departure. Gruzim remained, however, and the evil warrior's glowing eyes settled on Vecnor. The krukari harbored a desire to challenge him, that much was obvious. And now the undead parted between them, as if inviting Vecnor to that very event.

Chapter 28

Throne Room

Eslimil journeyed east after his meeting with Elgarroth. The West Twin River posed some difficulty, but he found a path across a fallen tree on the outskirts of Tarn Arum. He rode for two days with only a few hours of rest, and fields surrounded him as the jungle faded into the southwest. Herds of large cats, wolves, and harmless animals returned, seldom showing interest in Eslimil beyond a glance. A few predators gave chase, but the speed of Landolice was yet unmatched, even after the distance the steed had traveled, and pursuit never lasted very long.

The following day, an expanse of bright blue captured the eastern horizon. A part of the Endless Sea. Eslimil veered northeast until the mass of water faded, and early the next morning, the East Twin River forced him eastward. That evening, trees appeared in the distance. They were similar to those in the jungle, and vines draped from tree to tree, but it was not so dense as Tarn Arum. Instead, many rivers and ponds were visible. Dright Swamp lay ahead.

As Eslimil neared the marsh, swarms of parasitic insects welcomed him and Landolice. It was almost enough to hold his breath and dissolve into shadow, but he could not subject his horse to brave the critters alone. The pests increased in frequency when he entered the bog late into the night.

No roads or paths existed, and the mess of tangled vegetation slowed Landolice's progress. As well, ponds forced Eslimil and his steed left and right and they trudged across several streams to maintain an easterly trek. As the sun rose, the swamp grew less treacherous. Willows, river birches, and aspens replaced the jungle trees, but the soil remained saturated and the waterways plentiful.

Just after noon, a wide river passed from east to west, sporting colorful water lilies atop a green-speckled surface. Probably a tributary of the East Twin River. Eslimil followed its course for two days, and Landolice disturbed the stagnant water whenever they crossed one of its many branches extending to the south. Throughout the journey, animals did their best to remain unseen, but Eslimil spotted a line of sunbathing turtles, a nine-foot snake, and various birds he did not recognize.

The next evening, things changed. Snow coated every inch of the swamp ahead and ice covered all water surfaces. Eslimil donned his warm cloak, and he and Landolice pressed on. Beyond the snowline, the frozen air stung Eslimil's lungs and the clouds cast deeper shadows, and although the bog lacked any wind, the biting chill was worse than when they traversed the Fire Hills. A direct path was now attainable, however, as snow-covered ice made crossing ponds and streams an easier task, and Eslimil urged Landolice to a quickened pace with no stops for rest.

The night stretched long, and Eslimil's face, hands, and feet lost all feeling. Landolice's shivers proved the animal suffered as well. Just when Eslimil thought he could endure the icy atmosphere no longer, the morning sun peeked over the horizon to reveal the marsh's border, and with it, the snow's end. Landolice needed no urging as the horse sprinted, and soon Nomedd's sweltering heat and humidity replaced the wintry torment.

Though weary from days of hard travel, Eslimil turned northeast toward the looming mountains miles away. The journey to the Varlimor giants claimed the day, and Eslimil veered eastward until the tall peaks dwindled and the hills began. He entered the rolling terrain, and after half a mile, headed east until the Trethel River allowed no farther advancement. There, he dismounted to gain some much needed rest.

❖❖❖

Eslimil found only a few hours of sleep. The heat remained uncomfortable through the night, but his restlessness was due to the stronghold only a couple of miles to the southeast. It had been the same when he spent years spying on the castle. And though the evil fortress was hidden from view, he knew it was there.

In the distant northeast, flashes of lightning momentarily interrupted the darkness. But there were no clouds that Eslimil could see. Selanna's doing? A Death Lord? Time would tell.

A few hours passed, and the sky turned a brighter shade of blue with the arrival of a new day. Eslimil fed Landolice an apple and rubbed the mount's nose.

"I must continue without you," he said. "It grows much more treacherous from here."

The horse whinnied and nodded.

Eslimil patted the animal's neck. "Do not wander far. If I do not return within a week, you must find your way home. Understood?"

Landolice snorted and stomped a hoof.

"Take care, my friend."

The horse's ears twitched, but it said nothing more.

The Trethel River moved swiftly downhill, no less than twenty yards wide at its narrowest point. Eslimil took in a deep breath and floated across, regardless of the discomfort the brightening sky imposed. Upon reaching the opposite bank, he breathed freely, just as the first ray of sun arrived.

Continuing east, Eslimil climbed and descended the rugged terrain. It was a slow trek, and perspiration quickly drenched his underclothes. As he reached the hottest part of the day, he gazed at the black structure now visible to the south. The Nomedd heat could not prevent a chill from coursing down Eslimil's spine. Years of watching the stronghold and the horrors he witnessed had left his mind scarred forever, but he suppressed the memories, refusing to relive them.

A nearby gathering of trees offered shade, and Eslimil climbed into their midst to relax as best he could. He spent the day drinking from his waterskin, carving TUX onto an elm, and tossing pebbles into a hole in the trunk of an oak. An hour after the sun set, he detected voices to the east.

Eslimil left his cover to investigate, and fifty yards away he spotted Selanna, Eraim, Greyor, Brem, and Arrikan. Millord was not present. Eslimil remained in the shadows and watched as the group attempted to sleep, but they appeared as restless as he felt and eventually abandoned the task. As dawn approached, Brem meditated on a wet patch of grass, Arrikan spoke quietly to Greyor about the loss of Millord, and Selanna and Eraim stood on a ridge overlooking Trannum's stronghold. None of them were immune to the swarm of insects that had settled over them, and they constantly swatted at the pests and scratched the resulting bites.

"Selanna!" said Arrikan, staring at her palm. "The bugs! Have you looked at them?" The ranger ran to Selanna, holding out her hand.

Selanna's eyes grew large while gazing at Arrikan's discovery. The mage then inspected her own body and scanned the insects fluttering about. "We have to go!" She turned back to the stronghold. "They are from *him*. He knows we are here!"

Eraim slapped at her arms and legs. "What vile poison have they been infecting us with?"

"Shouldn't we wait for Soren?" asked Arrikan. "We'll arrive too soon."

Selanna gathered her gear. "We have no choice. We must go!"

The company lifted their packs and hastened down the hillside. The bugs pursued. After forty yards, Selanna halted and turned to the priest.

"Brem," she said. "Is there anything you can do?"

The marteese pursed his lips. "Maybe for some of us. But I doubt I have the strength —"

"Whatever you can manage, you must," Selanna insisted. "And hurry!"

Brem rushed to a maple tree and placed his hand on its bark. His eyes closed as he mouthed a prayer, and upon completion, he said, "Please, as much as you can spare." The priest dragged a knife across the bark, releasing a few ounces of sap. He collected the thick fluid into a vial before waving his hand over the cut and whispering. The tree's wound vanished. Brem returned to Selanna and offered the small bottle. "Use as much as you need and no more," he instructed, his voice hoarse.

Selanna accepted the vial and glanced at the stronghold. "Perhaps I should expend some power of my own."

She recited a short incantation, and a breeze swept over the area. It grew in strength, dancing with Eslimil's hair as it carried the flying pests away. The wind faded, and Selanna passed the container of sap to Eraim.

Eraim used her fingertip to apply the sticky substance to her arms and face. She then handed it to Arrikan.

Arrikan lifted the vial. It was half empty. She sighed and offered it to Selanna. "Your skills are more important than my own."

Selanna accepted the bottle and applied the sap in the same manner Eraim had. She then held what remained—less than a quarter—toward Arrikan and Greyor. The ranger and dwarf eyed the container and turned to each other.

"You have been most skilled in your arts," said Greyor. "You use it."

Arrikan placed her hand on the dwarf's shoulder. "Nonsense. This is a battle for Clanghorr! And only *you* can wield such a weapon."

Greyor nodded and took the vial.

Arrikan faced Selanna, scratching her arm. "I'll do what I can."

"I'm sorry," said Brem, scratching his neck.

Selanna's smile for the marteese, though worn, was genuine. "You have done more than enough. I only wish there was something more I could do."

Once Greyor finished treating as many bites as the remaining elixir allowed, the company resumed their downhill trek beneath the brightening sky. Eslimil followed at a distance beyond Eraim's detection—he was well aware of her abilities from years of observation. They trudged over the dried-out vegetation surrounding Trannum's home, and though Eslimil could not detect the chill of the Death Lord that was surely present, it was obvious when the others did. Their frosty exhales defied the heat, and they ceased moving to rub their hands or cradle their arms while searching the cloudless sky. The sun shone brightly, and no undead kings flew above.

Selanna's party held a quiet conversation and proceeded to the front of the structure. They then spoke again before retracing their steps, and Eslimil darted behind a boulder for cover. After several seconds, he chanced a peek. The group aimed for the castle's western side, where the large opening for the release of newly animated dragons existed on the top floor. Once they rounded the building, Eslimil followed and peered around the corner. The company stood in a circle while holding hands. Selanna recited an incantation, and they floated up and through the opening.

Eslimil waited a minute. He then crept along the wall until the entrance was directly overhead. The sun remained on the eastern side of the castle, casting a shadow over him, and though it was not a particularly dark shade, it would do. He took in a deep breath.

Blending with the weaker shadows placed added pressure on Eslimil's lungs as he ascended to the hole. Inside the stronghold, comforting darkness partially obscured piles of large bones and worktables in the corners of the dragon laboratory, but the company was still present. Eslimil feared he might have to risk discovery as he became lightheaded and his chest burned. But then Selanna opened the chamber's only door, and after a small light appeared above her, she passed into the corridor beyond with her companions close behind.

Eslimil bolted to the nearest corner and released his breath. There, he panted for several seconds, his heart pounding in his head. But there was no time for rest, and he hurried to the door to listen. Greyor uttered an exclamation—the company was still nearby. Additional words followed, first from Selanna and then Arrikan. The ranger's voice quivered, as one who was shivering. They moved on.

Eslimil cracked open the door. The hallway was silent. He stepped through and scrutinized the floor. There was little dust, but the group had obviously headed left. As he took a few steps, the sound of combat confirmed his suspicion. It was a short-lived battle, and Selanna's voice afterward revealed her company's success.

Eslimil proceeded until arriving at the top of a staircase. From Greyor's heavy footfalls, the dwarf was in the room below. A door opened.

"These are laboratories," said Selanna. "Keep moving around the bend."

How often had the mage visited Trannum's castle to know it so well?

Eslimil descended into a chamber containing several empty vats. Splayed on the floor were five destroyed dunarchins. He continued to the room's door and detected Greyor's metal boots on the flagstones beyond. As the sound grew faint, he opened the door.

A fifty-foot corridor bore many doors to either side. At the far end, the hallway went left, and Brem was just making the turn. Dark spots covered the marteese's blue skin, oozing red, black, and clear fluids. Eslimil wrinkled his nose.

He raced to the corner and listened. A door opened, and a gust of frozen air made its way along the corridor, penetrating Eslimil's clothing and casting a shiver from his head to his feet. He peered into the adjoining hallway to see the company entering the third of several doors to the left. Arrikan and Brem moved last, the ranger sharing in the priest's ailments.

Eslimil arrived at the door as it shut, and he placed his ear to the wood. There was shivering on the other side—likely Arrikan and Brem. The trembling persisted, as the ranger and priest did not move away, and Selanna spoke in a harsh whisper.

"Where are you going?"

"Thank you," Eraim responded after a moment, barely audible through the door. "I guess I could not resist his command."

"What command?" asked Selanna.

More silence, followed by Eraim's strained whisper. "He's down there."

A scratchy voice spoke aloud. Eslimil heard it clearly, as if he were in the same room.

"Ahh! Selanna. You've returned. Your appearance was much more appealing the last time you passed through these halls."

"Do not listen!" Eraim's tone held urgency.

Another pause before Selanna spoke.

"Today you shall meet your end! Your reign is crumbling as we speak."

The dry voice cackled again. "Fools! Do you think I care for your armies to the north? Even with your petty victories, your dead litter the land! There will always be soldiers waiting to rebuild my forces."

Eslimil's mind raced. Was this an elaborate trap? Had Elgarroth been wrong?

"You cannot raise the dead once you are destroyed!" Selanna retorted with a slight shaking in her voice.

There was a muffled crash, followed by a distant shout. "By Soleran's Might! Your tyranny has reached its end!"

"To battle!" Selanna commanded.

Greyor's boots rushed away from the door, and the clash of steel ensued.

Remaining in the corridor was useless. Eslimil took in a breath, and his shadowy form passed beneath the door and into the room beyond. To the right, Arrikan and Brem shivered violently while pus and blood decorated their blue faces and arms. Next to a wide descending staircase ahead, Selanna stood against a solid-wood railing overlooking the ruckus below. A male voice called out amid the clamor, reciting a forceful prayer to Soleran—no doubt Nilborg—and a blue glow emitted from the lower chamber.

Moving to a darkened corner away from the ranger and marteese, Eslimil exhaled. He was beyond all light sources, and there was no chance of being noticed. Forcing his breathing to slow, he watched and listened.

"Prepare to taste Clanghorr's edge!" Greyor bellowed.

Selanna moved her hands, as if to work her magic. But something distracted her and she gasped. "No!"

A clap of thunder sounded within the castle, and the shouting below intensified. A glow then emanated from the torchlight below. Selanna released several green spheres into the melee, casting the spell again and again.

Eraim appeared, backing up the stairs while four dunarchins pressed. She severed the head of one with Mithkahr, and as she did the same to another, one of the final two gashed her leg. Selanna sent fire from her open palm to wash over the attackers as Eraim fell, and the burning corpses tumbled down the steps. Eraim's leg was in a horrible state.

Do not engage, Eslimil told himself.

Despite her ailments, Arrikan rushed to the small elf's side.

"I can no longer fight!" Eraim cringed, holding her hand over the bleeding wound as the ranger helped her to sit against the railing. "They need me down there!"

Arrikan gazed into the lower chamber, and her eyes widened as she gasped. Somehow, she found strength enough to pull her sword and descend, regardless of the shivers and poison running through her veins.

"Arrikan!" Eraim called, to no avail.

Selanna resumed launching green spheres into the room while Eraim positioned herself at the corner of the staircase and pulled her bow. As the small elf released arrows into the melee, Selanna's jaw dropped, and the frozen air warmed slightly. Something had changed. Did they defeat the Death Lord?

A darkness emitted from the battle, followed by a flash of bright light. Selanna's expression became determined, and she issued a ball of fire. An explosion ensued. Seconds later, Eraim cringed, and Selanna jumped back as a bolt of pure blackness struck the railing. The elegant wood splintered, and Selanna flew across the chamber to hit the wall near Brem, her robes badly scorched.

Eraim loosed additional arrows until her face went ashen, and she froze. What had she witnessed? Her expression calmed when Selanna returned to her side, and she resumed the attack. Selanna cast a ball of flame, and upon the resulting explosion, the mage and Eraim gasped in unison. A moment later, Greyor roared, and a loud *crack* sounded as a chunk of the ceiling dropped into the room below, cutting his bellow short. Eraim's quiver was then empty. The small elf had sent every last one into the scrum, and the frustration in her sigh was unmistakable.

Eraim was correct about the orbs, said Elgarroth in Eslimil's mind. *The final one lies in Trannum's skull. You must help her destroy it.*

Eraim's gaze was suddenly blank. Eslimil recognized the stare. Elgarroth spoke to her — a task the wizard had told him centuries ago was risky to perform. Elgarroth could see through the eyes of nearly everyone with which he was familiar, without their knowledge. But to speak into Eraim's mind… She might sense his presence.

Eslimil shook the thought. He had a job to complete. Inhaling, he merged with the shadows and floated to the demolished railing — hopefully Brem was too occupied with scratching and shivering to notice him. As he released his breath, he pulled one of his special arrows and placed it into Eraim's quiver. He then returned to shadow as a second black dart arrived, and Eraim's head whipped to the side while Selanna raised a magical shield to absorb the attack.

Eslimil glanced at Brem. If the priest had seen him, it was not obvious. He hovered closer to Eraim, careful to remain out of her peripheral vision. Focused on the combat, she reached for her quiver as if by reflex, and her eyes widened slightly when her fingers grabbed the wooden shaft. She put the arrow to her bow. Eslimil floated near enough to hear her whispered prayer to Galenfial as she pulled back the string. He placed his shadowy hand over hers, unknowing if his idea would work. But he had to try.

Below, the necromancer stood amid a chaotic scene. Soren, Nilborg, and Pallit were unmoving, Greyor was stunned next to the chunk of ceiling that had fallen, and Rholmar and Lorylla battled dunarchins while Arrikan protected Pallit's body. There was no Death Lord. Trannum was near a throne of bones, his glowing eye brightening as it focused on Selanna. As one, Eslimil and Eraim released the bowstring. Eslimil concentrated, and his mind melded with the arrow—it worked! The undead wizard's head turned, and he shifted the missile's path to pierce the illuminated eye socket. He then pulled away, drifting to the ceiling as the skull exploded. The rest of the skeleton disintegrated.

Floating across the chamber, Eslimil slipped through the cracks of the door next to Brem before releasing his breath. He then raced from the stronghold by the same route he had entered. It was time to find Landolice.

CHAPTER 29

THE FINAL VERSE

Vecnor awoke. It was obviously nighttime, and he lay upon a cot within a large tent, surrounded by dozens of other cots holding wounded soldiers. A few attendants moved about by candlelight, cleaning wounds.

He sat up. He recalled fighting Gruzim on the battlefield, and the krukari's evil spear jolting Xorlunder with lightning. The poor elf was launched several yards away. The Death Lord then turned a steady stream of energy on Vecnor, and his muscles spasmed uncontrollably until Gruelenor cut the spear in half. Vecnor was pretty sure Gruelenor survived the confrontation. After severing Gruzim's head, Vecnor remembered only pain and fatigue. Now, his injuries were gone, while those in the surrounding bunks sported blood-soaked bandages.

"Sir?" A woman approached. She carried a candle and a bowl holding water and a saturated towel. "I know your wounds were mended by divine power, but you really should remain in bed. At least until morning, to allow your full strength to return."

Divine power? Vecnor glanced at the wounded. Apparently there wasn't enough priestly magic to go around. He smirked at the woman. "I'm Vecnor! Now, where are my armor and weapons?"

Her eyes darted to the floor and her lips moved without words. "Well… um…" she managed at last. "They were placed under your cot. Queen Elloria said you would want them."

"Queen?"

Excitement replaced the woman's doubt. "Oh, yes! She was pronounced queen on the battlefield. Wasn't much of a ceremony, from what I heard, but they'll do it up right later this week."

"What about the war?" Vecnor asked.

The nurse took in a deep breath, her shoulders rising and lowering as she sighed. "Northern Kalmaar is free. But who's to say how things fare in the south?" She held half a smile, gazing at the tent flap. "Perhaps I can return home soon… To Barraday." Her joy faded. "I'll never forgive that Tarm for what he started." She turned to Vecnor, and her eyes brightened. "But Queen Elloria won't let something like that happen again. You mark my words."

Vecnor chuckled. The nurse was oblivious to the necromancer's role in her plight. Ignorance was truly a treasure to cherish.

Bending over, he found his equipment. "I thank you for your care, good woman. But I must be off."

She didn't try to stop him while he donned his armor and placed his swords across his back. Once finished, he exited.

The hour was late, and guards carrying torches moved about. At least fifty other tents were present, likely housing additional wounded soldiers. Each bore a flag showing the realm of residency for its occupants. Vecnor had been in the one for Kalmirans. He grinned.

The encampment was just east of Burmagaard, a mile from where the battle had taken place. Farther east, the dead were being laid in rows. At least two hundred bodies occupied each row, and the corpses stretched into the darkness. So much loss. To the south, an enormous fire burned—likely the remains of the enemy.

Vecnor headed westward in the night, avoiding patrols as he rounded the city. Upon reaching the copse of trees where the secret door to the dungeon was located, he called out.

"Umbarc!"

The horse exited the trees and snorted.

"Good to see you too, my friend." Vecnor patted the large animal's neck.

He mounted and followed the Morimont River. It was time to go home.

❖ ❖ ❖

Vecnor returned to the clearing in Vermallon, arriving before Tux—a rare occurrence. Maybe the Salenti-gray elf would be the one serving the drinks this time! Elgarroth sat near the fire, smoking a pipe. Dark circles underlined the elf's eyes—Vecnor had never seen Elgarroth appear so exhausted. It was surely a testament to the power the wizard had employed over the past month. And beneath the fatigue was concern.

Vecnor's heart raced as doubt invaded. "Did we not succeed?"

Elgarroth expelled the smoke from his lungs. "Trannum's skeleton has been destroyed."

Vecnor frowned. "But did we win?"

The wizard's brows lifted. "We won the battle. But I am afraid the war is far from over."

Vecnor sat heavily upon the log opposite the elf, his mind numb. How could the war be far from over?

Tux arrived, looking haggard. Though the half-gray elf bore no visible injuries, he appeared every bit as drained as Elgarroth. Vecnor suddenly felt guilty about the energy he possessed.

"Far from over?" Tux echoed Vecnor's thought while taking a seat by the fire.

Elgarroth nodded. "The last verse of Seac's prophecy… It is an unfinished piece of work. And when I take into account all I have seen… The war is not yet over."

"But the necromancer was destroyed," Tux pointed out. "I witnessed it."

"Yes, Trannum was destroyed," Elgarroth said. "But then there is the final line of the prophecy. *Eyes open in shadowy hall.* Though I know not to whom these words refer, my visions remain plagued by

267

the undead. There is more to come, but I cannot see it clearly just yet."

Vecnor sighed. He didn't feel much like having a drink anymore.

"But what is to come will not happen too soon," added Elgarroth.

The wizard proceeded to relate all he had seen of the war. He began with the North Army battling through Nira and to Orlenfel Forest. The gray elves replaced those lost along the way, and their abilities doubled the strength of the entire force. The army faced a legion of dunarchins and Benasti warriors as they neared Burmagaard, and Gruzim joined the fight with a battalion of undead from behind the allies. Elgarroth paused to gaze at Vecnor, and Vecnor completed the tale, beginning with the triumph in Burmagaard and ending with the battle for Kalmaar.

Elgarroth then spoke of the South Army. Vecnor shook his head when learning of Landerik's folly on the mountain pass and the lives it cost. The wizard also described the taking of Ironside Keep, and the duel between Arkor and Vikur.

"It would seem that Vikur's spirit was too strong," said Elgarroth. "You see, the transformation to a dunarchin drives the subject mad. They yearn for the life they cannot regain, and hate those that have what they no longer possess. But it does not erase all of their memories, and Vikur possessed a good soul. A spark of that goodness still existed deep down. Radaam might have been better off had he killed Vikur and created a lesser undead soldier. For similar reasons, that is why Karrak was imprisoned for so long. I believe Trannum was searching for a way to bend the king to his will."

Elgarroth returned to the tale, speaking of Merssa and her company's passage into Denvale, and the magic Wezlok employed to see them safely from the city—the Lorian wizard was more powerful than Vecnor realized. The journey continued into Mentrial Forest, followed by Merssa's sacrifice. Somehow, the Cafior paladin bested Cadorn in single combat, but she found her own end as well, and a shockwave with her passing destroyed all onlookers.

Watching the fire dance, Vecnor fought back his anger, frustration, and sorrow while swallowing the lump in his throat.

Elgarroth advanced the story to the infiltration of Castle Lambrak and the existence of zhokards. Like the zhomians, zhokards were among the offspring of the Andrian women of Dimarr's tribe. But unlike zhomians, the zhokards detested Trannum and sought the necromancer's destruction. Elgarroth then spoke of the battles within the castle and Cavalor's discovery of his relationship to Mayry and Tarm, as well as his duel against his half-brother, Horx.

"As I foresaw," Elgarroth said, "Trannum had progressed Horx's aging. The krukari was to be king of Marcove, so he could undergo the same procedure as his father, Gruzim, and become a Death Lord. Luckily, Mayry's resistance to relinquish the throne delayed that process."

Elgarroth finished the tale of the South Army with the arrival of the Dales and Wezlok dropping Anduiff from the sky. He also mentioned that the Death Lord's body was never found.

"I'm glad Landerik got his," mumbled Vecnor.

"Do not place too much blame on his young shoulders," Elgarroth said. "Had Merssa's force retreated from the pass, as she desired, she would have perished with Arkor, and the leadership would have fallen upon Cavalor. Though wise for his years, I doubt he would have succeeded." The wizard frowned. "This was the way it needed to proceed. It was the path Merssa needed to follow to achieve her full potential. I know not what that means for the future, but I feel her sacrifice has yet to yield its true resolve."

Vecnor shook his head, still stung by the loss. "At least she defeated Cadorn."

Tux nodded.

Elgarroth returned to the story, touching on the company trekking across Fire Hills and Dright Swamp, as well as the horde of undead they faced and Rybeal's heroic death while battling an undead dragon. The journey into the mines of Lornibur followed, and

Elgarroth described a creature called Maak Maak, and the ice demon, Marfesna.

"And with Marfesna vanquished," Elgarroth said, "the torment of winter ended, and summer broke through. This was the only reason those traversing Dright Swamp escaped the bog alive, and it allowed those in Castle Lambrak a chance for success."

Elgarroth shifted to the hills north of Trannum's stronghold and the clash with Velgaad. After describing Greyor's victory over the Death Lord, he turned to Tux.

Eslimil picked up the story, speaking of undead bugs and the path taken to face Trannum. But he did not witness most of the battle against the necromancer, so Elgarroth filled in the gaps. Tux then explained how he assisted Eraim's final arrow.

"I was not even sure I could perform the feat," he admitted.

"It was a risk," Elgarroth said. "But our best chance centered on you helping Eraim. I, myself, was uncertain how you would do so. I had to take it on faith that you would figure it out."

A shiver raced down Vecnor's spine. Faith? What if Tux's little trick had failed? They could have lost everyone in that battle. Eraim might have perished. Vecnor pursed his lips. Why did his mind always turn to her safety? Several brave souls were present in that fight. He changed the subject to quash the thought.

"So what now?"

"Now," Elgarroth lifted his brows, "you two will disappear. It is time to drift back into legend."

That was no surprise. Vecnor's free rein to wander and conquer evil always came at the same price. It was surely easier for Tux. No one knew of the elf's existence; only the stories that followed him.

"But you will not sit idle," Elgarroth added. "There are tasks to be done. Investigations to conduct."

And there would be no joining in Vaeldor's celebrations of the war's end. Vecnor sighed.

"But there is time before we get started." The wizard turned to Vecnor. "Please fetch the tray from the kitchen."

So much for Tux serving the drinks.

Vecnor entered the cabin. The kitchen was tidy, as usual, and on the counter was a fine decorative tray with a crystal decanter and three goblets etched with silver. The liquid in the bottle was a golden color, and its aroma contained hints of citrus. He took the tray and returned to the fire.

Elgarroth smiled while Vecnor poured the libation into the goblets. "This is a grand mead from Holindale called *Bruulu Damiss*, or Nectar of the Gods," the wizard said. "I first tasted it nearly nine hundred years ago. They do not make it anymore; the recipe was lost. Luckily, I preserved this bottle for the right occasion." He looked from Tux to Vecnor. "And this seems an adequate time."

Vecnor handed a goblet to the wizard, one to Tux, and he sat with the third. Elgarroth raised his cup and spoke.

"To the most recent triumph; to a job well done by both of you; to Merssa, Soren, Vikur, Poluran, Pallit, Rybeal, Xorlunder, Solinin, Dellen, Landerik, Millord, King Karrak, Olinin, Hubrid, Krelnamir, Ballrik, and thousands more. Their sacrifices were necessary to achieve victory."

They drank.

The liquid was thicker than wine, slightly sweetened by honey, and smooth going down. The first gulp nearly set Vecnor's head spinning, and he slowed its flow to take only a sip for his second taste. It didn't escape his notice Elgarroth had fit Landerik into the toast, and it saddened him to realize Xorlunder didn't survive the encounter with Gruzim. But another name struck him, and he lowered his goblet.

"Ballrik?"

Elgarroth took a moment to savor the drink while gazing at the stars. "In a manner of speaking."

"Isn't he still here?" Vecnor asked.

"He is." Elgarroth lowered his gaze to Vecnor. "But he shall soon leave."

"Then he's not dead," Vecnor pointed out.

The wizard shrugged. "His sacrifice was no less important. And a sacrifice it was, for that life is lost to him."

Vecnor frowned. It was confusing. And it was obvious Elgarroth did not plan to elaborate.

❖ ❖ ❖

Two weeks passed, and Vecnor and Tux filled most of their time caring for the flower and herb gardens. Vecnor also chopped wood. Elgarroth rarely left the cabin.

In the back of Vecnor's mind, the unfinished work of evil was ever present. Maybe it would take another thousand years before the undead plagued Vaeldor again. Then it would be someone else's problem. He had fought enough battles to last ten lifetimes, and that was what Elgarroth promised him: ten lifetimes. And though he had a couple of centuries left, he wondered if he possessed the strength to go through such a war again.

That evening, Vecnor and Tux ate dinner by the fire. There was an hour of sunlight remaining, and they perspired from the swordplay they had just finished. Halfway through the meal, Vecnor transformed into Tewlon. He looked at Tux.

Tux shook his head, his expression curious. He set down his dish and walked swiftly beyond the trees.

Tewlon collected their plates and placed them aside before reporting to the old stump to chop wood. While he lifted the axe, the cabin door opened and Elgarroth exited, followed by an elderly man Vecnor recognized. It was Morsum, an aged gatekeeper from Ironside. How had the guard survived the fall of the keep? What was he doing in the house?

"Tewlon!" Elgarroth hailed. "Please fetch some supper for our guest."

Tewlon entered the kitchen to find a plate holding roasted duck, steamed carrots, a slice of cheese, and a piece of bread. Ignoring the temptation to eat the cheese — something his dinner had lacked — he took the plate and exited.

"I know it is difficult to comprehend," Elgarroth was saying to Morsum. "But this is the way it must be. It is the only way it *can* be."

The old man's eyes brimmed with tears as he stared blankly into the fire.

"This is a gift," Elgarroth insisted.

"But what about Lorin?" Morsum asked in a cracked voice. "And my son… Romik, you say?"

The old gatekeeper was Ballrik!

"You must try to understand," Elgarroth said. "I bent as many of Vou's Laws as I could without breaking them. You will know your son. But you will do so as his trusted soldier. And as long as you obey the rules I have set before you, you shall age slowly and live out the rest of the days you might have had."

Elgarroth and Morsum turned to Tewlon. How long had he been staring?

Morsum accepted the plate. "Thank you."

Tewlon bowed, and he walked a very slow pace toward the woodpile, listening to as much of the conversation as he could.

"I appreciate what you're saying." Morsum sighed. "I barely remember what happened after I passed through the gate. When I try to bring it to mind, I feel I might go mad."

"Consider the loss of memory a blessing." Elgarroth's tone was softer; sympathetic. "And put the experience far from your thoughts. It is not a remembrance you wish to achieve."

"But I still see flashes in my dreams," Morsum said. "Horrible visions. Can you not take those from me?"

"No," replied Elgarroth. "To alter one's mind carries terrible risks. Give it time, and they will fade."

Tewlon heard no more as he reached the woodpile and began chopping.

Elgarroth departed with the elderly man the next day. A week later, the wizard returned alone.

"Morsum?" Vecnor asked.

Elgarroth shrugged. "The poor old soldier died when the undead invaded Ironside Keep. Ripped to pieces. But no one that survived had witnessed it, and his body was unrecognizable afterward." He smiled. "Arkor was grateful to see his loyal gatekeeper healthy. Morsum explained he had left the keep for a holiday with his family in Sendorum before the attack." Elgarroth winked. "It was the best story I could think of."

Vecnor grinned. "And the rules were only *bent*?"

The wizard sighed. "To the point of fracturing." He shook his head. "I shall endeavor not to abuse Vou's trust again."

And that was all Elgarroth said on the matter.

A few weeks later, Vecnor performed sword exercises while wearing a blindfold. Tux moved around him, lunging with a wooden sword. Thankfully, Eslimil did not employ elements of stealth—the elf's approach would have been undetectable. Vecnor froze when his sword grew heavy and his blindfold loosened.

"Well, Tewlon," said Tux. "I guess our fun is over."

Tewlon pulled off the blindfold and gave Tux a wry smile before reporting to the woodpile. Tux disappeared beyond the trees.

"Selanna and Eraim are paying us a visit." Elgarroth stood in the cabin's doorway. He walked to the logs and sat. "They arrive shortly." He lifted his pipe, and the bowl issued smoke.

Sure enough, Eraim and Selanna entered the clearing moments later. They were beautiful, as always, and Eraim eyed Tewlon before taking her turn to embrace Elgarroth. Although Vecnor learned of her survival and triumphs in the war from Elgarroth and Tux, seeing her within the glade made breathing easier.

The visitors laughed around the fire, enjoying a pleasant conversation about everything but the war. While they spoke, Tewlon chopped wood, watered plants, and entered the cabin every so often to relax and write in his journal. When outside, he couldn't help looking Eraim's way now and again, but after she caught one of his glances, he decided it was time to focus on his chores.

As evening fell, Tewlon retrieved a couple of extra pipes from the house and handed them to Eraim and Selanna. He then returned to his room, pleased to see an open window on the exterior wall. Elgarroth was allowing him to hear their conversation, and Eraim and Selanna would never know he listened—the window was invisible to those outside.

"Just before I destroyed the orb," Eraim said, "a voice spoke inside my head. At first I believed it to be my own, but as I look back now, I am not so sure."

Vecnor peered out the window to see determination in the small elf's expression. She wanted answers.

"There was a lot of confusion," she continued, "and I was in a great deal of pain at the time, but I believe it to have been a voice different from my own. It was elfish, of that I am sure, but it seemed to be that of a male's. Perhaps… a wizard's?" Eraim stared intently at Elgarroth.

"That *is* intriguing." The wizard drew from his pipe.

"Then there is the arrow," Eraim said. "I have never lost count of those I have fired, but I had one more in my quiver than I should have. Beyond that, I purchase my stock from the greatest fletcher in Salenti. Though well crafted, they are otherwise unremarkable, but I swear that last arrow was darker in color and it changed direction in mid-flight." She tilted her head. "And how did a simple arrow shatter the orb? Many other weapons had failed to achieve such a task. Even Mithkahr needed help from Selanna."

More wood, please.

Vecnor obeyed Elgarroth's request, and he missed the wizard's response as he exited the house to gather firewood. He delivered it to the fire and returned to his room in time to hear most of what Selanna had to say.

"The first is Radaam. Why did he abandon his master? And where has he gotten off to? Or Anduiff for that matter?"

"Indeed, those are interesting questions," Elgarroth said. "You will let me know what you find?"

There was a pause. Selanna then spoke again.

"Second is the prophecy. The last verse, to be exact."

Did Selanna realize what Elgarroth pointed out to Vecnor and Tux earlier? Vecnor leaned closer to the window so he wouldn't miss a word.

"What do you mean?" asked the wizard.

Eraim recited the end of Seac's prophecy.

> *"Seek to end at dark throne,*
> *Might and strength of Evil Bone.*
> *Power shatters, dust does fall.*
> *Eyes open in shadowy hall."*

"The last line," Selanna said. "Whose eyes does it refer to?"

Silence again. Vecnor looked to see Elgarroth puffing on his pipe and staring into the smoke.

"Do not trouble yourselves with such matters," the wizard replied at last. "It is enough that the lands have been returned to their rightful owners. Enjoy life now, even if only for a while."

Some wine, please.

Vecnor opened his cabinet to find a tray bearing three crystal goblets filled with a deep-red wine. He took the drinks from the house and distributed a glass to each of the elves. As he handed Eraim her goblet, their eyes met, and a tiny smirk twitched at the corner of her mouth. She turned to Elgarroth.

"What do you know of Vecnor's whereabouts?"

"Why do you ask?" Elgarroth sipped from his cup.

"I have heard tales of his great achievements in the war," she replied. "I would like to thank him."

"Why do you think *I* know of his whereabouts?"

Eraim shrugged. "Years ago, he mentioned a wizard had convinced him to journey into Sistama. From the way he spoke, I assumed he meant you."

Perhaps Vecnor shouldn't have told her that.

Elgarroth glanced at Tewlon. "Interesting."

Tewlon reported to the woodpile and chopped more wood, drowning out the rest of the conversation. Moments later, he detected a presence. Eraim stood nearby, staring at him. He ceased in his actions.

"Many thanks, sir," she said. "You are quite a *strong* lad."

Tewlon nodded, not knowing what else to do. Rarely did anyone venture to speak to him.

Eraim flashed a charming smile, and Tewlon melted inside. He desperately wished to tell her he was all right. But he could not.

She returned to the fire.

"Master Elgarroth," Eraim said, loud enough for Tewlon to hear. "If you see Vecnor, have him drop by and see me." She looked Tewlon's direction. "I miss him."

Elgarroth smiled. "I am sure he misses you as well."

Tewlon's scalp tingled, and it was suddenly hard to breathe. It was a sensation he hadn't experienced since his youth, when Naya winked at him. Naya was the prettiest girl in the village where Vecnor grew up. But as he evolved into manhood and women threw themselves at him, the excited feeling of anxiety diminished and died. Or so he thought. Apparently, it had only been sleeping.

Tewlon resumed chopping while the elves said their goodbyes and exchanged hugs. Eraim and Selanna then departed, and Vecnor was himself again. Elgarroth sat and puffed on the pipe.

Vecnor approached the wizard, staring at the trees where Eraim had disappeared. "Do you suspect she knows?"

Elgarroth glanced at Vecnor. "She *is* a clever one." He followed Vecnor's gaze. "They are both quite clever."

Chapter 30

Ruins

A decade passed. During that time, Vecnor remained hidden from the world. Tewlon, however, was active, as were Norvec and Thalamir, Vecnor's human soldier and dwarfish forms. Tux had no cause for disguises—people rarely noticed the Salenti-gray elf. In Vecnor's alternate bodies, he traveled the realms, forests, and mountains and spoke with humans, elves, and dwarves. But the conversations were meaningless. His objective was to watch for the return of the thought-to-be-defeated evil. He saw little of Tux while the elf performed similar missions, wandering the wilds in search of dunarchins and signs of Radaam or Anduiff. There were none to be found.

Elgarroth was often absent or in the cabin library, and visits from Eraim and Selanna tapered off dramatically. When the two were present, Tewlon busied himself with chores if he was around, and he occasionally noticed Eraim watching him.

Over the next five years, Vecnor continued the search for signs of Trannum while Tux visited the Guardians of Lothen Forest. Upon returning home, Vecnor entered a conversation between Tux and Elgarroth that was most disturbing.

"You are sure?" asked Elgarroth.

"Did you not see what I saw?" posed Tux.

"Not necessarily," replied the wizard. "My research has kept me occupied."

"I am positive." Tux shook his head. "I searched Lothen from north to south. There were no Guardians. Nor were there any signs they had been in the forest recently. But there *were* tracks of another sort. Cold footprints of the undead."

Vecnor furrowed his brow. "What's this?"

He received no explanation, but the grave stares told Vecnor what he needed to know. Something dire happened to the Guardians.

"Undead in Lothen…" Elgarroth lifted his pipe.

"What does this mean?" Vecnor asked.

Elgarroth drew in a steady stream of smoke and released it. "That something stirs in Helmland." He looked at Tux. "We must discover what it is. You will head to Lormin Dmurr."

Tux frowned. "By myself?"

"No." Elgarroth turned to Vecnor. "You will accompany him." He puffed on his pipe and lost his focus in the smoke. "And *I* must redirect my studies. If the undead have settled in Helmland, it is Welmirth's journals I should be reading."

Tux's frown deepened. "Has the body been discovered?"

Vecnor's heart skipped a beat. There was only one body his companion could be referring to. "Trannum was in charge of finding the source behind Uustaag's power," he said. "Perhaps the necromancer awakened something."

"We will assume nothing," Elgarroth answered quickly. "There is a looming darkness, yes. But I cannot see it clearly. The Sight has been full of shadows. I fear it is Vou's punishment for the gift I bestowed upon Ballrik." He shook his head. "I knew there might be a cost… but…"

"We shall visit Helmland," said Vecnor. He hated when Elgarroth second guessed sending them into Hell to save the young warrior. What was done was done.

Elgarroth nodded. "Be safe. And confront nothing unless your lives depend on it."

❖❖❖

Tewlon and Tux journeyed across the realms to enter Beit through the Path of the Guardians. It was a trail through the Stone Eagle Mountains carved by dwarves of Rornibur and enchanted by elves to keep evil from discovering its location. According to Elgarroth, the dwarves no longer knew of its existence. The wizard claimed too many years had passed, but Tewlon believed they were magicked into forgetting it.

As they followed the winding path, Tewlon recalled the first time he traveled the route. The lush valley giving birth to the Shield River was an awesome sight, while the narrow bridge of rock spanning the chasm made his head spin at first glance. But he was nimble, and had crossed without mishap. Unfortunately, the bridge was unfit for horses, and they would need to leave Barcum and Landolice behind. When they reached the cave serving as a shelter for the animals, Tewlon was relieved to find it in good order. The make-shift stable provided oats and a trough of fresh water. An underground river fed the trough, and a separate basin drained the overflow. But who stocked the oats? Tewlon had believed it to be the work of the Guardians, but if they were missing… And asking Tux was pointless, so Tewlon pushed the query from his mind.

Neither Barcum nor Landolice appreciated staying behind, but they conceded with minimal complaints. Tewlon and Tux then moved on, crossing the bridge and turning north. Upon descending next to a waterfall to enter Beit a couple of days later, Tewlon changed into Vecnor—a welcomed occurrence. Though the region was uninhabited, as Beitians lived as far from Helmland as possible, Vecnor knew not what lay ahead, and he would rather fight as himself than as an elf.

He and Tux headed northwest toward Lothen Forest. Vecnor had met the Guardians only twice—both times as Tewlon. They were a tight-lipped group, even when meeting with Tux, but they eventually realized the Salenti-gray elf to be someone they could and should report to. Still, they said nothing of consequence unless Tewlon was out of earshot. The forest normally seemed an agreeable place, if one could forget the evil lands surrounding it, but as dusk arrived and Vecnor and his companion stepped among the trees, the air was thick and the woodland appeared darker.

"Be on your guard." Tux put an arrow to his bowstring as he scanned the forest floor. "Dunarchins have been here recently."

Vecnor squatted to search the ground. Many tracks were obvious, appearing as ordinary boot imprints. "How do you know they belong to dunarchins?"

"They bear the scent of the undead." Tux inspected the vegetation. "But they are confident in their placements, unlike the erratic steps of ghouls and zombies."

Vecnor looked for a pattern, but the tracks moved in every direction. "They must have been searching for something."

Tux frowned. "It would appear so. But I have no guess as to what it was, or whether they found it."

They pressed on, walking through most of the night and the next day. The only encounters other than a few passing animals were occasional gusts of wind. Upon reaching the far end, they exited the forest and entered Helmland.

Vecnor set foot on the dead realm's terrain for the first time. Tux had described it as a dry wasteland covered in a haze and sporting little plant life, and the elf's words rang true. The few trees daring to grow in the straw serving as grass barely rose any taller than Vecnor and held no leaves, and there were no signs of rivers or ponds. Thankfully, Tux made sure they brought plenty of food and water—Vecnor's special pouch contained almost nothing but rations.

To the northwest stood Darum Carumbor. Though Vecnor had never seen the tower before, he knew of its existence. Uustaag erected it to guard the eastern entrance of the realm, and its black stones resisted all attempts to topple it after the Great War concluded. What kind of stone could not be destroyed? Surely the dwarves of Rornibur could bring the structure harm. They were skilled at working rorbak, a seemingly indestructible rock. Perhaps they never tried. The tower was dark, and none of its windows showed signs of life. Vecnor and Tux approached.

"Palidurian clerics placed wards on this tower to keep out evil." Tux's voice was a bit muffled within the haze.

Bumps arose on Vecnor's forearms as he scanned the building from bottom to top. The structure oozed malevolence, but nothing moved. "Let's hope those protections have held."

After pausing for Vecnor to light a torch, they entered Darum Carumbor. The floor and walls radiated cool air, and Vecnor's steps echoed softly along the arcing corridors to the left and right. Ahead, stables lay in shambles. They rounded the tower to find all doors had been battered from their hinges long ago, and every room was empty. In the center of the first floor, Vecnor opened a trapdoor in the middle of a circular chamber to discover a prison cell below. Dark water hid the room's depth, but from the partial skeletons shackled to the wall, he guessed it to be fifteen feet to the bottom. He closed the door.

They checked every chamber as they ascended, finding barracks, offices, practice rooms, a smithy, and a dining hall and kitchen. There were no signs of recent occupancy. The topmost room encompassed the entire level. It was empty, save for a stairway rounding the opposite wall to a hole giving access to the roof. Tux led the way up. The rooftop held three ancient ballistae, all of them smashed and unusable. The tower was uninhabited.

As Vecnor returned to the stairs, Tux didn't follow. The elf wandered toward one of the ballistae.

"What is it?" Vecnor's voice didn't travel far, but he was certain Eslimil heard his words.

Tux lifted something from the wreckage and joined Vecnor.

"What is it?" Vecnor repeated.

The elf stared at a filthy scrap of gray wool in his hand. "A piece of cloth."

"And?"

Tux peered at both sides of the material. "It is torn. Probably caught on the ballistae." He looked at Vecnor. "And it is not so ancient."

"I thought evil couldn't enter."

Tux nodded. "That is what I have been told. But this possesses the odor of the grave. I believe something undead wore it."

Vecnor's heart rate increased as a sudden concern for being trapped in the tower struck him. "We should leave."

Tux vigorously agreed.

They descended Darum Carumbor in haste, and the fortress no longer seemed so empty. Every shadow appeared as a monster ready to strike, making Vecnor's skin crawl. But he and Tux were unhindered and soon passed through the gate. Nothing awaited them; no army of undead; no Death Lords. Vecnor took in a deep breath of relief. It tasted stale.

"It is a couple of hard days to Lormin Dmurr," said Tux. "We best get to it."

They walked across the wasteland, eating their meals without stopping to rest. The terrain was unchanging. At night, they proceeded a few hours in the darkness before breaking, and began again as the sky brightened. They saw nothing living or undead, and there were no sounds other than the buzz of a few adventurous insects, surprised to find guests within their realm. What did the bugs normally prey on?

An hour before the second evening after leaving Darum Carumbor, Lormin Dmurr appeared in the distance. A dark, crumbled wall surrounded equally deteriorated buildings. At the north end of the complex, the citadel rested atop an immense pillar of rock extending from the Blood River. Nothing moved. Still, Vecnor felt eyes upon him. Probably his imagination.

"This place never ceases to fill me with dread," said Tux.

Vecnor studied the elf. "Which belief do you own? Did Uustaag die in the Battle of Balgorn?"

"It was never a matter of whether or not he died," replied Tux. "He could only have achieved his strength by making a deal with a powerful being. The questions are with whom did he strike his bargain? And what happened to this power after the battle? Something that great does not simply vanish without a trace."

Vecnor frowned. "I never thought of it that way."

They proceeded into the ruins. The ancient gatehouse was completely destroyed, and a twisted portcullis lay rusted on the ground beyond what remained of the wall. As the feeling that someone was watching grew, Vecnor pulled both of his swords. Tux didn't tease him about being nervous or scared; the elf readied an arrow. They walked across the grounds, passing between partially collapsed buildings showing no signs of use. Upon reaching a bridge spanning the gap to the citadel, they halted.

Vecnor eyed the water flowing from east to west. It was greenish blue, and the crest of every wave reflected red in the dying light, giving it an ominous appearance. Tux didn't move. The elf did not wish to enter any more than Vecnor did.

"Have you ever been inside?" Vecnor asked.

"Once. With Elgarroth."

"What's it like?"

Tux looked at Vecnor. "Evil."

They crossed the bridge, slowly at first. As the river's current seemed to quicken, so did their pace. It was as if the water prepared to rise up and wash them away. But the Balgorn maintained its course, and they reached the stronghold entrance.

The entryway was fifteen feet high, and its doors were missing. Beyond, hallways stretched left and right while an archway revealed a long dining room ahead.

Vecnor forced a grin. "Should we split up?"

Tux's responding glare could have stopped a charging minotaur.

Vecnor winked. He had no intentions of searching the structure alone. He only wished to determine whether Tux was as uneasy as he was.

They moved systematically through the citadel, checking every room. Only furnishings of stone had survived the centuries, chipped, cracked, and broken as they were. There were barracks, guardrooms, lounges, and private chambers, as well as a kitchen, chapel, training room, library, and meeting hall. Several walls bore strange frescos, faded and uninterpretable, and all curtains and tapestries had rotted long ago. Throughout the building, nothing made a sound, but occasionally Vecnor swore he detected a presence; a creeping shadow in his peripheral vision that stabilized when he looked its way. A deep chill accompanied the visions — his nerves again.

Upon the top level, they entered a grand temple. Six pillars supporting nothing formed a circle around its center, where long, dark triangles pointed from the columns to a smashed stone altar. Old blood was evident. Beyond the pillars were three freestanding arches. Two faced each other while the third faced the altar, and faded runes decorated the stone frames. The room wasn't cold, nor was it hot, but a presence of dread, like an invisible fog, encouraged Vecnor to leave. Every step was labored, and from Tux's expression, the elf felt it as well.

They pushed their way to a staircase on the far side and climbed to the roof. Hinges on a square frame in the ceiling suggested a trapdoor once existed, but there was no sign of its whereabouts. Upon the rooftop, the disturbing force of the temple diminished, and a constant breeze played with all loose clothing. It was bare from parapet to parapet.

Vecnor scanned the surrounding territory. Mountains rose to the north beyond the Balgorn River, and the Stone Eagles were visible to the south. Miles of wasteland separated the forests in the west from Lothen in the east. But how was it he could see the Stone Eagle Mountains and Lothen Forest? A power surely remained atop Lormin Dmurr, and it turned Vecnor's stomach.

He made his way to the edge of the roof. The Blood River now seemed more red than greenish blue, and the crest of every wave held a face twisted in anguish. Vecnor looked away.

"It is no different from the last time I ventured up here." Tux stood next to Vecnor, and he averted his gaze from the water below. "Most unsettling." He turned to Vecnor. "There is nothing to report. We should leave."

Vecnor didn't require any further urging, and they descended into the citadel. As he set foot on the temple floor, a shadow moved down the stairway opposite them. Vecnor pushed through the imposing atmosphere and raced across the chamber, but upon reaching the steps, the shadows were motionless.

Tux joined him. "What is it?"

Vecnor shook his head. "I swear some shadows move. Must be this place."

"I am not so certain," said Tux. "We will report that to Elgarroth."

Vecnor probed his mind. Elgarroth wasn't there. It had been a week since he felt the wizard's presence.

They made their way down the citadel and across the bridge. Vecnor didn't look at the river. After exiting the ruins, they crossed the wasteland without rest, passed Darum Carumbor, and journeyed through Lothen Forest. At no time did Vecnor sheathe his swords until reaching the Path of the Guardians other than to eat, and Tux kept the sleek gray bow in hand.

Their hard march continued as they traversed the pass. After retrieving their horses, they exited the Stone Eagle Mountains at a quickened pace, and Vecnor enjoyed a breath of fresh air, as if he had been deprived since entering Lormin Dmurr. He transformed into Tewlon before reaching the nearest civilization in Virch, but he didn't mind—it was good to be free of the northern realms. He and Tux turned east and headed home.

CHAPTER 31
ANCIENT SHAFT

Elgarroth was home when Vecnor and Tux returned. Vecnor didn't know exactly where the wizard was, but the smoke rising from the cabin's chimney assured the elf's presence.

He and Tux unsaddled their horses and brushed the animals before heading to their chambers to freshen up. Vecnor exited just before Tux, and Elgarroth was sitting by the fire, appearing exhausted again. Vecnor and Tux claimed their usual seats.

"Are you all right?" asked Vecnor.

Elgarroth gave a slow nod, gazing at nothing. His attention then shifted to Vecnor. "It has been long hours in the library." He turned back to the fire. "That, and spending time with the Sight."

"Have you seen anything new?" Tux posed.

Again, Elgarroth nodded. "Things are coming into focus." He looked from Tux to Vecnor. "But first, some news."

Vecnor held his breath whenever the wizard began a meeting with those words. It usually meant the mage had kept something secret, and decided to reveal it at last. And it was typically information withheld from Vecnor and not Tux. Why did Elgarroth insist Vecnor wasn't ready to know as much as the half-gray elf? It had been eight hundred years since he spoke his oath.

"A baby was born in Kembald," the wizard said, "to King Cavalor."

Vecnor's heart leaped. "This is grand news!" The son of Merssa, now a father! This type of update was most welcome. "How is Cavalor's wife?"

Elgarroth's eyes saddened. "Humans are so fragile. She did not live long after the birth. And the king has his hands full with a spirited young girl."

Vecnor's elation deflated. He decided it was best to focus on the *good* news. "What's her name?"

"Vayla," replied Elgarroth.

It was a fine name.

"What about Borse?" Vecnor asked.

Elgarroth shook his head. "Borse enjoyed many years in this world, and his touch will not be forgotten."

Borse was gone as well. A pity. Vecnor held the utmost respect for the priest. And now Vayla was deprived of a mother and both grandparents.

"Take consolation in that Borse had a good life," added Elgarroth, "and he is where he wishes to be." The wizard smirked. "He even had a bit of influence over Vayla. She yearns to be a paladin of Cafior."

A respectable path. Vayla's father, Cavalor, once harbored such desires. But it was an unattainable goal, perhaps due to his birth parents, Tarm and Mayry. Would it be the same for Vayla? Vecnor then realized she must have been born years ago to be pursuing the life of a paladin. Why was this the first he was hearing of her?

"She is the very image of her grandmother," said Tux.

As usual, the announcement was not news to the Salenti-gray elf. Why hadn't Tux mentioned Vayla? Vecnor had been traveling with him for weeks.

Vecnor frowned as Eslimil's words sank in. "Wait. How's that possible?"

Elgarroth shrugged. "It can only be explained as divine intervention."

"Why am I the last to learn any of this?" mumbled Vecnor.

Elgarroth's gaze narrowed. "Now that you know, you wish to go see this for yourself. Your mind is working on an excuse to lead you into Marcove."

Vecnor's shoulders slumped. "Understood."

As usual, the wizard spoke the truth. Tux hadn't known Merssa the way Vecnor had. The half-gray elf's yearning to keep the little girl safe from harm could never be as strong as it now coursed through every muscle in Vecnor's body. But could it be her? Could Merssa have been reborn?

"I assure you, it is not Merssa," said Elgarroth. "But it explains why I have seen her leading an army. Vayla was born for a purpose. She has a destiny, perhaps to finish what her grandmother started. Time will tell."

A horrific vision of Merssa standing alone against a Death Lord filled Vecnor's head. Could this little girl be heading for the same grim fate?

"I only mention this because you will run into her at some point," explained Elgarroth. "And you must be prepared to interact with her as Vayla."

"Will she become a paladin?" Vecnor held his breath while awaiting the answer.

"All I can share is that I see her in New Palidur. Cavalor will send her there for training." Elgarroth's expression darkened. "And now, to more dire matters."

Vecnor nodded. It was time to focus on the present.

"A shadow lies over Vaeldor," Elgarroth said. "It is everywhere, and it is scheming. It grasps at an item just out of reach; an item it desires more than anything. With it, the Shadow's power is boundless. And beyond the Shadow is something even fouler: a giant of pure malevolence."

Vecnor shook his head. "We saw nothing to suggest any of this."

"That remains to be seen." Elgarroth looked from Vecnor to Tux. "It is time to tell me about your journey through Helmland. Perhaps you will fill in the cracks; provide clarity to the Sight. Leave nothing out, no matter how insignificant it may seem."

Vecnor and Tux described their expedition, and Elgarroth sat quietly until they completed their tale. He then addressed Vecnor.

"The moving shadows were *the* Shadow, and not your imagination. It seems to be settling in the north. But it is not ready to reveal itself just yet."

Tux's shoulders slumped. "I fear to ask… Could it be Uustaag?"

Elgarroth gazed at the crackling flames. "I do not believe so. At least, *I* have not seen him." He puffed on his pipe. "I see a frozen hand reaching out; darkness spreading through the light; a small girl holding a golden mace. And in the middle is Selanna." He looked at Tux and Vecnor. " These are *her* visions. You see, Selanna is the next seer. My successor. And she is advancing in her skills. Soon, I will have no choice but to divulge everything to her."

Vecnor held a wry smile. Somehow, the news didn't shock him. But how could Selanna guide the world? She was a prankster. A carefree mage concerned only with her own amusement. "Is she ready?"

"Apparently, Vou thinks so." Elgarroth smirked. "And who am I to say otherwise?"

"Eraim will be lost without Selanna," Vecnor mumbled.

"Perhaps," said Elgarroth. "Perhaps not."

The wizard's meaning struck Vecnor. Selanna would likely choose Eraim as her companion, as Elgarroth had chosen Vecnor and Tux. But would the little elf be accepting of a life in the shadows? A lonely existence with no time for perusing markets and exploring new lands for no other reason than to draw her maps? And who would Selanna pick as her second companion? Jealousy touched Vecnor's heart. If only he had been born eight hundred years later.

"I have a task for you both." Elgarroth changed the subject. "There is an item you need to procure."

Vecnor frowned. "Both of us?"

"Yes," the wizard replied. "It is not a safe journey."

Anxiety invaded Vecnor's chest. "Not Hell… Right?"

Elgarroth chuckled. "No. That shall not happen again." His expression turned serious. "The road before Vaeldor is even more dire than before the Necromancer War. Though the darkness in my Sight has yet to fully retreat, I see a weapon. And… Gruzim."

Vecnor clenched his fists as his blood boiled. "Don't tell me the krukari found a way to return."

Elgarroth took in a deep breath. "Not that. I do not know why I see Gruzim. Somehow, he is connected to this weapon, and I need you to fetch it."

"Gruzim's spear was destroyed," said Vecnor.

"Not the spear." Elgarroth concentrated on the fire. "I am yet to determine *what* it is, exactly, but you will recognize it when you see it. This must be accomplished, for proceeding without it could be devastating."

Vecnor didn't know what to think. The consequences of rescuing Ballrik still muddled Elgarroth's visions. Should they have left the warrior to suffer in Hell? Vou was a cruel god to hold such a grudge with Vaeldor's fate in the balance. Hopefully, Elgarroth saw things clearly enough.

❊❊❊

Vecnor and Tux departed the next morning on foot, traveling south to the ford. Tux had not been happy about constructing a new raft after Sullis sent the last one thrashing down the Great East River, but he completed the job and secured fresh ropes in a single day. Upon crossing the waterway, they proceeded up the slope along the Candermane Falls. They then entered the Candermane Tunnel and headed east. The passage was free of danger and only a few rats were present, and after a couple of days, they emerged among the mountains west of Benasti Forest.

Turning south, Vecnor and Tux pushed deeper into the rising terrain. The old dwarfish trail made the journey easier than it would have been otherwise, but as they drew nearer to Morimont, the presence of dwarves slowed their pace—their instructions were to avoid being seen.

On the eighth day after leaving the House of Elgarroth, they reached the path between Morimont and Kalmaar. Vecnor gazed west at the distant dwarfish city nestled between a pair of majestic peaks. He had been there on several occasions in the past, and it was a wonder to behold. Like a human city, Morimont possessed homes, guilds, and markets, but unlike the human settlements, there were no buildings. Instead, a wide road was carved into the mountainside, spiraling up the slope for five stories, and the dwarves bore into the core to create grand chambers to accommodate their citizens and businesses. Humans were allowed to visit for trade, but they were never permitted inside the mountain. Vecnor had enjoyed free access as Thalamir, his dwarfish form, but he always kept a low profile and spoke only to those Elgarroth bade him to speak to. Within the mountain, he marveled at exquisite rooms and tunnels with ceilings higher than any dwarf would ever require, as well as veins of copper, silver, and gold that lined the walls, often accented by formations of gemstones. Though larger deposits existed in the High Riser Mountains of Philen, Varlimor dwarves left much of the precious metals and minerals untouched, preferring to bask in the natural splendor rather than line their coffers with riches.

"What a horrible place," mumbled Tux, staring at the mountain home.

Like most elves, Eslimil abhorred the thought of living underground, regardless of the grandeur the dwarfish cities offered. Vecnor chuckled as they crossed the road and continued south.

The trail became more difficult. Though the footpath avoided the major pitfalls on its way to Ironside Keep, the frequency of traveling dwarves increased, and Vecnor and Tux left the path in favor of a more treacherous route to keep their passing secret. At least, it was more treacherous for Vecnor. Tux was not only nimble, but the special abilities of his gray elf heritage allowed him to make climbs and descents more easily. Several times, Tux insisted they journey at night, so he could utilize his shadow blending and simply float up or down the sheerer cliffs. But finding handholds in the dark would have been detrimental for Vecnor, so they did most of their traveling beneath the sun.

A couple of days later, in a valley a few miles north of Ironside Keep, they discovered the area Elgarroth had marked on their map. The hunt then began for a shaft the wizard claimed to be there. They searched among trees, brush, under boulders they could move, and everywhere the shaft might exist over a region nearly a mile long and wide. After three days, they were unsuccessful. As Vecnor's water supply ran low on day four, concern crept in.

"Over here!" Tux called.

It was a few hours past midday, and Vecnor was searching among a group of pine trees. Needles had adhered to his vambraces and gauntlets, bringing him great annoyance—the sap would be hard to clean. He exited the grove to find his companion on a ledge twenty feet overhead.

"This might be it," the elf said.

Vecnor looked for a way to ascend. There was nothing. "I suppose you jumped up there?"

Tux smirked. "I will lower my rope."

Eslimil pulled his long, thin cord from his pack. It was a special weave crafted from plant fibers found deep in Orlenfel Forest, and was both lightweight and strong. He disappeared for a few seconds and returned to drop the coil.

Vecnor tugged on the rope. It seemed secure. He climbed, bracing his boots against the hard wall to reach Tux's location. He then saw what had caught the elf's eye: the edge of a shaft delving into the rock. Next to a lean evergreen where Tux had fastened the other end of the rope, thirsty foliage concealed most of the hole. Had the leaves not browned and blown away, the shaft might have been missed. Tux pushed the brittle branches aside, snapping most of them, and revealed the remainder of the pit.

"This must be it," said Vecnor.

Tux collected the rope and lowered it into the hole. "I will go first."

Vecnor didn't argue. Though his eyesight and hearing were beyond the skills of humans, Tux's senses were yet superior.

The elf descended into the darkness, and Vecnor followed. The shaft was roughly five feet wide, and centuries of rain and rockslides had left it chipped and pitted. Vecnor lost sight of Tux as deeper darkness enveloped them, but the shaking of the rope assured him Eslimil hadn't dissolved into shadow.

"Halt!" Tux's hushed voice echoed. "I have reached the end. It is another ten feet to the floor."

Vecnor squinted. The outline of his companion was barely discernible, and it disappeared when the elf released the rope. He descended until he dangled, and let go. It was a short drop to a soft floor.

"We'll need light," Vecnor said.

There was a sudden glow, revealing Tux's grinning face. Eslimil held a bauble Elgarroth had given him for the trip. It was a magical ball capable of shedding light enough to make it seem the sun had risen, or it could illuminate only things within a few feet — Tux had complete control. Like Selanna's magical lights, the orb hovered, rising to the ceiling only six feet high, and it brightened to show they stood at the end of a crude tunnel. The corridor was four to six feet wide, and it headed in what Vecnor assumed to be a northerly direction.

He ducked as he stepped from beneath the shaft, so as not to hit his head. "Where are we?"

Tux shrugged.

A vision entered Vecnor's mind: the remains of a battle. Judging by the armored skeletons and the cobwebs streaming from corpse to corpse, it was fought some time ago. The vision faded, and he knew Tux had seen it as well.

"Only one direction to go," said the elf, and the light followed as he led the way.

The floor was as uneven as the walls, as if someone had excavated the tunnel in haste, and there were no obvious tracks in the moist dirt.

"This place is unused," murmured Vecnor.

"Forgotten," Tux corrected him.

The passage connected to a perfectly chiseled hallway going left and right. The new corridor was fifteen feet high and twenty feet wide, and finely crafted arches with hammers and anvils in bas-relief just below the ceiling were ten yards to either side. Beyond the arch to the right, the corridor turned.

Vecnor stepped onto the level stone floor, grateful to stand up straight. The tunnel they had used was obviously not part of the system where he and Tux now stood. He looked at the elf. "Which way?"

Tux narrowed his eyes along the passage. "It is hard to say. Everything is covered in dust and smells… dead."

"We have to start somewhere," said Vecnor, and he headed right.

They followed the corridor around the bend and stopped. The tunnel had collapsed many years ago, judging by the thick dust.

"Odd," commented Tux. "Dwarfish construction such as this does not normally deteriorate."

"Perhaps it was intentional," suggested Vecnor.

Tux shrugged. "In any case, it is not our concern."

They headed the other way.

The hallway stretched another two hundred feet, with additional arches every twenty yards, and the quality of the craftsmanship did not wane. An intersection was then before them, turning left and right as well as continuing forward, and a single rusted rail ran along the former.

"Mining," said Vecnor.

"What else would there be this deep underground?" Tux sniffed. "Surely dwarves did not make homes in this place."

Vecnor turned right, following the railing, and Tux pulled a piece of chalk and marked the wall before trailing after. The tunnel progressed a couple hundred yards and split into seven directions. The rail continued straight.

"Listen," Tux whispered.

Vecnor focused on the silence. There was a rustling to the right, like shuffling feet.

Tux cocked his head, and the light withdrew to the strength of a candle. He stepped from the intersection, back the way they had come, and Vecnor and the floating bauble joined him.

The shuffling drew nearer, but it slowed, as if moving cautiously. Shadowy forms standing four-feet high then entered the intersection. They were humanoids, obviously unused to the light as they shielded their red eyes with their free hands, and their pale faces displayed both fear and curiosity. Stringy black hair sparsely covered most of their scalps, while others were bald, and a few had patchy beards. They held crude spears made from thin rusted metal and wore reptilian skins over their torsos like armor. A few had old helmets that left their eyes and mouths exposed.

There was no time to dawdle, and Vecnor drew his swords and stepped forward, releasing a roar that echoed into the distance. The humanoids bolted, running back down the corridor.

"We should follow them," said Tux.

Vecnor lowered his brow. "Why?"

"Did the helmets not look familiar? Surely they procured them from the corpses we seek."

A good point. Vecnor nodded.

Tux marked the wall with chalk, and the orb's light expanded as they pursued the clamor of the retreating creatures. But after fifty yards, the noise diminished and silence returned.

Vecnor halted, gazing into the darkness ahead. "Fast little creatures."

"That," said Tux, "or there are paths of which we are unaware."

They moved on, and forty yards farther, a larger hallway crossed their path. The tunnel was thirty feet wide, with pillars in the middle at twenty yard intervals, and rails ran along either side. The columns were as exquisite as the arches, and a sapphire decorated the top of those to the left, while a ruby adorned each heading right.

"Those are fine stones," whispered Tux.

Vecnor had no cause to doubt the elf. Tux was never wrong about such things.

They followed the path of blue gemstones, and Vecnor looked back to see a red jewel marking the opposite side of each pillar they passed. After sixty yards, smaller archways dotted either side of the corridor, but they did not display hammers and anvils in bas-relief. Most had images of picks or mine carts, one had a mushroom, and another a pair of wavy lines.

Tux fitted an arrow to his bowstring. "Watch yourself!"

Vecnor followed the elf's gaze, but saw nothing. A second later, Tux's arrow flew at the nearby pillar, halting just before striking the stone, and a ten-foot lizard fell to the floor. Its color had matched the column perfectly, but it darkened to a deep green as blood seeped from between its eyes where the dark shaft protruded.

"Thanks," murmured Vecnor, scanning the walls for the reptile's friends.

"This creature's hide is similar to the skins the small folk wore," said Tux.

Were the mine people short enough for Tux to call *small folk*?

Vecnor and Tux walked along the hall with weapons ready, peering through each archway. Rails passed through those displaying picks or mine carts, and the first arch adorned by a pick led to a large room with a few wagons, ancient digging tools, and several piles of rubble. Beyond the arch with the mushroom was an expansive chamber. The prominent odor of musty, wet dirt caused Tux's nose to wrinkle, and from the dark soil covering the room's floor sprouted mushrooms of various sizes, from a couple of inches to six feet in height. Vecnor never saw such a room in Morimont, but he had not ventured into the city's lower levels. Some of the larger fungi appeared to have been cut down, judging by the stumps left behind.

Tux lifted his arm to his mouth to block the smell, and they moved on.

An archway bearing a mine cart opened into a chamber with dozens of carts in various states of ruin. A pick topped the next arch, which led to a downward slanting hallway. As Vecnor and Tux approached the entrance with wavy lines, Tux halted a couple of feet away and held up his hand.

"I hear water," the elf said. "An underground river."

Did it lead to any rivers Vecnor was familiar with? Peering through the opening revealed nothing but an empty room stretching beyond the light. But the echo of racing water became obvious.

They checked half a dozen more archways before finding what appeared to be a dining chamber. The bas-relief above the entrance was a simple square. A score of stone tables that survived centuries of neglect adorned the hall, and a second arch on the far end showed only darkness. But what held Vecnor's attention were the armored skeletons strewn about. All had been dwarves in their living days.

He followed Tux into the room, keeping watch for lizards. Nothing moved. Eslimil inspected several nearby bodies.

"They fought one another," the elf said.

Vecnor frowned. "Strange."

Tux stepped deeper in, and an enormous lizard gnashed its teeth from beneath a table. Vecnor reflexively swung his sword downward, decapitating the creature before it could strike.

Tux nodded his thanks.

In the middle of the chamber, between a couple of tables, was a skeleton slightly larger than the others. It sat against a stone bench with head bowed, and on its lap was a battleaxe. The blades of the weapon were of bronze, with runes inscribed along their edges. A ratty leather strap wound about the haft, the only part of the axe appearing to have known the passage of time, and at the bottom protruded a bronze spike. Vecnor didn't need to handle the battleaxe to know its blades were sharp.

Tux squatted to examine a pendant around the corpse's neck. "This is crafted from platinum, and bears a crest: two hammers resting on an anvil with a six-pointed star made of picks." He looked at Vecnor. "A noble house of Lornibur."

Vecnor narrowed his eyes on the symbol. Lornibur... The ancient home of the dwarves. Of *all* dwarves, before they separated into the clans Vaeldor was familiar with. Rumor held the stout folk to have collapsed the entire network of tunnels, but Poluran disproved that belief when he discovered a point of access in a secret passage between the Fire Hills and Ironside Keep. Vecnor returned his attention to the axe. "It's a king's weapon."

Tux shook his head. "I do not believe this skeleton to have been a king. I do not even think it was a dwarf."

Vecnor leaned closer. The bones were not so thick as the others around the room. "Then what?"

"I know not." Eslimil eyed the weapon. "But this is surely what we seek."

Vecnor reached for the battleaxe and balked. Upon the leather strap was a marking he hadn't noticed before. It was a blackness, darker than the wrappings. "What do you make of this?"

Tux scrutinized the haft. "Someone had grasped the handle, and they were burned. Badly."

Vecnor looked from the body's skull to its hands.

"I do not believe it was this individual," Tux added. "The handprint is too large."

Vecnor raised a brow. "So... someone tried to take it?"

"It would seem."

Vecnor gazed about. The corpses lay over twenty feet away, and none of their hands appeared big enough to have made the imprint. "Whoever it was, the burn didn't kill them. They're not here."

Standing there was accomplishing nothing. Vecnor reached for the axe, and Tux cringed when his fingers wrapped around the handle. As he lifted the weapon, he swore the skeleton exhaled, and its head fell from its shoulders to roll a few feet away. More importantly, Vecnor did not get burned.

Return home.

Vecnor looked at Tux. The elf received Elgarroth's message as well.

"We have company." Tux aimed an arrow at the ceiling.

A twenty-foot lizard made its way silently overhead. Though its coloring nearly matched the stone, its movements betrayed its location. Tux's arrow drove into its skull, but the monster didn't die. It jumped onto a table, shaking the furniture but not breaking it.

Vecnor dropped the axe and pulled his blades as the reptile lunged. Its massive jaws clamped onto his forearm, piercing the armor and penetrating his flesh. He struck its head with his pommel, inadvertently pushing the fangs deeper, and lost hold of his right sword. Tux's next arrow sank into the lizard's eye, and it relinquished its grip to hiss at the elf. Thrusting his remaining sword, Vecnor forced the entire blade down the creature's throat. The reptile thrashed a few seconds before becoming still.

More lizards crawled along the walls, ceiling, and floor. None were as large as the one they just faced, but the scaly beasts were formidable nonetheless. Tux launched three arrows, each striking with deadly precision and dropping a reptile.

Vecnor held his right arm close and charged a lizard scrambling onto a table. He decapitated it with a single swing. His second slash passed through another's skull and sparked on the flagstones. He then sidestepped a reptile leaping from the ceiling and bashed it with his pommel. Though the monster surely weighed over five hundred pounds, his blow steered it headfirst into a table. He placed his boot onto the lizard's neck, and the reptile squirmed while he brought his weapon across, slicing it in half.

"We must go," said Tux.

Ten lizards lay still while six others moved around the chamber, as if studying their prey. Vecnor's arm wound burned, but he could ignore it for the time being. Sheathing his sword, he fitted the battleaxe into his belt and retrieved his other weapon before addressing Tux.

"Lead on."

Eslimil slung his bow over his shoulder, and as he pulled his sword, the blade issued smoke. They raced back through the mines toward the shaft, slaying five lizards along the way.

CHAPTER 32

DUNARCHINS

No lizards pursued once they reached the shaft. Vecnor didn't need to jump very high to reach the rope, and he pulled himself up, despite the pain in his forearm. Tux made even easier work of the task with his bounding ability. Upon exiting the mine, the elf coiled his rope and secured it in his pack.

An hour of sunlight remained, and they headed north until nightfall. Vecnor then removed his vambrace to allow Tux to tend to his bite wound with an herb concoction. By morning, the burning ceased. The only proof of the injury's existence were pink dots permanently etched into Vecnor's skin.

The rest of the journey passed quietly, and they arrived at the cabin. Elgarroth was in his usual position near the fire.

"Welcome home," the wizard said without looking.

Tux took a seat to Elgarroth's left while Vecnor leaned the battleaxe next to the mage.

"A fine weapon," murmured Elgarroth after paying the item a glance.

Vecnor nodded as he sat across from the wizard. "It is at that. How is it that thing has gone undiscovered for so long? The bodies surrounding it were centuries old."

"It is old indeed," said Elgarroth. "Forged with a rare ore found only in Lornibur." He pointed at the runes on each blade in turn. "This one says *courage*, and this one says *honor*. And it is rumored the axe learns its wielder's fighting style, so they can work together in harmony."

"I recognized a crest of Lornibur on a pendant," mentioned Tux.

"Yes," Elgarroth said. "It was a part of Lornibur you found. I was not certain it was so until you entered the first hall."

"It was a royal symbol," Tux added. "But it did not adorn a dwarf. A thief?"

Elgarroth shook his head. "Not a thief, but a dwarf-friend. And to answer your question," he looked at Vecnor, "there was one other who tried to take the weapon. But it protected itself, and that fellow was deeply wounded."

"The burn marks," said Vecnor.

Elgarroth gave a confirming nod.

Vecnor frowned. "Why didn't it burn *me*?"

"It did not wish to do so," the wizard replied. He glanced again at the axe. "I will not bore you with the details, but this is no ordinary weapon. If there exists items that possess souls, this is one of those items."

Vecnor eyed the battleaxe. "It's alive?"

Elgarroth chuckled. "In a manner of speaking. But that is not important at the moment. You will both depart tomorrow."

"Where to now?" asked Vecnor.

"There have been dunarchin sightings across the realms," Elgarroth replied. "No proof to support these claims has been found, but reports of missing people accompany them. It is my suspicion these missing folks are firstborns."

"They're building their numbers," Vecnor murmured.

"It would seem so." Elgarroth's expression was grim. "And we must hamper their efforts."

"Another war is coming," said Tux.

Elgarroth nodded. "You will need to split up. But avoid places where you are too well-known." He aimed the last instruction at Vecnor.

"Where should I go, then?" Vecnor posed.

"Cover the realms west of King Arman, beginning with Virch. Do what you can to protect Vaeldor's inhabitants from these attacks, and report everything you discover to me."

Vecnor nodded. Elgarroth was steering him away from the eastern lands; away from Vayla and Ballrik. The wizard surely realized his growing desire to visit the two. It was probably for the best.

❖ ❖ ❖

Vecnor maintained his own body while heading west—a sign Elgarroth wanted him at full strength. He journeyed across Virch, spending no less than a month in every village and city he encountered. During the daytime he stayed out of sight and slept, and through the dark hours he patrolled the streets, concentrating his efforts near taverns, where folks were most vulnerable to attacks. Vecnor saw nothing of the undead firstborns, but he often witnessed thugs harassing people in alleyways. His presence was all that was necessary to disrupt these events, and as rumors of a savior roaming the darkness spread, he moved on to another settlement.

Five months passed before Vecnor discovered the first sign of dunarchins. While standing in the shadows outside an open window of a tavern, he heard a patron speak of being accosted by bandits with glowing eyes in an alleyway. The man claimed to have barely escaped.

Vecnor made his way from alley to alley, finding no undead firstborns. But in one alleyway, empty crates and debris were scattered, as if kicked about, and a crate bore a groove, as if struck by a sword. Perhaps the man told the truth. But if dunarchins created the mess, they were gone now.

Another week expired with no additional reports, and Vecnor moved on.

He arrived in Neja nearly two years later. There weren't many folks in the kingdom that would recognize him, so long as he avoided Larman's Haven in Eastgate. Larman, the innkeeper rescued from Ellaville by Merssa decades ago, was no longer the proprietor after passing from old age, but according to Tux, Larman's sons spoke often about Vecnor, especially in Lindow's case. Lindow's motivation arose during the rescue, and the lad chose the life of a soldier. Vecnor was told the inspiration came from Merssa and himself, but he felt it was more the paladin's doing. The boys, now men, would know Vecnor right off, so when he entered the city, he stayed clear of their establishment.

After a week of roaming Eastgate's alleyways, a ruckus caught Vecnor's attention. He raced to find the source of the noise, expecting more thieves, but glowing eyes revealed the culprits to be dunarchins. There were six, and one dragged a limp body.

Vecnor drew his blades, and five of the dunarchins came with swords. He flailed his weapons, knocking aside their attacks and slashing their bodies, and they collapsed either due to decapitation or dismemberment. Only the creature holding the victim remained, and it released its prize to pull its weapon. Before the blade was halfway out, Vecnor skewered its skull and its eyes went dark.

Vecnor took the unconscious man to a nearby home and placed the body on the doorstep. He knocked, and headed back to the alley without awaiting an answer. When he arrived, the dunarchins were missing. Further investigation revealed at least a couple of undead warriors had not shown themselves or advanced in defense of their comrades. They waited out of sight until the melee was over to drag their dead away. They certainly did not want their passing to be known.

Vecnor thought hard for Elgarroth's attention. When the wizard's presence was felt, he relived everything he had seen. Elgarroth was then gone, and Vecnor moved on.

For six more years, Vecnor patrolled western Vaeldor. In all that time he encountered no more dunarchins within cities or villages, but he discovered small encampments of the monsters. The gatherings were in reclusive areas, a couple of miles away from the nearest settlements, and there were no less than a dozen in each, though a score of horses were normally present. Vecnor exterminated the abominations with Umbarc's assistance, including the undead mounts that barely resisted. Once the dunarchins were defeated, Vecnor awaited the return of those that had entered the nearby city or village, in case any had gone hunting for victims, but none ever arrived. During the fourth skirmish, a dunarchin mage struck Vecnor with lightning, and he pushed through the pain until lopping off the undead wizard's head. Other than the lightning, Vecnor received only a few minor injuries through it all, but they were nothing well-prepared herbs couldn't cure.

Presently, Vecnor sat atop Umbarc in Fendora, observing a fifth grouping of dunarchins, and a pair of humans lay face down over the saddles of two of the undead horses. The captives were bound and gagged and appeared unconscious. The temptation to follow the dunarchins crossed Vecnor's mind. Perhaps he might learn where they were hiding, if they were working together, and who was leading them. But what horrors would the prisoners endure if left in the care of the undead? A morbid thought.

He sighed.

Destroy them, said Elgarroth. *Following them will not change the fate of Vaeldor. Save those men and return home.*

Vecnor smiled. This was the way he preferred it.

Urging Umbarc into the enemy, Vecnor cut down three dunarchins while his mount trampled a few more. He then dropped from his saddle to continue the fight and allow Umbarc to do as much damage as the horse desired. They defeated the undead firstborns and animals in minutes.

Placing the unconscious men on Umbarc's back, Vecnor delivered them to a temple in a nearby city and set them next to the front door. He departed without speaking to the gathering onlookers marveling at his awesome presence, some of their eyes showing fear. After using the last of his healing herbs to tend to his injuries, as well as Umbarc's, Vecnor began his journey home.

CHAPTER 33
LONG JOURNEY SOUTH

Upon arrival at the House of Elgarroth, Vecnor learned that Tux's travels differed very little from his own, and the half-gray elf was in need of arrows. Elgarroth granted Eslimil leave to return to Orlenfel to gather the necessary supplies. Vecnor sat at the fire on the evening Tux departed, staring at Elgarroth. The wizard scanned exhaled pipe smoke for several moments before focusing on Vecnor.

"Vayla's training in New Palidur is complete," the elf said.

Vecnor smiled. A thought then occurred to him. "Isn't she only eighteen years in age?"

Elgarroth raised his brow. "Nineteen. Nearly twenty. And a most interesting young lady." He placed the pipe between his lips, and the bowl glowed bright orange as he inhaled.

Vecnor sat on the edge of the log, desperately wishing to know more. As a smirk spread across the elf's cheeks, he couldn't help feeling the wizard was being cruel.

"Yes, Vayla is a paladin," Elgarroth said at last. "And Romik is Lord of Ironside Keep under Arkor's watchful eye… as well as Morsum's, of course."

Vecnor relaxed. This was good news. Still, he felt a twinge of irritation that he had not seen these events for himself. Perhaps it would have been better to remain ignorant. "Why share this knowledge with me?"

Elgarroth maintained his grin. "Because you will be entering Nomedd. And… I'll allow a route through Sardina and the mountain pass."

Vecnor's spirits lifted, and he couldn't contain his joy.

"But I'm afraid Tewlon will have to make the journey."

Vecnor scowled. The expression didn't last long, however. Making the expedition as Tewlon was better than not making it at all. He then realized where he headed. "Nomedd?"

Elgarroth's smile vanished. "Yes. There is something we require. It is in no danger of being claimed by another, but you must arrive at Trannum's stronghold by early spring. I will give you instructions when the time comes. And…" he lifted a small silver jar, "you'll need this."

Vecnor accepted the item. He then went to his room to make sure he received sufficient rest for the journey ahead.

❊ ❊ ❊

Vecnor awoke with the dawn. Upon exiting the cabin, Elgarroth was not at the fire and the smoke issuing from the chimney slowed to a trickle. Vecnor was alone.

Vermallon was quiet while he rode Umbarc west through the trees. As he reached the forest's edge two days later, his gear adjusted as his height reduced, and Umbarc became leaner and smaller. Tewlon then crossed the wilds of Sendorum.

After a couple more days, they arrived at Tedonis. It was just past noon, and Tewlon gazed at the village named for Merssa, recalling when the compound was young. He remembered tents where the buildings now stood, and the wooden fence surrounding them, presently a wall of stone. Vecnor had never set foot within, but the human soldier, Norvec, had. Unfortunately, even as Norvec he was not permitted to interact with Merssa, and deep down he regretted it. He had not known it was the last time he would see the paladin.

Tewlon urged Barcum across the Palidur Bridge, and New Palidur came into view. The city appeared just as it had before the undead left it in ruin, prior to the Necromancer War. Unlike those days, an elf visiting the Holy City was not too uncommon, and the gates were open to allow access. Only three decades ago, outlanders had to give sufficient reason for their visit before being allowed entry. Rholmar and Nilborg changed all that when they rebuilt the city, and New Palidur welcomed most visitors.

The streets in the Cafior Sector were brown, and the buildings ranging from one to five stories were white. Palidurians added fresh coats of paint often enough to keep the buildings bright and unmarred, and though the color of the cobblestones became dark blue and light blue within the Soleran and Arronaus Sectors respectively, the structures did not change.

Tewlon's first stop was at the statue of Merssa in the middle of the Cafior Sector, where several Palidurians milled about on their own business and paid him no heed. Although Merssa had been small in stature, the monument made her seem giant. Of all of Vecnor's acquaintances, he respected no one more than the late paladin, and Tewlon's eyes moistened while gazing upon her likeness.

"Well, Merssa..." He detested his boy-like, elfish voice. "I'm going to meet your granddaughter today. I only wish it was as myself."

"Please tell me you're not talking to that statue!" said a female.

A tingling sensation raced to the top of Tewlon's head. It was Merssa's voice. He spun to see her standing with a handsome young man. Merssa bore the same sour expression he had known, but she was too young.

"Come now, Vayla," the woman's companion said. "One of these days you're going to have to recognize the good she did for Vaeldor and show proper respect."

Vayla eyed the statue and twisted her lips. "Thank you, Lady *Merssa*!"

Conflict gripped Tewlon. The tone in which Vayla spoke stirred anger deep within, but he was yet in awe of the image before him.

Vayla turned to Tewlon. "I apologize for—" She scowled. "If you're here to pay respects, by all means do so, and I shall leave you be. But if you've come to stare at me, you best turn and exit the city."

Tewlon averted his gaze first to the rooftops and then the brown bricks making up the street. He glanced again at Vayla as she and her companion headed back the way they had come.

"Lady Vayla," the young man said. "Have you learned nothing about the treatment of outlanders?"

"Quit with the title, Macurak!" she said, as if for the thousandth time, and the two disappeared.

Tewlon did not move for several seconds. His mouth was dry, and he had no idea what to do next. Follow Vayla? Finish his conversation with Merssa? Leave?

"Sir!" called the man Vayla addressed as Macurak. He had returned. "I apologize. Lady Vayla is having a bad day. Please do not allow her words to cause negative opinions about her, the city, or the grand monument before you. Lady Merssa was the best Palidur had to offer. And I'm certain Lady Vayla will be equally renown in the years to come."

Tewlon liked this warrior. He smiled and bowed his head. "Thank you, sir. I take no offense. Your city is quite lovely."

Macurak bowed before hastening to the south.

Tewlon took in a deep breath and slowly released it. He turned to Barcum. "Did you see that?"

Barcum snorted.

"I agree." Tewlon gazed down the street. Though Vayla was gone, her image remained etched in his mind.

With a sigh, he led his mount along the brown streets to the center of the city. There, the walls separating New Palidur into its sections of worship connected to a wall encircling the Grand Cathedral. The dome of the Holy City's largest building rose high above, adorned with statues of angelic warriors. Beyond the open gate, silver cobblestones held several more statues of the city's greatest heroes. A representation of Merssa was there, smaller than the one in the Cafior Sector, and so were sculptures of Soren and Hubrid—other High Paladins killed in the war against Trannum. To the right was a majestic fountain, as white as the cathedral and all the other buildings of New Palidur, and above it burned a single flame — the Eternal Flame. It was a tribute to Silcor for the heroics of Nidor during the Necromancer War. To the left was the Grand Cathedral, its long, covered porch accessible by any one of three staircases. The closest steps were painted brown, the middle ones dark blue, and the far stairs light blue, and the doors nearest to them matched their colors. A pair of guards stood atop each staircase. The sentries were not there to turn away outlanders like they might have done in old Palidur, but to make sure visitors had sufficient reason to enter their most treasured structure.

Tewlon did not approach the building. He could think of no purpose to do so. Instead, he sat on a bench next to the fountain to pass the time, and Barcum meandered by the wall. After half an hour, Lord Rholmar exited the cathedral.

The retired Grand Paladin leaned upon a staff with every other step, but his expression appeared strong. Beside him was Lady Ladonia, also aged, but as beautiful as she had been years ago. Growing old was an event unknown to Vecnor. Would he experience it once his service to Elgarroth ended?

An hour later, the reigning Grand Paladin emerged from the building. Montac was extremely muscular, with a mind to challenge most mages. He was son to Rholmar and Ladonia, and he inherited the couples' greatest assets and more. The Grand Paladin walked alongside a white-haired elderly man Tewlon knew to be Nilborg. The priest surely enjoyed a strong connection with Soleran the Protector, for he aged very slowly. By Tewlon's estimation, Nilborg was a hundred and twelve years old, yet he required no devices to keep his balance.

Tewlon smiled. Although he knew them only from afar, through the eyes of his elfish guise and from stories told by Elgarroth and Tux, he felt as if they were old friends. And it would have to do. It was the life he chose.

That evening, Tewlon stayed in the city. New Palidur inn rooms were expensive, but Elgarroth never failed to supply an adequate amount of gold for their journeys. Tewlon always procured a room with two beds, and he pushed them together, end to end, before lying down to sleep. Just as expected, he reclaimed his own body for the night. Sleep was better that way, and Vecnor appreciated Elgarroth granting him that favor.

Tewlon remained in New Palidur for a couple of weeks, catching several glimpses of Vayla. The young lady's attitude did not soften, but that didn't bother Tewlon—Vecnor had journeyed with Merssa enough to build a tolerance. Vayla caught him staring on a few occasions, and during the last instance, she held a steady glare for him. It was time to move on.

Tewlon rode Barcum southeast from New Palidur, and three days later, he arrived at Charndova. The walled city was observing some obscure festival, but he skipped the celebrations and turned in for the night. Come morning, he entered the mountain pass.

Evening was yet an hour away when Tewlon reached Ironside Keep. He walked Barcum up the winding slope to the stronghold's entrance, where a soldier attempted to lead his mount to the stables. Tewlon nodded to his horse, receiving a disgusted snort in response, but Barcum reluctantly headed to the horse prison without another word.

At the gate, an elderly gentleman stood beneath a raised portcullis. Morsum.

"Ah, an elf," Morsum said. "We don't get too many—" The blood drained from his face. "Tewlon?"

"Yes?" Tewlon blurted without thinking. He normally didn't confirm his elfish name outside the House of Elgarroth, but he wasn't used to being recognized while traveling. Whenever he happened upon Eraim and Selanna outside the glade in Vermallon, he hid until they were from sight.

"I have kept my word." Morsum glanced over his shoulder. "I know not how Arkor…"

Tewlon furrowed his brow. Obviously, Morsum thought he had come in an official capacity. "I am passing through. Nothing more."

"Oh." The old man's shoulders relaxed. "Very good." He frowned. "You never spoke back at the house. I thought you were mute."

Tewlon chuckled. "Please, don't tell. It's better no one else knows."

"You're secret's safe with me!" Morsum forced a smile. "So long as you don't tell Elgarroth…"

"What does Arkor know, exactly?"

"Well…" Morsum glanced over his shoulder again. They were alone. "I'm not sure *exactly* what he knows. But there might have been an occasion that I used *uncle* instead of *lord* when addressing him. I thought I covered it up with a cough, but… I'm not so sure."

"What did he say?"

"Not so much what he said." Morsum checked once more to see that no one else could hear. He sighed. "He gave me better accommodations. In the central tower, even. He explained to the other soldiers that it was due to my long service and loyalty."

"Not your old room?"

Morsum raised a hand. "No, no. That's Romik's." Moisture glistened in his eyes. "My son—um, Lord Romik moved in a while back. Permanently." A tear worked its way down his wrinkled cheek. "He's such a fine lad… A beautiful man. And he treats the soldiers well, just like Father—um, Lord Vikur did. In truth, he appreciates this rock better than I ever did."

"There, there." Tewlon placed a gentle hand on the guard's shoulder. "I've not met him, but I understand he is a well-respected young lord."

"What's this?"

A finely dressed man with graying hair uttered the question. And though he seemed shorter than in days when Vecnor last saw him, the missing left arm just below the elbow was unmistakable. Lord Arkor.

"What's wrong, Morsum?" Arkor appeared genuinely concerned, and he shot an accusatory glance at Tewlon.

"Nothing, Lord Arkor." Morsum wiped his eyes. "Nothing at all. This here's Tewlon. He was one of the folks that helped me find my way back." There was no deceit in his smile or words.

Arkor measured Tewlon. "Well, then. A friend of Morsum's is a friend of the keep! Your coins are no good here. And you may stay as long as you like."

The gleam in Arkor's eye made it obvious he had figured something out. Whether he was completely correct, Tewlon could not know. But the one-armed warrior had seen a lot in his lifetime, and he was probably close enough.

"I'll show him to a room, if you'll allow," offered Morsum.

Arkor studied his gatekeeper's face. His eyes softened. "You do that. Give our elf friend the best room in the place." He turned to Tewlon. "A pleasure to meet you."

Tewlon nodded.

Morsum led the way deeper into the keep. The structure's original intention had been to stop bandits, hobgoblins, and barbarians from using the mountain road to raid settlements in the west, but after six generations of Ironsides, peace ruled the lands to either side and the keep became more of an inn for travelers. The undead uprising returned the fortress to its military status, and now, over twenty years since the war's end, it was a combination of the two. Vecnor had been to the stronghold several times, as had Thalamir, his dwarfish guise, but this was a first for Tewlon. Still, he knew his way around.

They entered the heart of Ironside Keep: the tavern. Vikur spared no expense when transforming the old dining hall into the grand meeting place for food and drink. A bar was to the left, next to a door leading to the kitchen, and to the right, a plush chair sat atop a dais where Vikur once related embellished stories for his guests' entertainment—Vecnor often wondered if Vikur truly remembered things the way he told them. Several tables covered the floor, and patrons occupied half of them.

Morsum left Tewlon at the door and spoke with the barkeep. The barman glanced at Tewlon before relinquishing a key, and Morsum returned. They headed back down the hallway.

"Nidor has been through here many times," Morsum mentioned while they walked. "My, how he has made a name for himself in these parts."

Tewlon let go a small chuckle. Nidor's fame traveled much farther than the mountain pass.

"I knew there was something special about that man," Morsum continued. "He's a good soul, through and through. I'm sure it was him that saved the others from Ragab back in that cave in Selt."

"I have it on good authority that it was you that did so," said Tewlon. "And that the demon had just gained the upper hand on Nidor."

Morsum stopped before a door and frowned at Tewlon with disbelief. Though his face was elderly, his eyes were young. Surely Arkor noticed as well.

Tewlon lifted his brow. "I speak the truth. Ragab was pulled into the portal when you jumped through. Didn't you see it on the other side?"

Morsum's eyes widened. "Vecnor?"

Great. The last sentence had slipped. Tewlon should not have said as much, but his sympathy for Ballrik got the better of him. He sighed.

"Not to worry." Morsum grinned. "Who am I going to tell?"

Tewlon relaxed. But had he truly slipped? Or did a part of him want the gatekeeper to figure it out?

Morsum opened the door. Beyond was a lavish chamber with two beds, vanities, wardrobes, and washbasins. On a table before a hearth was a silver tray holding a decanter of red wine and two goblets, and a pair of overstuffed chairs were to either side. One bed and a chair were unusually large. Vikur had provided the oversized furniture to accommodate Vecnor whenever he visited.

"Here you are." Morsum waved his wrinkled hand. "The best Ironside has to offer." He gazed at the fixtures. "Father made this room for you. But you never returned. I remember cleaning this room so many times…" He shook his head.

It was obvious the gatekeeper had more to say.

"Please," Tewlon walked to the table, "have a drink with me."

Morsum glanced over his shoulder. "I suppose they can do without me a few more minutes." He sat in the smaller chair. "Most soldiers constantly bother me about taking it easy." He shook his head. "I know this body is old, but I *feel* my age."

Tewlon smirked as he poured the wine and handed a glass to his guest. He took the other goblet and sat, and in an instant he was Vecnor, and Morsum was Ballrik.

Ballrik looked himself over, felt his cheeks, and stared at Vecnor in disbelief. His skin was tighter, though he was still middle-aged, and he was a handsome man. "What…?"

Vecnor's smile broadened. "Consider it a gift from Elgarroth. Even if only for a moment."

Elgarroth had surely foreseen this visit, and Vecnor realized he hadn't made a mistake in speaking with Morsum. Perhaps this was for Ballrik's benefit.

"Tell me," Vecnor eyed Ballrik, "what troubles you?"

"It has been a difficult adjustment." Ballrik's eyes moved to his goblet. "It's like watching my life pass me by instead of living it."

"I see." Vecnor took a sip. The wine was excellent.

"I forgot how often people I know use this road," Ballrik added. "So many familiar faces… And they think me strange for staring."

"You *are* a guardsman," Vecnor said. "It's your job to scrutinize visitors. Perhaps you're mistaken."

Ballrik shrugged. "Perhaps. But it sure is good to see them doing so well. I thought I might lose myself the first time Gruelenor brought Romik to visit." He looked at Vecnor. "Probably another clue for Arkor that I was something other than an old soldier returning for duty."

Vecnor finished his drink and poured a second.

Ballrik's eyes were downcast. "I heard about poor Solinin. And Merssa."

"Many lost their lives in the Necromancer War."

Ballrik smirked. "I heard *you* were quite the hero."

Vecnor waved off the comment. "I'm sure things are exaggerated."

Ballrik shook his head and chuckled. "I doubt that." He took a drink.

"What else troubles you?" asked Vecnor.

Ballrik had another sip before responding. "Lorin visited." He looked up. "Did you know she married…?"

Vecnor nodded. "I know." There was no sense in making the poor man finish the question. Ballrik's widow took Gruelenor as her husband—one of Ballrik's dearest friends.

"I don't blame her," Ballrik said as a tear escaped. "And she couldn't have chosen a better mate. I asked Gruelenor to take care of her, and he has fulfilled that wish." He held a wry smile. "But I must say, I was relieved when Romik didn't call him Father."

"Don't feel guilty about that." Vecnor winked. "You've earned a few less-than-pleasant thoughts."

"To be sure." Ballrik released a nervous chuckle. "And that boy of Gruelenor's… Baylun?"

"I've not met him."

"Well," Ballrik's brow rose, "he's not much to look at."

"That's what I hear." Vecnor could not contain his smirk.

"Some say he looks like Gruzim."

Vecnor froze. He had forgotten Baylun was related to the late Death Lord. But also he remembered Elgarroth's words. The wizard mentioned seeing the axe Vecnor and Tux retrieved from the mine shaft in a vision, and with the weapon was Gruzim. Was it truly Gruzim that Elgarroth saw?

Ballrik's expression moved to concern. "Did I say something wrong?"

"No." Vecnor shook the thought. He would discuss it with Elgarroth later. "Not at all."

Ballrik sat back. "It's just that… you look like you've seen a ghost."

"Nothing to worry about." Vecnor smiled. "How was Lorin?"

Ballrik searched Vecnor's face, as if to make sure he hadn't gone too far. He then relaxed. "Lorin's beautiful. And happy. And I shall have to take solace in that."

"If you could go back," said Vecnor, "would you deny Elgarroth's gift?"

Ballrik's sigh transformed into a chuckle. "Not in a hundred years. Some things I see and hear bring me pain, certainly. But I shouldn't even exist. And here I am, getting to know Romik better every day. I wouldn't trade this for anything."

"That's good."

Ballrik's cheerful expression faltered. "Right now, Romik is planning a hunting trip for his brother's birthday." He shook his head. "It's only for six weeks, but I'll miss him terribly while he's gone." He set down his goblet and stood. "This has been most beneficial, speaking with you. You could say you arrived just in time to keep me from walking a dark road. But I really should get back to my duties."

Vecnor nodded. "Before you go, how did you know it was me and not Tux?"

Ballrik scrunched his brows together. "Your eyes. And the way you talk. But mostly the eyes."

Vecnor chuckled. "It has been grand sitting with you."

"If you need anything," Ballrik said, "even a bit of conversation, please, *please* don't hesitate to ask."

He walked to the door, and as he did so, he resumed his aged appearance. Vecnor transformed as well. Morsum looked back with a smile and a nod before departing.

✷✷✷

Tewlon received excellent care during the week he remained at Ironside Keep. Arkor spoke with him on several occasions, always probing with seemingly innocent questions. "Are you a friend of Selanna's or Elgarroth's?" the one-armed lord posed the first day. The next day, he asked, "Where exactly did you find Morsum?" On the fourth day, he said, "Morsum reminds me of someone. How about you?" Tewlon offered very little in his responses, consisting of nods, headshaking, or shrugs. He also sat with Morsum a couple more times, but they maintained their guises. Morsum seemed disappointed.

On the evening of the sixth day, Tewlon went to his room to get some rest, and Tux was there. As Tewlon shut the door and locked it, he became Vecnor.

"What brings you here?" he asked.

Tux gazed at a battleaxe leaning against the normal-sized chair. It was the one they procured in the mine. "It is time to give this a home."

Vecnor frowned. "A home?"

"Elgarroth heard your conversation with Ballrik. And you were correct. It was not Gruzim in his vision," Tux's lips twisted in disgust while uttering the name, "but someone looking too much like the knave."

"So why bring it here?"

"Apparently, Romik seeks a grand gift for his brother's birthday." Tux furrowed his brow. "I do not know why humans celebrate birthdays."

"Well," Vecnor responded, "when you don't live through hundreds of them, they tend to have a bit more meaning."

The elf shrugged. "I suppose."

"So, what are we doing with it?"

Tux grinned. "Not *we*. Thalamir."

Vecnor sighed. Now he was to be a dwarf.

"And there's no time to lose," added Tux. "Romik leaves tomorrow morning for Morimont. You can save him the trip."

Vecnor changed the topic. "What have you been up to?"

All hints of joy vanished from Tux's expression. "Elgarroth is reading Welmirth's journals again."

A chill traversed Vecnor's body. "He fears Uustaag's hand in this?"

"If he does," replied Tux, "he will not say as much. He claims he is preparing."

Vecnor nodded. Tux probably knew nothing more on the subject.

"As for me," the elf continued, "I have been tracking the dunarchins' movements." He shook his head. "But always the trail vanishes. I recently discovered an arch drawn upon a cliff wall at one of my dead ends. Someone had tried to remove it, and it was greatly faded. Elgarroth confirmed it had been a gate, and that lingering magic showed it to have transported the undead to Sistama."

"Sistama?"

Tux nodded. "It seems the swamp has new denizens. That is where they have been living, no doubt."

Dread crept into Vecnor's chest. "Don't tell me we're heading back to the marsh."

"No." Tux poured himself a goblet of wine and took a sip. "There are too many dunarchins for us to defeat. That, and Elgarroth does not believe they will remain there long. He surmises the portal in the swamp still exists, but he hesitates to guess as to where it now leads."

"It could go anywhere," murmured Vecnor. "Is it the Shadow's doing? The one Elgarroth spoke of?"

"More than likely. He also said the Shadow will soon make itself known."

Every nerve in Vecnor's body tingled. Was it fear? He could use a few more years of preparation before facing another great war; one worse than the fight against Trannum, according to Elgarroth.

Tux studied Vecnor's face. "Yes. The thought makes it hard to breathe."

Vecnor nodded.

"You best leave before the dawn." Tux drained his goblet and set it on the table. "I am off to spy on Selanna and Eraim."

Vecnor smirked. "Want to trade?"

Tux chuckled. "Elgarroth has seen fit never to force me into the body of a dwarf." He headed toward the exit. "But you look great with a full beard!"

Vecnor grinned as Tux faded into the shadows beneath the door.

❊ ❊ ❊

Tewlon packed his gear and strapped the axe to his back, careful to make it appear as something other than a weapon. He then cracked open the door. The hallway was dark and empty. He crept silently along the corridor to the guardroom at the gate. Soldiers would be present, but they wouldn't stop a guest from departing in the middle of the night. Tewlon only hoped Morsum wasn't there; the goodbye would surely be a tearful one. Upon arrival, a pair of guards roused from their boredom. Morsum was not in attendance. Tewlon released a silent sigh of relief.

"Leaving at this hour?" asked a soldier.

Tewlon nodded.

"That's your business," said the man. "But I don't recommend traveling the pass in the dark. It can be treacherous."

"He's an elf," the other soldier pointed out. "He'll be just fine. It's Morsum *I* worry about." He looked at Tewlon. "Poor old guy has taken a shine to you."

Tewlon remained silent.

The first guard worked the winch to lift the gate, and the other fetched Barcum. Relief shone in the horse's eyes to see Tewlon, and they walked side by side down the snaking trail to the mountain pass.

The road was dark beneath the aging moon, but Tewlon's sight revealed every pitfall while they headed east. He did not travel far before reaching the hidden door used by dwarves traveling between Morimont and the keep. It was created long ago, and to Vecnor's

325

knowledge, the rulers of Ironside were the only humans aware of its location, a secret they protected. Tewlon pushed in a loose rock a few feet away, and the wall slid to the right to reveal a staircase.

Barcum followed Tewlon down the steps—it was a good thing the horse wasn't Umbarc's size! They reached the first landing, a twenty-foot hallway leading to a stairwell descending in the opposite direction, and continued at a steady pace. This happened again and again as Tewlon and Barcum worked their way downward a thousand feet to a stone wall. There, Tewlon opened the secret panel to the floor of the chasm below Ironside Keep.

The moonlight struggled to illuminate the valley of boulders, discarded scraps, and ancient bones and pieces of armor left by thousands of victims of falls over the ages. Tewlon saw them almost as clearly as if it were daytime. He then became Thalamir, and he led Barcum toward the Morimont Trail.

Being a dwarfish path, the road was not easily discernable from the surrounding mountains, especially in the dark, but Thalamir had used it often enough and found it without delay. He and his mount followed the footpath for an hour before stopping to camp. After staking a blanket to a cliff wall and employing a couple poles to create a simple shelter, he lit a fire. He didn't intend to sleep, but he needed the campsite to look authentic, and he ate bread and dried meat, allowing scraps and crumbs to litter the ground.

It wasn't long before the sky brightened and the sun peeked over the mountains in the east. An hour later, a young warrior came wandering along the path on horseback. The Ironside sword strapped to his waist gave him away as Romik.

"Hail!" Romik called as he neared.

"Morning." Thalamir cleared his throat while eyeing the lord. He saw Ballrik in the lad's cheekbones and jawline. "How'd you get here?"

Romik held up a hand. "It's all right. I am Romik, Lord of Ironside. And by treaty, I have shared the secret route with no one."

Thalamir stared a few seconds before nodding. "Yeah. You look like your father."

"You knew Ballrik?"

"Sure did." Thalamir stroked his beard. "Good man. Sorry to learn of his passing."

"Thank you." A genuine appreciation shone in Romik's countenance. "Are you heading to Morimont? Or were you on your way to the keep?"

"The keep." Thalamir wiped his bulbous nose. "Looking to unload a couple things. Thought maybe someone there might be in the market for a battleaxe."

Romik's eyes narrowed. "Battleaxe, you say?"

"Yes, Lord Romik," Thalamir replied. "In fact, I was hoping to sell it to you. It is, after all, a special weapon. One fit for a lord. But, of course, you have your heirloom." Thalamir's gaze fell to the sword hanging from the warrior's belt. He then pulled the axe from under the shelter. The bronze blades gleamed in the sunlight, and a new black leather strap showing no signs of use spiraled about the handle until reaching the bronze spike. Tux had done a fine job.

Romik patted his scabbard. "Yes. The ruling sword of Ironside is all I need." His attention fixated on the axe. "I am, however, looking for something for my brother. And that is why I aim for your city. What can you tell me about that weapon?"

Thalamir scratched his beard—he missed his goatee! "It is a grand creation of my own design, made from the rarest metals deep below the mountains. The best I have ever forged." He pointed at one set of runes. "This says *courage*." He pointed at the other runes. "And this says *honor*." He hoped he had gotten them right.

"Why not sell it to one of your own?"

Thalamir smiled. "If only I could. But it's not meant for a dwarf hand. It's for a dwarf-friend. I originally crafted it with King Karrak in mind. But… that cannot be. So my next thought was the line of Ironside. Yours have always been true friends."

"Would my half-brother be considered part of my lineage?"

Thalamir looked up, as if seeking the answer among the peaks. "Yes." He nodded. "Yes, I believe he would do just fine."

"May I see it?"

Thalamir handed over the weapon. "As I said, it's special. Its blades never need sharpening, and it will learn the fighting style of its wielder, so that they might work together in harmony."

Romik tested its weight. "It's a bit heavy." His brows lifted as he swung it to and fro. "But its balance is perfect!" He peered closer at the blades and grinned. "How much were you planning to sell it for?"

"Well," Thalamir scratched his hairy cheek, "it's very valuable—"

"Sold!" Romik produced a small bag and poured gems into his hand, including a ruby, a diamond, two emeralds, and three sapphires. They were surely worth several thousand gold coins. He returned them to the pouch and offered it.

Thalamir balked. He didn't feel right taking the lad's treasure.

"If this isn't enough…"

Thalamir snatched the bag. "It's plenty."

Romik's eyes became distant. "It needs to be Baylun's greatest birthday ever." He looked at the axe. "This is perfect!"

"Very good." Thalamir clasped arms with the lord.

"I thank you, good sir!" Romik looked again at the weapon. "But I must take my leave."

Thalamir bowed.

Romik climbed onto his horse and rode back down the path. Thalamir thought it strange the lad hadn't ask for his name. Probably better that way.

It is time, said Elgarroth. *Proceed to Trannum's stronghold. Use the silver jar and collect the dust of his bones. They should be in the black robe before the throne.*

Vecnor cleaned up his campsite, and he and Umbarc headed east toward Kalmaar.

CHAPTER 34
THE SHADOW STRIKES

Eslimil sat on Landolice outside the walls of New Palidur. Elgarroth seemed certain the Shadow would first strike in the Holy City, though not where or when. The wizard still relied heavily on Selanna's visions, combining them with his own. Would he ever regain his full Sight? Given the choice between the life of a human and Elgarroth's precognitive abilities, they should have left Ballrik to the consequences of his actions. But then, Elgarroth probably did not expect Vou's punishment to be so severe. Perhaps the mage was getting soft. Eslimil saw firsthand the horrors Elgarroth had endured over the centuries, watching good people pay the ultimate price for doing the right thing. Would the wizard alter his decision if given the chance? The answer would remain a mystery.

A chill captured the night, and tiny bumps arose atop Eslimil's arms. He searched the surroundings. The moon shone and stars dotted the sky; that was unchanged. But an ill wind now played with his cloak and the air tasted like dirt. He traced the path from Palidur Bridge to the Holy City, and he saw it: a dark presence hovering above the wall, unnoticed by the sentries.

He urged Landolice into a full run as the mass of darkness darted around the city toward King Arman Lake. It was all Eslimil could do to keep the Shadow in sight until it stopped to hover outside the Soleran Sector. He slowed his approach as he spied glowing blue dots serving as the spectre's eyes, reminiscent of a Death Lord. Was it Radaam? As Eslimil drew to within forty yards, the Shadow passed over the wall.

Eslimil took in a breath to fly in pursuit of his quarry. The apparition descended and seeped through the cracks of a window near the back of a Soleran church—the church where Nilborg resided. Eslimil moved swiftly toward the temple, but a flash of bright light beyond the curtains caused him to balk. The Shadow reemerged, and it took no notice of him as it headed over the wall.

Eslimil followed, his eyes never straying from the wraith-form, and he materialized upon reaching his saddle. He pushed Landolice as the ghost flew north. It was like chasing a patch of darkness in the night, a blurry spot in his vision, and he dared not blink or look away. Landolice's hooves pounded the stones of Palidur Bridge, and as the Shadow entered Sendorum, it veered northwest toward Virch.

Leaving all roads behind, Eslimil managed to keep sight of the Shadow for an hour. But it was too swift and eluded him. In its wake was a path of frozen vegetation, however, and even after the sun rose, damaged grass, flowers, and bushes, as well as leaves that prematurely fell from their homes among the branches of scattered trees, marked the Shadow's passing.

Eslimil pressed on for three days without rest and reached the Shield River, several miles east of Darmoor. It was nearing dusk, and he spied the continuing trail on the far bank.

"You will have to wait here," he said to Landolice.

The horse nodded.

Eslimil drew in a deep breath before floating over the broad waterway, and released the air upon entering Beit. He then ran through most of the night, walking at times to conserve energy. The countryside was clear of Beitians through the dark hours, but come morning, a platoon of soldiers obstructed his path as they traveled a road from east to west. They were likely headed for Zurzak. Eslimil remained unseen until they passed, and he continued north, following the trail of withered flora. An hour later, his throat developed a scratchy sensation. Perhaps the cost of so little sleep.

Another twenty minutes expired, and Eslimil spied a village to the northwest. He narrowed his eyes to see dozens of Beitians lying on the ground, unmoving. He ventured closer. Still nothing moved or made a sound. Approaching to within forty paces of the nearest bodies, he gasped. They were dead. Every one of them. Dark blood issued from their pink noses and ears, their skin was pale, and they appeared to have rapidly lost weight.

Moisture coated Eslimil's upper lip. Wiping his nose, he discovered mucus flowing from both nostrils. He swallowed, reminding himself of the scratchy pain in his throat. As fear crept down his spine, he sprinted toward the Shield River.

A plague invaded Eslimil's body; he needed to escape before it was too late. The arrival of dusk was a blessing, and he inhaled deeply to become weightless, but a fit of sneezes expelled the breath. As the outburst ended, he suppressed the urge to cough and pulled in as much air as he could hold. He flew south, aided by a northerly breeze, and renewed his breath only when dizziness threatened to overwhelm him. In this manner, Eslimil arrived at the water faster than he had made his way north and floated across the river to join Landolice.

Upon reaching the saddle, he panted, sucking in air as if Vaeldor had a sudden lack of oxygen. It took several minutes to slow his breathing, and it was then he realized his throat had returned to normal.

The sickness did not take hold, Elgarroth said. *You are safe. Selanna and Eraim are on their way to New Palidur, and you must keep an eye on them. Go now.*

Although appreciative of the wizard's reassurance, Eslimil swallowed hard, sensing for the slightest discomfort. Nothing. He gazed across the river, certain he spied the plague hanging like a fog over Beit. It was likely his imagination. He steered Landolice to the southeast.

❖ ❖ ❖

Eslimil remained outside Tedonis until Selanna and Eraim arrived, riding their Salenti horses from the direction of Virch. It was not yet dawn, and the two gazed upon the settlement, obviously touched by memories of Merssa. They then rode across Palidur Bridge, stopping at its midpoint to gaze at the enormous monuments of Vennimor and Bormungdaher, the founder of Palidur and the dwarf king that commissioned the bridge's construction as a gift to the Holy City. From there, the elf maidens entered Sardina and passed through the gates of the Cafior Sector and into New Palidur.

Leaving Landolice outside the walls, Eslimil proceeded on foot with his hood concealing his face. He nodded at the tower guards regarding him with furrowed brows as he walked beneath the raised portcullis, and once from their sight, he ducked into the nearest alley.

He made his way toward the Soleran Sector, figuring the elves would go there. And he was right. Selanna was speaking with Cafior soldiers stationed before the closed gate of the divider wall. But the conversation did not last long, and the two departed. Eraim's expression revealed confusion, and frustration soured Selanna's.

Eslimil trailed them to the Grand Cathedral. Upon the silver cobblestones outside the enormous church, he wandered near the fountain and watched the elves enter the domed building through the Arronaus door. Fifteen minutes later, they exited, and Lord Rholmar was with them. The retired paladin led the maidens past a group of soldiers guarding another closed gate to the Soleran Sector.

Eslimil wandered to an area of the inner sanctum engulfed by shadows. The handful of people walking about paid him no mind. He glanced at the guards on the covered porch of the cathedral. They were busy talking to one another. He took in a breath.

Floating over the wall, Eslimil spotted the elves. Just as expected, they headed toward Nilborg's church. He passed through the darker alleyways, arriving before them, and settled next to the building. There, he materialized.

Shortly after, Selanna and Eraim approached the front doors of the temple. Eraim glanced Eslimil's way, and he slinked deeper into the shadows. She narrowed her eyes, searching the alleyway until she entered the church.

With sunrise close at hand, Eslimil dissolved into shadow and followed a waning path of darkness over the wall and out of the city. Selanna and Eraim would surely head north after their investigation. He whistled, summoning Landolice, and crossed Palidur Bridge to wait near Tedonis.

Sure enough, the maidens returned across the river. They rounded Tedonis and continued northeast, and Eslimil followed at a distance until they reached Vermallon Forest a couple of days later. It was obvious they aimed for the House of Elgarroth.

He took a direct route to the cabin, and upon arrival hid Landolice among the trees and climbed a tall maple. No smoke issued from the chimney. Where was Elgarroth? The Salenti elves entered the clearing, and Selanna was disappointed to find nobody home. A few minutes later, after the mage attempted to expel her frustrations with a forceful sigh, they departed.

Again, Eslimil took a direct route through the forest. A half hour after he exited the trees, Selanna and Eraim emerged along Vermallon Road, and he trailed them for days across Sendorum, Virch, and over Korban Bridge.

Seac is dead, said Elgarroth. *His body was discovered this morning in the same state as Nilborg's.*

A vision entered Eslimil's mind, and he pulled Landolice to a halt. Nilborg's skin was blue, and the priest lay in bed, extending a hand toward the bedroom door. Then Seac, almost in the exact same pose. *Frozen, righteous hand shall fall; Sight is blinded in Shadow's wake...* Nilborg and Seac. Selanna's prophecy was taking shape.

Are you in Tikken City? Eslimil asked. But he knew the answer and did not wait for a reply. *I am sure Selanna heads your way. Should I continue?*

Yes.

It was past noon when Selanna and Eraim reached Tikken City. Eslimil dismounted a quarter mile away and allowed Landolice to wander while he continued on foot. Entering the massive city during the day posed no problems, and he pulled his hood further over his head as he passed through the gate and proceeded to the Council Building. Selanna and Eraim were there when he arrived, and it appeared a tower guard had denied them admittance. After quartering their horses within nearby stables, and a lengthy conversation between Eraim and a groom, the pair walked to a tavern down the street.

Shadows crept across the city, and no one paid attention to Eslimil as he wandered to the rear of the building. Loose shutters covered all windows, save for where the Salenti elves sat. The two were sipping wine. Locating a vacant table in the corner, Eslimil held his breath and passed through one of the shutter's many cracks.

The tavern room was two-thirds full. Everyone kept to their own affairs, and Eslimil materialized unnoticed on a seat. He was a few tables away from Selanna and Eraim, but close enough to hear them. Unable to resist the urge, he pulled his dagger and worked its tip into the tabletop while keeping an eye on the maidens.

"I cannot believe this," said Selanna, staring at her goblet. "Nilborg was murdered. Seac is dead, and we know not how. We can neither find Elgarroth nor talk to the Council. It is almost like that prophecy…

> *"Eyes of old are kindled,*
> *Master returns from below.*
> *Frozen, righteous hand shall fall,*
> *Sight is blinded in Shadow's wake…"*

She shook her head. "Or something like that. You probably remember it better."

Eraim narrowed her eyes. "I know not of what you are saying. Where did you hear this?"

Selanna twisted her lips. "Never mind." She gazed out the window at the late sun. "We best get going."

As they headed for the exit, Eraim paused to look directly at Eslimil. He had just finished etching his name onto the table. Selanna called to her friend from the door, and Eraim looked away for a second. That was all Eslimil needed to depart the same way he had entered.

He rose to the rooftop before releasing the air and grabbing hold of the eaves to pull himself up. Though the sun was low, it illuminated the shingles and he could float no higher. From his vantage point, he watched Selanna and her companion walk back toward the Council Building. Positive that was where they headed, he descended to the street and used alleyways to arrive at the same destination.

He found the Salenti elves outside the Council grounds, in a discreet location hidden from watchtowers. Selanna scaled a rope to join her companion, who crouched atop the wall, and Eslimil smirked at the golden-haired elf's technique. Surely a human would have thought the mage a graceful climber, but she exhibited several hesitations, and the slack below her thrashed about. Eraim pulled up the rope once Selanna finished, and lowered it into the courtyard beyond. The maidens descended.

Eslimil eyed the late sunlight illuminating the crenellations. There was not enough shade to travel the quick way. After making sure he was alone, he extracted his rope and tossed his grappling hook up and around a merlon. He ascended, and upon reaching the top, he returned his rope to its place and used Eraim's to climb down.

The Council grounds possessed many trees casting shadows, allowing Eslimil to float to the servants' entrance and seep through the opening at the bottom of the door. The corridor beyond was dim, as always, and Selanna and Eraim were gone. But that did not matter. Eslimil knew where they aimed for.

He exhaled and walked the hallways at a steady pace, making no sound. On three occasions he detected another's approach, and each time he held his breath to hover near the ceiling until the servant passed. Upon reaching the final passage to the audience chamber, he found the double doors closed. He floated through the crack at the top, over Mordan the steward, and settled into a dark corner, unnoticed.

The Council of Wizards glared from their semicircle of chairs at Elgarroth, Selanna, and Eraim. Their frowns deepened while Selanna whispered to Elgarroth about Nilborg's death. She failed to notice the extra attention until mentioning she had seen the murder in a dream, and one of the wizards spoke.

"Please. Tell us all about your *dream.*"

Eslimil despised the arrogance of the human wizards. Without the Seer, their relevance in Vaeldor would dwindle until the next Seer was ready to assume Seac's duties.

Selanna described her dream about the Shadow and Nilborg, and her words were met with rolling eyes, dismissive hand waves, and silent sighs. But she did not back down. Good for her. Trannum was then brought up, as was the Ancient Enemy of the North. More scoffing ensued.

Next, they debated the resurgence of dunarchins. The Council refused to grant the rumors any merit, whether driven by fear or ignorance, and they hid behind the lack of proof to empower their resolve. When the Council was young, the members did not rest until peace reigned, and they were not above subtle threats to push their agenda. They even managed to create a common language to unite the realms all the more. Today's Council cared more about pacifying the masses and playing politics. Seac had attempted to reclaim the old ways, but he was only one man, and now he was gone. What a useless bunch of aged humans.

Elgarroth spoke, mentioning Seac's past interest in Selanna's dreams, and at that moment, Eraim turned Eslimil's way. He stepped deeper into the shadows and took in a breath. She narrowed her eyes, attempting to pierce the darkness, and nudged Selanna. The mage followed Eraim's gaze, and Eslimil floated to the ceiling. Abandoning the search, the maidens returned their focus to the Council.

The conversation became distorted while Eslimil remained in shadow form, but he understood every word as Eraim stole the room's attention.

"What about the *Frozen, righteous hand*? And *Sight is blinded in Shadow's wake*? From what prophecy are they?"

The verses were a product of Selanna's mind, so of course the Council had never heard them, and they dismissed them.

After some indignant words from Selanna, she and Eraim exited the chamber. Elgarroth remained, casting a glance at Eslimil. Once the doors closed, Eslimil lowered to the floor and took some much needed breaths.

"You will find Seac's curiosities were well placed," said Elgarroth to the Council. "He believed the Prophecy of Trannum was incomplete. And the Shadow has indeed opened its eyes, as if awakened by the destruction of the necromancer."

"And where do you come by this information?" posed a wizard.

Eslimil heard nothing more. He blended with the shadows and floated across the chamber and through the doors.

The corridor was empty, and he materialized and moved swiftly toward the Council Building's exit. As he neared, he detected men around the next bend, speaking about "those blasted elves" while approaching his location. Eslimil inhaled and drifted along the ceiling, passing over four servants. Once out of sight, he alit and continued.

The front entrance bore a single guard. The man gazed through the open doors, likely making sure Selanna and Eraim departed the grounds before shutting them. It was dusk, and Eslimil held his breath to float past the soldier, across the courtyard, and over the wall.

The maidens had just exited, and they walked in the direction of the tavern where they had sipped wine earlier. Eslimil moved from building to building until they entered the establishment, and he settled on the roof. This time, he would not go inside. Eraim was too alert.

The Salenti elves returned to the street an hour later and headed back to the Council Building. Eslimil followed, leaping from rooftop to rooftop and floating across the greater distances. At the closed entrance, Selanna spoke to the gatekeeper, inquiring about Elgarroth. The sentry eventually replied.

"I suppose it wouldn't hurt to inform you he left." The soldier glanced over his shoulder at the empty courtyard and turned back. "And it might not be my place, but the wizard didn't look too happy. Trouble was in his eyes, mark my words."

Selanna's expression darkened. She thanked the man, and she and Eraim walked away.

Eslimil descended to the street to follow at a distance. The maidens carried a conversation about Elgarroth for a couple of blocks until Eraim's attention snapped Eslimil's direction. He bolted into an alley devoid of lights, and the faint sound of tiny feet pursued. After sixty feet, he reached a dead end. Eslimil floated up the wall to the right and materialized on the roof. There, he stilled himself to listen as the alleyway lit up.

"Was it Tux?" Selanna asked.

"Hardly." Eraim's reply was drenched in sarcasm. "But it *was* the cloaked figure. Whoever it is, they are very skilled to have climbed this wall so quickly."

"Why is it following us?" inquired Selanna.

"Perhaps it is keeping watch on us," was Eraim's response.

"But who is it?" Selanna posed. "And why?"

Eraim sighed before speaking again. "Should you not use your magic next time? So we can get some answers?"

"Yes," said Selanna. "We need answers."

"You will get them soon enough," Eslimil murmured. "And you may not like what you learn."

The Salenti elves stayed the night at an inn. Eslimil made himself comfortable atop the building, and come morning he watched them retrieve their horses from the stables. They shared several words, but the only part that interested Eslimil was that Selanna wished to return to the House of Elgarroth. With this knowledge, he climbed down the backside of the inn and swiftly exited the city.

Landolice was not far, and the horse came running after Eslimil whistled. He mounted, and pushed the animal hard up the northern road to remain ahead of Selanna and Eraim.

The day passed, and it was not quite dusk when Eslimil crossed the Squire River. He had surely put an hour between himself and the maidens, and he rode north of Rivercross to dismount and allow Landolice a chance to recuperate. Seated upon a hill, he monitored Korban Bridge.

It is time to speak with them, said Elgarroth. *The enemy is on the move. Tell Selanna what you know about the Shadow, and make sure she does not proceed to Vermallon. Then return.*

Eslimil detected a darkening of the night sky. Was it his imagination? Elgarroth claimed the approaching evil would be worse than the Necromancer War, and Eslimil sensed those words to be true. Hopefully, the pair of maidens riding their little horses across the bridge of white stone were the answer.

Chapter 35

The Rising Evil

Vecnor sat across the small fire from Elgarroth. Tux was on the log to his right, facing them both. Vecnor had been there a few days already, alone until Elgarroth appeared yesterday. Tux arrived just before dinner. Elgarroth had relayed to Vecnor most, if not all, of what Tux had been up to, and now Eraim and Selanna headed for the Path of the Guardians to learn more. Presently, the wizard was quieter than usual, watching pipe smoke drift into the night sky.

"I can no longer deny the Shadow is Trannum," Elgarroth said, breaking the silence. He drew from his pipe. "It always seemed the logical conclusion. But with the destruction of the orbs and his skeleton, I had to leave room for the possibility it was one closely connected to him."

Vecnor clenched his jaw. Trannum! But it could have been worse, he supposed. It could have been Uustaag.

"The Shadow has usurped control over Beit," Elgarroth continued. "And it has released a plague onto the realm's citizens." He glanced at Tux. "A plague that kills all living things."

The half-gray elf shifted slightly on the log.

"The obvious purpose would be to raise an undead army, as Trannum did in Nomedd," Elgarroth added. "And from what I have learned, several firstborn Beitians disappeared before the plague was released, no doubt to boost the dunarchin force."

"Hasn't he failed at this type of warfare already?" asked Vecnor.

"As a skeletal necromancer, yes," replied Elgarroth. "But I believe the Shadow is his true form. The skeleton was nothing but a puppet controlled by his subconscious mind from afar. And when Eraim's arrow struck the final orb, he was awakened."

Vecnor found no words. *Awakened?* They fought a sleeping wizard twenty years ago? If that were so, what was Shadow-Trannum capable of?

Elgarroth looked from Tux to Vecnor. "I will not try to explain it in full, but let me say that his mind was functioning, carrying out his plans while his form was at rest. Hibernating, if you will."

Vecnor frowned. "For more than a thousand years?"

"Evil is patient," Elgarroth said. "Trannum discovered something while researching the fall of Uustaag, something so powerful that he could not resist its allure. Perhaps the same temptation that seduced Uustaag."

"Thard'Dun," muttered Tux.

Elgarroth nodded. "A malevolent deity so vile and corrupt that even Shadia and Demoligius refuse to align with Him."

Vecnor knew those evil deities all too well. Shadia, the Mistress of Darkness; Queen of the Underdark. Demoligius, Father of Dragons. The extinction of the giant beasts after the Dragon Wars weakened the latter, but He found strength again in fire and demons, and over the centuries He evolved ordinary reptiles into monsters.

"In fact," Elgarroth continued, "Shadia and Demoligius opposed Thard'Dun, and were aided by Soleran, Cafior, Arronaus, and Frayorna to imprison Him, weakening His influence over Vaeldor to mere nightmares. The priests of the fallen deity lost their power, and the religion all but faded into memory. Welmirth believed Uustaag's intentions were to free Thard'Dun."

"Has Uustaag returned?" Tux inquired. "Did Thard'Dun escape the prison?"

Elgarroth drew from his pipe and blew the smoke overhead. "No, on both counts." He gazed at the fire. "Had Uustaag returned, we would know. The warlord would not hide, of that you can be certain."

"How close did he come to freeing Thard'Dun?" asked Vecnor.

Elgarroth raised his brows. "Close enough to once again empower His priests. According to Welmirth, the arches you saw in Lormin Dmurr once contained openings to Thard'Dun's world, and from them issued horrific creatures to aid in Uustaag's mission. With these monsters, the warlord conquered the north, including all realms from Urell Coast to Nira, before Vennimor and Welmirth overthrew him."

"Does Trannum search for Uustaag?" posed Tux.

Elgarroth sighed. "He searches for something. And he looks for it in the north. That is the only explanation for the missing Guardians in Lothen Forest. From Selanna's visions, he seeks a key of some sort."

"Do Welmirth's journals mention any keys?" inquired Vecnor.

"His journals are many," Elgarroth said. "I have spent several years going through Trannum's books, and only returned to Welmirth's a few months ago."

"What do you *feel* is Trannum's quest?" Tux pressed.

Elgarroth eyed the Salenti-gray elf. "He desires the key to restore the openings in Lormin Dmurr. Trannum wishes to finish Uustaag's work."

Tux's gaze drifted to the soil. "A war that killed hundreds of thousands."

Elgarroth nodded. "And if he adds the monsters that aided Uustaag to his horde of undead, the price will be higher. There have already been sightings of Blackfoot goblins, unseen since before my days."

An image of Eraim faced with a colossal shadow invaded Vecnor's thoughts, and anxiety gripped his chest as a realization struck him. "Wait. Aren't Eraim and Selanna marching into the north right now?"

"And several others," said Elgarroth. "Romik and Baylun, Desser, Daymyn, and Vayla."

Vecnor's mouth ran dry. "Romik and Vayla?"

"The Sight is unclear." Elgarroth turned back to the fire. "But I foresee Vayla returning to New Palidur. As for the rest, the vision is fractured. Romik is badly broken, but aid arrives in the form of a maple tree. Desser has a painted face. Baylun and Daymyn are hiding, surrounded by the enemy, and Baylun's fate lies on the edge of a knife. I see Selanna and Eraim with another marteese warrior we have not met. They battle soldiers in black armor."

Vecnor clenched his fists as rage chased away all fear. "Radaam and Anduiff?"

Elgarroth shook his head. "I know not who they are, but they are plentiful. And they are not Death Lords."

"Will your Sight ever be unobstructed?" posed Tux.

Elgarroth's shoulders slumped. "I have taken strides. But I still cannot see far enough. I am relying on Selanna's mind, but I must teach her to do more. Perhaps then I shall uncover more."

"What are we to do?" Tux asked.

"The war approaches much faster than I would like." Elgarroth flashed an angry expression—with himself? He looked at Tux. "You will go to Beit and learn what you can of the enemy."

Tux sat up straight. "What about the plague?"

"I sense the plague to be diminishing," the wizard replied. "All the same, you should remain in the north. Onzac shows no sign of the illness, so venture no farther south than that."

Tux nodded.

Elgarroth turned to Vecnor. "You will head to the Path of the Guardians and enter Lothen Forest."

Vecnor frowned.

"The area should be free of the plague by the time you arrive," the wizard added.

"Should?"

Elgarroth shrugged. "That is the best I can offer at the moment. If anything changes for the worse, I will let you know."

That wasn't very reassuring. Vecnor stared at the fire.

Chapter 36

Beit

Eslimil journeyed across Harbnum to Maple Lore Forest. He could not simply float over the Shield River because he needed Landolice upon entering Beit, and the armies stationed on either side of the bridge outside Arbornum complicated the more direct route. Luckily, at the behest of Elgarroth, he had become familiar with the Lorians centuries ago, and they tolerated his presence.

The journey through the woodland was not difficult. The wildlife was in check for the most part, and he avoided areas where territorial predators made their dens. Nearing the end of the first day in the forest, he encountered the easternmost village. Like Salenti and Dakreal elves, Lorians lived in the trees. They constructed platforms about the boughs of towering maples to support buildings of wood, and stairs and ramps led to higher platforms. Most of their villages had three or four tiers, but a couple of them possessed eight. One of the larger settlements rested in the center of the forest, near the Grand Maple, and the other was beyond the Shield River, closer to the Beitian border. Eslimil skirted the village before him, not wanting to waste time mingling with the locals. A few elves spotted him, but paid him no mind.

The next day brought him to the lake west of the Grand Maple, the tallest tree in all of Vaeldor. Lorians believed the divine plant to house the realm of *Galenfial*, the elfish deity. Their largest city encircled the mammoth tree, beginning forty feet above the ground and reaching out to hundreds of neighboring maples to support housing for its citizens. Higher still, the layers continued above the normal treetops to allow a spectacular view of surrounding territories, but its clever construction went unnoticed by those beyond the woodland's border.

The nearby lake was called Westessimer by Lorians — Eslimil did not believe humans ever gave it a name. It was a serene visage, fed by the Shield River and giving birth to the Maple River, which eventually formed a natural barrier to separate Virch from Harbnum and Sendorum. Fish were in high supply within the calm water, and three elfish boats of exquisite make floated a hundred yards out. Each bore green sails, and their bows arced upward to display carvings of Nelceana, Goddess of Water. Lorians prayed to her daily to ensure a good day's haul.

Eslimil rounded Westessimer to its northwestern edge and followed the tributary feeding the lake until reaching the Shield. There, the Lorians had built up the riverbed for fording. The water was swift, but easily traversed. Thirty yards to the north, the ground sloped steeply downward to increase its flow all the way to the Icy Sea.

After crossing, Eslimil rode to the next Lorian settlement — the only village west of the Shield River. He hoped to gain some news about the plague before entering Beit. Many of the inhabitants there did not know him, and a few issued suspicious glares. Every Lorian had the freedom to deal with outsiders as they saw fit, but they hesitated, perhaps because Eslimil was an elf, and seemed content to allow the approaching soldier to handle the issue.

Eslimil immediately recognized the warrior as Captain Dresnian. The captain's elegant leather armor always reminded him of a gentle summer breeze with its finely embroidered swirls. It was almost peaceful. But Eslimil had met Dresnian on several occasions, and the Lorian's general attitude was anything but peaceful.

"Eslimil." Dresnian offered no pleasantries, his expression grim. "You have caught us on a bad day."

Eslimil scanned the forest, as if the plague might come billowing around the trees. It was not so. In the center of the clearing, a large cage held well over a hundred occupants. Eslimil had never seen more than a score of prisoners inside. To the southern edge, a rope corralled a gathering of elves with pink noses, and sneezes sounded from within.

Dresnian followed Eslimil's gaze. "There is a plague on Beit. But it has not penetrated the forest."

Eslimil nodded at the sniffling elves. "What about them?"

"They returned from Beit, where they battled disturbing creatures. Hairless black gorillas with violet mist for eyes." He shook his head. "There were at least fifty of the monsters. But after we killed a few, they retreated."

Eslimil narrowed his eyes. "Retreated?"

"Well," Dresnian looked away, "they headed west at any rate."

"Black gorillas…" Eslimil tried to picture the beasts.

This is most disturbing, said Elgarroth. *I do not believe the portals of Lormin Dmurr are open. Selanna has not seen what he describes. Trannum must have opened another gate somehow. A powerful one, to allow so many through.*

"Eslimil?" Dresnian was frowning.

Eslimil looked at the cage. The occupants appeared to be commoners in their unimaginative, plain garb. Their hair was unkempt and their hands dirty, as if having put in years of hard work. "Where did you find your guests?"

The captain sneered at the prisoners. "*Beitians*. Thought they could invade our home."

"Did the gorillas drive them into the forest?"

"Does it matter?" Dresnian sniffed. "They can seek shelter from their own. They will not drag us into their war."

Eslimil eyed the captain. "A shadow passes over Vaeldor, and it will consume all that fail to stop it. Mark my words: this is a battle in need of all realms; human, dwarf, and elf."

Dresnian held a measuring gaze. "That is not up to me. The elders shall decide where our interests lie."

"Where is Wezlok?" Eslimil asked.

Dresnian's expression soured. "Gone. Rode into Beit with Palidurians!" He shook his head. "Ever since he aided the humans in their war two decades ago, he has not been the same."

"Careful." Eslimil raised a brow. "I would not want to be you if you are overheard uttering such things."

Dresnian paled, as if he had just seen a ghost. "I apologize."

"Palidurians, you say?" Eslimil inquired.

The captain scowled. "Yes. Vale was her name. A baby paladin."

Eslimil almost smirked. "Vayla?"

Dresnian nodded. "Thinks she will defeat the plague and the new Beitian king. Wezlok left with her yesterday."

Eslimil sighed. There was no time to waste. "Thank you, as always, for the conversation. I must take my leave."

Dresnian gave a firm nod. "Watch yourself. If you plan to enter Beit, the Death Fog rests just outside our border."

Eslimil turned to depart. "Think on my words. I shall return."

He left the village before mounting. After a slow, steady breath, he patted Landolice's neck. "How are we to survive this plague?"

It was not his steed that answered, but Elgarroth.

Follow the river north. Onzac remains free of the sickness.

Eslimil prayed the wizard's statement remained true once he arrived.

Riding quickly along the Shield River, Eslimil exited Maple Lore as evening arrived. He crossed the open field to the north, pausing between inhales, but the irritation that invaded his throat the last time never presented itself. This realization allowed him to breathe easier.

Night captured Beit as Onzac came into view. Half of the windows revealed torchlight, and the dark stones making up the walls and buildings made for a depressing scene. Across the river, Arbornum glowed in contrast, every window alive.

Eslimil turned west and rode beyond the range of the city watch before veering northwest. He continued until morning, picking up the pace as the heat of the rising sun touched his back. The plague remained absent, and no Beitians, gorillas, or anything else hampered his progress.

As dusk arrived the next evening, the sparse lights of Benzon dotted the horizon. Eslimil expected to see more of the tower windows aglow as he continued toward the northern end of the city, but it was not so. Benzon seemed almost lifeless. He then detected the unmistakable chill of a Death Lord, and his heart pounded in his chest.

Ease your mind, said Elgarroth. *Vayla and Wezlok will confront the undead king. I feel there to be something more. Something farther in the north.*

Eslimil's nerves calmed slightly with Elgarroth's words, and he pushed Landolice to pick up speed. As the few lights of Benzon dwindled into the south, he detected enormous shadows in the night. Smoky, violet eyes atop the shapes gave away their position, and he estimated there to be no less than fifty of the massive gorillas Dresnian mentioned. But the Lorian's description did not prepare Eslimil, and he found it hard to breathe. They made ogres seem small. One of their fists could pulverize him and Landolice in a single strike. An invisible essence, a feeling of true evil, oozed from their smooth, hairless bodies to churn Eslimil's stomach, and only the occasional shuffling of feet proved they were not statues. The scene made his head spin.

Continue north, said Elgarroth. *Remain unseen.*

The creatures seemed uninterested in everything around them, making the command an easy one to carry out. Eslimil averted his gaze and focused on the way ahead.

Only a mile existed between Benzon and the Icy Sea. The body of water normally reflected every light source, as glass-like ice constantly covered its shore, but something more twinkled in the distance. As Eslimil neared, he found a free standing arch ten feet from the massive lake. It stood twenty feet high and displayed a shimmering violet fog. A gate.

It is as I suspected, said Elgarroth. *The power of this gate is enough that I can sense it through you. You must find its key.*

What if more of those creatures come through? Eslimil asked.

From what you saw, I doubt it can sustain any more. You need to close it before it is too late.

Eslimil neared the portal and slowed. From his years with Elgarroth, he knew the gate would not function if the key was too far away. He dismounted.

The ground was hard, and a frozen breeze drifted from the north. Eslimil searched around the rocks and vegetation, but found nothing. He turned to the sea. The ice, normally pristine, bore a patch of jagged shards near the shore. It had been disturbed recently.

He raced to the water and discovered fresh ice covering the suspected area, roughly six inches in diameter. He pulled his dagger and began chipping. Though the surrounding ice was thick, Eslimil broke through after digging only half an inch. He plunged his bare hand into the hole, and the cold stung his flesh — it would not be long before it went numb. Feeling along the murky bottom, he touched something round and smooth, and withdrew it. Filling his palm was a pearl, the largest he had ever seen.

With the chill penetrating deep, Eslimil moved the gem to his other hand and ran to the portal. He tossed the pearl into the purple mist, and the glow of the haze shifted to gray. It swirled counterclockwise, pulling in a massive stream of air, and although the rushing wind drowned out all sound, Eslimil's clothing and hair danced as if caught in a mild breeze. Dozens of smoky representations of the gorillas rushed into the gate. A moment later, the wind ceased and the gray mist vanished. The arch was a freestanding window between Benzon and the Icy Sea.

It must be destroyed, said Elgarroth.

Eslimil nodded.

He was not strong like Vecnor, so he could not simply smash it. Looking at the sea, he extracted his rope. He tied one end to the side of the arch and the other to Landolice. The horse understood his intentions and pulled with all its might, toppling the arch and snapping it in half. Next, Eslimil had his mount drag the pieces to the

Icy Sea, and he put forth every ounce of his strength to roll them onto the frozen water. The heavy stone broke through and disappeared.

Very good. Elgarroth seemed calmer. *Now make haste to Lothen and join Vecnor.*

Panting from his labors, Eslimil wrapped his frozen hand in a rag and tucked it under his armor to gain some warmth. Once feeling returned, he climbed onto his saddle and headed west.

CHAPTER 37

THE ENEMY REVEALED

Vecnor followed the Path of the Guardians through the Stone Eagle Mountains. Upon reaching the stable-cave, he found several horses within, and immediately recognized Lilli and Dandi. How far ahead of him was Eraim? Also in the cave was a pouch with Vecnor's name on it. Elgarroth's doing, no doubt. A rolled parchment was inside, along with a small note from the wizard. The note read:

TAKE UMBARC TO THE BRIDGE
AND READ THE SCROLL

Vecnor took the scroll and departed. After reaching the two-foot-wide stone bridge, he unrolled the paper and read its words aloud. None of them made any sense, but once he completed the final syllable, the stone before him widened to five feet. He quickly led Umbarc across, unsure of how long the effect would last, and as they stepped onto the far side, the bridge reverted to its natural width.

Having his mount made for a swifter journey, and upon exiting the mountains the next morning, Vecnor spied a trail of rotting animal carcasses along the river. The poor creatures must have sensed something foul in the air and attempted to wash it from their systems with fresh water. Vecnor took Elgarroth's silence as a confirmation of the plague's absence, and he proceeded.

The fumes of decay stung his eyes and lungs. He pushed Umbarc northwest to Lothen Forest, but there was little relief from the odor after entering the woodland—Lothen held its share of scattered remains, though not nearly as many as the riverbank. As evening arrived, Vecnor camped beneath the trees, awaiting word from Elgarroth. It came while he ate dinner.

Remain where you are until Eslimil arrives. Selanna has witnessed something dire. Trannum used the key, and the portals are open. Uustaag has returned.

The air seemed to thin, and the pounding of Vecnor's heart filled his ears. How could this be?

Selanna will face resistance upon reaching Darum Carumbor, Elgarroth continued. *She and her companions are weary and will need your help.*

Darum Carumbor? So much for the tower being warded against evil occupation.

Vecnor found no sleep. He paced the forest floor, desperately awaiting Tux's arrival. At least Eraim was alive. But how had Uustaag returned? Was Trannum the master of the warlord now? Or was it the other way around?

Tux appeared in the middle of the night, obviously fatigued from long days of riding. From Eslimil's expression, he was aware of Elgarroth's discovery. He made no pleads for even a small break as Vecnor mounted, and they headed west.

Tux spoke of his experiences in Beit while they rode. Although it was only a matter of time before the Death Lords returned, news of the undead king in Benzon sent a chill down Vecnor's spine, nonetheless. The gorillas sounded fearsome indeed. At least Tux had been able to close the gate. It was bad enough Vayla faced a Death Lord without adding strange monsters to the situation. Vecnor prayed Wezlok kept her safe.

The thickets didn't allow for a quick pace, and the horses worked hard, receiving only a short break to drink from a stream as the forest illuminated with the dawn. Morning ended while they pressed on, and the afternoon sun reached its apex and began its descent. As the undergrowth thinned, Tux pulled Landolice to a halt.

"Armored horses," said the elf.

Vecnor urged Umbarc forward while Tux disappeared to the northwest. The trees spread out, allowing the horse to pick up speed, and the end of the woodland approached. As the field outside Darum Carumbor came into view, Vecnor spied several mounted warriors in dark armor charging Eraim, Selanna, and a marteese woman. The half-elf wore a golden breastplate and held a matching sword. All three appeared haggard, their cloaks tattered, hair singed, and faces streaked with filth.

Joy at seeing Eraim lasted only seconds. Evil surrounded her and her friends, and the threat stirred a fire in Vecnor's stomach. He donned his helmet and emerged from the trees at last. Eraim spotted him, and she rushed him with her tiny sword—such courage! Vecnor's heart lightened when she slowed and shouted his name. He outstretched his free hand to lift her onto the saddle as he rode past.

Without losing a step, Umbarc carried them to the battle. Vecnor's blade and Tux's arrows helped to rout the warriors, at least for the time being, and Selanna joined Vecnor and Eraim on his massive steed. The marteese, who Vecnor learned to be Kiryanna, sat atop an enemy horse. They hastened to the forest's edge, where Tux awaited, and it surprised Vecnor to see Eraim's disgust for the legendary elf. The tower, meanwhile, issued another wave of soldiers.

Having no trust for the enemy-trained mount, Vecnor insisted Kiryanna release the animal and join Tux on Landolice. The marteese complied, but not before swearing to return for Brem. Vecnor had forgotten about the priest of Frayorna, and his mind drifted to Romik, Baylun, Desser, and Daymyn. He prayed they all remained safe.

There was no pursuit while they made their way through the forest, and they continued until dusk. It was then that a chill enveloped the trees, a sensation Vecnor had not felt since his battle with Gruzim. A Death Lord flew overhead, shaking the branches of Lothen, but the bone dragon did not slow, and the air warmed as the distance between them grew.

"I was wondering when they would arrive," muttered Selanna.

"We best move a bit farther," Vecnor said. "If the Death Lords are arriving, it's only a matter of time before the dunarchins follow."

"Dunarchins?" Eraim stared at Vecnor, her face pale.

The little elf's bravery through the worst of odds never failed to amaze Vecnor. Still, she recognized fear. He winked, hoping to grant her some comfort, but her darting eyes proved it an impossible task.

They rode farther, and fatigue deepened on the maidens' weary faces as the night grew late. Though Tux would have preferred to continue, the half-gray elf confirming this with a headshake, Vecnor halted. He didn't make a habit of ignoring his companion, but on this occasion, he dismounted and pulled blankets from Umbarc's packs. He could feel Tux's sigh as the elf accepted the decision. While Vecnor prepared the campsite in the darkness, Eraim approached.

"Are you a human?" She had obviously moved past the fear that recently drained her face of blood. "Or an elf?"

"What is that supposed to mean?"

Eraim produced one of her impish grins—Vecnor loved those smiles. "Nothing. But I am never sure if I address Vecnor the human, or the wood chopping—"

A rush of air penetrated the forest, returning Eraim's ashen complexion. Vecnor detected faint screams riding on the wind, and from Tux's expression, the elf heard them too. They both moved toward their horses.

Selanna raised her arms. "Hold!" The gust tossed her robes and hair about, adding to her already haggard appearance. She closed her eyes, and upon opening them, she said, "They want us to follow them."

Vecnor reached for one of his swords. "Who?"

"I am not sure," Selanna replied. "But they did not lead us astray the first time. We must go before they vanish."

Vecnor didn't trust this wind. But as Selanna ran off, what choice was there? He grabbed as many blankets as he could and pursued the mage.

Selanna led them north at a running pace, and Umbarc and Landolice followed. When she halted at last, the wind intensified, causing the trees to dance. The air then abruptly calmed.

"We are safe here," said Selanna. "We must sleep."

The notion of stopping to rest no longer seemed a good idea, and Tux's level gaze revealed the half-gray elf to be equally concerned. But Vecnor conceded—the maidens needed the break. He supplied food from his packs while Tux climbed a nearby tree, and once everyone was settled, Vecnor pulled a sword and left to walk the perimeter. He didn't make it far when Eraim's voice halted him.

"Vecnor?"

He paid her only a glance before turning back to the forest. If he stared longer, he might not have the strength to resist her charms. Even in her raggedy state, she was beautiful. "It's good to see you," he said.

"It has been too long… as usual." She frowned. "But I must ask you about Tux. Do you *know* him?"

Of course she had questions about Tux. It was obvious in her doubtful stare at the edge of Lothen. Vecnor nodded. "I've known him for some time. Don't worry. You can trust him."

"But is it really *him*?"

He grinned to one side and looked back. "The legend himself."

Her frown deepened. "But the tales are old. And he appears as young as I."

Vecnor shrugged, hoping he had not said too much.

"Then again," Eraim wore another one of her grins, "age probably holds little meaning for you."

Vecnor needed to guard his response. Too often she made him slip; swayed him into uttering things he ought not to. He furrowed his brow, as if considering her comment about Tux. "I've never put much thought to it. All elves appear young to me."

That should do the trick.

She held a wry smile. "Of course." She then returned to her line of questioning. "What *is* he? He appears as one from Orlenfel. But he is shorter, like my kin."

"He's both."

Eraim stared, as if he were mad.

"Take my word for it. Tux is trustworthy." Vecnor smirked to lighten the mood. "Now, you really should get some sleep."

"All right." She turned away. "But if you hear anything, you are to wake me. I do not want you getting in over your head."

Her tone carried a serious note Vecnor was unused to.

She shot him another glance. "And we are not finished with this conversation."

He opened his mouth. Eraim had earned an explanation. But the vow of secrecy held, and he gave a single nod.

She headed to her blanket.

An hour passed, and Vecnor returned to see Eraim, Selanna, and Kiryanna fast asleep. They looked tiny and helpless on their blankets. He felt pity for what they must have endured, and he imagined the worst. Trannum and Uustaag... The maidens were lucky to be alive.

"Kiryanna is a wild spirit," said Tux.

Though Vecnor didn't flinch from his companion's sudden appearance next to him, his heart jumped into his throat. "She is at that."

"Do you know this Brem they spoke of?"

Vecnor shook his head. "Only in conversation. He is a respected priest of Frayorna."

Tux grinned. "Mother of Nature. The greatest of all human gods." The smile faded. "Do you think the marteese really means to return alone?"

Vecnor thought for a moment. "I doubt Selanna will allow that to happen. She'll find a way to make Kiryanna see the folly of such an action."

Tux raised a brow. "Dare I believe you have found respect for the silly mage?"

Vecnor released a small chuckle. "She has her moments."

"What about the boys left behind?" Tux frowned. "You know some of them, do you not?"

Vecnor sighed. "I know their parents. And my heart goes out to them. They have endured too much loss already."

Tux nodded. "Well, I best get back to my post." He sprung into the air, grabbing hold of a branch fifteen feet overhead, and somersaulted before disappearing among the branches.

Vecnor sat against a tree. With his sword resting across his lap, he closed his eyes and allowed his senses to keep guard.

***

Vecnor's eyes snapped open. Selanna had released a gasp. With a bewildered look, she searched the trees.

"What is it?" Vecnor tightened the grip on his weapon as he scanned the area.

Eraim rose with Mithkahr in hand. The blade did not glow, so no evil was near. Kiryanna also awoke, and Tux dropped from above. All attention focused on Selanna. The mage shook her head, and everyone relaxed, though only slightly.

Selanna's eyes shifted to the ground next to her. "We are not safe here any longer," she said, without looking away from whatever held her interest. "Do not ask me how I know, for I do not think you would believe me. But our protection has diminished."

She moved from atop her blanket and placed it over what appeared to be a stick. She then wrapped the item in the cloth and stuffed it into one of Umbarc's saddlebags.

Vecnor waited until she finished, deciding it best not to pose any questions. "Let's go."

They rode through the remainder of the night and exited the forest an hour after sunrise. The river was then before them, and they proceeded south amid the odor of rotting animals. Shortly after, Eraim hissed a warning.

"Mees!"

Something approached from the north.

"A score of horses," Tux said. "But only half bear riders."

The horsemen slowed, and Vecnor pulled one of his swords while Eraim and Tux fitted arrows to their bowstrings. Eraim then announced another observation.

"Wezlok?"

Vecnor squinted. His vision didn't travel far enough.

Eraim lowered her brow. "Vayla?"

Vecnor breathed a sigh of relief and relaxed the grip on his weapon. Vayla was alive.

The two groups met, and Vecnor saw Vayla and her companions clearly. The paladin rode at the lead with a look of determination. Next to her, Wezlok appeared as he did many years ago when helping Merssa retrieve the orb in Andria: emotionless. The soldiers riding behind them all bore wounds. Vecnor recognized Macurak from New Palidur, and a warrior dressed in Beitian garb and a chain shirt held a scowl. The latter was obviously a Beitian.

After a brief conversation between Eraim, Selanna, and Vayla, they joined forces. Selanna and Kiryanna borrowed a couple of the spare mounts Vayla had in tow while Eraim remained upon Umbarc. The small elf's decision stirred deep feelings in the pit of Vecnor's stomach once again, though he couldn't show it. Vayla stared quizzically at him and Eraim, but the paladin's gaze didn't last long.

They continued to the mountains at a decent pace. As they neared the waterfall, Eraim turned to Vecnor.

"We need to release the horses," she said softly, her eyes filled with pity. "I am sorry."

Release the horses? The thought of Umbarc trapped in Beit consumed Vecnor with dread. Perhaps the scroll Elgarroth supplied to expand the bridge would work again. But how could he bring it up without rousing suspicion from Eraim?

Do not worry about Umbarc, Elgarroth said. *I will guide him.*

A weight lifted from Vecnor's shoulders, and he smiled at Eraim. "Umbarc will be fine."

He pulled his mount to a halt, and the others did the same. Eraim then explained that the way ahead was not for horses, and though Vecnor assured Vayla Umbarc would lead her treasured mare back to her, the paladin refused to part with the animal. Wezlok spoke for the first time since the union of their companies, insisting he would take care of the situation. Selanna relented.

Vecnor trusted Elgarroth. Still, a touch of fear for Umbarc entered his heart as the steed led the other horses into the wilds of Beit. Was the plague truly gone? Did walking corpses infest the realm? Eslimil seemed unconcerned for Landolice's safety, and Vecnor pushed the thoughts from his mind. Elgarroth had never steered him wrong before.

They continued south with Vayla leading her mount, a Batorn mare named Star. The sun set shortly after they scaled the side of the waterfall, and they followed the Path of the Guardians beneath Selanna's magical lights until reaching the first campsite.

The presence of the horse cramped the area, but there was sufficient room. To one side were Vayla's holy soldiers, speaking softly among themselves, except for Macurak. The Palidurian was pallid, and perspiration on his forehead defied the cool breeze. Kiryanna sat between Macurak and Selanna while the mage used her finger to conjure flame and bring life to a pile of firewood. Apart from everyone stood the Beitian, maintaining a sour look. Or was the man pouting? Tux was atop a boulder inspecting his arrows, and Eraim walked away from the half-gray elf's pack with a grin splitting her pretty, dirt-smeared face. In her hand were healing herbs surely procured from Eslimil's stock. If Tux had noticed her pilfering the supply, he didn't show it.

With a smirk, Vecnor pulled enough food for everyone from his bags, and he joined Selanna while watching Eraim deliver the herbs to Vayla. The small elf and the paladin shared a conversation he could not hear, but from the gestures, Eraim imparted directions for using the plants—unicorn's blood, they were called. Vayla listened, revealing not a single scowl, then retrieved a bowl from Star and went to work. It was like seeing Merssa…

Upon completion of her task, Vayla moved from soldier to soldier, administering the healing concoction. She visited Macurak last, and Vecnor caught sight of a nasty gash along the soldier's side. After tending to the wound, Vayla eased Macurak onto a blanket and fed him from Vecnor's rations. She then procured some food for herself and wandered to the southern edge of the camp.

Once everyone was eating, Vecnor helped himself to a generous portion. While he ate, it was Selanna's turn to converse with Vayla. The paladin had every one of Merssa's facial expressions mastered, exhibiting interest, remorse, and annoyance, the latter taking control when Eraim joined the little party. Shortly after, Eraim uttered Vecnor's name, and Vayla gazed at him with disbelief.

Vayla and the elves shifted to other matters, and their eyes moved about the campsite as each was informally introduced to those they didn't know. Vecnor heard mention of the Beitian being a general of Zurzak. Burnod was the man's name, and there was no trusting the soldier's repulsive countenance, his red mustache curled into loops, nor the way he chewed his food like a cow grinding a cud. Vecnor inhaled deeply to expel the thoughts—it wasn't his place. Eraim and Selanna then appeared to tease Vayla about something. Macurak? It was time Vecnor rescued the paladin.

"Selanna!" he bellowed. "When will you share with us the item you took from Lothen?"

After a moment of shock, the mage closed her mouth and went to the packs Vecnor had removed from Umbarc before releasing the animal. Everyone watched as Selanna pulled the blanket she had wrapped around the item, and she carefully unrolled it a few feet from the fire to reveal a black stick.

Just a stick? There was nothing more to it?

"What is it?" asked the angry marteese. Kiryanna's glare seemed a permanent feature.

Selanna frowned. "I do not know. I suspect it is a key. Trannum used it in Lormin Dmurr."

It must be the key Elgarroth mentioned. But there were three gates…

"One key for multiple gates?" Vecnor spoke his thought aloud. "Is that possible?" he added, trying to cover up the utterance.

"I did not believe it to be so." Selanna sighed. "But—" She turned to Vecnor. "How did you know about the gates?"

He shrugged. "Someone must have mentioned them."

It was a lame attempt, and Selanna wasn't buying it.

"Lormin Dmurr?" Vayla stole the mage's attention.

Selanna studied the paladin before responding. "We shall speak of that later. As for the stick, it is a key Trannum used to open three portals. I did not think it was possible that a single key could create multiple gates," she glanced at Vecnor, "but I also have doubts as to where this item has come from. I hesitate to touch it."

"Who was the krukari?" asked Kiryanna. "The one who chased us across the bridge? The one standing twenty feet tall?"

Vecnor forced himself to show no reaction. He still hoped Elgarroth was mistaken about Uustaag.

"It was only twelve feet," mumbled Eraim.

Vayla frowned at Selanna. "Krukari?"

"And how is it that Trannum is still alive?" Kiryanna split an accusatory glare between the mage and Eraim. "I thought you two destroyed him."

Selanna nodded, her cheeks flushed. She was growing frustrated. "Indeed. But then there is the final verse of Seac's Prophecy."

"*Power shatters, dust does fall; Eyes open in shadowy hall,*" Eraim recited.

"They were Trannum's eyes." Selanna looked at the fire. "I know not how, but he has survived." She turned to Eraim. "I am not even sure it was Trannum you destroyed."

Eraim spun on Vecnor with her fists on her hips. "Did you know?"

Vecnor put up his hand in defense. "I wasn't there."

Eraim's face reddened. "That is no answer! You are not Elgarroth!"

Vecnor had never been on her bad side before. He didn't like it.

"We need more minds on this," said Selanna.

"What about Elgarroth?" asked Eraim, instantly converting from inquisitor to her beautiful self.

"Apparently we can't get answers from *him*," Vecnor muttered, receiving another glare from the small elf.

"He has been hard to track down as of late," Selanna said. "I doubt he is home." Her eyes drifted to Tux at the edge of the camp, who gave a slight shake of the head.

So many questions. So much uncertainty. With the expressions surrounding the fire, the whole campsite would be up all night. They needed sleep.

"We best get some rest," Vecnor said. "There is still a distance to travel."

No one argued, although Vayla's suspicious glare for Selanna lasted several more seconds. Everyone then found their places to get as comfortable as was possible.

❈ ❈ ❈

Vecnor awoke to Tux's hand on his shoulder. It was late. The elf had disappeared hours ago to guard against intruders, though it was an unlikely event. Eslimil returned to the shadows as Vecnor assumed that duty.

The night was cool and quiet. Vecnor wandered about the campsite for the first hour, careful not to wake the others, and his eyes often drifted to Eraim and Vayla.

Eraim's hand rested on the handle of Mithkahr. Though Vecnor understood her frustrations, he did not enjoy being the target of her heated words. She had worked tirelessly over the past couple of decades, attempting to uncover his association with Elgarroth. It pained Vecnor that her prying made it difficult to spend time with her. But it was for the best.

Vayla slept peacefully, and in the moonlight she looked like an angel. Vecnor wished terribly to turn her away from the impending danger; to have her live on a farm or work in a church in some far off place. What would Merssa say if he allowed her granddaughter to perish at the hands of the same enemy that claimed her life? Surely, the old paladin was watching.

It was twilight when Kiryanna arose. Vecnor sat against one of the many boulders encircling the campsite. The marteese was fierce; there was no doubting that after seeing her fight outside Darum Carumbor. Vecnor didn't blame her for wanting to return to Helmland. If he could, he would go with her to rescue Romik and the others. Kiryanna gave Vecnor a nod, and she pulled her golden sword and retrieved a whetstone from her pack.

Vayla stood, and she quietly checked on Macurak's wound. The soldier awoke while she changed his bandage. Vayla said something, and Macurak smiled and nodded. Vecnor recognized that smile. The man was in love with her. Did she know? Dellen came to mind, and the captain's death within the jaws of the demon Hezeb while defending Merssa. Hopefully, Macurak didn't meet the same fate.

With a stern expression, Vayla approached Vecnor. "I have been told you defeated a Death Lord single-handedly. Is that true?"

That was blunt. She had that part of Merssa's personality covered as well.

"Do you always say what comes to mind?" Vecnor raised a brow. "I suppose you would. That's the way—"

"Yes, I know!" Her countenance chased away all traces of the angelic glow the moon had provided. "You obviously knew my grandmother!"

"I was *going* to say that's the way of paladins." Vecnor did nothing to hold back his smirk, and her scowl deepened. After that, he couldn't help himself. "But now that you mention it—"

Vayla stomped off, speaking loud enough to stir the rest of the camp. "When do we depart?"

Everyone readied, and they moved on to the narrow bridge crossing the gorge. It was obvious Vayla was unaware of its presence by the anxiety-filled tone she used.

"How are we to cross that?"

Vecnor chuckled. "Very carefully."

She didn't appear to appreciate his humor, and it took all of his self-control not to laugh harder.

Vayla, Star, and Wezlok were soon the only ones on the far side, and the Lorian summoned magic to float Vayla's mare across. It was touching. Elgarroth had informed Vecnor of Wezlok's altered outlook on life since Merssa's sacrifice during the Necromancer War, and the elf's assistance was surely due to that transformation.

They arrived next at the cave stabling the horses Eraim and her group had left behind. Everyone mounted up, and the journey became easier. The following night, jealousy tugged at Vecnor as Eraim conversed with Tux away from the fire while they camped. Why? It seemed a silly reaction. As always, he quashed the feeling, focusing instead on the hope Eraim was now accepting of Tux's identity. Once their meeting ended, she returned to the campfire and sat beside Vecnor.

"Am I a legend?" she asked.

Vecnor grinned. "You are to me."

Her ensuing smile nearly caused him to melt.

The company journeyed several days more to Tikken City. Before approaching the gates, Tux gave Vecnor a nod, and the half-gray elf lagged behind until disappearing altogether. No one seemed to notice.

They arrived at the Council Building, and it didn't surprise Vecnor to see Elgarroth in the audience chamber. Ten wizards sat upon their thrones, the middle chair empty, and the meeting began. Selanna talked about her journeys into Beit, Lothen Forest, Darum

Carumbor, and Lormin Dmurr. After describing the opening of the gates and the emergence of the krukari, Elgarroth spoke.

"It seems Uustaag has returned."

Several statements and questions followed as fear enveloped the room. Vecnor swallowed all emotion, refusing to let it consume him. Uustaag had been defeated before, and there was no choice but to perform that task again. The next step was to figure out how to accomplish the feat, but until everyone moved beyond the shock and hope that Elgarroth was wrong, that step could not be taken. As that reality sank in, the conference concluded with Vayla speaking in Merssa-like fashion.

"The problem is that Uustaag has returned, Trannum is not dead, Helmland and Beit are massing their forces, and Vaeldor lacks a proper Seer!" Her final point was aimed at Fenreil, the new Seer, who joined the meeting late and offered no additional wisdom.

Vecnor withheld his chuckle, but couldn't contain his smirk. Selanna supported the paladin's opinion after Vayla and the holy soldiers exited, and she, too, led her company from the room. After a nod from Elgarroth, Vecnor followed them toward the Council stables.

Selanna thought aloud while they traversed the hallways, wrapping her mind around the situation. Upon reaching the rear door of the building, she spun on Vecnor.

"Can we count on you for counsel? Or do you plan to disappear for another ten years?"

Vecnor was at a loss. Luckily, Elgarroth was listening.

Go with them.

"I am at your disposal." Vecnor bowed to the mage.

"Good." Selanna looked around the corridor. "Where is Tux?"

Eraim shrugged, seemingly not surprised by Tux's absence. Vecnor said nothing.

Selanna pursed her lips. She then instructed everyone to meet at The Jeweled Scabbard, a fine establishment on the southern edge of town. Vecnor had eaten several meals there many years ago with

Dellen, captain of the city watch at the time. Selanna gave them an hour to prepare before the meeting was to begin.

Vecnor had planned on finding Tux, but then Eraim joined him. So instead of visiting places his companion frequented when passing time, Vecnor walked aimlessly, trying to think of things to pretend to be doing.

"I cannot believe the Ancient Enemy is back," Eraim said while they wandered. "And Trannum, too? It is not fair."

"Fair?" Vecnor furrowed his brow. "Since when is evil fair?"

"That is not the point," she retorted. "We destroyed Trannum —"

"*You* destroyed Trannum." Vecnor preferred she take credit for her actions. Even though Tux assisted her, it was her idea that another orb existed.

Eraim looked up with a frown. "I am still not sure that was completely my doing." She narrowed her eyes. "And do not think I have not noticed the similarity between the arrow I used, an arrow I was certain I did not possess, and those in Tux's quiver."

"So… Tux was there?"

Eraim twisted her lips. "I doubt that. But he obviously gets them from Elgarroth. I suspect the wizard put it there." She gazed up again. "Have you ever seen arrows like that in Elgarroth's cottage?"

Vecnor chuckled. Another attempt to catch him off guard. "I'd be surprised if that tiny cabin has more than a single room in it."

Eraim rolled her eyes.

Vecnor entered a shop to buy a whetstone. It was a frivolous purchase, since his swords never needed sharpening. But there was little else he could think of to do. He also purchased a small knife, oil, and soap. Eraim inspected each item, and replaced his knife choice for another before he paid.

"Is this what you do when you disappear?" she asked once they returned to the street. "Buy trivial equipment?"

Vecnor shrugged. "Everyone needs trivial equipment."

"Staying away so long is rude." Her tone became serious as she changed the subject. "You cannot ride around saving people, making friends, and then vanish for a decade or two."

"You seem to have gotten along just fine."

She glared at him. "It is mean. What if someone grew attached to you? And missed you terribly? I am sure someone like that could keep your secrets."

Her words touched him. But they weren't his secrets to tell. Lacking any more clever responses, he said, "I think our hour is up."

Eraim sighed. "Yes. We should head to The Jeweled Scabbard."

Upon reaching the tavern, a barmaid informed Eraim where to find Selanna, and she headed toward the door indicated. Vecnor followed, but a couple of elderly patrons delayed him. The retired soldiers recalled Vecnor from the days of the undead invasion.

"My, you haven't aged a day!" one beamed. "You must let me buy you a drink."

Eraim entered the private dining chamber.

"Sorry, my good man," said Vecnor. "Another time."

The veteran grinned. "I'll hold you to that."

The gentlemen clasped arms with Vecnor before allowing him to proceed.

Kiryanna's glare greeted Vecnor as he stepped into the small room. "You're late!" she scolded.

Though her tone and the daggers issuing from her eyes were daunting, Vecnor fought back a laugh. The marteese's passion was admirable.

"My apologies." Vecnor bowed and took a seat next to Selanna, where a tall mug of beer awaited.

A knock fell on the door. To Vecnor's relief, it was Elgarroth. Vecnor wasn't certain how much he could share.

"You're late!" Kiryanna said to the wizard.

The meeting began. Vecnor listened while they discussed things he already knew, including the final verse of Seac's Prophecy of Trannum. Elgarroth divulged additional information afterward, enough to prod Eraim and Selanna in the right direction, and as usual, Eraim deduced where they needed to go next.

"Rorbak?" she asked the room.

Elgarroth then led Selanna to think on the prophecy he claimed to be swimming about her mind—a swirling mist of words and images she couldn't quite pull together. They were verses Elgarroth had been relying heavily upon lately. Selanna focused, and she slowly recited the entire prophecy for all to hear. Once finished, Vecnor realized it was to be the night Elgarroth revealed her destiny to her. Big changes were coming.

They broke the prophecy apart, figuring out which verses had already transpired so they might determine what was yet to come. Vecnor offered help, but he didn't provide any significant insight. He mainly reminded everyone he was there. The conversation turned to the black stick, and Selanna set the item on the table. It was perfectly smooth, but otherwise unremarkable.

"Trannum used this to open the three gates," she said to Elgarroth. "But does not every gate need a key unique unto itself?"

Elgarroth explained that the stick was not from Vaeldor, but from another world. The world of Thard'Dun. It was Uustaag's tool, intended to join the Dark Realm to Vaeldor so the evil deity might spread His reach and grow in power. This was news even to Vecnor, as was Welmirth's knowledge of the key and the fact that the ancient wizard had hid it from the enemy. And of all locations, Welmirth placed it on the very doorstep of Helmland. A risky decision. Why not the Arman Forest? A place where nothing could be found, and no one could exit once having entered—no one but seers? Vecnor would have to ask Elgarroth that question.

More discussions about the key followed. According to Elgarroth, it was the item Thard'Dun used to rescue Uustaag when Welmirth and Vennimor defeated the krukari and his army of monsters. And Uustaag wanted it back.

Selanna reasoned they should return the stick to Lormin Dmurr and cast it through the portal Uustaag emerged from, to send the warlord back. Her fear allowed her to overlook the obvious, and Vecnor pointed it out.

"But what of the other gates? Do we allow whatever lies on the other side free rein into Vaeldor?"

Her folly showed in her eyes, and her shoulders slumped.

The meeting continued, and Vecnor learned the portals were not mere gates as he understood them. Elgarroth called them openings, as he had back in Vermallon. And apparently, they did not follow the same rules. In the end, a different method was necessary to close them, and even Elgarroth didn't know that procedure. He would return to Welmirth's journals to learn more.

In conclusion, they pieced together that without the black stick, Uustaag was bound to Lormin Dmurr. They understood hunting parties would search for the key, and that whomever carried it was in constant danger. Vecnor wished to volunteer, but Elgarroth would never allow that to happen. Selanna kept it, and dread filled Eraim's eyes.

Kiryanna stated her desire to return to Helmland, a notion that was dismissed. They could not do so until they were ready to confront Trannum and Uustaag, and the rescue of those left behind would have to wait. It was also decided that a second expedition into Trannum's crypt among the rorbak was necessary, in hopes of finding a way to defeat the necromancer. Elgarroth would work on the rest. Vecnor desperately hoped to accompany Eraim and Selanna into the crypt, but that was not his choice to make.

"We must also spread word," he said, to remind everyone of the wider perspective. "The kingdoms of Vaeldor need to know what is coming. Especially the realms of Virch and Harbnum."

Selanna's expression was grim. "But it will not be like last time. Merssa is not here to lead us."

How true those words were. Could Vayla capture that element of Merssa's personality, as she had so many others?

Selanna sighed. "As much as my heart wishes it to be so, Vayla is not her."

Evidently, Selanna didn't believe so.

"I only pray Montac can unite the kingdoms," the mage added. She looked from Vecnor to Elgarroth. "And we cannot assume the enemy will sit idle for years while we arrange a coordinated attack. They may very well strike first. So the realms must rally soon."

Vecnor agreed. Perhaps Selanna was better prepared to guide the world than he previously believed. "I'll spread the word," he said. "Most kings will listen to me."

The meeting adjourned, and Vecnor, Eraim, and Kiryanna walked to the stables to gather the horses. Selanna remained with Elgarroth, where Vecnor was sure she would learn things about herself.

The night was pleasant and the stars sparkled, but Vecnor sensed the weight of the Shadow on his shoulders. From Eraim's lack of conversation, the small elf certainly felt the same way. Kiryanna also said nothing, and Vecnor detected worry in her eyes. Did she use anger to mask her true feelings?

Upon returning with the mounts, Selanna appeared occupied. The mage was processing information Elgarroth shared in the company's absence. How would this affect her relationship with Eraim?

While Elgarroth exited Tikken City, Vecnor rode with the others toward the northern gate. As they neared, Selanna announced they would stay the night and get a fresh start come morning, but Vecnor sensed there to be more on her mind. She still struggled with Elgarroth's news and searched for a way to explain some aspect of it to Eraim.

"I must be off if I'm to enter every realm," Vecnor said. "The sooner the kings and queens are aware of the approaching evil, the better."

Selanna seemed disappointed. Kiryanna either did not hear his words, or she didn't care. Eraim's eyes moistened. With a lump in his throat, Vecnor urged the horse he had ridden from the Stone Eagle

Mountains toward the gate. As he reached the large wooden doors, Elgarroth spoke.

Do not stray far. Eraim shall join you in your journey.

Vecnor pulled the mount to a stop. So he would actually have to ride to *every* realm? He had counted on Tux to share in that task. A grin stretched to one side. At least he would be in good company.

The next morning, Eraim smiled from ear to ear upon finding Vecnor eating breakfast in the tavern.

"Excellent," said Selanna. "You are still here." She appeared conflicted, as if unsure of how to convey what she wished to say. "I have somewhere I must go alone." She glanced at Eraim's confused expression and back to Vecnor. "Could Eraim accompany you for a time?"

Eraim's perplexion evolved into a hopeful smile.

Vecnor chuckled. "I couldn't think of a better way to tour Vaeldor."

"What about me?" asked Kiryanna.

Selanna considered the marteese. "You should remain here."

She nodded to Eraim, who dug into a pouch and extracted a few gemstones.

"These should sustain you," Selanna added as Eraim placed them on the table. "And I promise we will return soon and set things to right."

Kiryanna shook her head at the stones. She scooped them up and headed for the door.

"You do not think she will go without us, do you?" Eraim asked Selanna.

"There is no way to know for sure," the mage replied. "I can only pray she sees reason."

As Kiryanna exited, Vecnor caught the slightest glimpse of a figure cloaked in black following her. Tux would make certain she stayed put.

Chapter 38

Stroll Across the Realms

The weather was fair when Vecnor and Eraim left Tikken City. Umbarc was yet absent, and Vecnor continued riding the horse from the stable-cave of the Path of the Guardians. Though a fine breed, it wasn't what he was used to, and he yearned for his mount's return.

Eraim decided they would first speak with King Merdain of Moclen. The castle was less than a day's ride, so it was the obvious choice. Eraim smiled often as they passed the time with small talk about places she had been over the past twenty years and things she had seen. One tale involved a recent visit from a Dakreal elf to Dominelli, an arrogant male boasting of the quality of life for denizens of the forest in Philen being superior to those of Salenti elves. Eraim took everything the elf owned while he slept, including his horse, to teach him a lesson about bragging. Though some of her words were hard to decipher through her giggles, Vecnor followed the story, for Tux had already shared much of it with him. The half-gray elf had been in Dominelli to spy on Selanna, and witnessed most of the affair before being called away to watch for the Shadow at New Palidur.

Upon reaching the castle, King Merdain received them without delay. Vecnor had never met the king before, but the young ruler was receptive and listened carefully to what he said. In the end, Merdain promised the soldiers of Moclen would be ready when the time came.

Vecnor and Eraim then headed into Fendora to speak to Queen Helni. During the first day's ride, Vecnor found no harm in touching on a few comical times from his youth. He mentioned his early growth spurt, and how awkward he was for nearly a year.

"I could barely swing a sword," he said once Eraim's laughter paused long enough to get the words in.

"I am still trying to imagine you that thin!" Her hysterics began anew.

On the second day, they rounded Queen Arman Lake, and Eraim regaled Vecnor with her expedition through Tenvale several decades ago, when she played the part of a handmaiden to Selanna. She and Selanna had traversed the Wizard Kingdom with Arkor, Rholmar, Ladonia, and Nilborg to claim one of Trannum's orbs, and it ended in a battle bringing about the death of a wizard named Solett. But Eraim focused only on the journey, and bounced from made-up accent to made-up accent while telling it from her "handmaiden" point of view.

The weather remained pleasant as the next two days sped by, and they reached the queen's castle. Just as the Moclen king, the Fendora monarch had never met Vecnor, but knew of his reputation and showed respect. Queen Helni responded in the same manner as King Merdain, more or less. She exhibited disbelief, followed by ire, followed by fear and more disbelief. After receiving a promise of soldiers, Vecnor and Eraim headed for Philen.

"Was growing up in Kalmaar difficult?" Eraim asked.

Vecnor never told her where he grew up. She was very astute. "Growing up anywhere is hard."

Eraim momentarily twisted her lips in a sarcastic grin. "Not in Dominelli. It is a wonderful place full of friends, animals, love, and laughter."

"And Salenti elves," added Vecnor, still seeing Eraim as one very different from her kin.

She tilted her head with mock offense, eyeing Vecnor—he sat much higher than she, even on the normal horse. "Do not make fun of my home! You have never been there!" She looked forward. "At least, not as far as I know. Maybe if we had a bigger need for firewood…" she muttered the last part.

Vecnor chuckled. "Salenti elves probably can't swing a proper axe."

They stopped in West Palidur, and Eraim insisted on accepting a dinner invitation from Magneer and Gruelenor. Nidor was present when they arrived, in town for a visit. Of the three, Nidor was most pleased to see Vecnor and gave him an embrace. It was the hardest squeeze Vecnor had ever received. Eraim remained quiet and her demeanor humorless. As they sat to the meal, she broke the news of the boys that were left behind, and the return of evil. Magneer's glare was rife with anger and fear. Gruelenor stirred, the krukari's face unreadable. Nidor's eyes dropped to the table.

"Why were they in Helmland?" demanded Magneer. "They were supposed to be on a blasted hunting trip."

Nidor faced the ranger. "This is most grievous news. But take heart. When I arrived, I told you I felt a need to come here. It is clear Silcor sent me for this reason. If Trannum is truly behind this, and… Uustaag… has returned," he had the slightest difficulty uttering the warlord's name, "we must oppose them."

Magneer's expression remained unchanged. A flicker of hope entered Gruelenor's eyes.

Nidor turned to Eraim. "When do we leave?"

"Um…" Eraim looked at Vecnor. "We… uh… We begin in two months. But not in Helmland. There is a task we must first perform in the Stone Eagle Mountains."

"What?" Magneer's cheeks flushed.

"It is a place your father had journeyed with us," Eraim said to the ranger.

Magneer's frown deepened. "Trannum's crypt?"

"He told you?" Eraim seemed surprised. "Well… yes. Selanna feels something is there that might help us defeat Trannum."

Magneer's face reddened. "But Trannum doesn't have my son!"

"We do not know that for a fact." Eraim's shoulders slumped. "I am very sorry we allowed them to accompany us. But we had no way of knowing what the future held."

"And it's a good thing they entered Helmland," Vecnor added, disliking Magneer's anger toward Eraim. "Otherwise, evil would be gathering in secret."

"This is correct," said Nidor. "As painful as it is to know your sons and nephews are in that gods-forsaken place, do not lose sight of the larger issue. We have seen what Trannum is capable of. If this crypt can provide us an advantage, we must seize it."

It had been too long since Vecnor enjoyed Nidor's company. The barbarian paladin was wise beyond his years and radiated goodness. Perhaps Selanna would choose the Dale as her second champion after taking Elgarroth's role as Seer. She could do much worse.

Magneer was unconvinced.

"It is something we *must* do first," Eraim insisted. "Until then, there is no hope of saving Desser or any of the others."

Was Eraim lying? Or had she been informed the young ranger was alive?

Magneer's eyes softened and brimmed with tears. "If that is the case, I shall be ready."

"Why two months?" Gruelenor's voice was more gravelly than Vecnor remembered.

"We must first spread word to the realms," Eraim replied. "They need to know what lies on the horizon so another allied army can be mustered. We will then meet in Vol Maren, and Selanna will be there."

Magneer appeared as though he wished to say something, but as his eyes moved to Vecnor, his mouth closed. It was likely unpleasant or unproductive. Probably both.

"I have it on good authority that your boys are alive," Eraim added quickly, as if to appease the ranger. "And this is the only hope of rescuing them."

Magneer sat back. Gruelenor sighed. Nidor nodded, ever respectfully.

"We will inform King Rybex," said Gruelenor of the Philen king. "That should help move things along."

Vecnor couldn't imagine Gruelenor being welcomed in any royal castle. Such a hideous face. How had Ballrik's widow grown to love the half-hobgoblin and bear him a child? Vecnor then recalled when the krukari cut Gruzim's spear in two. The Death Lord, Gruelenor's father, might have gotten the better of Vecnor with the lightning issuing from the weapon had Gruelenor not arrived. Surely the king was aware of the krukari's heroic status.

"I will inform the chiefs of Holindale," Nidor added.

"We'll then head north and do the same." Magneer's attitude appeared unchanged while he stared at Eraim. "And then we will meet you in Vol Maren."

Eraim shifted in her seat. "We have visited Fendora and Moclen already. If you could speak to the kings of Urell Coast and Neja, that would save us some time."

To this, Magneer and Gruelenor acquiesced.

Vecnor and Eraim departed the next morning. Magneer wasn't present when Nidor and Gruelenor wished them a safe and speedy journey.

There was no need to enter Tenvale—the Wizard Kingdom would suffer warnings from no one. Vecnor doubted they would listen even to Elgarroth. Turning north, Vecnor and Eraim traveled back through Moclen and into Virch. The reception they received from the Vircan king was displeasing.

"You are well respected," said King Onivar to Vecnor, "and your reputation, though beyond your years, precedes you. However, Palidurians have recently returned from Beit, and they have reported nothing so dire as you suggest. Even if Trannum and the Ancient Enemy have somehow reappeared in Vaeldor, we have already mobilized most of our forces to the Shield River to oppose the massing Beitians." He spread his hands. "We cannot deploy more than we have."

That was the problem with disappearing for decades at a time. Monarchs came and went, and some knew Vecnor only from stories. He would never convince the Vircan king beyond New Palidur's claims. But why did the Holy City not warn them about the source behind the growing evil? Vayla had been present for Elgarroth's revelation. Perhaps Grand Paladin Montac awaited more proof before stirring the masses.

The response in Harbnum was the same as in Virch, but Sendorum's King Yavell was old and recognized Vecnor. And although the aged ruler seemed delighted to see the Rogue Knight, the news visibly haunted him.

"Our resources are few," Yavell said. "We will offer what help we can. But Virch and Harbnum will not allow a military force to cross into their realms unless they are convinced it is absolutely necessary. Until then, all I can promise is that we'll be ready."

That was good enough for now.

There was no need to pass into Andria—barbarians were too difficult to organize or convince—and New Palidur had certainly informed Sardina already. So Vecnor and Eraim followed Vermallon Road. As they passed north of the House of Elgarroth, Eraim stared southward, as if she could see the cabin.

"Surely you are not felling trees in Vermallon for all that firewood," she said. "There would be none left south of the road."

Vecnor rolled his eyes. Before he could offer a response, Umbarc came dashing out of the forest.

"Whoa!" Vecnor pulled the horse he rode to a stop.

Elation for his mount's return invaded, and he couldn't contain his grin. He dismounted and climbed atop Umbarc, feeling stronger for the massive steed beneath him. Eraim appeared even smaller now, and she frowned.

"How are we to converse with you sitting way up there?"

Vecnor chuckled. "My ears work just fine."

She gave a mocking smile. "But they are not pointy at the moment."

Vecnor looked at the animal that had borne him for weeks. "What do we do with him?"

"Drop him off at the next village," replied Eraim. "In truth, he has been slowing us down."

She wasn't wrong.

They continued into Nira. The nearest settlement was Steadshire, and there, Eraim gifted the horse to a middle-aged farmer.

"Do you know him?" asked Vecnor after they left the farmhouse.

Eraim shrugged. "No. But he is the younger brother of a soldier named Delarrin, who died when the enemy pressed north of the Great East River. Poor lad wanted to be a hero." She craned her neck to look up at Vecnor. "Nidor spoke fondly about him."

Eraim had a kind heart.

King Raynek of Nira had yet to receive word from New Palidur, and he was receptive to Vecnor's warning. Vecnor and Eraim then headed south, as Selt would be unwilling to ally with other kingdoms, regardless of the reason. The theocracy of Demoligius joined Trannum during the Necromancer War, and had the realms not been so depleted once the battles ended, the Seltans might have paid a suitable price.

Queen Elloria of Kalmaar welcomed Vecnor with open arms, and King Sullis was all smiles. But their moods darkened upon hearing his news.

"We will be ready," said Elloria, the priestess-queen. "You have but to give the word, and Kalmirans will lead the charge!"

There was no reason to doubt her. Kalmaar was unmatched when it came to training warriors in Brondor's name.

Though he wished to remain in Darmhorng longer, Vecnor continued south. The conversations with Eraim resumed, and by the time they reached Marcove, he was sure he knew most of the major events of her life, as well as several less-significant moments. She really was a treat to speak to. He divulged as much as he could about his past, including the challengers wanting to make a name for themselves; those dying on the end of his sword for the sake of pride.

Horror was plain on Eraim's face. "How many duels have you fought?"

"Too many." Vecnor sighed. "The vanity of warriors is hard to reason with."

"You poor man."

Vecnor smirked. Was she humoring him?

"No one in Dominelli would ever challenge you," she said. "I can promise you that."

He chuckled. "But I'd hit my head on many a bough on those tree platforms."

She grinned, as if she had tricked him into admitting something.

"Or so I've heard," he added.

Castle Kembald was next. Though only Norvec had met Cavalor before the Necromancer War, Elgarroth allowed Vecnor to visit Borse a few times during the year following the affair. King Cavalor had been aware of the mutual respect between Vecnor and Merssa, and always welcomed him with open arms.

Cavalor beamed with delight when Vecnor and Eraim arrived. Unlike Queen Elloria, he had already received word from New Palidur. Vayla had likely visited, as the king was cognizant of everything they had to say, and not just the mobilization of Beit's forces.

"My soldiers prepare as we speak," Cavalor said.

Vecnor bowed his head. "Very good."

"Are you headed for the mountain pass next?" the king asked.

"We are," replied Vecnor.

"Please give Arkor advanced warning of my approach. That would save time."

"It will be done." Vecnor bowed again.

Unfortunately, they could not stay. Eraim embraced Cavalor for several seconds.

"It has been too long since my last visit," she said.

"I agree." Cavalor smiled as he released the elf, and he eyed Vecnor while still speaking to her. "But at least *you* have visited."

"Vecnor is very busy and goes only where he is needed." Eraim gazed about the chamber. "How is your stock of firewood?"

"We must be going." Vecnor urged her toward the door, as one corralling a child.

"Ride through the northern part of the realm," said Cavalor. "You should say hello to Mother."

Vecnor had visited Merssa's statue dozens of times already. He never passed through Marcove without stopping at the hill where the paladin fell, and this time would be no different.

The monument of Merssa stood tall and proud when Vecnor and Eraim arrived the next day. A small shrine marking Borse's grave stood next to it. Vecnor felt a chill whenever he climbed atop the mound, but it wasn't the remnants of a Death Lord's aura. His nerves always came to life, as if Merssa were there, and he found it hard to speak. He had known many deaths throughout his lifetime, but none hit him harder than the paladin's. On this occasion, Eraim spoke for the both of them.

"We are here," said the little elf. "Vecnor and I. Sorry, Selanna is busy doing... who knows what? But you know Selanna. Oh, and Trannum is a big stupid liar. He did not perish after all. And he let Uustaag loose." She looked at Vecnor. "Am I leaving anything out?"

Vecnor's eyes moistened.

Eraim turned back to the monument, and her tone softened. "Vayla is special. But she needs guidance. Please look after her." She sighed heavily. "I feel this will be much worse than the last war. And like you, she will be at the brunt of it all."

Vecnor controlled his breathing to hide further emotions. Eraim spoke the truth, whether or not she knew it.

After saying their goodbyes, they rode into Denvale. From there, they followed the mountain pass to Ironside Keep.

"It is hard for me to go to Ironside," said Eraim while they walked their horses along the snaking path to the stronghold. "I never know what to say to Arkor. He has lost so much."

Vecnor thought about Ballrik—Morsum—and he smirked. He then remembered Romik's predicament, and the smile faded quicker than it had arrived.

Morsum greeted them at the gate with as large a grin as Vecnor had ever seen. The gatekeeper played his part well, however, and Eraim didn't appear to notice anything out of the ordinary. At Vecnor's request, Morsum led them to Lord Arkor.

Like Cavalor, Arkor was aware of the situation. Unfortunately, the one-armed lord was too old to assist personally. But he vowed to lend support in any way he could.

"Have you any news about Romik?" Arkor asked.

Vecnor cleared his throat to gain Eraim's attention, and he bowed to whisper in her ear. "Could you please explain things? I need to take care of something."

Eraim's brow furrowed, and she slowly nodded.

Vecnor returned to the gatehouse to find Morsum whittling a piece of wood. It would obviously become a dog.

"Ah, Master Vecnor!" Morsum glanced beyond Vecnor to see if anyone accompanied him. The aging gatekeeper then spoke in a hushed tone. "You're here as yourself?"

Vecnor didn't look forward to this conversation. "I have to tell you something."

Morsum's grin faded. "It's Romik. Isn't it?"

Vecnor took in a deep breath and blew it out. "All I can say is that he is alive. What shape he's in… I do not know."

Tears rolled down the old man's cheeks. "The hunting trip?"

"No."

Vecnor looked over his shoulder. They remained alone. He informed Morsum of Romik's plight—the soldier would learn of it from Arkor anyway, and it was better he be prepared. After mentioning Helmland, Morsum's eyes grew distant and his lower lip quivered, making him appear as old as his wrinkles suggested. Vecnor pushed through, bringing up Trannum and Uustaag, and the blood drained from Morsum's face.

"Then everything was for naught." The guardsman's voice struggled to escape. "The Necromancer War... The loss... It was all a waste of time." He wiped his tears with his arm.

"No." Vecnor put his hand on Morsum's shoulder. "Do not question the bravery shown by those that did their part, including yourself. The threat Trannum posed was very real. Had Vaeldor not fought against him, the current state of affairs would be much worse."

"Yes, you're right." Morsum sniffled. "Of course."

Vecnor helped the guardsman to sit. "And we will get Romik back."

Morsum forced a smile. "If anyone can do it, it's you. Thank you, Vecnor."

Vecnor detected the slightest noise behind him. It was Eraim.

"We must be off," he said to the gatekeeper. "Thank you for listening to a warrior's prattle."

"No need to mention it." Morsum did his best to compose himself, rising and wiping away another tear. "I just wish these old bones worked a little better. Thank you for bringing me some water." He sniffled again.

Vecnor saw a mug on the gatekeeper's table. It was dry. Hopefully Eraim didn't notice.

They collected Umbarc and Lilli from the stables and headed west on the darkened pass. The moon revealed the canyon on the northern edge and the winds were calmer than usual, so the way was not treacherous. As the cliff walls closed in and the chasm fell behind, Eraim spoke.

"You took him water?"

Vecnor shrugged. "Sure."

She frowned. "Why did you speak to him about Romik?"

"I mentioned all of those left behind. Just spreading the word."

"To ancient gatekeepers beyond their fighting days?'

Vecnor nodded. "It's news for everyone, to do with what they will."

"I see." Eraim wrinkled her little nose. "How is it Morsum is still the gatekeeper? He was old before the Necromancer War."

Vecnor shrugged again. "Some folks have all the luck."

"But there is something about his eyes," Eraim said. "I swear they used to be green. They are brown now."

"I'm sure you're mistaken." Vecnor chuckled. "How could you possibly remember the color of a gatekeeper's eyes?"

Eraim scoffed. "You doubt me?" Her offended expression pierced the darkness. "Even Selanna knows better than to do so."

"Perhaps the lighting was wrong."

"Perhaps he drinks the same water as you," she retorted.

Vecnor sensed Eraim's growing anger or frustration—maybe both—and he stilled his tongue. As the sky brightened, they exited the pass, and Elgarroth spoke in Vecnor's mind.

Return home. Alone.

What? Vecnor asked. He must have misunderstood. *Am I not going into the crypt?*

No. You are needed elsewhere.

Vecnor took in a deep breath as anxiety invaded. Exploring the unknown depths of Trannum's lair with Eraim and Selanna was the only plan that made sense. But he couldn't disobey Elgarroth. Not again. He dreaded his next conversation with Eraim.

"Isn't it time to head to Vol Maren?" he asked.

"Yes." Irritation had not abandoned Eraim's tone. "And we best pick up the pace."

"Sorry." Vecnor looked down at her. The sun peeked over the Varlimor Mountains, but he and the elf remained in the shadows of the giant mounds. "I have affairs I must attend to."

"What?" she practically yelled. "What affairs? What could be more important than Trannum's crypt?"

Vecnor shook his head, trying to think of an excuse she'd accept. But she didn't leave him room to speak.

"Do you not care about the impending war? About Vaeldor? Do you not care about… me?"

"I care about all of those things," he insisted. "Especially the last part."

Her eyes welled up. "You have a fine way of showing it."

Times like this made Vecnor hate his life. It was worse than sneaking away in the night while others slept, or steering his horse into a forest to disappear while no one was watching. This was personal. This inflicted pain to one he cared for deeply. And at the moment, it was unforgivable.

"Believe me," he said, "I would love nothing more than to accompany you. And you deserve an explanation. But… I…"

"You cannot give me one." Her angry expression resurfaced. "So go ahead. Return to your *mysterious* life." She pushed Lilli to a quicker pace. "I, on the other hand, have a world to save."

Vecnor watched Lilli break into a run, and the small horse carried Eraim swiftly away. His chest and stomach ached. And for the first time, he said a prayer not to Brondor, but to Soleran the Protector.

"Please, Almighty Soleran, see them safely through. Let this not be our last meeting."

With a heavy heart, he turned Umbarc northward.

CHAPTER 39

A BLEAK FUTURE

Five days passed while Vecnor followed the Varlimor Mountains to Vermallon Forest. He then rode along the southern bank of the Great East River and used the ford to cross. It was nearing evening when he entered the clearing of the House of Elgarroth. He had stewed throughout the lonely ride about being denied the mission into Trannum's crypt; rehearsed what he would say to Elgarroth. But as he looked upon the wizard, all words were lost.

Elgarroth smoked his pipe by the fire. No calm existed in the mage's eyes—a foreign expression.

"What is it?" Vecnor asked.

Elgarroth slowly shifted his focus to meet Vecnor's gaze. "The shadows obscuring my visions have all but faded. And what I see is most disturbing." He turned back to the flames. "Just as I had hoped, Selanna will defy her destiny for a time yet." Elgarroth sighed. "But she heads into peril. Strong evil awaits her. There is no guarantee of her survival."

Vecnor sat across from the wizard, his frustrations beginning anew. "Then why not send me into the crypt?"

Elgarroth studied Vecnor. "That was my original intent. But it is not the crypt alone I speak of. Yes, there is much danger there. But I sense Nidor will see them through."

"What about Eraim?"

Elgarroth revealed a wry smile. "By now, you know Eraim can take care of herself. Though I offer no assurances that she escapes this whole affair with her life, she has as good a chance as anyone. Maybe better."

Vecnor let out a slow breath. The wizard spoke the truth. But he couldn't agree out loud, as if doing so would bring Eraim bad luck.

"Uustaag will have a massive army," Elgarroth continued. "One larger than we anticipated. Every day, Thard'Dun's monsters enter our world. And they hunt for the stick."

"Why does Selanna carry it?" asked Vecnor. "Why not me or Tux. Why not throw it as far as you can into Arman Forest?"

Elgarroth shook his head. "That is a question on several minds. But it would not work. Arman Forest is a mystical place, as you are well aware, but its powers are of *our* world."

"And Thard'Dun's minions are not," Vecnor murmured.

"Precisely." Elgarroth lowered his brows in thought. "I know not if the enchantments of the forest can withstand the krahluks and zreekans."

"The what?"

"I apologize," Elgarroth said. "The gorillas and floating tentacle creatures. You have not encountered them yet. Welmirth documented them in his journals. Krahluks possess the strength of ten ogres, and zreekans wield evil magic; deadly powers I believe they have shared with Trannum. Because they are not of our world, Welmirth could not risk hiding the stick in Arman. In fact, I suspect that is the first place Trannum looked. I know not how long he has been allowing these beasts access, but I am certain it is not only recently. He likely hid them from us, so that no one would realize his true intentions."

"I see." Vecnor tapped his fist on his chin.

"As to your other queries," added Elgarroth, "Selanna will not carry the stick for much longer, and you know we cannot be the ones to possess it."

"Yes, I know," Vecnor growled. "But all of Vaeldor lies in the balance. Can we not break a few rules for the good of the people?"

Elgarroth raised a brow. "I broke a small rule already. And it has hindered me ever since. What do you think would be the punishment for breaking a much larger one?"

Vecnor gazed at the darkening trees. He had no idea, and he didn't want to know. He released his frustrations with an exhale. "What must we do now?"

"The enemy has horrific soldiers," Elgarroth replied, "including monsters from both our world and Thard'Dun's, as well as a horde of undead. It will be too much for the force of the united realms. Even if Desser is successful in recruiting the Pavish, it is not enough. We will lose."

"The Pavish?" Vecnor frowned. "What—?"

Elgarroth lifted a finger. "We need another army."

"Where do we get another army?"

"There are many that do not fight for their kings or queens for various reasons." Elgarroth eyed Vecnor. "But they might fight for you."

"Me?"

The wizard continued, as if Vecnor hadn't spoken. "Some are mercenaries, some are aging warriors, discarded and forgotten by their lords. Some of them are undesirables: krukari, criminals, and such."

Vecnor gazed at the dancing flames. "An army of misfits…"

"One capable of blending with the enemy."

"Will I lead them into Beit or Helmland?"

"Helmland." Elgarroth took in a deep breath. "That is where the final battle will be fought. And with an allied force among the enemy, perhaps side by side with the Pavish, we might just gain the edge we need to win this war."

The Pavish again. Perhaps Vecnor would learn more later. "Where do I start?"

"Begin in Kalmaar, where your legend is most known. In the southern region. Recruit those overlooked by lords; folks possessing courage and a will to protect their homes and loved ones. Then work your way west. I will supply treasures to offer, and you shall promise more to their families afterward, whether or not they survive."

At least he would travel as himself, Vecnor supposed. "Once I gather this... army... how do I get them into Helmland?"

"The Path of the Guardians, unfortunately, needs to be revealed," said Elgarroth. "You must sneak them through and hide them in the valley below the waterfall."

"And then what?"

"A Beitian army will enter Helmland," the wizard replied. "It, too, is a band of *misfits*, as you call them, unworthy of being Dun Soldiers or much else. Expendables. You shall insert yourself and your warriors into their ranks." He stared intently at Vecnor. "And you will make yourself their leader by any means necessary, before they reach Lormin Dmurr."

"How can you be sure they'll be there when we arrive?"

"There are no guarantees in life," Elgarroth stated. "But I have seen this force. I have heard their orders."

"Tux?"

Elgarroth shook his head. "There is one among those we consider an ally that desires more than his family and friends realize."

Vecnor's mind went to Baylun. But he dismissed the thought. From stories he had been told, only one of the boys ever gave a reason for concern. "Daymyn?"

"His fate is not yet decided," Elgarroth said. "He may yet do the right thing."

By the wizard's expression, the odds weren't favorable. But Elgarroth always held onto hope, as long as there was hope to be found.

"When do I leave?" Vecnor asked.

"At once." Elgarroth turned to the fire. "You will find a set of pouches in your room. Be sure to take them with you."

Vecnor rose. "It shall be done."

Without awaiting a response, he entered the cabin. Two bags rested on the table in his bedchamber. They didn't appear to hold much, but when he checked their contents, one contained a king's wealth and the other possessed gray flatbread and blue apples.

Vecnor exited the house. Elgarroth was gone. The fire was extinguished, and the chimney smoke eased to a trickle.

CHAPTER 40

ARMAN FOREST

The hallways were dark, but Eslimil's vision revealed every seam in the flagstones. He moved with speed and purpose, his ears alert, but nothing made a sound. The servants had turned in for the night.

He approached the double doors at the end of the corridor. Pressing his ear against the wood, he detected nothing. He inhaled and passed through the seam between the doors.

The audience chamber was bare and the eleven thrones were vacant, just as expected. The Council of Wizards had no cause to anticipate Eslimil's visit. He released his breath and moved swiftly across the room to the small door leading to the wizards' quarters. Again, he heard nothing. He repeated his process and passed into the corridor beyond.

The hallway stretched thirty feet, with a pair of doors to either side. At the end, it turned right and left. Eslimil hurried to the intersection—sneaking around wizards' personal chambers was enough to put even *his* nerves on edge. To the right, a fifty-foot passage held four more doors split between the side walls. In the opposite direction, it traveled forty feet, with a single door on the left, two on the right, and an iron-bound door at the far end.

Eslimil turned left.

A typical burglar might think the reinforced door protected the Council's most prized possessions. But it was a ruse. It led to the bedchamber of Fenreil the Seer—Eslimil knew the layout well. He halted before the lone door on the left. It matched the other bedroom doors with its simple lock and a gap along the bottom, one large enough to accept Eslimil's entire hand. But passing through as shadow would alert the wizards to his presence. Worse still, the alarm would summon bright lights to illuminate every inch of the chamber and assault his vaporous form with excruciating pain. Eraim had visited too many times, and the Council took extra precautions to foil future thieving attempts. Eslimil had to first disable the trap.

Pulling a couple of small tools from his pouch, Eslimil went to work. The lock was a complex set up with several barriers, both mechanical and magical, to hinder his progress. Prodding the wrong spot would trigger the protections. Fortunately, Eslimil recognized those obstacles from centuries of practice. He concentrated, and just as his mind guided arrows in flight, he became the tools and saw every intricacy the mechanism offered. He bypassed three false pins and reached the end. From there, he worked his way back, setting each tumbler in its proper place and avoiding a tiny rune etched onto the metal—a magical trap he believed held paralytic powers. As he exited the keyhole, he pushed down the latch. It opened.

Eslimil allowed the door to swing a few inches—enough to fool the trap into believing the appropriate key was used. Holding his breath, he blended into the shadows and entered. Within were a score of tables of various sizes, all of them displaying items as if they were trophies. To the left was a giant wolf skull. Eslimil remembered the legends of the Great White Wolf of the North, an animal constantly obscured by a torrent of snow and ice. Although an Andrian hunter eventually defeated the monstrous hound, the barbarians feared its spirit haunted the skull still. Thus, they turned it over to the Council. To the right, three wide straps secured a mighty warhammer to a table. The cursed weapon drove anyone daring to wield it mad. Deeper in the room, the tiara Mayry wore while ruling Marcove rested atop a pillow. No one could fathom a human going to the lengths she had to gain power, and the Council obtained the item to conduct research for signs of Trannum's influence. Eslimil knew better. Mayry was simply a horrible person. On a few tables across the chamber, Eslimil spied what he sought: a burnt tome, a few black iron bars, and a purple shard that had once belonged to the Dun crystal Baylun destroyed in Darum Carumbor.

He drifted until the items were near and released his breath. Pulling the sack Elgarroth provided, Eslimil readied his free hand while eyeing the objects. He seized the purple shard and put it in the bag, and as he did so, an alarm sounded. It was the voice of Fenreil, shouting from everywhere.

"Thief! Thief! You will never see beyond these walls again!"

Eslimil shoved the remaining items into the sack while green gas seeped from beneath the tables. The fumes made his skin tingle, and as it reached his shoulders, he took in a breath. He flew across the ceiling, arriving at the door as a wizard entered and scanned the room. A golden glow surrounded the mage's mouth and nose.

Eslimil floated over the man and into the hallway. More wizards exited their bedrooms, and one cast a spell down the corridor leading to the audience chamber—obviously an enchantment to restrain anyone attempting to flee. Eslimil passed through the cracks of the door at the end of the hall and into the Seer's room, where Fenreil was donning his robe and mumbling to himself.

"This had better be important. If this is another one of their blasted tests..."

The wizard stormed out.

Eslimil materialized, eyeing the fireplace while catching his breath. The hearth was cold. He could not determine when it was last used, as it was free of soot and ash. Like many wizards, the Council members probably kept their bedchambers warm with magic. He inhaled and floated up the chimney.

Upon the rooftop, Eslimil landed to renew his breath. Below, most of Tikken City slept while merriment drifted from a few distant taverns on a light breeze. Eslimil again merged with the shadows, and he flew two blocks away to where Landolice patiently waited in an alleyway. He reformed on the saddle, and the horse snorted in recognition of his arrival.

They headed to the southern region of the city, where Elgarroth's steed rested in a stable. In all the centuries Eslimil had known the wizard, he was yet to hear of a name given to the mount. Dandi was in the neighboring stall, and no grooms were around. Eslimil crept in and tied the sack to Elgarroth's saddle before speaking the command word.

"*Wississtenance.*"

The bag vanished.

⁂

Eslimil waited atop Landolice to the south of Tikken City. He stayed well off the road, sitting in the dark and beyond detection of even the keenest-eyed elf. Except for Elgarroth, of course. It was where the wizard told him to wait after completing his task.

He thought of Vecnor raising an army. It was a mission the tall warrior could accomplish better than most. Vaeldor teemed with warriors hoping for a chance to do something good in their lives. How many Vecnor recruited remained to be seen, and Eslimil prayed his companion exceeded expectation. They needed all the help they could muster.

Elgarroth and Selanna rode forth from Tikken City, both on their Salenti steeds. Eslimil often wondered if he would be more comfortable on one of the smaller mounts. But he had only ever ridden Batorn horses, and he trusted Landolice with his life. He urged his horse, slowly at first, and then paced the two mages, remaining well to the west. Though Elgarroth never glanced his way, the wizard was surely aware of his presence.

Why did Elgarroth need to enter Arman Forest with Selanna? Eslimil knew only that his task was to monitor their surroundings. Elgarroth did not fear the forest—its hazards were not meant for him. But the wizard expressed uncertainty as to whether the woodland's magical barriers would deter the foreign soldiers of Uustaag's army. According to Elgarroth, the Thard'Dun monsters were aware

Selanna carried the key to their master's freedom, and would stop at nothing to retrieve it. And while Elgarroth and Selanna attempted to remedy that situation, they could ill afford distractions. Having never faced krahluks or zreekans, Eslimil wondered what help he could offer.

Elgarroth kept a hard pace, and it impressed Eslimil to see Dandi keep up. Whenever they stopped, the wizard fed the horses the special apples that grew behind the cabin, and Selanna did not seem to notice the blue color beneath the night sky—had Elgarroth disguised the fruits?

On the third evening, Arman Forest shrouded the southeast in darkness. Trees lining the southern shore of the King Arman swallowed the Prince Arman River as it flowed southwest to link the King and Queen Arman Lakes. Elgarroth and Selanna halted to converse, and the wizard shared some sweetbread. Did Selanna realize the bread carried magical properties?

Eslimil dared to draw near enough to hear the two. Selanna would not likely notice him, as his senses were undoubtedly superior, and Landolice made no sound. The mages were discussing the Chant employed by Dun Soldiers to gain an advantage on their adversaries. Eslimil learned of it from Elgarroth after Selanna witnessed its power in Darum Carumbor. It slowed the muscles and minds of the enemies of Thard'Dun while removing pain and fear from the dark god's followers. The evil warriors' eyes would gloss over, and they acted as if compelled to destroy all that opposed their malevolent deity. Selanna gasped when Elgarroth revealed the Balgorn River draft's ability to bend others' wills to this effect, an elixir she and her companions imbibed to survive the plague while in Beit. But she relaxed when he explained they had not consumed enough to be turned to evil thoughts. Eslimil could not imagine being restrained so. Had Eraim and Baylun not resisted the vile magic, their entire company would have perished.

Selanna changed the subject to the tower guarding the road into Helmland, and the boys trapped within.

"But how is it you see Darum Carumbor?" she asked. "Is it through Daymyn or Baylun?"

"No," Elgarroth replied. "As I mentioned, doing so would risk their lives."

Elgarroth's probing of the mind was detectable by its target. Eslimil figured that out centuries ago, as well as how to resist the invasion. Until just before the Necromancer War, he had not realized powerful beings of magic could also detect Elgarroth's prying through others, and it seemed neither had Elgarroth. It was likely the reason Selanna's stay at Trannum's stronghold had not gone unnoticed, even with her disguised as undead. Since then, Elgarroth avoided using the Sight in that way when the enemy was too close.

Elgarroth pulled a pack from his saddle and extracted the black crowns Selanna procured from Trannum's crypt. After setting them on the grass, he opened the bag Tux had strapped to the saddle and removed the black iron bars and the shard from the shattered crystal in Darum Carumbor. Selanna unwrapped a blanket and handed Elgarroth the black stick, careful not to touch it directly. Elgarroth placed the item into his sack with his bare hand before adding the other contents. He fastened the pack to his horse, and they headed toward the forest.

Eslimil had to time it perfectly. He was to avoid notice by Selanna, but he needed to remain within sight of Elgarroth or become hopelessly lost. He counted on Selanna's awe of the ancient woodland to keep her attention as he pushed Landolice, risking the noise of his mount's pounding hooves. Neither Elgarroth nor Selanna looked back—the rushing water of the Prince Arman surely filled their ears. Elgarroth halted once they reached the tree line, pointing out various bits of scenery, and he and Selanna dismounted and grabbed their packs.

Eslimil was thirty yards away when the two proceeded without their horses. He leaped from Landolice, propelling himself and closing the gap. As he neared the trees, he took in a breath and dissipated into the shadows among the branches.

Selanna looked over her shoulder and peered into the night. Dandi and Elgarroth's horse were slowly making their way west — Landolice knew to get from sight once Eslimil made his move. The elf maiden returned her attention forward, and Eslimil exhaled, standing atop a sturdy branch of an oak tree. All three of them entered the forest.

The sound of the Prince Arman vanished, and although no clouds obscured the night sky, raindrops pelted Eslimil and the leaves — few droplets reached the forest floor. A full moon illuminated the trees with a soft glow, highlighting the vivid green vegetation. Strange, since a half-moon inhabited the blackness overhead before they entered. Unlike other woodlands, Arman was clear of debris, and not a stick or fallen leaf lay on the ground. But small streams were plentiful, some broad enough to require jumping over. Elgarroth walked an easy pace, speaking no words while Selanna gazed about with wide eyes. Eslimil sensed her fear and excitement. He followed, leaping from branch to branch while the rain masked any noises he made. After thirty yards, Elgarroth glanced back, briefly looking upward to confirm Eslimil's presence. The wizard then turned to Selanna.

"Are you ready?"

"Here?" she asked.

"No. Not here." He looked about. "You see, Arman is divided into elements of magic. When you use spells conducive with the area, you will have greater strength. Conversely, when you oppose that magic, you will be weaker. At the moment, we stand within the element of water. The air is moist, and the soil spongy."

Selanna took in her surroundings. She tested the ground with her boot and smiled. "I can feel energy from absolutely everywhere."

"Go ahead." Elgarroth spread his arms. "Test the element."

Selanna's grin broadened. She weaved her hands while speaking an enchantment, and there was a sudden downpour. Though already wet from rain, Eslimil was completely soaked, as were Elgarroth and Selanna.

Selanna laughed. "I only conjured a mist!"

Elgarroth smirked, his wet hair flat against his scalp and neck. "Try the other way."

Selanna pulled in her lips as she contemplated. She recited another spell while holding out her hand, and a flame appeared, as if she held an invisible candle. Her eyes widened.

"I summoned a ball of fire." She looked at Elgarroth. "It should be a hundred times this size!"

"Cast it at a tree," Elgarroth said. After her incredulous expression, he added, "It will bring no harm."

Selanna concentrated on the flame. It doubled in size. Her face reddened, but it grew no larger. She released the spell, and it dissipated upon a birch fifteen feet away, leaving not even a scorch mark.

She panted, as if having run a great distance. "This is amazing!"

"Yes." Elgarroth scanned the trees. "It is at that. But water is hardly useful at the moment. We will travel to another part of the forest."

"How far will we go?"

Elgarroth grinned. "Just around that birch you tried to incinerate."

She giggled. "How soon I forget distance means nothing here."

"Make sure you stay within sight of me at all times," Elgarroth said. "You do not want to get lost. And I have not yet taught you to navigate the trees."

"That is a lesson I await with great eagerness!" She again scanned the woodland, coming dangerously close to Eslimil's location.

"This way." Elgarroth stole her attention.

Eslimil leaped to the birch while Elgarroth slowly proceeded. He rounded the bole, keeping the wizard in sight, and the forest changed. The streams vanished, and the air became warm and dry. Better still, the moisture evaporated from his clothing and hair — Elgarroth and Selanna were dry as well. Though Eslimil remained high up, he could tell the ground was stone-like, almost as if the trees protruded from a dungeon floor.

"Fire?" Selanna asked, looking at the trees as if they had changed in some way.

They were unaltered.

"Not quite." Elgarroth searched the treetops, his gaze resting briefly on Eslimil. "Transformation."

Selanna wrinkled her nose. "That is not an element."

"Elements of *magic*. Not the elements as others understand them." Elgarroth held out his hand, and a table of rock arose from the hard soil. It was not crude, but intricate in its detail, as if carved by a Stone Eagle dwarf. Elgarroth then pulled the black stick from his pack and placed it on the tabletop. "This is where we will complete our work."

Selanna squatted to marvel at the new-made furniture. "Amazing!"

Elgarroth again glanced at Eslimil. *Be alert*, came the wizard's voice.

Eslimil concentrated. He heard Elgarroth and Selanna speaking and moving about, and also he detected animals romping from place to place, birds alighting and taking flight, and a light breeze dancing with the treetops. All was clear.

"Close your eyes," Elgarroth said. "Feel the surrounding energies."

Selanna gasped. "There is so much!"

"Calm your mind," instructed Elgarroth. "Focus on a single strand of power. Hold it. Breathe it."

"I have one." Selanna's voice bore a slight giggle.

"Good." Elgarroth walked around the table. "Do not let it go. What are you holding?"

"Energy from an oak leaf." Selanna tittered again. "How does a leaf contain so much?"

"Focus." Elgarroth left her question unanswered. "Allow the energy to take the shape of the leaf."

"I..." Selanna sounded strained. "I got it!"

"Do not lose hold," cautioned Elgarroth. "Now move its borders. Make it… a maple leaf."

Selanna breathed heavily for a moment. "Did it work?"

"Open your eyes."

Selanna released a gleeful squeal. "I did it!"

Eslimil shifted his position to see the result. Attached to a branch bearing dozens of oak leaves was a single maple leaf, as if adopted by the tree as one of its own.

"Very good." Elgarroth appeared satisfied. "You have transmuted one leaf into another, which is no small feat. But transforming something into a completely different object, especially an item of power, will be quite another task. While the leaf accepted its new form, the black stick will fight you."

"I do not think I am ready for that."

"No," Elgarroth agreed. "You are not. That is why I shall assist you."

Her expression was grateful.

"But first we must decide on what the key is to become," Elgarroth said.

Selanna pursed her lips. "It should be light in weight. And small."

"Small?"

"The stick is so bulky," Selanna complained.

"And someone other than yourself must carry it," Elgarroth added.

"Why?"

"While I respect your decision to delay your responsibilities," Elgarroth replied, "I insist you allow another to bear this burden. You will understand one day."

Selanna furrowed her brow. "There is only one other I trust." She sighed. "But she will never accept it."

"She will never *willingly* take it," Elgarroth corrected her.

"But… How can I do that to Eraim? She will never forgive me."

"I think she is the perfect choice," said Elgarroth.

Eslimil detected a noise. Something big approached. By the sound, it traveled on all fours, was covered in scales, and stretched thirty feet in length. A flapping joined in, as if it possessed wings. A dragon? It had been centuries since Eslimil heard such a beast — they were extinct. The creature snorted and moved away as quickly as it had arrived. The woodland fell silent, except for the conversation below.

"A dagger?" Selanna asked.

"A gift most befitting Eraim," Elgarroth responded, "and one she might readily accept."

"I am not so sure," Selanna said. "She has been very suspicious lately. I do hate keeping things from her."

"It is your responsibility to convince her," Elgarroth insisted. "You will think of a way."

The mages repositioned themselves around the table.

"Are you ready?" asked Elgarroth.

Selanna took in a deep breath. "I am."

"Reach out your mind to the stick. Feel the power within, but do not take hold of it. Observe it."

Selanna focused on the smooth black wood.

"Good." Elgarroth's voice grew eager. "Now pull surrounding energy to you. Just enough to encompass the stick."

Eslimil's attention shifted to a distant noise. Heavy footfalls belonging to no less than a score of large creatures brutally crushed the undergrowth. To his knowledge, the denizens of the forest knew better than to bring destruction. Surely these were foreigners. Krahluks?

Eslimil made a bird call. It was the ordinary chirp of a bluebird — the call Elgarroth instructed him to use. He then peered down, just as the stick shifted into a perfect black dagger with a metal handle.

Elgarroth glanced upward before scanning the area.

"What is it?" asked Selanna, her eyes darting about the trees.

"Nothing." Elgarroth smiled to ease her anxiety. "We are almost finished."

Selanna turned to the dagger and gasped. "It worked!"

Eslimil focused on the distant movements. They were drawing closer, but not at an alarming rate. He allowed the conversation below to mingle with the approaching monsters. The *clink* of metal on stone sounded—items placed onto the table.

"These crowns may be of use," said Elgarroth. "Being from the realm of Thard'Dun, I believe they can be made into weapons that will pierce the enemy's flesh more easily."

"They are so thin," commented Selanna. "There is not much to work with."

"No," Elgarroth agreed. "But enough for making more daggers. Ones similar to the key."

"An excellent idea!"

Additional instructions came from Elgarroth, but Eslimil's senses returned to the source of the trampling. Distance in Arman was difficult to fathom, but he had been in the woodland enough to know about ten minutes existed before the creatures arrived. How were they accomplishing it? Even Eslimil could not track within the boundaries of Arman Forest.

He glanced down to spy half a dozen black daggers on the table. The newer blades were almost identical to the first. Only a keen eye such as his could spot the difference.

"I have a thought for the shard," said Elgarroth. "I suspect we can harness its power for another purpose."

"What do you mean?" asked Selanna.

"Like the crowns, it is an element from Thard'Dun's world, and therefore possesses energy foreign to ours. I believe we can mold it to fit our needs, perhaps as a protection from the Chant."

"I could do nothing to counter those ill words." Selanna's voice softened, as if ashamed. "I have been thinking hard on how to defeat it."

While she spoke, Elgarroth lifted his palm upward, and several rocks broke free from the soil and floated onto the table.

"Transform these into pendants," he said.

"Me? By myself?"

"You are ready for that," Elgarroth assured her. "And while you do so, I will separate the shard and steer its power into protective magic."

Elgarroth surely heard the approaching monsters. It was not like him to do as much work during Selanna's lessons.

Eslimil closed his eyes while they chanted, their strange words mingling to make for complete gibberish. The invaders were a few minutes away. Seconds later, the incanting ended, and Elgarroth spoke.

"Very good. Next, fuse the crystals to the pendants."

More chanting.

"What about the bars?" asked Selanna once she had finished.

"Those are items best left to me." Elgarroth's tone then became serious. "I must leave you for a moment."

Eslimil gazed downward, surprised by the wizard's statement. Several golden pendants lay on the table, each with a dark, almost black crystal attached. Selanna's eyes were wide.

"Leave me?"

"You are safe," Elgarroth said. "As long as you do not stray from this spot."

"I… I will not move."

Elgarroth offered a comforting smile. "Please, put everything into your pack. I shall return momentarily." He glanced at Eslimil as he walked around the birch.

Eslimil rounded the tree and jumped down to join the wizard. The forest was no longer warm, but cold enough to see their breaths. He and Elgarroth were far from where they had been moments ago.

"There is very little time." Elgarroth spoke as if unconcerned with being overheard.

Eslimil focused. He detected nothing beyond small animals nearby. "Is it wise to leave her alone?" he asked.

"She will be fine," Elgarroth said. "I will return before they arrive." He looked to his right. "Eraim nears the house. She is early."

He turned to Eslimil. "I shall send you there immediately. Landolice will be there."

Eslimil nodded.

"And you must supply her with arrows."

Eslimil frowned. "Arrows?"

"I know you treasure your stock, but it is vital she be prepared."

Elgarroth had never made such a request before. How could Eslimil say no? The wizard gave a nod, understanding Eslimil's submission. Elgarroth then chanted several words before a cedar tree, and a shimmering portal filled with green fog and dancing yellow lights appeared. Eslimil stepped through.

He emerged from the back wall of the house in Vermallon Forest. The sky was bright, and birds twittered while vermin chittered and raced across the ground or from branch to branch. It was daytime, and the world was normal again. Not far away stood Landolice. The portal was gone.

After meeting with Eraim, said Elgarroth, *go to the bridges over the Shield River. Inform the allies of everything you know of the enemy they face. Then speak with the Lorians. They* must *follow Wezlok's example. Make them understand the impending doom of Maple Lore.*

Are you safe? Eslimil asked.

All is well.

The diminutive sound of boots and hooves grabbed Eslimil's attention. He peered around the corner to spy Eraim leading Lilli toward the house.

CHAPTER 41

MESSENGERS

"Over here," Eslimil said.

Eraim turned his way and wrinkled her nose. "What are you doing here?"

Great. She still held no trust for him. But why would she? At times, Eslimil pitied Eraim for the difficulties she endured. Her friend was a seer and kept secrets. She and Vecnor shared a bond they could not explore. And now, *he* entered her life: a legendary figure from ages ago. It amazed him Eraim maintained her sanity.

"I am here as a favor." Eslimil turned to the trees, trying to decide what else to say. Though he could not share the complete truth, he could provide a few clues to pacify her for a time.

"A favor to whom?" Eraim asked.

"Does it matter?"

Her lips twisted into a sneer. "Was it Elgarroth? Or perhaps the strong *elf* lad?"

He held a level gaze. "Please. It is obvious you have figured out much, but you are far from knowing everything."

Silence followed while Eraim searched his face for the meaning of his statement.

"Time grows short," he added. "You will learn everything you need to know soon enough."

He walked to Landolice and pulled one of his quivers from the saddle. It held a score of his special arrows. It had taken over five hundred years to perfect the craft, and never had he offered the results of his labors to anyone. He tossed the quiver to Eraim.

Her eyes lit up. "What...?"

"It is a gift. To fulfill a request."

Her brow rose. "What do you owe Elgarroth to honor such a request?"

"We all have done things," Eslimil replied. "We all have things to do. And we all owe somebody something, whether or not we wish to. In the end, what does it matter who I owe or who you owe? Or the reasons why? I have something to do, and so do you. Hopefully, this gift makes your something easier."

In truth, Eslimil owed Elgarroth his life. Had it not been for the wizard, he might have been hunted down for crimes against lords and nobles and died before he grew old. The more he thought about it, the more comfortable he became with the offering. And if anyone was deserving, it was Eraim.

"Thank you," she said, her words hesitant but sincere.

"May they serve you well." Eslimil climbed onto Landolice. "Wherever your path leads."

"Thank you," she repeated. She then frowned. "Wait. Where is it I am supposed to go next? Elgarroth told me to come here, and I assumed I would get direction once I arrived. In truth, I expected to find Vecnor."

"I see." Eslimil studied her. With Vecnor and Selanna busy, there was nothing for her to do.

Take her with you, said Elgarroth. *There is no harm in sharing your mission.*

"I suppose you can accompany me… for a while."

Eraim tilted her head, sizing up Eslimil. She then climbed onto Lilli, all anxiety melting from her expression. "Where are we off to?"

❈ ❈ ❈

Eslimil and Eraim left the House of Elgarroth, riding through the days and most of the nights. Not only was there a distance to cover, but Eraim informed Eslimil she must meet Selanna in Ellaville before too long — knowledge he already possessed. She kept up, but it came as no surprise. Eslimil had watched her for decades and knew she was up to the task.

Their first stop was in Arbornum. The large city in Harbnum played host to half of the allied forces, including the likes of Grand Paladin Montac, King Cavalor, and two of the High Paladins of New Palidur. Eslimil was aware of these people and their importance to Vaeldor; he had watched them from afar for most of their lives. But they were yet to make his acquaintance, an occurrence he dreaded. He lived in the shadows, and the fewer that knew of his existence the better. An idea formed when he and Eraim were less than a day from the city, and he spoke about krahluks and zreekans, making sure Eraim understood as much about the monsters as he. As it turned out, she had faced a krahluk already, and realized the folly of underestimating the creatures.

More tents occupied the fields north of Arbornum than Eslimil cared to count. The sentries for the united armies recognized Eraim, and escorted her and Eslimil to the command tent where the lords and generals were gathered. Eslimil remained a few paces back with his hood pulled low, allowing Eraim to do the speaking. She began with her council with Elgarroth in Tikken City. She then explained the impact of the Chant, described the strange monsters, and discussed the horror that was Uustaag. The assembly listened, asked questions, and Eraim provided answers as best she could, glancing at Eslimil more than once for input. He offered a single nod each time to confirm her facts were correct.

"Who is it you bring with you?" King Cavalor posed toward the end of the meeting. He had been eyeing Eslimil since they arrived.

Eraim hesitated, looking over her shoulder. She then faced Cavalor and spoke in a firm voice. "He is my escort. Nothing more."

She was a clever one, and Eslimil appreciated her discretion.

Before leaving the encampment, Eraim insisted they seek Vayla. Eslimil understood her attachment to the young paladin. She and Selanna exhibited the same glistening in their eyes as did Vecnor when Vayla came up in conversations. Eslimil knew Merssa only as a hero, for it was not his place to interact with others. But she must have been truly special for Elgarroth to mourn her death. The wizard disappeared for a time afterward, and though Elgarroth's absences never surprised Eslimil, the pain in the mage's expression was unmistakable.

Vayla was drilling soldiers with her captain, Macurak, when Eslimil and Eraim found her. The Beitian general, Burnod, was nearby, watching and shaking his head. Vayla allowed Macurak to carry on the exercise while she walked with Eraim and Eslimil to a place less busy.

Vayla's attitude toward Eraim was intriguing. Back on the Path of the Guardians, the paladin was aloof. Now she appeared relaxed and pleased with the visit. In fact, Vayla hung on every word, as if craving knowledge. She glanced more than once at Eslimil, as well as his bow, and it was not long before she asked him a question.

"Are you a gray elf?"

Eslimil removed his hood. "Do you believe me to be a gray elf?"

Vayla frowned. "Is there anything to add to Eraim's report?"

"I think she has conveyed all pertinent information."

Vayla sighed and turned to Eraim. "Thank you for bringing this to my attention. Are you and Selanna ready to play your part?"

"If I *see* Selanna again…" Eraim mumbled.

Vayla lowered her brow. "What?"

"Nothing." Eraim smiled. "We will end the Chant, do not worry."

Vayla gave a firm nod.

Eslimil and Eraim took their leave and rode for the bridge outside Darmoor in Virch, where the rest of the massive army prepared. Eraim again did the talking when they met with the commanders, this time without looking at Eslimil for assistance.

"Where to next?" she asked once they exited the command tent.

"We must await darkness," Eslimil replied.

Eraim furrowed her brow, but she posed no additional questions.

They spent the remainder of the day walking about the encampment. Armies of various realms were scattered, sometimes mingled in central areas. There were Vircans, Mocs, Nejans, Fendorians, Dales, Philanders, and Palidurians. For the most part, the soldiers ranged from determined to scared, and some seemed overly confident, if not arrogant. A particular warrior from the last category hailed from Fendora, and he caught Eslimil's eye.

The man was well aware of his beautiful appearance, and he obviously carried a fair amount of wealth. His golden hair was shoulder length, his eyes bright blue, and his lips too red to be natural. He strutted about with an entourage, poking fun at soldiers of other kingdoms and enjoying laughs at their expense. It was a bit too much for Eslimil's liking; the man's comments were boorish and had no place in the current setting. Eslimil sensed disdain radiating from Eraim as well.

That evening after dinner, Eslimil paid attention to which tent the Fendorian retired. And though he and Eraim needed to move on, he allowed another hour to pass.

"Before we depart," he said to Eraim, "there is something I must attend to."

She smirked. "Are you planning to teach the lout a lesson in manners? We have been following him all day."

"Perhaps." Eslimil shrugged. "Or I might just even the odds."

Her eyes brightened in the moonlight. She approved.

"All right, then." He allowed half a grin. "Follow me."

They crept outside the reach of the campfires and torchlight until arriving at the tent. Eslimil cut a slit to create a new opening and peered inside. At least a hundred double bunks filled the darkness, and a chorus of snores permeated the air. He turned to Eraim and whispered.

"Keep watch on the others."

She nodded.

They entered, and Eraim remained near the breach while Eslimil maneuvered around the beds. His elfish vision pierced the shadows, and he discovered the Fendorian sleeping on a bottom bunk, the man's hair draped to one side.

Eslimil grazed the man's ear. No response. Good. Drawing his sharpest knife, he gripped a lock of hair to minimize the pulling and dragged the blade across. The edge easily sliced through. He dropped the hair onto the floor.

Eraim giggled silently.

Repeating the procedure, Eslimil removed two more tufts of hair. While cutting a fourth time, the man stirred, and Eslimil took in a breath to become one with the shadows as his target's eyes opened halfway.

The Fendorian glanced about without seeing. His eyes rolled into his head as he returned to slumber with a smacking of the lips.

Eslimil awaited the man's rhythmic breathing to resume before releasing the air. Eraim's jaw was agape. He did not mind revealing this ability to her; she had earned it. He winked and continued with his undertaking. By the time he finished, the Fendorian's hair was a mess of various lengths, none of them greater than a couple of inches and a few spots trimmed almost to the scalp.

After a nod of satisfaction, Eslimil exited the tent with Eraim close behind. Outside, the night was quiet and the air cool. No sentries strolled nearby.

"How did you do that?" asked Eraim while they walked. "I have witnessed many things from elves of Orlenfel. But what you did was…"

Eslimil raised a brow. "Amazing?"

She smirked and punched his arm. "You cheat!"

"If you say so." His smile dropped. "It is time to go."

They exited the encampment and rounded Darmoor, the militant city tasked with guarding the bridge over the Shield River. The Darmoor soldiers focused on the black towers of Zurzak, failing to notice the elves in dark cloaks riding horses along the riverbank.

Eslimil turned to Eraim. "Ready for a run?"

Her eyes widened as her mouth opened, but before she could reply, Eslimil urged Landolice forward.

The Vircan guards shouted as he raced onto the bridge, and he heard Lilli close behind. They passed beyond the lights of Darmoor to reach the middle of the arched structure, and at the opposite end were silhouettes of armed soldiers atop the gatehouse of Zurzak. By the lack of torchlight, the Beitians were likely krukari or hobgoblins.

Although the evil sentries had surely detected the shouts of their longtime enemies, shadows would conceal Eslimil and Eraim for a few seconds more. Putting an arrow to his bowstring, Eslimil let go without aiming. His consciousness soared with the projectile and toward the Beitian guards—they were krukari. He veered the arrow at a merlon to the left, summoning a power shared by most of his Orlenfel kin. The arrowhead vibrated, and upon striking the stone, it exploded.

Eslimil was back on Landolice while the Zurzak warriors scrambled, searching for the source of the showering rocks. He entered Beit during the chaos and turned east along the river; a glance told him Eraim had kept up. No one pursued while they pushed the horses, and after a mile they halted to allow the animals a short rest.

"I wondered how we were to cross," said Eraim while she and Eslimil sat on the riverbank, watching the water rush by in the moonlight. She faced Eslimil. "Another handy talent. But I have seen your kin explode arrows before."

Eslimil grinned.

Eraim gasped. "Crossing back will not be so simple. And I must join Selanna before she leaves for Darum Carumbor. She cannot hope to succeed without me!"

Eslimil tossed a stone into the water. "We will find a way."

She calmed, seeming to accept his words. She then scrunched her nose. "What happened to you on the bridge?"

Eslimil glanced at her inquisitive expression before tossing a second rock. "What do you mean?"

"Your eyes glazed over," she said. "And your arrow did not strike anywhere near where it should have." She lifted a brow. "Another little talent of yours?"

"We should go." He stood.

"That is your answer?" Eraim smirked as she rose. "You cheat at archery too?" She gasped again. "The arrow that destroyed Trannum's skull!"

"You have a schedule to keep." Eslimil climbed onto Landolice.

Eraim maintained her sly grin. She was too observant for her own good. Combine that with her extraordinary talents and battle skills, and it was obvious why Vecnor held a strong respect for her. Were the large warrior not smitten with the elf, Eslimil might consider learning more about her hopes and dreams, a notion he had only experienced three times throughout the centuries.

"Okay, *Eslimil*." She climbed atop Lilli. "You can keep your secrets… for now."

Eslimil appreciated her not pressing the subject any further.

They continued across Beit, avoiding a couple platoons of soldiers while making their way to Maple Lore Forest. Once beneath the trees, Eslimil led Eraim to the only village west of the Shield River. Dresnian was on the ground floor when they arrived, and the captain issued a sidelong glare at Eraim while greeting Eslimil. Eraim ignored the Lorian, her attention captured by the caged humans, and she wandered toward the prison.

"Twice in a single year?" Dresnian said to Eslimil. "I am inclined to believe you enjoy our company."

Eslimil held a level gaze. "I have news." He checked to make sure Eraim was not freeing the prisoners. The Beitians did not appear as malnourished as he was accustomed to. Perhaps they received more than a meal a day. "The war is spreading."

Dresnian sneered. "Why do you concern yourself with human affairs? Let them kill each other. Good riddance."

"Maple Lore is the only elfish clan uninvolved."

"The other clans are fools!"

"I would watch my tongue." Eslimil glanced at the branches overhead. "I believe Wezlok feels differently. What if he hears you?"

Dresnian sniffed at the comment. "That paladin must have cast a spell on him. You should have seen the way he reacted when the silly girl spoke."

Eslimil raised a brow. "Wezlok? Enchanted?" He shrugged. "Perhaps. But not by spells or potions. He has unlocked a truth that you may never know. Not if you hide, hoping evil does not turn its eye on you."

Dresnian frowned. "You speak like a human!" he hissed, just above a whisper.

Eslimil glared until the captain's expression softened. "I am here to see an elf of higher import than you. I suggest you take me to Harnistae at once. Unless you prefer I find my own way."

Dresnian stood taller. "I shall bring Elder Harnistae to *you*. Outsiders are not permitted beyond the ground floor." The captain spun on his heels and headed for one of several ladders rising to the lowest platform.

Eslimil chuckled. He had visited most of the buildings already, and Dresnian knew that. But he allowed the captain's little rant. Dresnian was among the top archers in the forest, and the war needed such soldiers.

Eraim stood in the middle of the clearing, attempting to spy the highest level of the city. She probably did not see past the third tier. Her attention returned to the cage, and she circled it while nonchalantly peering at its occupants, perhaps making sure no one she knew was among the prisoners.

"Eslimil Tuxendora!" said an approaching elf dressed in robes bearing three different shades of green. It was Harnistae, and the elder embraced Eslimil. Like many residents, Harnistae believed Eslimil to be half-Lorian and not half-Salenti.

Dresnian remained several paces back, the captain's distaste for the encounter obvious.

"I have been expecting you." Harnistae released Eslimil. "Elgarroth visited only a few nights ago." His brow lowered. "Are things as dire as the Salenti wizard claims?"

"The outcome is uncertain," Eslimil replied. "The necromancer Wezlok opposed has returned in another form, and Uustaag reigns over Helmland once again."

"Yes, yes." Harnistae's frown deepened. "You echo Elgarroth's words. I have heard them already."

"Vaeldor needs everyone in this war."

Harnistae studied Eslimil. "We do not involve ourselves in human affairs. You know this. Elgarroth knows this. The Grand Maple will keep our forest safe."

Eslimil raised a brow. "Is that why Master Wezlok travels with the humans?"

"Wezlok..." The elder shook his head. "That wizard changed near fifty years ago, when he left in pursuit of knowledge; pursuit of the power behind the *Wind of the Dead*, as the humans referred to it." He held a satisfied smirk. "Did you know the Wind never penetrated our borders?"

Harnistae enjoyed reminding everyone of that fact. Eslimil responded with a wry smile.

"Yes." The elder's grin doubled in size. "The Grand Maple protected us, and it will continue to do so."

"Your history tells you that Lorians opposed Uustaag the first time," Eslimil said. "Though Trannum failed to breach your woodland, Uustaag's minions are from the world of Thard'Dun, and they resist much of the magic we hold to be absolute. I have it on good authority they passed through Arman Forest not two weeks ago."

"Bah!" Fear in the elder's eyes contradicted his tone.

"Your Grand Maple is of Arman," Eslimil added, causing Harnistae's brow to lower. "Yes, my knowledge runs deep. I am aware that the very roots of your divine tree burrow into the foundations of Vaeldor and across the miles separating Maple Lore and Arman. Your master tree is but a child from the Resting Place of Vou. And if the monsters can enter that forest, they will surely destroy yours." He turned and walked away.

"Eslimil!" Harnistae called. "Come back here!"

Eslimil continued, and Eraim was suddenly at his side. She said nothing as they mounted, and they rode east from the village despite several more orders for Eslimil to halt. He left Harnistae with much to think about. Hopefully, the elder made the right decision when the time came.

Upon reaching the Shield River, Eslimil revealed to Eraim the fordable stretch, and they continued. Eraim's eyes moved constantly, taking in everything and surely imprinting the route into her mind. They passed a couple more villages, but Eslimil stopped only to rest the horses and spoke few words to the residents. Eraim remained silent until they exited the woodland along the Maple River and entered Sendorum.

"Vecnor says you are part Salenti."

Eslimil glanced at Eraim. It was the darkest hour of the night, but he saw her clearly. It surprised him Vecnor would divulge such information.

"But from observing you," Eraim added, "I am wondering if he is mistaken. Perhaps you are part Lorian."

Eslimil held half a grin. "He is not mistaken. My mother was of Salenti."

"Maybe I know of her."

She was searching for clues again.

"I think not," said Eslimil. "She lived with my father in Vermallon Forest for centuries. And she passed long ago."

"Oh." Eraim's eyes softened. "I am sorry to hear that. My parents live in Salenti." She sniffed. "Of course, you probably know that already."

He did.

"My mother had no home in Salenti after wedding my father," Eslimil explained. "Her village was displeased with the union."

Eraim sighed. "That was not right. It *is* not right. Salenti Forest is a wonderful place, but there is too much my kin does not understand about life beyond the trees. Most live like Lorians, never venturing forth to see what a marvelous world is out there, or the fascinating people that fill it."

Vecnor was correct. Eraim was the least Salenti-like elf Eslimil had ever met. Outside of Elgarroth, of course.

Selanna and I have completed our tasks, said Elgarroth. *Proceed to Ellaville without delay.*

"I believe it is time you report to Ellaville." Eslimil turned to Eraim. "Are you up for a hard journey?"

Eraim's pity-filled eyes fell upon Lilli. "They have ridden so hard already."

Eslimil fished an apple from his saddlebag and tossed it to Eraim. She snatched it from the air.

"A blue apple?" Eraim scrutinized the fruit, rotating it from top to bottom in the darkness.

"Feed it to Lilli." Eslimil pulled another apple and reached around so Landolice could eat it.

"I am tempted to try it myself," Eraim said, "and see if it benefits me as well as it would her."

Thankfully, she fed the apple to Lilli.

They picked up the pace, riding with little rest across Virch. Upon entering Ellaville, Dandi stole Eraim's attention. Selanna's mare stood outside the Happy Ranch with several other horses. Eslimil steered Landolice south and sped away while Eraim hurried toward the inn.

Chapter 42
A Quaint Inn Room

Following Elgarroth's instructions, Eslimil headed east to a tavern in Tribenor. The capital city of Sendorum was not as busy as in the recent past, as the soldiers that once crowded the streets had moved on to Arbornum to prepare for the march into Beit. Eslimil passed through the tavern without a word, scaled the stairs to the second floor, and opened the third door on the left within the ensuing corridor. He entered a cramped inn room with a single bed, shuttered window, washbasin, and a table holding a candle and a mug. Elgarroth sat on the bed. Eslimil had never seen the wizard surrounded by such mundane accommodations. If Elgarroth wanted rest, why not magically travel to the cabin?

"This is quaint," said Eslimil.

Elgarroth looked around and smiled. "It serves its purpose." He turned to Eslimil with tired eyes. "With everything I have done over the last month, I am nearly drained."

"Did you visit Arbornum?"

Elgarroth nodded. "I spoke with Grand Paladin Montac again, imploring him to put Vayla in charge of the force bound for Lormin Dmurr. He still insists it should be him."

"Montac is not as thick as many past leaders of the Holy City," Eslimil said. "He might yet hear your words. You are positive Vayla needs to lead?"

Elgarroth sighed. "I know it seems folly to place the fate of Vaeldor in the hands of one so young. But my visions are clear. And she is the key." He stared at Eslimil. "And I mean the actual *key*. It is hard to explain. It is like there is a chest full of divine energy within reach, but it is locked tight. Only Vayla can open it, but she cannot see it. She must be pushed harder than she believes she can endure. Only then will the treasure be visible."

"And without this chest?" posed Eslimil.

Elgarroth shook his head slowly. "There is no hope of defeating Uustaag. We will put up a grand fight, and victory will seem within our grasp. But we will fail. And Vaeldor, as we know it, will end."

Eslimil puffed out his cheeks with a long exhale. With all the skills, the strength, and the knowledge the heroes of Vaeldor possessed, it was not enough. How could so much depend on one so young? So inexperienced? What could the paladin possibly do?

"What is my part?" he asked.

Elgarroth stood. "You shall assist Vecnor in Helmland. He marches to Lormin Dmurr with his Army of Misfits, as he calls them. There is a secret entrance into the compound, and you must find it for him. After that, you will seek Vayla. But you cannot give her aid." He held a level gaze. "Not until the lock has been opened."

Eslimil shook his head. What if Vayla dies before finding the lock? What if Montac fails to make her general of the collective army? What then? And how will he know if or when this *lock* opens?

"You shall know when the time comes," said Elgarroth. "It will be her shining moment. But it will not arrive until all seems lost. That is all I can tell you."

It was not like Elgarroth to say things in such plain terms. No verses? The future must surely rest on unsteady ground.

"So… is Vecnor to face…?"

"He will likely oppose Uustaag," Elgarroth replied. "I am still working that out, so mention nothing to him."

What a nightmare! Eslimil sat on the bed, as if his legs might give out. For the first time since his parents' passing, his eyes grew warm with tears. Vecnor had been the only true friend he had known. Would his next meeting with the human be the last?

"This is the very reason we exist." Elgarroth placed a comforting hand on Eslimil's shoulder. "I am sorry."

Blinking away the tears, Eslimil rose. "I will not fail."

"There is no time for riding all the way to Lormin Dmurr," Elgarroth said. "I shall have to open a gate and get you as close as I dare. That is one reason I stay in this *quaint* little room, to shorten the distance. I must conserve what power remains." He turned to the closed window, as if looking outside. "Once you and Landolice exit Tribenor, seek a green light in the north. That will be your portal."

Eslimil left without a word.

He rode north through the city at a steady pace. The streets remained empty, and few windows bore candlelight. As the buildings fell behind, a green light flashed ahead among a small grouping of trees. Eslimil entered the grove and followed the flickering to a wide tree. Its trunk contained an archway of green fog with dancing red specks. He pushed Landolice to enter.

They exited an enormous boulder. There was no return gate. Eslimil recognized the shadowy mountains behind him to be the Stone Eagles, and to the north stretched the wasteland of Helmland, greatly altered from the last time he and Vecnor visited. The land was broken. Fissures reached out from the direction of Lormin Dmurr, ranging from a foot to twenty feet in width, and the larger ones glowed orange and issued steam that seemed to thicken the haze.

Eslimil took a moment to adjust to the new environment. With the obstacles, he estimated three days to reach the dark citadel. He and Landolice would make it in two.

They headed north, remaining as far from the smoking crevasses as possible. The smaller cracks, Landolice jumped. The way was slow at first, but as morning arrived, Eslimil got a feel for the terrain and the pace quickened.

Nighttime brought little relief, for the paths narrowed as the steaming fissures doubled, and the heat grew almost unbearable. Perspiration saturated Eslimil, and his mount slowed as it surely suffered twice as much. He fed the horse two blue apples, and it regained its gait.

Halfway to morning, Eslimil spied a force of large creatures a couple hundred yards to his left. Minotaurs. The bull-men marched northward, but at a much slower speed than Landolice. The evil army headed for the citadel.

Eslimil urged his steed to run faster.

The sky brightened, and Eslimil fed Landolice another apple before eating a piece of sweetbread. The day was then long and hot, and as dusk approached, a platoon of monsters appeared in the northeast. Lanky arms dangled from their hunched shoulders, and drool hung from the fangs of their open mouths. The trolls were marching westward.

Eslimil veered the same direction.

Nighttime returned, and shadows interrupted the orange glow of several gaps ahead. Bridges spanned the fissures. Eslimil took advantage of the fortuitous path, and well before the dawn, he and Landolice reached Lormin Dmurr.

The compound was in order. The walls were whole, the gatehouse intact, and the crumbled buildings stood erect. Surely magic played a role in rebuilding the complex. The citadel was at the rear, rising into the shadowy sky. From the rooftop shone a sickly glow, no doubt cast by the gray, red, and violet portals within the topmost floor.

Eslimil scanned the surrounding terrain. The fissures ended short of the wall encompassing the compound, and nothing moved or made a sound. No sentries manned the ramparts; the enemy did not fear an invasion. He rode forward until reaching the wall and dismounted east of the portcullis.

"Find a place to hide," he said to Landolice, feeding the horse an apple. "I will look for you in the east."

The horse whinnied. It nuzzled Eslimil's neck, and he patted it lovingly. Landolice darted into the haze.

Eslimil removed his gloves and felt along the wall. There were no seams in the rough, dark stone—it was as if it had been raised from the soil and shaped by unworthy hands. With so much surface to inspect, a feeling of dread touched his heart. What if he did not find the door before Vecnor arrived? What if it did not exist? He shook the despairing thoughts. There was no time for doubt.

Eslimil continued his search, moving away from the gate and to his right. A half hour later, he found the door forty yards to the east of the portcullis. Were the wall not so dark, it might have been obvious. As it was, those of lesser skill would have easily missed it.

Though every fiber of his being told him to leave, Eslimil sat against the wall, ignoring the evil essence behind him. How long before the armies of monsters arrived? Would Vecnor come first?

Eslimil sighed.

Chapter 43

Army of Misfits

Vecnor began his journey across the realms to build his army. He began in Kalmaar, as Elgarroth suggested. The southern region was infamous for bandits, discarded soldiers down on their luck, bullies lacking direction, and cutthroats looking for excitement and wealth. Unfortunately, the first group he happened upon had no interest in hearing his offer and assailed him. It had been necessary to slay half of the thugs before they realized the error in their decision and fled.

The second encampment consisted of thirty men, and he employed a different tactic. To appear less imposing, he dismounted and approached with a pearl necklace wrapped around his fist.

"What do we have here?" laughed a bandit while five archers fitted arrows to their bows. Curly black hair fell to the man's shoulders, and the confidence in his eyes said he would do the talking. "Looks like a knight has lost his way."

"I am Vecnor."

The speaker's grin dropped momentarily. "And he's a jester as well!"

"You can ride a mile north if you doubt me," said Vecnor. "What's left of them didn't believe me either."

The smile vanished. "Them's Mainin's boys."

Vecnor pressed his brows together. "I failed to catch any names. Sorry."

The bandit eyed the jewelry in Vecnor's hand. "Why are you here, bearing such a shiny trinket?"

"It's an offering." Vecnor tossed him the necklace. It was easily worth five hundred gold coins. "That one's a gift. The rest, you'll have to earn."

The leader inspected the pearls, likely hearing nothing since catching them. He looked up with narrowed eyes. "Who you need killed?"

Vecnor chuckled. "Trolls, minotaurs, goblins, humans, and other horrors. About eighty thousand or so."

The man turned to his cohorts and laughed. Most of them joined in, while some watched Vecnor with nervous expressions. A few ogled the necklace and licked their lips.

"So… Vecnor…" The leader looked back. "An army of monsters, you say? And where shall we find this horde?"

"Helmland."

The camp was silent for several seconds. No one smiled, smirked, or released as much as a chuckle.

"We don't fight for the *queen*." The man threw back the pearls, much to the disdain of his following. "Find your pawns elsewhere."

Vecnor tossed the necklace again. "I said you can keep it, and I meant it. But it isn't pawns I seek. I look for courage. Bravery. Those among you that tire of making a living on the road, hoping for a fat merchant to let down his guard. Those with mouths to feed. Those wishing to make their mark in this world before their time comes."

The leader sneered. "You've come to the wrong camp, my friend." He held out the necklace on a single finger. "And I'm keeping this. Now be on your way." Though he voiced a command, his eyes begged Vecnor to go.

"I shall leave." Vecnor scanned the faces before him. "And I'll keep searching for those willing to face the greatest evil of our time; a shadow that has settled over all of Vaeldor, threatening everything we hold dear. Everything." He emphasized the last word. "And in death, all that enlist will have payment forwarded to their families and loved ones."

The spokesman didn't avert his gaze, but several of his men exchanged worrisome glances. Of the bowmen, only two still held arrows ready.

Vecnor climbed onto his saddle and turned Umbarc.

"When the Ancient Enemy arrives," yelled the leader as Vecnor urged his mount eastward, "I'll buy him a thousand drinks!"

Vecnor returned to the roadside half a mile away and dismounted. He lit a small fire before setting down a blanket, and fed Umbarc a blue apple and sat to enjoy a piece of flatbread. An hour later, as dusk captured the sky, the pounding of hooves drew near.

Vecnor bit into another piece of bread.

The horses halted outside the firelight, and shadowy figures approached. At least half of the bandits had come, and their weapons remained sheathed.

"You mean what you said?" asked one. "Payment even after death?"

Vecnor nodded once.

"Why would he pay after we die?" a man with a patch over his left eye posed. "What if *he* dies? Why did I let you talk me into this?"

"He's Vecnor!" hissed the one who spoke first. "Do you know nothing?"

"I don't care much about jewels," said a bandit with a scar from his ear to his nose. "I was dismissed from service because of my limp. They don't even care how good I can still swing my blade."

"What if my family already thinks me dead?" asked a man standing half a foot shorter than the rest. "Will they still receive my share?"

Vecnor stood. "I have a contract. Once you sign the names of those to be paid, it will be done. On my honor."

"Honor..." The first man chuckled. "Never thought I'd do anything *honorable*." He grinned. "I'm in. And I know others that would jump at the chance, if you don't mind a few krukari."

"This war knows no races," said Vecnor. "Only good and evil."

"No one ever accused me of being good," laughed a bandit toward the rear. "But I ain't evil. And it might be nice to provide something for my kids besides shame. I'll sign."

Several nods ensued.

Vecnor pulled the parchment Elgarroth had given him. With a magical quill, each of them made their mark. Not all of them could write, and Bornuk, the man with the scar, took charge of listing those to receive payment upon their deaths.

"Time is short." Vecnor rolled the scroll and returned it to its container. "Take this evening to do what you must." He grabbed the treasure bag and handed each of them a gem. "Be back here by noon, or I vow to hunt you down when this is over."

The edge to his voice during the last several words led most of them to eye one another. It was obvious they believed him capable of fulfilling that promise. They nodded and returned to their horses.

And that was the beginning. The bandit claiming to know of others brought ten additional men—six were half-hobgoblins. They all signed and received payment.

"Make for Virch without delay," Vecnor said to the recruits. "There is a village called Ellaville on the western end of the realm, near the border of Neja. Do not rob *anyone* on the way, *or* after you arrive. I will know if you do. Set up camp north of the village, and I'll meet you there."

After they departed, Vecnor packed up and continued his journey—there was no time for sleep. He enlisted over five hundred Kalmirans before passing through Marcove and Sardina, who yielded six hundred more. Sendorum had little to offer, but Vecnor bolstered his muster while crossing Virch, adding another four hundred. He then visited the encampment north of Ellaville.

Over sixteen hundred thugs inhabited a field half a mile outside the town. They segregated themselves by kingdom of origin, and tensions were high. It took Vecnor pushing several around and dismissing a few to calm matters, and those departing were never seen again after Vecnor's threats to inflict horrible deaths—another promise he'd never have to act on. He promoted three men he believed to be trustworthy to keep the peace: Bornuk, the scarred Kalmiran with a limp; Cramnil, a Vircan dismissed from the army because of his age; and Driliz, an orphaned krukari from the slums of Charndova in Sardina that stood up against his taskmaster. The latter commanded a group of orphans that rebelled against authorities, and they were known as the Vengeful Deviants. Although they led lives of crime, it was crime for the sake of survival, and once Driliz joined the cause, his cohorts did the same.

Vecnor was confident the captains were up to the task, and he entered Ellaville, where the villagers exhibited several levels of stress, unsure of what to do about the gathering army of undesirables. Vecnor assured the mayor the stay was temporary, but also that more would be coming. He gave the rotund man a couple pieces of jewelry as payment for the food his men would require, and promised to produce twice as much upon his return. The mayor thanked him profusely and shook his hand, though the man's eyes showed little relief.

Vecnor returned to camp and led his captains along the Path of the Guardians on horseback, pointing out landmarks so they wouldn't lose their way on future trips. They reached the stable-cave in good time.

"On our final trip," he said, "we'll leave the horses here."

The captains frowned.

"We cannot take them into Helmland," Vecnor explained. "Horses are not in large supply, and we'd likely see them taken by the enemy."

"Or eaten, by the sounds of it." Driliz's voice resembled Gruelenor's, though he wasn't nearly as hideous to look at.

Vecnor could not argue the krukari's point.

"What if someone steals them?" posed Cramnil.

Driliz smiled. "We're not that far from Neja. Shouldn't be hard to sell 'em there."

Vecnor gave the krukari a level stare.

Driliz held up a hand. "Only teasin'!"

"No one can find this path unless shown the way," Vecnor said. "So I'll know it was one of you three."

Bornuk gave Driliz a meaningful glare before speaking to Cramnil. "You have nothing to worry about."

Cramnil showed little comfort with the statement. "It's just… this is *my* horse."

"You'll be able to buy a hundred horses!" chuckled Driliz.

Cramnil's attachment to his mount was understandable. And although Umbarc would keep watch over the herd, the captain would never believe an animal capable of such a feat.

"Your horse will remain yours when you return," Vecnor said. "You have my word."

"*If* you return." Driliz grinned. "Otherwise, he's mine."

Cramnil pursed his lips, his cheeks reddening.

"Follow me." Vecnor headed up the path, ending the conversation.

Upon reaching the bridge, Bornuk's face blanched as his eyes alternated between the strip of rock and the distant trees below. "I don't know what you *think* we're doing at this point." His voice held the slightest shudder.

Vecnor chuckled. "It's a bridge built for elves." Before anyone commented, he added, "But there's a way."

He handed Bornuk the scroll he used when he last crossed. The other captains were illiterate.

"Read that aloud," Vecnor instructed.

Bornuk stared at the parchment and frowned. "I don't speak elf."

"Just read it," Vecnor said.

Bornuk carefully sounded out each word. As he finished, the bridge expanded.

The captains gazed in wonder.

Vecnor walked Umbarc across, and once the others joined him, the bridge contracted. They mounted and headed along the trail to the north.

Traveling on horseback allowed them to bypass the next campsite, and they arrived at the final one at dusk. They stayed the night and continued early the following morning to the top of the waterfall.

Driliz dismounted and walked to the edge to peer down at the water issuing from the cliff wall. "There's nothin' like this around Charndova!"

"The world has many wonders to behold," said Vecnor.

"A reminder of what we're fighting for," commented Bornuk.

Driliz nodded.

Vecnor pointed past the waterfall. "There are steps descending just a bit farther. They'll lead you into the valley. There, you'll make camp." He eyed his captains. "Then you take the horses back and return with the next group."

"Two hundred at a time…" mumbled Driliz, recalling the orders from days ago.

"Not only is that all the reliable horses we have," said Vecnor, "but—"

"It will be done." Bornuk gave a firm nod. "We need no other reason than your orders."

Vecnor appreciated Bornuk.

They headed back, stopping to camp at the site nearest to the bridge and again on the other side. The next day, they exited the mountains into northern Virch and halted a few miles from the encampment.

Vecnor and Umbarc were exhausted—they had pushed the benefits of the apples and bread to their limits. Regardless, Vecnor said farewell to his captains and rode west to continue the search for soldiers. After scouring Neja, he journeyed into Urell Coast, Moclen, Fendora, and Philen, adding over seven hundred to the muster.

The encampment was empty when Vecnor returned with the Philanders—the final recruits. The captains had done well. Bornuk, Driliz, and Cramnil arrived the next day, fatigue heavy in their eyes, but none of them complained and they headed north the following morning for their final trip. Vecnor's only regret was for the debris they left behind—a mess of tent stakes, ashes of past fires, and scraps. But it was a small price for Ellaville to pay compared to what the Misfits were sacrificing.

Upon reaching the stable-cave, Vecnor brought the group to a halt.

"We shall walk the rest of the way."

Many frowns greeted his words, none deeper than Cramnil's.

Vecnor led Umbarc away from the others to share a private word. "Take them to the fields south of the mountains. Keep them together and out of sight as best you can."

Umbarc released an angry snort. The horse hated babysitting.

Vecnor chuckled and patted his steed's neck. "I will see you when it's over."

The massive animal whinnied and stomped its hoof.

Vecnor fought back a tear before returning to his captains, who had just explained to the Philanders the procedure for continuing. He nodded at Bornuk, and they marched toward the bridge. As they reached the next bend, Vecnor glanced to see Umbarc leading the herd south.

They arrived at the waterfall two days later, and Vecnor took a moment to view his army spread along the river. He never expected to find so many undesirables ready to die for a world that discarded them. He proceeded down the steps, reaching the valley just after noon, and as everyone gathered before him, he spoke.

"Vaeldor thanks you for your service, whether or not the powers in charge know it. There is no army more important than this army." Head bobbing followed his words. "As I told you, we will pose as soldiers of Uustaag." Several men flinched at his use of the Ancient Enemy's name. "It is vital we play the part."

"So…" a man up front looked at those around him, "you want us to be ourselves?"

Raucous laughter ensued.

Vecnor grinned. "That is precisely what I want." His smile vanished. "We will join forces with another army. They are the enemy. And although I encourage you to mingle, they cannot learn of our true mission. And none of them refer to the warlord as *the Ancient Enemy.*"

Many faces paled. Several recruits bore looks of determination.

Vecnor raised his fist. "We do this for honor, for our loved ones, and for all of Vaeldor!"

"Brondor!" shouted a smattering of soldiers.

They packed their gear, and Vecnor led the way north, walking deep into the night until reaching the southern edge of Lothen Forest. There, they made camp.

Vecnor settled away from the others and sat against a tree. As the air cooled, he pulled a blanket over his shoulders. Bornuk approached moments later, carrying the scroll Vecnor gave him to enlarge the bridge.

"Lord Vecnor?"

Vecnor held up his hand. "Just Vecnor."

"Yes, sir." Bornuk glanced at the rolled parchment. "I was wondering… might I keep this?"

"It has no use elsewhere," Vecnor said. "In fact, I doubt it will work again."

"Right, right." Bornuk nodded. "All the same, can I keep it?"

Vecnor grinned. "It's yours."

"Brondor bless you!" Bornuk bowed, and he limped away.

Vecnor chuckled.

❈ ❈ ❈

The Misfits followed the eastern border of Lothen Forest the next day, beginning the march before dawn. Upon reaching the northern edge, they settled within the trees and waited. The air was crisp, much cooler than what they were used to, but it wasn't winter, so the soldiers merely fidgeted in mild discomfort. An hour later, as the sun began its descent, an army approached from the east, following the road from Beit. The unit matched the Misfits in size, and according to Elgarroth, they aimed for Lormin Dmurr.

Vecnor raised his hand, and his captains readied the men. He motioned forward, and they exited the trees. The opposing force stopped fifty yards away while eight men continued.

Vecnor signaled the captains, and they followed him to meet the advancing group. While they walked, Vecnor noticed nearly half of the enemy were krukari and hobgoblins. His focus shifted to the approaching warriors. They were humans. A man with dark eyes and a nose bearing a long scar was clearly the leader by the arrogant expression and elevated chin.

"By whose authority do you march?" Scar Nose demanded.

"Mine," growled Vecnor. "And I'll be taking command of your company as well."

The man's brow furrowed, and his lips moved without words until finding a response. "Who do you think — ?"

"Now you get to make a choice." Vecnor stepped forward to glower over the man. "Do I kill you? Or will you be a good lad and assume your role?"

"I… um… That is, we are — "

Vecnor reached over his shoulder to grab one of his swords.

The cowering worm bowed. "Muzmar at your service, my lord."

Vecnor grinned. "Excellent. Have your men fall in behind mine."

And he took charge of the entire force.

They followed the road as it turned south around Lothen, and Darum Carumbor came into view. Firelight shone from several windows while the topmost were dark, and the stronghold silently watched from across a field.

Vecnor's mind went to Baylun and Daymyn. The boys were in the tower at that very moment, enduring… He didn't wish to imagine what the two faced, or which path Daymyn chose. He glanced at the Misfits. Many stared at the structure, unknowing of its history or what lay within, yet their eyes were nervous, nonetheless.

Vecnor picked up the pace.

The road turned west, and Vecnor's heart raced while passing the face of the tower. Bullying the general of a ragtag unit was not a difficult task, but if the master of Darum Carumbor interfered…

The portcullis remained in place. Nothing issued from the keep, and the dark building fell behind. Vecnor breathed easier, but he didn't halt until Darum Carumbor was more than a mile away.

His men erected a tent procured from Muzmar's troops. It was the only one within the encampment, and large enough to house Vecnor and his captains while the army found places to lie beneath the hazy sky. Vecnor took a moment to watch his soldiers make "friends" with the enemy before turning in. Hopefully, they didn't get too close.

The night sped by, and the force resumed their march early the next morning. Vecnor kept a hard pace throughout the day, hoping to arrive at the citadel before any others. The following night passed without mishap, and the succeeding day was as vigorous as the last, but shortly after noon, a squadron of Dun Lancers paid his army no heed while riding past. Unfortunately, there was no reaching Lormin Dmurr before the cavalry.

The third day saw the arrival of the fissures Elgarroth had mentioned. How could Uustaag cause such destruction without leaving the citadel? They were widespread and narrow, so they didn't impose too much of a hindrance, but that would change. Vecnor could not show uneasiness, and he pretended the cracks were a welcome sight.

Since combining the armies, Muzmar often grumbled to the Beitian soldiers. Still, he did not openly challenge Vecnor's command. In return, Vecnor demeaned the man as much as possible. "Be a good lad and fetch me a bowl of stew," he said the first evening. "You might need to rub my feet later," he teased after lunch the second day. It came as no surprise when Muzmar sneaked into the tent that third night.

Vecnor lay on his blanket, staring at the ceiling. Bornuk, Driliz, and Cramnil were asleep. He was about to drift into slumber himself when a noise captured his attention. He detected light footfalls making their way toward him. It was dark, but his eyesight was unmatched by any human's, and he spied Muzmar carrying a dagger. A dagger? Vecnor closed his eyes, allowing his senses to take over. Muzmar was six feet away... Four feet... The man knelt over Vecnor. Next came the swoosh of Muzmar's sleeve as the dagger descended.

Vecnor opened his eyes and moved his hand to intercept. He caught Muzmar's wrist, and easily snapped the bone as he bent it at an awkward angle. The would-be-assassin cried out, waking the captains as the dagger fell.

Vecnor rose, lifting Muzmar by his mangled arm until his feet dangled. The ex-general's screaming stirred the encampment as Vecnor exited the tent, and soldiers gathered to see what had disturbed their slumber. Many eyes widened and jaws dropped.

"This man tried to kill me in my sleep." Vecnor lifted Muzmar higher. "Do with him what you will!"

He tossed Muzmar on the ground twenty feet away, where the fool cradled his broken arm and whimpered. The first to approach was a Beitian krukari. The warrior grinned while dragging the weasel by the foot and into the onlookers.

Vecnor returned to his tent, and Muzmar's screams ended before the flap closed.

"You knew he'd try it?" asked Bornuk. He held a candle.

Vecnor shrugged. "There can be only one leader. He had to, sooner or later. But that's that. Let's get some sleep."

Bornuk grinned at the other captains. Driliz laughed. Cramnil laid down and resumed his gentle snore.

The next day saw the fissures grow closer together and the temperature rise. The march became laborious, forcing the army to veer left and right, but Vecnor pushed them without sympathy. Come night, he didn't stop to camp. Besides the space being too cramped and the heat too uncomfortable, his desire to reach the citadel grew. The only complaints comprised fatigued expressions and slumped shoulders as far as Vecnor could see. The following day, bridges spanned many of the larger crevasses, making for a direct trek, and they arrived at Lormin Dmurr that evening.

Vecnor controlled his breathing while gazing at the compound; he couldn't gasp in front of his men. Atop the citadel, strange lights danced, as if disturbed by movements within the temple floor. Outside the surrounding wall to the left of the gatehouse was gathered an army of trolls—thousands of monstrous swamp creatures outside of their element. The Dun Lancers were nowhere to be seen.

Vecnor scanned the base of the wall. Nothing moved. He scrutinized it again, and a light flickered to the eastern side of the portcullis. Tux. He proceeded toward his companion, halting thirty feet from the complex so the upper level of the citadel remained within view.

"Set up camp," he said to Bornuk. "I'll return shortly."

"Where are you...?" Bornuk's frown disintegrated. "Yes, sir!"

Vecnor walked to the wall, where the shadows were thick. He saw nothing, but he sensed a presence.

"It is about time you showed up." Tux materialized, not far from Vecnor. "I have been waiting for days."

Vecnor chuckled. "It's not easy leading this bunch around chasms of lava." He glanced over his shoulder. "Any luck?"

"I am standing next to the door." Tux traced a line on the wall with his finger.

Vecnor saw nothing.

"The mechanism is here." Tux circled an area two feet from the hidden panel.

"I'll never remember that," Vecnor mumbled. "But that's not important. The position of my army is what matters. I'm sure Eraim will find the door when the time comes."

"I am certain she will." Tux looked at Vecnor's soldiers. "A fine bunch you have assembled."

"The Misfits?" Vecnor chuckled. "Only half are mine. The others are here to fight for the enemy."

"How do you tell them apart?"

Vecnor shrugged. "I need only remember my captains. They take care of the rest."

Tux gazed at the trolls. "I never knew so many of those wretched creatures existed." He turned back to Vecnor. "Minotaurs should arrive shortly. I am surprised they are not here already."

An army with thousands of minotaurs and trolls… A daunting thought to say the least.

Vecnor changed the subject. "Where are you off to next?"

"I am to watch over Vayla."

"Good." One of several weights lifted from Vecnor's shoulders. "I fear for so many, it almost makes me ill. It's a relief to know you'll keep her safe."

"If only it were that simple." Tux hesitated. "I am not to intervene until all seems lost; after a sign I will evidently recognize." He shook his head. "But if the leaders make the wrong decisions, that sign will never come."

Vecnor took in a deep breath. He needed to remain positive. "Cavalor has a sound mind. He'll not like putting Vayla in charge, but he'll realize Elgarroth's words must be heeded."

"Have you seen the lights?" Tux glanced upward, though the wall hid the tower from view.

Vecnor nodded, remembering the dancing glow.

"The gates." Eslimil shook his head. "Every passing shadow is another monster entering our world. By the size of them, I suspect krahluks. It started a couple of days ago."

Vecnor had yet to face a krahluk or zreekan. He hoped the information Elgarroth gathered from Welmirth's journals was accurate.

"I guess this is goodbye." Tux held out his arm.

The tears welling in the half-gray elf's eyes didn't escape Vecnor's notice, and he grabbed Eslimil and squeezed. "I'll see you when it's over, my friend."

Upon being released, Tux straightened his leather sleeves. "Yes. When this is over, we will take a long holiday."

Vecnor smirked.

Tux inhaled and dissolved into darkness.

Back at the encampment, Vecnor's tent stood ready and fires burned. Apparently, the Beitians brought several skins filled with beer, and the brew was flowing. A party had begun.

Vecnor summoned his captains. Driliz held a drink; Bornuk and Cramnil did not.

"More armies will arrive," Vecnor said. "Minotaurs, goblins, Dun Soldiers, and such. I doubt they'll mingle with our group." He glanced at the trolls. The monsters' camp was dark—they detested fire. "If everything goes well, an army of Pavish will settle next to us."

"Barbarians?" posed Cramnil.

"They're on our side," Vecnor assured the Vircan. "It's important our men know this."

"How long do we stay here?" asked Bornuk.

Vecnor shook his head. "I'm not sure. A couple days maybe. So enjoy a few drinks." He turned to Driliz. "But not too many."

Driliz grinned. "Yes, sir!"

The next day, the minotaurs arrived and situated themselves between Vecnor's force and the gate. Their dirty, matted hair assaulted the air worse than any uncleaned stables, and there was no shortage of stares aimed at Vecnor's men. But fights were unlikely to arise. All the same, Vecnor cautioned his soldiers to steer clear of the bull-men. That evening, Blackfoot goblins came from the south and claimed a spot west of the trolls. The following day, Dun Soldiers chose the area next to Vecnor and opposite the minotaurs—so much for having the Pavish as neighbors. A day later, hobgoblins made camp beyond the Dun Soldiers.

The Pavish approach, said Elgarroth. *Selanna and Eraim are among them.*

Vecnor scanned the landscape, his heart lightening. Selanna's group had survived. Would he see Eraim? Did Soleran hear his prayer months ago? He spied only smoking fissures, and a couple hours of daylight were all that remained.

Selanna has devised a plan so the barbarians do not attack allied forces, Elgarroth added. *Have your men tie something white around one arm, and bring no harm to any with a face painted blue and white. You must also get the bag of bone dust to Selanna. A way shall present itself.*

It will be done, Vecnor thought.

He looked again to the south, and the silhouette of a large force appeared in the haze. Surely it was the Pavish.

"Bornuk!" Vecnor called. "Bring the captains to me!"

❈ ❈ ❈

That evening, Vecnor entertained the evil members of his army with feats of strength and agility. He sparred with several, showing off his aptitude to use any weapon, and wrestled ten at once. The soldiers roared with applause. While he distracted the Beitians, his captains made sure the Misfits received a strip of white cloth to tie around their arms when the time came.

"Hey, General!" said a muscular krukari once the contests ended. Rumor held him to have once been a Zurkan warrior. "I think I ran into your mum in Benasti. Ugliest ogre I ever laid eyes on!"

Raucous laughter ensued.

Vecnor laughed as well, and he grabbed the krukari's breastplate and issued a headbutt, breaking the warrior's already crooked nose. The mirth escalated as the half-hobgoblin fell to his knees.

"Funny or not," Vecnor shouted, "there will be no more jests about my mother being an ogre!"

The laughter continued.

Vecnor glanced at the wall, and in the darkness near the secret entrance was a tiny figure. He caught only a glimpse before it retreated into deeper shadows and disappeared. Eraim!

He took in a deep breath to conceal his excitement. Though grateful to Soleran for this opportunity, Lormin Dmurr was no place for silly emotions. "I must relieve myself," he announced.

He headed toward the wall and discovered Eraim crouching among the shadows. Strapped to her shoulder was a quiver of long, black-shafted arrows. Had she stolen them from Tux? She moved to his left, and he veered with her. She pulled Mithkahr.

"Put that away!" he said.

Eraim slowly complied, but her hand never strayed from the handle.

Vecnor stepped a few feet to her right and faced the wall, stifling a laugh as she turned away in disgust. "I'm not relieving myself." He kept his voice down. "But I must play the part."

"Then... you are not...?"

How could she doubt him after all this time? Perhaps he deserved it. "You think me capable of evil?" He raised his brow without looking at her.

She didn't respond.

He saw the angst in her eyes and felt small for having put it there. "Of course I'm not evil. The door you just located was discovered weeks ago by Tux." Weeks sounded better than days. "That's why I led this contingent to this very spot. To keep it clear."

"Tux?" Eraim frowned. "Does Selanna know you are here?"

"I don't think so." Vecnor lowered his brow. "I'm not entirely sure how much she knows... yet."

"What are you doing here?" Her eyes hardened. "*How* are you here?"

"I'm here to help," he replied. She should have known that. "And I have been here for a month." Another small lie, this one to avoid further questions as to his whereabouts. "It hasn't been easy."

A smug expression replaced her anger. "Is that why the servant was not chopping wood at Elgarroth's house when I met Tux there?"

Vecnor couldn't hold back his grin. How badly he wished she'd figure the rest out.

"It seems Elgarroth's servant has been absent a lot over the past decade," she added. "How *has* the old wizard gotten along without all that firewood?"

Now that he thought about it, Tewlon hadn't made many appearances since the end of the Necromancer War. Missions had kept Vecnor busy.

"I have been sneaking soldiers into Helmland for weeks now." He attempted to steer the conversation to more important matters. "Even so, we are greatly outnumbered, and we have to blend in."

"Have you not been *relieving yourself* for some time?"

Eraim's tone carried more sarcasm than Vecnor cared for.

"No one will be surprised by my long absence for such a task." He winked, and her glare softened again. "But time is short." He pulled the bag of bone dust from his waist and dropped it onto the ground. "Get that to Selanna. She'll know what to do with it." He looked at Eraim. "Don't open it."

Her blue eyes tore into his heart. But he couldn't explain any further, and to prolong the meeting would only cause her more heartache. He walked toward his army.

"Wait!" she said, just loud enough to be heard.

He turned back, lifting a brow. She needed to go before someone noticed them talking.

"I…" Her mouth hung open, but nothing came out. She sighed. "Be safe."

Vecnor winked again and forced himself to leave. How badly he wished to scoop her up and take her from this evil place. But Selanna needed her. Vaeldor needed her.

Upon reaching his soldiers, Vecnor caught the end of an anecdote and laughed with the others. A glance at the shadows told him Eraim had gone.

Vayla arrives soon, Elgarroth said. *It begins tomorrow.*

Vecnor's heart raced.

You will enter Lormin Dmurr with Selanna, Elgarroth added. *Do what you must to achieve victory.*

Vecnor breathed a sigh of relief. Though he had spoken often in his youth of how he would have defeated Uustaag, he no longer felt so confident, but at least he could keep Eraim safe while Tux watched over Vayla. Outside of Elgarroth and Eslimil, the maidens meant more to him than anyone.

He summoned his captains into the tent.

"Bornuk," Vecnor said once they arrived. "You'll be in charge when the battle begins tomorrow."

"Me?" Bornuk's frown was fraught with anxiety. "Tomorrow?"

Vecnor nodded. "All three of you have served me well, and you shall receive additional compensation for your extended duties."

"What about you?" asked Cramnil.

"I'm going after the Enemy."

Driliz paled—a foreign look for the krukari. "Tomorrow, huh?" He looked at the others. "We knew this day would come, but now that it's here..." He turned to Vecnor. "You can truly make sure my reward reaches my family?" Driliz's "family" comprised the orphans still living in Charndova. The krukari hoped the funds would give them a better life.

Vecnor nodded. "It will be paid."

Driliz sighed. "If any other than you made that promise, I'd tell them to jump in the Blood River. But I believe you. And I thank you for allowin' me this opportunity."

Cramnil raised his fist. "Here! Here!"

"I think we need a round of drinks," said Bornuk.

Cramnil moved swiftly to his blankets to retrieve a flask from his pack. "Thought an occasion might arrive when this came in handy." He distributed mugs before filling each with wine.

Bornuk lifted his cup. "To Vecnor!"

"To honor!" added Cramnil.

"To Vaeldor!" Driliz grinned. "Though She never gave me much of a chance, I love Her still."

"To our enemies lying at our feet!" Vecnor said.

"Brondor!" cheered Bornuk.

They drained their mugs.

❊ ❊ ❊

Vecnor was up before the dawn. Drums had pounded a mesmerizing beat throughout the night, and it was impossible to discern whether it came from inside or outside the black wall. They pounded still.

He exited the tent. Everyone remained asleep. The air was dry, and he took a deep swig from his waterskin before performing his sword exercises. He swung the blades about, pausing to glance at Lormin Dmurr after every dozen slashes or so. Shadows continued to interrupt the bizarre lights atop the citadel—additional monsters entering the upper floor of the structure.

The sky brightened an hour later, and the mass of creatures surrounding the wall stirred all at once, as did the evil muster of Vecnor's army and the Dun Soldiers. The Misfits remained asleep.

Vecnor ducked into his tent. "Get up! Something's happening."

His captains rose and began donning their armor without delay.

Back outside, the Beitians readied their gear while the Misfits were just waking. Vecnor grabbed the arm of a Beitian.

"What's going on?"

The man frowned. "Did you not hear the whispers? The enemy approaches."

Vecnor had heard nothing. He nodded and let the soldier go. Returning into the tent, his captains were nearly ready.

"Did any of you hear whispering?" he asked. "Possibly in your mind?"

They looked at one another with furrowed brows and shook their heads.

Great. Lormin Dmurr was communicating with the evil forces, and Vecnor and the Misfits didn't receive the news. Was the enemy aware of their presence? As long as the monster armies remained ignorant, it mattered little.

"Make sure our men get ready immediately," Vecnor said, and his captains scurried from the tent.

He finished dressing, and a thought occurred. Did the Pavish get the message? He exited and saw his soldiers running about. A Beitian krukari walked by, and he halted the half-hobgoblin with his hand on the warrior's chest.

"I had too much to drink last night," Vecnor said. "What did the whisper say?"

The krukari's eyes went up in thought. "Um… The enemy is near… Ready to march…"

"Yes, I remember that part," Vecnor snapped. "What else?"

"Oh, uh, just the marching order."

"Marching order?"

"Yes, General." The warrior scrunched his brow in thought. "We are to march behind the Dun Soldiers and beside the Pavish. We break right at the second bridge to flank the battlefield."

Vecnor pursed his lips. "I remember now. Carry on."

"Yes, sir!" The soldier hastened away.

Vecnor looked at the Pavish. They had sense enough to realize the armies prepared to move, and they were applying their blue and white face paint.

Bornuk approached.

"Our Beitian soldiers can hear the message," Vecnor told his captain. "We march next to the Pavish, following the Dun Soldiers."

"Yes, sir." Bornuk frowned. "For how long?"

Vecnor gave it some thought. "When the Pavish attack, you do the same. If you cross the second bridge prior to that event, strike the Dun Soldiers from behind before they enter combat." He never mentioned the Chant to his men, for fear of disheartening them. It was crucial they acted before the evil warriors employed their spell.

Bornuk nodded. "I pray we meet again, Vecnor."

Vecnor clasped arms with the captain. He hoped so, too.

He turned back to the Pavish while Bornuk left to speak with Driliz and Cramnil. The barbarians continued decorating their faces. Around Vecnor, everyone focused on preparations. He slipped away and skirted the minotaur camp.

"You there!" he yelled, gaining the attention of several Pavish. He pointed at his army. "You march next to my force."

The barbarians looked away.

"I'm speaking to you!" Vecnor growled, regaining their attention.

One of the Pavish said something he didn't comprehend. But he knew better. Elgarroth had informed him most Pavish understood at least some of the common tongue, for trading purposes. He pulled a white cloth and showed it to them.

"You march beside my army. On our left. That was the order given by the citadel. Make sure your chief knows this."

They continued pretending not to understand, and Vecnor walked away. After ten paces, he glanced back. The barbarian that spoke was missing. Hopefully, the warrior carried the news to their chief.

Upon returning to his force, Vecnor gazed into the distant haze. The sky illuminated much of the land, and amid the smoking fissures was an impressive gathering. Vayla and the allied armies had arrived. The crevasses compressed their ranks, making it impossible to know their true numbers.

A horn emitted from Lormin Dmurr, its low tone shaking the ground. None of Vecnor's soldiers responded beyond gazing at the citadel—not even the evil half. Moments later, the Blackfoot goblins marched by, followed by the trolls, and the hobgoblins moved to walk beside the swamp creatures. To either side of Vecnor's army, the Dun Soldiers and minotaurs mobilized to march fifty yards behind the trolls and hobgoblins.

Half of Vecnor's men began assembling, and Bornuk shouted orders for everyone to fall in line. Vecnor looked back. The Pavish headed his way, veering to his left. Good. As the barbarians arrived, his battalion marched beside them.

Vecnor walked at the rear of his force. He attempted several times to spy Eraim's company among the Pavish, but it was like trying to spot a particular tree within the middle of a forest without entering. There were no armies behind him, and he turned to the secret entrance. Eraim's group was there, and she stepped through the opening in the wall.

Vecnor ran to join them as Cavalor entered. Selanna followed the Marcove king, then Magneer and a couple of Pavish, the male barbarian small for one of his tribe. Romik went next, and then Baylun, Kiryanna, and Brem. Gruelenor moved through last.

Vecnor thrust his gauntlet in time to prevent the door from closing — he would never locate the mechanism on his own. He stepped into the courtyard, greeted by a mixture of fear and relief.

"Vecnor!" gasped Magneer. "Thank the gods!"

CHAPTER 44

THE CITADEL

Vecnor stood with Eraim's company behind a row of buildings lining the road from the gatehouse to the citadel. A twenty-foot-wide path of dried grass ran left and right. No enemies were present, but a frozen aura engulfed Vecnor and his companions as Radaam and Anduiff flew overhead on their way to the battlefield. Had the Death Lords been so inclined, they might have noticed the trespassers in the courtyard.

"We're in the open." Vecnor spoke with urgency. "We need to move."

Eraim led them to the nearest building, and they hugged the wall.

"The krahluks have been entering our world for the past couple of days," Vecnor said. "They are tough, so don't underestimate them."

"What do you know of the zreekans?" Magneer asked.

"Only that their magic is deadly," Vecnor replied. "But they're not strong. If you can get in close, they are easy to kill." At least, that's what Elgarroth had claimed. "But beware of their tentacles."

"I will see what is going on," Eraim said.

The rough exterior of the near building wasn't lacking for handholds, and Eraim made a quick job of scaling the wall. As she disappeared onto the flat roof, Selanna's eyes glazed over. Vecnor recognized the look. The mage was using the Sight.

He viewed the others. Romik appeared thinner, but healthy. Baylun was much larger than Vecnor remembered—the krukari's arms would have rivaled Nidor's. The male Pavish was actually Desser with a painted face; Vecnor didn't recognize the female barbarian. Black spots infested Brem's skin, and the marteese scratched a few of them — was his complexion blue? Kiryanna's scowl was absent, and she glanced often at Baylun. Were they holding hands?

Eraim returned. As she opened her mouth, Selanna spoke.

"I know. But we cannot split up."

Eraim frowned.

Of course. Selanna had been peering through Eraim's eyes; hearing her thoughts. The mage could have at least allowed Eraim to first impart her idea, so it wasn't so obvious.

"Then what do you suggest?" asked Vecnor, hoping to distract Eraim from additional frustration.

Selanna shook her head. "I am at a loss. Perhaps we can just run across the bridge."

"Through the giant gorillas?" posed Magneer.

Selanna sighed. "They will not be expecting it. We might catch them by surprise, and I will destroy the bridge so they cannot follow."

Magneer frowned. "And how do we get back out?"

Cavalor looked at the ranger with a raised brow. "You mean, after we scale the citadel, defeat Trannum, defeat Uustaag, overcome their minions, and figure out how to close the gates?"

Magneer's shoulders slumped.

"The problem is that the bridge is indestructible," said Vecnor. "Even Welmirth couldn't bring it to harm after defeating Uustaag the first time."

"Yes, I know." Selanna pursed her lips. "But perhaps I can find a way." She turned to Vecnor. "I see no other choice. We must enter, and soon."

Eraim's eyes betrayed her lack of faith in the plan. But she led them from building to building, getting as close as possible before they would have to make their presence known. Just as they readied to run, a golden light radiated from the battlefield; an aura reminiscent of Merssa's, but on a much larger scale. Inspiration coursed through Vecnor, and for a moment the krahluks no longer appeared so daunting.

The ground trembled as the enemy horn blared again, and the rattling of the gatehouse winch resonated across the complex. Vecnor and Eraim peered around the building to see the Dun Lancers, minotaurs, and krahluks heading for the rising portcullis. From the looks of it, no one was to remain in the courtyard. As the riders and monsters exited, none of them looked back.

Eraim bolted onto the bridge, and everyone followed. Nothing opposed them as they reached the entry chamber of Lormin Dmurr, but a fog of shadow billowed from the corridors to the left and right and seeped from the large doors straight ahead, limiting their sight.

"Trannum!" Selanna said with anger. "He knows we are here!"

"Of course he knows," Magneer muttered under his breath. "He *always* knows."

"He does not know all." Selanna lifted her chin. "And he will learn that truth."

Rushing feet reached Vecnor's ears, and from the shadows of the adjoining corridors charged Dun Soldiers. He pulled a sword and stepped left to meet the advance, dropping three warriors before knocking aside a Dun axe. As Baylun, Kiryanna, and Romik joined him, an explosion behind them stole his attention.

A portion of the entryway lay in ruin — stone thought to be indestructible. Magneer climbed to his hands and knees amid the resulting debris, shaking his head, while the rest of the group concentrated their efforts on the warriors in the opposite hallway. Except for Eraim. The small elf faced a zreekan in the short passage to the large doors, her bow in hand. The strange monster hovered, its skin crawling as if thousands of black worms made up its form, and four tentacles flailed in place of its legs. Serving as its body and face was a single lump, and the violet pupil of its one yellow eye pulsed while a purple tongue lashed behind a score of fangs. In a dark pool of slime beside the creature, a long black shaft slowly dissolved — Eraim must have pierced a second zreekan's eye. As she pulled back an arrow, a tentacle wrested the weapon from her grasp while another wrapped around her wrist. Her face contorted with pain.

Vecnor struck down two Dun Soldiers with a single swing before kicking a third in the chest and launching the warrior into several others. He then abandoned the fight to rush the zreekan, thrusting his sword through its potato-like body. The creature collapsed into a heap, but it didn't liquify. It did, however, leave disgusting black juices along Vecnor's blade.

With Eraim's arm released, Vecnor turned back to the hallway. Romik, Baylun, and Kiryanna had been driven several paces. Worse still, the Chant began, and the enemy's expressions were blank while they mouthed inane words.

A ringing filled Vecnor's ears, muffling all sound—Elgarroth protected him from the vile spell. Baylun remained strong, while Kiryanna and Romik slowed, and in the opposite corridor, their companions fell victim to the dark magic. Eraim pulled Mithkahr and moved freely.

Vecnor charged the opposing hallway—hopefully Baylun and Eraim handled the rest. The enemy made no attempts to prevent his assault, and he sliced through their black armor with enough force to slay or knock down an evil warrior with every strike. Attacks came Vecnor's way, and those he did not parry failed to penetrate his steel plates. He lowered his shoulder and advanced, slamming Dun Soldiers into each other and off the passage walls, and the Chant weakened as its participants dwindled. His company then fought with renewed vigor. As the last Dun Soldier fell, the Chant ended, and Vecnor's hearing returned to normal. The shadowy fog remained.

"Thank you," Selanna said to Vecnor, eyeing the massive amount of blood adorning his armor.

Vecnor nodded, looking back to make sure everyone was all right. Amazingly, it appeared they had avoided taking injuries from the evil weapons. Baylun tucked an orange jewel into his pouch, and Magneer stood next to Eraim, the two gazing at the puddle left by the zreekan Eraim had defeated.

"Brem?" asked Selanna. "Are you okay?"

The priest shivered, and his skin was definitely blue. He aggressively scratched at his dark spots, which oozed pus and blood. "I shall be well enough," he insisted. "I'll not stay behind this time."

Selanna gave a nod while Kiryanna's lips parted, as if to object. The marteese's shoulders slumped and her mouth closed.

Eraim led the way through the large doors and into the long hall. The room was in order, new furnishings having replaced the destroyed fixtures. But the tidiness didn't last as krahluks crashed through the chairs from the opposite end, three to either side of the table. Their monstrous bodies were deep black and hairless, and their arms like tree trunks. From their eye sockets issued purple mist, and while their snarling mouths displayed pointed black fangs, no sound was forthcoming.

Vecnor charged left to meet the first krahluk. The giant gorilla towered overhead, reminiscent of an ogre, but the evil essence radiating from it was far worse than any fear an ogre could generate. Vecnor ducked its fist and pierced its chest with his right sword. The krahluk countered, striking Vecnor's gauntlet—his hand throbbed with immense pain, and he dropped his weapon. The creature bared its teeth, still emitting no voice, and Vecnor thrust his left blade into the krahluk's mouth, burying it to the hilt. As the mist serving as eyes faded, the ape fell.

Around Vecnor, black pulses descended from zreekans upon the balcony surrounding the chamber. But even as they sped toward his companions, they changed directions, as if bouncing off invisible shields, and exploded furniture or chunks of the walls. To Vecnor's left, the second krahluk slammed Romik through a couple of chairs. Vecnor retrieved his lost sword and turned on the monster while Magneer opposed the third krahluk.

The explosions continued.

The giant ape brought down both fists, and Vecnor jumped back in time to escape the massive blow that marred the flagstones forever. He swung his weapons despite the pain in his hand, scoring deep gashes that splattered him with purple blood. The krahluk narrowly missed Vecnor's nose, and he slashed his right sword and lunged with his left. The first cut into the krahluk's upper arm, and the thrust pierced beneath its chin and emerged from the top of its head. Its eyes went dark.

As Vecnor pulled his weapon free, searing pain coursed along his right side—the third krahluk bit his shoulder. Magneer had inflicted very little damage to the beast, evidenced by purple lines interrupting the monster's perfectly black skin, and the ranger leaped aside to evade the krahluk's fist. Vecnor swung his left sword with all his might. The blade sliced through the krahluk's neck, and its head dropped to the floor.

"We must stop the zreekans!" Cavalor shouted.

Magneer looked at Vecnor, as if seeking permission. Vecnor nodded, and the ranger raced to join Cavalor on the wide staircase at the far end of the room. Desser and Barrelda were close behind.

Across the table, Baylun fought the final krahluk. Vecnor planted his left fist on the tabletop and leaped over the furniture. As he landed, he crashed into the ape, and a momentary chill spread through his body. He followed the action with his right sword, but the pain in his shoulder prevented him from cutting too deep.

"Use no more arrows!" cried Eraim.

The elf spoke to Gruelenor, who trained his bow on the zreekans above. Their companions had reached the balcony.

Baylun's axe drove into the krahluk's thigh, staggering the beast and allowing Vecnor a moment to recover. He thrust his left sword into its eye, and Baylun's next attack sliced through its lower jaw. The krahluk fell.

Baylun and Kiryanna raced up the stairs, where the remaining zreekans lashed their tentacles and issued devastating bolts of darkness at those opposing them. The evil spells continued missing their marks as Selanna frantically worked her hands—she was disrupting the zreekan magic!

The pain in Vecnor's shoulder became unbearable, and he dropped his right sword.

"Are you all right?" Eraim stood beside him, concern in her eyes. Vecnor winced and nodded.

Romik joined them, holding his arm close and lowering to one knee. "I think my bone is shattered!" he said through clenched teeth.

The battle against the zreekans ended. The balcony lay in shambles, and the walls behind what remained of the railing were blackened and cracked.

Vecnor focused on shutting out the pain, but it was too intense. Baylun then arrived with the orange gem. Elgarroth had informed Vecnor of Nidor's demise in a blast of divine fire, and that the paladin's soul now inhabited the fire opal. It had the power to heal, just as Nidor had, or so Vecnor heard. Knowing Romik to be in worse shape, Vecnor nodded for Baylun to tend to the Lord of the Keep first.

Baylun held the jewel against Romik's arm, but nothing happened. The krukari frowned and touched it to Vecnor's shoulder. Nothing. Gruelenor stepped next to Baylun, gazing at the gem. A fire burned within.

"Even when he lived," Gruelenor said in his gravelly voice, "Nidor only had so much energy to give." He turned to his son. "And I saw you struck twice while you fought the krahluks. You're lucky to be alive."

"Yes." Kiryanna appeared as a mother scolding her child. "You are a great warrior. But you need to take more care to defend."

Baylun nodded slightly. "I promise."

Kiryanna nearly concealed her smile—it vanished as quickly as it arrived. She gave a firm nod.

How was this beautiful marteese smitten with Baylun?

While Eraim prepared healing herbs, Brem applied a salve to Cavalor's neck, where the mark of a zreekan tentacle was obvious.

"Hold still," Eraim told Vecnor.

He did as instructed, and she pushed the herbal concoction into the holes the krahluk fangs left in his right pauldron—there was no time to remove the armor. Each thrust of the mixture brought stabbing pain, but he bore it, grateful for the elf's aid. He opened and closed his gauntlet while she worked. The ache in his hand persisted, but it would not hinder him. Hopefully, his shoulder mended enough to face Uustaag.

"You must hurry." Selanna stood at the bottom of the stairs. "The enemy continues to prepare for us."

Eraim turned to Brem. "Is there anything you can do for Romik?"

The priest still shivered. "I'm sorry. His arm is beyond my ability at the moment."

Eraim sighed. She pulled a cloth from her pack and tied a sling around Romik's neck to support his arm.

Once everyone was ready, Magneer led the way up the steps, with Cavalor close behind. Vecnor went next, ignoring the throbbing pain as best he could. They passed through large doors and into an adjoining guardroom occupied by two krahluks and the largest minotaur Vecnor had ever seen. It was every bit as giant as the apes flanking it, and the blood of its past victims stained its filthy black hair.

"Take the krahluks!" Vecnor ordered, pushing his way into the chamber to stare down the minotaur.

The bull-giant snorted, and a grin stretched beneath its red eyes as it advanced.

Vecnor met the beast, slashing his right sword with more power than he thought possible—the herbs were working quickly. The minotaur brought up its axe, but it did not completely knock aside the attack, and the tip of Vecnor's blade sliced its cheek and erased its smile. The creature slammed the butt of its weapon onto Vecnor's forehead, making the room momentarily spin. Vecnor recovered swiftly and gashed the monster's stomach with his left sword.

The minotaur released a distorted, bovine-like roar while lowering its head. Vecnor dropped his swords as it rushed him, grabbing hold of its long horns to avoid being trampled. The beast drove him several feet before twisting its neck and tossing him aside, and the wall greeted him with crushing force. He fell into a seated position.

Baylun and Eraim moved to oppose the minotaur, and the krukari's axe bit deep into the monster's back. Baylun dropped to the floor as the creature spun with its oversized battleaxe, and the attack sailed harmlessly over the young warrior. But it was not so for a krahluk not far away. The massive weapon cleaved the giant ape's neck, killing it.

Vecnor regained his feet while Eraim cut into the minotaur's leg and Kiryanna thrust her golden blade into its side. He roared as he charged, ramming the beast with his shoulder before it could focus on the maidens. The minotaur stumbled, and Vecnor pushed it across the chamber. As they passed over his swords, he scooped a blade and jammed it into the monster's nose, piercing its skull. They hit the far wall, and the impact drove the weapon to the hilt. The bull-fiend slid to the floor and ceased to move.

The battle ended, and the company seemed in good shape, all things considered. Cavalor's sword was broken, cloven by the errant swing of the minotaur that slew the krahluk. Vecnor pulled his weapon free and retrieved his other sword. They were too big for the king, but what choice was there? He handed one of his blades to Cavalor.

"Do your best," Vecnor said.

They rested briefly while Brem prayed over healing herbs and treated each companion in need. He approached Vecnor last. The marteese was pale, and dark circles underlined his eyes, barely noticeable beneath the fluids covering much of his skin.

"Are you certain you can continue?" asked Vecnor.

Brem smiled weakly. "What choice have I? Now hold still."

Vecnor knelt so the priest could inspect his injuries. But Brem didn't apply the herb concoction to his wounds. Instead, the marteese smeared the mixture on Vecnor's forehead while reciting a prayer. A tingling sensation encompassed Vecnor's head, and warmth spread to his extremities. The pain in his hand from the first krahluk vanished, his shoulder throbbed less, and the jarring ache from slamming into the wall faded. He nodded his thanks, noticing Brem had paled further, practically glowing within the shadows. How much longer could the marteese last?

For Romik, Brem provided only encouraging words. Vecnor's concern for the young lord increased.

While the company readied to move on, Vecnor reached out with his mind.

How does the battle fare?

No answer came. Either Elgarroth focused elsewhere, or something terrible had occurred. Vecnor took in a deep breath. Neither possibility mattered at the moment.

He moved to the lead beside Magneer, and they exited the guardroom into the long, arcing corridor that approached the temple. As they proceeded, an eerie chill touched Vecnor's soul, and Selanna brought them to a halt.

"Wait!"

Vecnor turned to see her pulling the small pouch he had given Eraim. Selanna untied the strap, and her body quivered while she gazed at the bag's contents. She looked at the faces staring at her.

"Hold your weapons forth," she said.

The company hesitated, so Vecnor stepped forward and presented his blade. Selanna scooped a handful of bone powder, the dusty remains of Trannum's demise, and rubbed it onto his weapon. Her focus was impressive, and she didn't flinch or reveal the slightest disgust as her hand passed over a mixture of minotaur and krahluk blood.

"What in Cafior's name?" Magneer offered his sword.

"Bone dust." Selanna smeared some on the ranger's weapon. "Trannum's bones." She coated Baylun's axe. "It is believed that fighting him with his mortal remains will afford us an advantage. Perhaps make your weapons more effective."

"Perhaps?" Magneer shook his head. "I know I have not faced Trannum before, but trusting our lives to *perhaps* and *maybe* seems extreme."

Selanna looked at the ranger. "The dust is not the only plan. Now ready your mind for Trannum. He is near." She nodded to Eraim and Cavalor, and the two returned the gesture.

Vecnor knew not what Selanna's plan entailed. He searched his mind for Elgarroth, in case her strategy didn't work. Nothing.

After treating everyone's weapon, Selanna completed the procedure by dipping Gruelenor's arrows into the pouch and coating their tips. She then closed the bag and placed it within the confines of her robe. "Let us move on."

Vecnor and Magneer continued. Baylun and Kiryanna walked to their left flank; Desser and Barrelda were to the right. Gruelenor followed with an arrow held to his bowstring, and beside him, Brem appeared as a shivering zombie. Behind the krukari and priest, Selanna walked between Eraim and Cavalor, and Romik was at the rear.

A large door filled an archway at the corridor's end, and Magneer pushed it open. Thick shadows greeted them, nearly concealing the stairway rising to the temple. A pair of blue eyes interrupted the darkness and hovered in the middle of the chamber.

"Selanna…" came a whisper. It was Trannum. "I knew you would come."

Vecnor and Magneer stepped forward to allow the others entry.

"This will be the last time we meet!" Selanna said from the hallway.

"How true those words are." The whispery voice moved about the room while the eyes remained affixed. "I have no more need of you, other than to procure that which you carry. Tell me. What form have you and Elgarroth chosen this time?"

Selanna's complexion blanched, and she didn't answer.

"No matter," said Trannum. "It shall be mine soon enough. Please, enter my chamber."

A yearning to obey the necromancer tugged at Vecnor's mind, and he walked deeper into the room against his will. Where was Elgarroth?

"Stop!" yelled Selanna.

Vecnor overcame the compulsion, as did his companions. He and Magneer stood ten feet from the hovering eyes. Baylun, Kiryanna, Desser, and Barrelda were close behind.

"Oh, it is too late for that." Trannum emitted an unnerving cackle. "You lost the moment you entered Lormin Dmurr. You see, I am here; in the corridor; in every chamber. I am everywhere. Including inside your very bodies!"

With Trannum's last words, Vecnor's limbs stiffened, making it nearly impossible to move.

"We must act quickly!" Selanna's voice was strained.

Vecnor forced his head to turn. Selanna, Eraim, and Cavalor struggled to kneel in the hallway, where a blue glow emitted.

"Destroy it now!" Selanna commanded, sliding away from the source of the light.

Trannum laughed. "You have been to my old home. I forgot that little item existed. Thank you, Selanna. I shall keep it somewhere *very* safe."

A light flared inside the chamber, and for an instant, Nidor was wreathed in flame and holding Baylun's axe. But it wasn't Nidor. It was Baylun, and the krukari defied Trannum's evil magic and raced through the doorway. Glass shattered, and the necromancer's control over Vecnor and his companions again dissipated.

"What?" Trannum hissed as the fog from the corridor rushed into the room, collecting around the floating eyes to form a humanoid shape.

Vecnor advanced, and Baylun was soon beside him. The krukari's body no longer burned, but fire surrounded the bronze axe and flickered in the warrior's eyes. Before they reached Trannum, Vecnor's stomach tingled as weightlessness encompassed his body, and he and Baylun were cast into the far wall by an invisible force. The air in Vecnor's lungs escaped with a grunt.

The chamber filled with destructive magic, as lightning, beams of red light, and exploding black darts launched from the shadow-being. Selanna frantically waved her hands from the doorway, steering the spells away from her companions as best she could. To Vecnor's right, Magneer twitched on the floor as traces of energy coursed about his body. To his left, a dark bolt caromed from Eraim and into the ceiling, raining debris onto Desser and Barrelda. Baylun's flaming eyes turned Vecnor's way. He and the krukari nodded at each other, and they regained their feet.

Another force impeded Vecnor as he charged, but he pushed through, as if bursting through the webs of a giant spider, and reached the Shadow. Baylun again crashed into the wall. Vecnor's blade left a violet line in its wake as it sliced the wraith-like form, and Trannum shrieked, sounding like one of the undead dragons. An arrow passed through the dark presence, resulting in a purple dot that grew three times its size. The necromancer cried out.

"Master!"

Trannum glided toward the stairs, but came to an abrupt halt, as if an invisible barrier denied farther progress. Selanna's doing? The eyes turned back to the room and the assault of deadly spells resumed, but none of them found their marks. Vecnor slashed, inflicting another line upon Trannum's noncorporeal body, and the attack spells diminished. Kiryanna and Desser added wounds while a second arrow passed through the necromancer's head.

"Master?" Trannum's voice grew weaker.

Baylun arrived, and his fiery axe left a violet wound larger than any weapon before it. The gash expanded until no shadow remained, and faded into nothingness.

Vecnor stood with his sword poised, in case Trannum's demise was a trick. His companions did the same. A deep voice from the opening atop the stairs rattled the citadel.

"You may enter. And bring me the Starrifix."

The Starrifix. The key Elgarroth had described to Vecnor. He looked at Selanna.

"The easy part is over," she mumbled, turning to Brem. "Please, do everything you can. And hurry."

Though the priest appeared even more like the walking dead than when they had entered the room, his shivering had ceased and he moved with renewed energy. He immediately prayed over the wounded.

CHAPTER 45

THE BATTLEFIELD

Eslimil left Lormin Dmurr behind, hoping he had not seen Vecnor for the last time. More so, he prayed the war was a success, lest the former become meaningless. He whistled to summon Landolice. The horse was not far, and he mounted and began his eastward journey.

With the rising sun, Eslimil spied the army of minotaurs. He gave a wide berth. The next day, a platoon of Dun Soldiers headed for the citadel, and a few miles farther marched hobgoblins. Eslimil remained unseen.

He continued east without rest, arriving at Darum Carumbor just past noon. Amassed outside the tower was the allied force, preparing to depart. Eslimil breathed a sigh of relief to see Vayla in attendance. Though he refused to entertain negative thoughts while awaiting Vecnor at Lormin Dmurr, he had been unable to shake the fear she might perish in Beit before the final battle.

Vayla leads the allies, said Elgarroth. *That part, at least, is on the correct path, although the decision was not attained by favorable means.*

Eslimil did not care how the humans reached the decision. It gave him hope just knowing that it was so.

The army began their westward trek, and Eslimil moved north to avoid detection. The size of the force was impressive. Though marching as a single unit, the troops were understandably segregated by kingdoms of origin; they would operate more efficiently with those trained in a similar manner. Vayla rode at the lead with members of various realms. Some of them, Eslimil recognized. There was Greyor, Macurak, and Melac—Eslimil had not seen the wizard out of

Kalmaar in years. It encouraged him that King Cavalor's Royal Guard, the zhokards, had made the journey. The warriors were an unplanned creation of Trannum's that were difficult to kill, but unlike zhomians, they had aided the allies in the Necromancer War. Lorylla, daughter of Xorlunder, was in attendance as well, as was Eimell, the only Vermallon elf among the massive force—a few thousand had joined the war. Other soldiers were present, but Eslimil could not put names to them.

Behind the lead squad marched the Palidurians, then the Sards, Kalmirans, Nejans, Philanders, Marcs, Harbanians, gray elves of Orlenfel, Mocs, Dales, Sendors, Nirans, and Salenti elves. Varlimor dwarves made up the final ranks, toting their giant ballistae and several log missiles of twenty to thirty feet in length.

Eslimil watched the allies until they were beyond sight, and turned his attention to the southeast. Elgarroth warned him of an enemy force flanking Vayla. With the field clear, he rode into Lothen Forest and concealed himself.

A couple of nights passed within the woodland, and a few hours after dawn the next day, the evil battalion arrived. There were no less than twenty thousand dunarchins dressed as Dun Soldiers, and a thousand krahluks followed. Farther back, zreekans floated across the ground—about two hundred of the deformed creatures.

The army marched south along the road and rounded Darum Carumbor. At that moment, sentries appeared atop the tower. Throughout the night, Darum Carumbor had remained silent and dark, but now it teemed with allied soldiers launching arrows from the rooftop and through windows.

The tactics made no sense. The allied warriors would never survive the ensuing onslaught.

The undead firstborns did not react like living troops. They stayed in rank, unaffected by the missiles piercing their bodies, and nothing barred them from entry—the portcullis lay twisted on the charred ground. They stormed the tower with weapons drawn. From the surrounding field, dunarchin archers released arrows while zreekans cast exploding black darts upon the roof. Strangely, no allied soldiers accompanied the blasts.

The dunarchins suddenly halted the advance, as if having received a mental command, and the archers and zreekans ceased their assault. Several hundred undead had gained access, and they now retreated. Fire burst from the roof and through the windows and entryway as an explosion erupted inside the tower. It had been a trap—Wezlok, no doubt. Every dunarchin within the stronghold was destroyed.

There were no conversations about what had just transpired. The evil army simply reformed their ranks and proceeded west.

The enemy did not stop for rest, and Eslimil followed them for two days, keeping a greater distance than usual—he knew not the reach of the zreekans' senses. If they were aware of him, they showed no concern. The second night, they halted a few hours after sunset, and dunarchins ignited hundreds of campfires.

Campfires? The undead had no use for fire. Did krahluks and zreekans need warmth? The fissures were not much farther, and Eslimil could not imagine the Thard'Dun creatures requiring light. Once the task was complete, the evil force settled a mile to the south, and Eslimil noticed many bonfires in the distant north. Vayla's encampment. Were the campfires an attempt to intimidate the allied soldiers?

A few hours before dawn, Eslimil detected marching feet behind him, pounding the ground with short steps. From the jingle of mail, it was certainly dwarves. He moved closer on foot to investigate. They were indeed dwarves, from the Stone Eagle Mountains by the looks of them.

Additional marching feet assailed Eslimil's senses, much lighter than the dwarves' and to the north. He crept four hundred yards to spy a Lorian force of five thousand—surely half the forest's entire muster. Every elf carried a bow and two quivers of long arrows, and Dresnian was among them. Eslimil returned to Landolice, grateful for the Lorians' attendance.

The sun rose, and the evil army followed Vayla into the northwest, remaining a couple of miles back. Eslimil estimated the dwarves to be yet a mile farther. He moved southwest to avoid being spotted by the Lorians and Stone Eagle warriors, and hastened until he was parallel with Vayla.

The four armies continued, each seeming to pace the one before it. A day later, the fissures slowed all progress. Eslimil detested the heat, and he drank water and wiped his brow often. As well, he ate a piece of Elgarroth's sweetbread every night and fed Landolice an apple, and they remained awake all the way to Lormin Dmurr.

Eslimil gazed at the citadel the morning they arrived. The complex lay to the northwest, surrounded by armies, and a pair of Death Lords circled above on armored dragons of bone. Vecnor's force appeared small amid the monsters and Dun Soldiers, and beyond the wall were Dun Lancers, additional minotaurs, and krahluks. Vayla's army stretched long between fissures, appearing adequate for the task ahead. But with the horrors the enemy employed, would they be enough?

Vayla halted. The trailing forces must have done the same, for they remained out of sight. A wave of activity cascaded through the allied ranks as they tied white strips of cloth to their arms to mark themselves as friends of the Pavish army. Eslimil did the same, breathing in deep and exhaling through his nose. The battle for the fate of Vaeldor was at hand. He needed to make every arrow count.

A horn emitted from Lormin Dmurr, a low tone that shook the ground. Landolice shifted beneath Eslimil, and he understood the horse's fear. Dismounting, he grabbed his bow and quivers and patted the animal's neck.

"Be on your way," he told his mount. "I will find you when this is over."

Landolice snorted, and Eslimil fed the animal an apple before sending it into the haze. He turned back to the citadel. The enemy was marching, with Blackfoots in the lead.

Eslimil moved into bow range, choosing an elevated position. The armies then clashed, and several images of Vayla and her surrounding soldiers emerged to assail the goblins—strong magic. Eslimil smirked at the enemy's confusion. The allies held the advantage.

The minotaurs charged, and Vayla retreated while other forces met the bull creatures. Meanwhile, the gray elves abandoned their bows to confront trolls approaching from the left, and humans opposed hobgoblins to the right. Human archers continued releasing arrows beyond the melee, attempting to weaken the enemy before they arrived.

Between the battlefield and Lormin Dmurr, Vecnor's men and the Pavish attacked those loyal to Uustaag, including the Dun Soldiers. Hopefully, the element of surprise prevented the Chant from becoming a factor.

Eslimil returned his focus to Vayla. She charged again, and hundreds of illusionary duplicates appeared. But the minotaurs barely noticed as they trampled images and real soldiers alike, and several allies flew left and right, tossed by the creatures' powerful horns.

Eslimil put an arrow to his bowstring.

The flanking army of Lormin Dmurr arrived, with dunarchins leading the charge. Half of the Varlimor dwarves challenged the foe, and Salenti elves added support with spells and bows. The allies looked to be superior until krahluks entered the battle. Giant fists then pulverized dwarves or knocked them through the air. The elves' magic seemed ineffective against the black gorillas, and the Salenti folk concentrated on the dunarchins. The undead firstborns countered with wizards of their own that cast bolts of lightning.

A dark presence caught Eslimil's eye. The Death Lords arrived from Lormin Dmurr to attack the dwarfish archers with evil spells and dirty yellow clouds of withering gas. The Varlimor warriors only managed to release one log missile, and it proved ineffective against the bone dragon's armor.

Eslimil made sure Vayla fared well before turning his bow on the rear force. Was it really interfering if he dropped a few krahluks? He pulled back the bowstring, but before releasing it, arrows rained out of the east. The Lorians had joined the fray.

Unlike the illusory attack at Darum Carumbor, the Lorians' long-shafted arrows pierced deep into the skulls of the undead firstborns, and dunarchins fell at a rapid rate. The undead then split their attention between the main battle and the elves of Maple Lore. The krahluks focused on the dwarves and Salenti folk, leaving in their wake a bloody mess of flesh and bones no longer resembling living beings. The Varlimor and Salenti denizens showed amazing resolve as they held their ground.

Another log missile sailed across the sky, striking a dragon's skull. The beast crashed, sweeping scores of enemies into a large fissure. Vayla battled toward the crash site with Macurak at her side, facing zombies of hobgoblins, Blackfoot goblins, and minotaurs—newly risen undead. Eslimil spotted Anduiff, and realized Vayla aimed for the Death Lord. The undead king must have abandoned the dragon before the ground swallowed it.

Eslimil controlled his breathing while training his bow on Anduiff. Every one of his nerves was alive—he could not fail Vayla. She approached the Death Lord, unaware of Radaam swooping low above the melee. Eslimil shifted his target to the mounted enemy and pulled back the string. But the sign Elgarroth mentioned had not arrived, and he reluctantly relaxed his grip.

As Radaam cast a black dart at Vayla, a spell reminiscent of the ones used by zreekans, Eslimil worried he had misread the situation. Macurak and Wezlok then jumped to intervene, and it was the wizard that suffered the dark magic. Before the missile struck, the briefest flash of green surrounded the Lorian—surely a defensive spell. The explosion sent Wezlok, Macurak, and Vayla sprawling.

Eslimil gasped. Vayla lay unmoving. Then something odd happened. Hovering above her was a golden ball of light, barely discernable in the daytime. A golden version of Vayla formed and reached down to touch prone-Vayla's chest. The image transformed back into a ball and lowered to the paladin's side.

Vayla sat up. She scanned the battlefield as she rose, and in her hand was a mace of gold. How was that possible? As Vayla raised the weapon, a golden aura enveloped her. It reminded Eslimil of Merssa, except the light extended fifty yards in every direction. Within the glow, allied soldiers fought with strength renewed, undead crumbled to dust, and smoke billowed through the seams of Anduiff's armor. This had to be the sign Elgarroth mentioned: Vayla's shining moment.

I have lost contact with Vecnor, said Elgarroth. *I cannot see through his eyes nor hear his thoughts. I am blocked.*

Eslimil lowered his bow. This was not good. Was it Trannum's doing? Or Uustaag's? And now Lormin Dmurr sounded its horn again, its tone barely audible through the clamor. From the complex's gate issued reinforcements.

We must take it on faith that he will succeed, the wizard added. *I will enter Arman Forest to see if I can break through.*

Eslimil nodded to no one.

Vayla defeated Anduiff, suffering a wound that caused her left arm to dangle, and she readied for Radaam as the Death Lord descended again. But the undead dragon could not withstand the divine power of the golden aura, and its bones blackened and deteriorated. Radaam steered the mount outside the glow to crash among enemy forces, buying Vayla a moment to catch her breath. What she saw was surely discouraging.

The battlefield was a mess, her troops spread thin. The Pavish arrived, but so did hundreds of Dun Soldiers. To the rear, Stone Eagle dwarves fought valiantly, but a dozen krahluks had broken through the defenses and the Varlimor archers turned their ballistae on them. Of the Salenti folk, very few stood. The Lorians dealt with zreekans now assaulting them with dark magic, and the reinforcements from Lormin Dmurr drew nearer, including Dun Lancers with minotaurs and krahluks close behind. Not much would separate them from Vayla once they entered the combat. The walls were closing in.

Vayla returned to the fray, working toward Radaam with the aid of the zhokards while her arm remained useless. Did paladins lack common sense? The Death Lord wielded two swords, one larger than the other, and defended itself from Greyor. Clanghorr failed to land a single blow as Radaam used magic to cast the dwarf away.

Vayla reached the undead king with three krahluks approaching her flank, and though a protective circle of allies had formed, Eslimil could not risk them failing. He rapidly released three arrows. His mind soared, and the first missile needed little guidance to pierce a krahluk's skull. He shifted the second arrow into another's eye. The last arrow, he veered into the third krahluk's nose. The apes collapsed.

Vayla now lay defenseless at Radaam's feet. Eslimil raised his bow, but Lorylla's arrow pierced the dark helmet, foiling the Death Lord and allowing the paladin to roll to safety. Radaam turned on the gray elf and released a black missile. Lorylla leaped safely away while the ensuing explosion sent Eimell tumbling.

Radaam became a blur of shadows and streaked across the battlefield until exiting the golden glow. There, the undead king reformed and commanded the surrounding enemies like a general.

The Dun Lancers arrived.

Vayla barked orders, and hundreds of allies gathered to form a shield wall while gray elves launched arrows into the krahluks and minotaurs trailing the cavalry. The Dun Lancers trampled the wall, both sides suffering heavy casualties, and as Vayla charged to meet the horsemen, more images of her and her companions materialized to assist.

Eslimil chanced another glance to the east. Nirans joined what remained of the Stone Eagle and Varlimor dwarves, and a second force of Lorians made themselves known as they felled a group of krahluks approaching the rear of the main host. Each gorilla received over fifty arrows to accomplish the feat. But the black apes continued breaking through, and the dwarves and Nirans would not be enough to halt their momentum. Soon, they would be attacking Vayla from all sides.

Focused on the krahluks before her, Vayla detected Radaam's return too late. The Death Lord struck her wounded arm as she attempted to dodge, dropping her to the ground. Eslimil pulled back his bowstring, but Wezlok released a spell to stagger Radaam, allowing Vayla to regain her feet.

The paladin and Death Lord faced each other while allies prevented Dun Lancers from aiding their evil king. A few krahluks approached, and Eslimil ended their charge with well-placed arrows. Vayla then dropped to her knees when Radaam's eyes brightened, her scream rising above the clamor as she befell a dark enchantment. Before Eslimil could intervene, a ball of fire conjured by Melac struck Radaam and freed her. The Death Lord turned on the mage, using magic to pull Melac from forty feet away and onto its smaller blade. The wizard slid from the weapon to the dead, trampled grass.

Vayla smashed Radaam's smoking vambrace with her mace, knocking the smaller sword to the ground. Radaam's arm went limp. The undead king countered, and the paladin foolishly rolled in an attempt to cripple the Death Lord. Radaam was too skilled for such a maneuver, and she was left defenseless. Eslimil nearly released an arrow, but Macurak shouldered the Death Lord aside, allowing Vayla to escape; and though a weapon did not strike Macurak, he collapsed.

Greyor joined Vayla as she charged Radaam, and the dwarf sliced through one of the Death Lord's legs, toppling the mighty foe. Vayla dropped to her knees and pounded the black helmet until the eyes faded.

The battle continued.

To the north, the surviving hobgoblins and Dun Soldiers combined forces. To the south, trolls and less than fifty minotaurs attacked like feral beasts. Krahluks smashed every allied soldier within reach to the east and west, and zreekans continued their assault of deadly magic. The Stone Eagle dwarves possessed only half their original number, while scattered Varlimor dwarves fell to a third—the ballistae were completely destroyed. Still, the dwarves did everything they could to slow the enemy's advance. Less than five hundred gray elves remained, and by the amount of arrows out of the east, the Lorians were failing fast. Eslimil saw no Salenti elves. Of the humans, he could no longer tell most of them apart for the dirt and blood covering them, but the painted warriors were obviously Pavish, and more than half of the barbarians still fought.

Vayla helped Macurak from the ground, and around her, soldiers readied to combat krahluks only moments away. The gorillas smoked upon entering the golden aura, but they did not slow; and as Vayla and her contingent charged, the false images appeared—more than double the number from before.

Eslimil held his bowstring taut while observing. A gathering of soldiers remained with Vayla at all times, and they utilized the illusionary warriors to fell several krahluks. The enemy pounded the ground with their enormous fists as they became frustrated with the false images, and they abandoned their brutish tactics, collecting into groups and making them harder to defeat.

Vayla and a pair of humans faced four krahluks, and Lorylla alit on the shoulders of one to pierce its eyes with a sword and a dagger. Another ape grabbed the gray elf by the leg and threw her high into the air, and she landed hard a hundred feet away. The Vermallon scout, Eimell, slew the offending krahluk, but he was unaware of a zreekan ten yards behind him. A dark bolt tore through the elf, exploding him into hundreds of bloody pieces. Moments later, a band of Pavish slaughtered the zreekan, preventing it from inflicting further harm.

Vayla and her companions continued exploiting the illusionary warriors to defeat the other two krahluks. But six more approached, and she appeared exhausted. Eslimil released three arrows to slay half of them, and he launched four more, piercing the skulls of the other three and another one nearby. All four collapsed.

Two zreekans crept up on Vayla, releasing darts of blackness. Wezlok intercepted the magic with spells of his own, redirecting the missiles into a pair of krahluks. The gorillas exploded. The Lorian wizard then crumpled, and the false images of Vayla and her warriors vanished.

Eslimil released two arrows, steering them to pierce the tentacled creatures, one in the top of the head and the other in the mouth — he knew the dangers of attacking their eyes. Both perished.

Vayla ran to Wezlok, and Eslimil hastened onto the battlefield. He leaped three fissures, loosing arrows to clear zreekans and krahluks from Vayla's vicinity while soldiers formed a protective circle. The golden aura faded as Eslimil arrived, and the circle parted to allow him access.

"Do not waste your Palidurian waters on me," Wezlok insisted as Vayla knelt beside him. "You will be in need of it."

"He speaks the truth," Eslimil said. "*Your* health is more important."

Eslimil detected the pounding of two approaching krahluks, and he released a couple of arrows to end their advance.

"I need you!" Tears streamed from the paladin as she pulled the stopper from a vial with her teeth — her left arm remained useless.

"Please, no," Wezlok said, just above a whisper. "There is no time to argue. Your grandmother bought my life. And now I have paid her in full. With no regrets."

"No!" cried Vayla, and she thrust the vial into the wizard's mouth.

Eslimil exited the circle. There was nothing more he could do for Vayla from his current location. She should have taken the potion herself. He dropped three krahluks as he leaped the wide cracks to reclaim his elevated position. A krahluk and two zreekans pursued, and he slew the one-eyed creatures before dropping the bounding ape.

As Vayla and her soldiers reentered the melee, the golden glow returned. The krahluks had established a stronger presence during the aura's absence, but the allies now fought with strength and inspiration, and the gorillas resumed smoking.

An explosion stole Eslimil's attention. It was not a zreekan's spell, but the distant eruption of stone. Half of Lormin Dmurr's temple floor had crumbled and fallen into the Balgorn River, and from the wreckage flew a swarm of man-sized demons with four arms and scorpion tails for legs. Their heads were skull-like, lacking noses and possessing hollow eye sockets, and gray hair streaked back from their scalps, appearing as thin daggers. Eslimil's mind moved to Vecnor, but he pushed away the thought. He needed to focus on Vayla.

The krahluks and zreekans paused in their fighting to gaze at the damaged building, as if unsure of what the explosion meant. Vayla and her warriors did not hesitate to slay several of the gorillas, and the beasts did not defend or retaliate. To the east, the Stone Eagle and Varlimor dwarves drove into a group of motionless zreekans while Lorians assisted with arrows. The enemy then snapped from their trances, and the battle resumed.

A krahluk closed on Vayla's flank as she eyed the flying monsters. Eslimil sent an arrow through the ape's head. Vayla then ordered nearby soldiers to establish a front, and Eslimil dropped three more krahluks to aid in that task.

The demons arrived, and the majority of them descended onto the Pavish. The fiends viciously attacked with swords and daggers while their leg-tails struck like snakes, and the venom of their stingers needed only seconds to slay their victims. Eslimil turned his bow on the newcomers, dropping one with every shot. Unfortunately, he did not possess enough arrows to make a significant difference.

A score of demons approaching Vayla suddenly smashed into each other, as if crushed between invisible walls, and a *clap* echoed across the battlefield like thunder. Wezlok knelt twenty yards behind the paladin with his arms extended and hands firmly together.

Vayla and Macurak charged a nearby krahluk, and a pair of demons descended toward them. Eslimil released arrows to drop the enemies from the sky. As the second one fell, Macurak tumbled and became still. The gorilla had struck him.

Eslimil pulled back an arrow, but he did not release. Every krahluk stopped fighting to clutch at their throats—some dropped to their knees. It was as if they could not breathe. As well, the zreekans cast no more magic, and their tentacles lashed wildly at nothing. Was it a result of the temple's destruction? The Thard'Dun creatures collapsed, almost in unison, and the demons crashed down and ceased to move.

Silence ruled the battlefield while everyone looked about in confusion. But then a smattering of unhorsed Dun Lancers lifted their weapons and began anew. The minotaurs and hobgoblins did not share in the lancer's desire to continue, and fled as fast as their feet could carry them while the allies overwhelmed the Dun warriors.

The battle ended, and Vayla rushed to her fallen captain.

Eslimil turned to Lormin Dmurr. Was Uustaag defeated? Did Vecnor survive?

Chapter 46

Uustaag

Vecnor led the way up the temple steps. Baylun was close behind, and the rest of the company followed.

The room differed from when Vecnor last saw it. The pillars and altar were repaired, and the archways beyond the circle of columns emitted lights: the right one gray, the left one red, and the central one violet. To either side of the pillars stood four krahluks, and within the circle, behind the altar dripping with fresh blood, a zreekan larger than all others of its kind hovered, its eye red instead of yellow. Past the zreekan, amid the arches, was a krukari no less than twelve feet tall. It wore black armor, and impaled upon spikes on its shoulders were freshly decapitated heads of men with euphoric grins.

Uustaag was the most hideous krukari Vecnor had seen—worse even than Gruzim. The warlord's skin was like old leather, fangs protruded from either side of his prominent lower jaw, and his jutting, bushy brows failed to conceal that one of his eyes was red while the other was violet. Beneath Uustaag's arm was a full helm bearing teeth reminiscent of Hezeb's, and ram horns adorned the top, like the demon Ragab. Hanging at the krukari's side was a sword Vecnor doubted any other could wield, and strapped to the giant's back was a massive hammer.

The Enemy took in a slow breath. "You will surrender the Starrifix," his voice vibrated the floor, "and I'll allow you to leave this place alive."

"You will return to your world." Selanna's words trembled slightly as she uttered them. "You are no longer meant for ours."

"I see." Uustaag drummed his fingers on the pommel of his sword, his demeanor eerily calm. "How many of you must I kill to change your mind?"

Baylun stepped past Vecnor with the flaming axe. "You can try!"

Uustaag's eyes widened for the briefest moment. His sights narrowed on Baylun, and some of the composure faded from his voice. "Where did you come by that weapon? Torrac was lost long ago."

So the axe had a name.

"I care not for your words," Baylun spat.

"No matter." All evidence of stress vanished from Uustaag's expression. "Though the fire is new, I killed its owner once. I shall do so again." The krukari donned his helmet and unsheathed his sword. His multi-colored eyes glowed from within the Hezeb jaws while violet wisps of smoke arose from the wide blade. "This is your final warning." His words carried a demonic growl when spoken through the helmet. "And there will be no retreat."

The zreekan's tentacles flailed, and a muffled explosion sounded. It came from outside the citadel.

"You will not find us easy foes." Selanna's voice continued to shake.

"Welmirth is long gone," said Uustaag. "Vennimor is dead. And now it's your turn." He moved into the pillars and stepped around the zreekan and altar. "Dispose of these mortals!"

The krahluks seemed to smile as they advanced.

"Baylun left!" Vecnor ordered. "Cavalor right! Eraim and Gruelenor, your bows!"

The rest of the company could fall in line wherever they chose; Vecnor didn't care. He focused on the Enemy.

Uustaag stepped forward, eyeing Vecnor. "You're the people's champion?" The krukari sniffed. "This won't take long."

The warlord lunged, and Vecnor knocked the smoking blade away. He countered, and Uustaag slapped his thrust aside—the krukari's strength was much greater than Vecnor's. They continued watching each other.

Green spheres raced at Uustaag—Selanna's magic. They dissolved before reaching the krukari and brought no harm. A pillar then toppled toward the warlord, but the column changed course and flew over Vecnor's head to crash into the wall a second later.

Uustaag advanced, swinging again and again. Vecnor gave ground, parrying the blows before countering. The krukari knocked his weapon aside. They danced back and forth with more of the same, Uustaag attacking three times for every one of Vecnor's, and Vecnor worked to keep the Enemy in the middle of the room. As Uustaag released a barrage of slashes, Vecnor called upon all his skills to avoid being struck—he was no match for the warlord.

Baylun joined the fight, and Uustaag thrust his shoulder at the young krukari. Baylun twisted at the last moment, narrowly avoiding the occupied spike. Still, the pauldron knocked Baylun to the floor. Kiryanna screamed as Uustaag followed with an overhead chop, but a surge of fire surrounded Baylun, halting the fiendish weapon before it landed.

The Enemy spun with the evil sword as Vecnor charged. Vecnor barely pushed the wide blade over his head, and retreated several steps as the warlord again drove him back. He needed to find an opening.

Uustaag turned and lunged, targeting Baylun as the young warrior returned. Baylun steered the thrust aside to where his brother now stood, and the blade sliced through Romik's good arm. The appendage dissolved into ash spotted with purple cinders. To make matters worse, Baylun crashed into Kiryanna while performing the maneuver, knocking her to the floor.

Wicked laughter issued from the demonic helmet.

Uustaag lifted the unholy sword in defense as Vecnor swung, but Vecnor surprised his opponent with a low slash, cutting into the Enemy's leg. Unfortunately, the tactic was ineffective and left Vecnor exposed. But the warlord didn't strike. Baylun released a barbaric roar, bearing down with the flaming axe, and Uustaag parried the attack. There was a flash of light as the evil weapon snapped.

Uustaag bellowed with rage, shaking the citadel and making it hard to remain standing. The Enemy pulled the hammer, swinging it in a wide arc; and though Vecnor dodged most of the blow, the hammerhead grazed the side of his head and breastplate.

The room spun. Through blurred vision, Vecnor saw Baylun flying through the air. His sight stabilized, and Baylun was gone. Kiryanna stood before Uustaag, raising her golden sword as tears streamed down her cheeks. The krukari paid her no mind and advanced on Vecnor.

Vecnor ducked one swing and dodged another, and the wind following the hammer challenged his balance. The lights beyond the pillars then grew brighter, drawing Uustaag's attention. Vecnor knew not what had transpired, but he dared not take his eyes from the Enemy while shaking the final traces of dizziness.

Uustaag renewed the attack with a fury, swinging the hammer from the side, overhead, and from below. Vecnor ducked, sidestepped, and steered the weapon aside. There were no opportunities to counter. The next swing struck his chest, launching him across the room until the wall halted him.

Vecnor lay on the floor, bleeding from his mouth, nose, and probably eyes and ears. His ribs pressed into his lungs and his heart barely found the strength to beat. He had failed.

Everything went dark…

A light appeared in the darkness. A golden light. Vecnor squinted. Before him stood Merssa, reaching out.

"Take my hand," she said.

The temple was gone. Vecnor and Merssa were alone in some kind of void; a black nothingness, except for the golden aura. Could it be her? Or was Vecnor having one last dream before passing on to the Halls of Brondor?

"You lummox!" she scolded. "Get on your feet. You're no good if you're dead!"

Yes. It was her.

Vecnor reached out a trembling hand, and she grabbed hold. A surge of energy shot along his arm and throughout his body. Every bone mended. His lungs healed. His heart beat a steady rhythm.

She pulled him to his feet.

Vecnor stared, dumbfounded. "How…?"

"That's not important." Merssa eyed him. "How *have* you managed without me?"

"It hasn't been easy." He released a nervous chuckle. "Your granddaughter's a handful."

Merssa smiled. "She's lovely."

Vecnor's vision blurred from tears. He wasn't there for Merssa in her final days, when she needed him most, and the thought haunted him still. "I'm sorry."

"Save your apologies. Everything is as it needs to be." Her grin stretched to one side. "I have watched you for some time." She shook her head. "You were not completely honest with me."

"I—"

"You need not explain." Merssa chuckled. "I understand." She glanced over her shoulder at the nothingness and turned back with a stern gaze. "I must return. Are you ready?"

Vecnor took in a deep breath. There was so much more to say. He nodded.

Merssa vanished. The void dissolved.

Vecnor stood near the temple wall where he had crashed. Among the arches across the room was… Nidor? Fire surrounded the barbarian paladin, and he relentlessly hacked at krahluks, zreekans, and flying demonic creatures with four arms and scorpion-tail legs. The original eight krahluk guards lay dead. Amid the three remaining pillars, the zreekan slumped over the altar, unmoving. Before the columns, Brem's corpse was barely recognizable, and Eraim assisted Nidor with arrows while Cavalor, Baylun, Kiryanna, and Gruelenor fought Uustaag.

Selanna stood at the entrance, holding a dark jewel that burned with a violet light deep inside. Black tendrils extended up her wrist, disappearing beneath her robe and reappearing on her neck and across her cheeks. Her eyes glowed purple while staring at nothing. Shaking her head, she rapidly blinked away the glow, and the dark lines retreated into the gem. Her focus shifted to the Enemy.

Uustaag approached Selanna with determination. The item she held was the Starrifix, and the warlord wanted it. Baylun cut into the krukari's leg with the flaming axe, the weapon biting deep, but it failed to deter the giant warrior. Cavalor stepped between Selanna and Uustaag, only to be slapped aside by the Enemy's gauntlet.

You must stop him, said Elgarroth.

Hearing the wizard's voice lifted Vecnor's spirits further. Surely, the chance for victory still existed.

There was no time to reclaim his sword from across the chamber, so Vecnor advanced on the warlord. His bearings were a bit muddled and his first step shaky, but as he took a second and a third, his head cleared and he began running. So focused was Uustaag on Selanna that Vecnor arrived unnoticed, and he crashed into the dark warrior with every ounce of strength he possessed, knocking the monstrous krukari to the floor.

The jaws of the helmet clamped onto Vecnor's arm while he scrambled to keep the Enemy from rising. His armor turned away the metal fangs, but they pounded again and again until penetrating the steel and ripping into his flesh. Baylun joined the scrum, leaping on Uustaag's stomach while Vecnor pinned the warlord's chest. The Enemy swung a spiked gauntlet into Baylun and the Hezeb teeth bit Vecnor's shoulder.

"Nidor!" shouted Selanna.

Vecnor prayed the mage had figured out what to do next. He wasn't sure how much longer he could hold the krukari down.

Cavalor wielded Kiryanna's golden sword, and the king sought openings to thrust the weapon. Gruelenor did the same with his own blade. Kiryanna flopped onto Uustaag, wrapping her body around the warrior's massive forearm and holding on with all her might. She was a brave little marteese indeed.

"No!" roared Uustaag, reaching his free arm toward the gates where a golden glow emanated.

An explosion shook the citadel.

Uustaag arose with a surge of power, launching Vecnor several yards away. From the floor, he saw the arches were gone, as were the back half of the room and most of the roof. Around the warlord, Vecnor's companions scrambled to their feet.

Vecnor climbed to his knee, fighting a searing pain that coursed through his arm, shoulder, and leg—the Hezeb teeth had surely injected venom with every bite. He forced himself to stand.

Selanna's focus bore into Uustaag, and the Enemy struggled against an unseen force to move toward her. She worked her hands in quick motions while mouthing unintelligible words, crashing one of the remaining pillars onto the giant krukari. The column rolled harmlessly from the black armor. Shortly after, green bolts of light raced from her fingers and disappeared beneath the warrior's protective plates. Uustaag howled in pain—an occurrence Vecnor believed impossible. One of Selanna's lights emerged from the breastplate, climbing Uustaag's neck, and it tore open the krukari's flesh.

As the Enemy roared again, portions of the crumbling walls fell and what remained of the temple shuddered. Baylun drove the bronze axe into the warlord's side, Cavalor pierced the Enemy's armor with the golden sword, and Eraim thrust Mithkahr into Uustaag's stomach. The attacks only seemed to fuel the evil krukari's bellow as he dropped his head back. It was as if he was trying to cast everyone into the Balgorn River.

Rattling on the floor near Vecnor was his sword—the one he had lent Cavalor after defeating the giant minotaur. He pushed away all pain and snatched the weapon as he charged. Leaping higher than he thought possible, Vecnor plunged the blade into the Hezeb jaws and down Uustaag's throat.

The roar ended. Uustaag fell.

A flame erupted from nowhere, briefly washing over what remained of the temple. But it brought no harm. A comforting warmth filled Vecnor, and his injuries vanished. Nidor's doing, no doubt. The healing fire appeared to have mended everyone's wounds, except for Romik's missing arm and Brem's crushed body.

"We must flee!" Selanna said, her eyes wide.

Baylun went to his brother to offer support, and Selanna uttered a hasty spell, lifting Brem's mangled corpse onto a floating green light that moved to her side.

"This way!" Eraim said, racing down the stairs.

Selanna and her magical stretcher followed, and Vecnor ushered the others along, descending last.

Dust fell from the ceiling while the company avoided uneven fractures in the arcing hallway. Everyone then struggled to remain standing in the guardroom bearing the giant minotaur when Lormin Dmurr sank a few inches. As the quaking eased, they hastened into the long hall.

The stairs were mostly intact, and the company sped downward and past the dead krahluks as Eraim led the way across the room. Beyond the large doors, they maneuvered around the corpses of Dun Soldiers littering the entry chamber. A gap outside the citadel then halted them. The bridge was gone.

Selanna stood at the edge of the drop off and recited another spell. "Cross now!" she said upon completion.

Nothing had changed.

Eraim stepped over the water without hesitation, running atop the air as if an invisible bridge supported her. Everyone followed. The farther they moved, the more Lormin Dmurr crumbled, and as they set foot on solid ground, the structure collapsed altogether. So did Selanna. The poor mage appeared exhausted, and her eyes closed.

Eraim knelt beside her friend with alarm. "Are you all right?" She shook the mage. "Selanna? Are you okay? Are you hurt?"

Selanna's bloodshot eyes gazed at Eraim. "I am just tired."

"Oh." Eraim removed her hands from Selanna's shoulders. "I am sorry."

Selanna rose upon shaky legs and scanned the compound. The dark buildings were quiet. But were they empty?

"Vayla shall arrive soon," the mage said, revealing a fleeting smile. "We should remain here until that time."

Vecnor's heart lifted to hear Vayla had survived. He briefly wondered if Tux was all right, but he shook the thought. The half-gray elf was a master of escape when the situation called for it. He took in a deep breath and gazed at the sky. The haze was thinning.

Anticipation of the survivors' arrival drove Vecnor to walk along the road. No one seemed eager to follow, and Eraim's concern for Selanna kept her from leaving the mage. He eyed the buildings' fifteen-foot-high entrances on either side of the wide path. No windows existed, only doorless archways, and the dark interiors revealed nothing.

Vecnor continued until reaching the closed gate. A thick chain led him to enter the gatehouse on the right, and he employed all his strength to crank the winch until the portcullis lifted. Locking it in place, he returned to the road and waited.

The army of allies arrived shortly after, with Vayla at the lead. Her left arm rested within a sling, several strands of her hair had escaped the knot on the back of her head, and dirt, blood, and scorch marks marred her face. She halted and smirked at Vecnor.

Vecnor noticed the golden mace on her belt, and all he could do was grin. It suited her. Beside Vayla was Macurak, covered in more blood than any soldier should be, and Wezlok trailed behind with Greyor and Lorylla. The dwarf allowed the gray elf to lean on his head for support. Wezlok spared Vecnor only a glance, while Greyor and Lorylla gave respectful nods.

"It's great to see you, Master Vecnor," Vayla said.

Vecnor found himself speechless. In that moment, Vayla appeared as a child too young to have led troops into battle; a ray of sunshine among a most vile collection of buildings. She was the version of Merssa that married Borse; the one receiving an orphan baby to raise as her own. Vecnor's eyes grew warm, and he bowed while holding back the tears.

"You must thank Tux for me," she added. "His assistance was most appreciated."

"It will be done." Vecnor bowed again.

In an instant, Vayla's smile vanished, and she was the militant version of her grandmother while barking orders for the buildings to be searched. Soldiers from various kingdoms responded, working together to complete the task.

Vecnor followed Vayla as she continued along the road to the river. Cavalor ran to embrace his daughter, allowing tears of joy to flow, and he kissed her forehead, much to her halfhearted chagrin. Several more cheerful greetings ensued.

Vecnor thought of leaving while everyone was occupied—Tux surely headed home already. Even with his stock of flatbread exhausted, he had strength enough to return to the Path of the Guardians, and it wouldn't be long before he found Umbarc to carry him the rest of the distance. A lump arose in his throat when he spotted Eraim staring, as if waiting for him to do just that. How could he disappoint her again so soon?

Stay with your friends, Elgarroth said. *I will see you in a month.*

Vecnor winked at Eraim.

She grinned from ear to ear while moving to his side. "You are not leaving?"

There's no place else I'd rather be at the moment, he thought. But he said, "There's a lot to do. Helmland remains a dangerous realm." He looked around. "I'll make sure everyone gets out safely."

Chapter 47

Change of Masters

Vecnor allowed the allied forces to clear any monsters hiding in the compound without his help. They discovered two minotaurs, three trolls, a dozen hobgoblins, and an equal number of Blackfoot goblins. A score of krahluks lay in the cellars of a couple buildings, already dead. From what Vecnor heard, the creatures that had emerged from the arches perished all at once.

After Vayla declared the complex empty, the army returned to the battlefield, where they discovered many wounded soldiers and cared for them with what supplies existed. Among them was Bornuk. The bandit sat on the blood-stained ground, grinning, and his bad leg was mangled. Vecnor shared a laugh with the Kalmiran.

"You'll need to pay me extra!" the injured captain said. "A survivor's bonus, if you will."

Eraim frowned, looking from Vecnor to Bornuk and back.

Vecnor narrowed his eyes at the warrior. "I can do better than that. Have you ever met Queen Elloria?"

Bornuk scowled. "I told you I was turned away. And I'll be slower still, if this leg don't mend."

"She's a good friend of mine." Vecnor smirked. "I believe she'll find work for one with your skills."

"I would think King Sullis would be empathetic," Eraim said. "He has only one arm, after all."

Bornuk scowled again, obviously unappreciative of the comparison.

Vecnor chuckled while Eraim applied a splint. "I shall speak to the queen and king." He stared pointedly at Bornuk. "You just make sure you arrive in Darmhorng before the end of next month. It's north of Burma—"

"I know where the blasted castle is!" Bornuk glared at Eraim. "Do you know what you're doing?"

Eraim raised a brow and returned to her task. Once completed, her results were as good as any experienced healer's.

The search for survivors took the rest of the day—Bornuk was the only Misfit. They camped half a mile from the battlefield once they finished. The land remained scarred by fissures, but the cracks were dark, as the lava had receded, and several fires were lit with the cool night. While at the fireside, Vayla vowed to return and transport every slain ally to their homeland so proper arrangements could be made.

Come morning, the army marched east while the Pavish headed west, save for Barrelda. The female barbarian remained with Desser. A few days later, Darum Carumbor was before them, a gravestone exhibiting remains in dark armor. The allied force slowed to gawk at Wezlok's handiwork.

As the road turned northward on its way to Beit, Vayla halted. Vecnor had informed her that he aimed for the Path of the Guardians, and all those that faced Uustaag joined him, except for Cavalor. Vayla hugged each of them before they parted, saying, "Thank you."

Nothing opposed Vecnor's group while they traversed the forest and entered the Stone Eagle Mountains. Selanna, whose strength returned with every passing day, giggled when they reached the narrow bridge—it seemed some of the company had chosen to forget about the gorge. Magneer joined his son and nephews in not wanting to cross the valley a second time, Gruelenor was hard to read, and Barrelda appeared as if she had just rubbed the white paint over her entire face. Selanna eased their anxiety when she used magic to expand the bridge, much like Elgarroth's scroll had done, and they proceeded.

The stable-cave contained several horses, including Lilli and Dandi. But there weren't enough for everyone. Baylun rode with

Kiryanna, Romik shared a mount with Gruelenor, and Magneer surrendered his horse to Desser and Barrelda while he squeezed onto Nidor's steed behind Vecnor.

Upon exiting the mountains, the world they knew returned, and everyone's expression brightened. It was as if the past weeks had been a nightmare. While Eraim and Selanna led the way across the grassy fields sloping gently downward, Eraim shared a look with her friend, and the elves rode farther ahead for some privacy. Although Eraim spoke softly, Vecnor heard every word.

"I cannot believe you gave me the black stick! And without telling me!"

Selanna sighed, offering no defense for her actions.

Vecnor smiled. He didn't blame Selanna. He would have done the same thing, given the mage's options. Eraim was a lot like Tux: resourceful and nearly impossible to corner.

For the rest of the journey, Eraim rode beside Vecnor and said nothing to Selanna.

Upon reaching Ellaville, some of the company procured additional mounts, as the town had been inundated with the horses that transported Vecnor's army through the mountains — so much for Umbarc keeping them together. New fences penned in the animals, and the community showed obvious signs of prosperity from the resulting sales. Vecnor searched the herd until locating Cramnil's horse, and he purchased it as well. It would make a fine gift to Cramnil's family, in addition to the captain's compensation.

Vecnor exited Ellaville under the watchful eye of Eraim and whistled for Umbarc. Minutes after, the Andrian horse galloped out of the north. Vecnor chose not to scold his steed for allowing the animals to be corralled — he was just happy for the reunion.

A few days later, the company camped a mile north of Rivercross, and Vecnor walked the perimeter, as he did every evening. He didn't fear attacks through the night — the region was relatively tame — but it made the world seem normal. Eraim joined him.

"How long before you disappear?" she asked.

Vecnor shrugged. "As soon as home calls me."

She scrunched her brows. "Where is home?"

Vecnor chuckled. "In a room seemingly too small for one such as myself. Yet, it has everything I need."

Eraim shook her head. "Inn rooms are not a home."

He smirked, knowing she'd believe that to be his meaning.

"Have you never wanted a place of your own?" Eraim looked up at him. "A real home?"

Vecnor sighed. "As tempting as that sounds, it wouldn't fit my lifestyle. I'm on the road too much."

"That would be no bother to me." Eraim gazed forward. "I am used to you being gone for years, though I dislike it. And this way we can see each other more often."

Vecnor frowned. "What?"

"A home." She halted, prompting Vecnor to do the same. "I have found the perfect spot. It is not in Salenti, mind you. But for you, I would live anywhere."

Vecnor held his breath. He hoped he misunderstood.

"I love you, Vecnor."

His heart ached. He loved her too, but it wasn't fair to say so. His time was nearly spent. Elgarroth would soon hand over the occupation of Seer to Selanna, and Vecnor's duty would end. It was time to fade away and become a true legend. He looked into her eyes; her smiling eyes. Nothing he said would spare her the pain he was about to inflict. He could only try to minimize it.

"You are very special." He knelt to look her eye to eye. "And were it my choice, this *home* sounds beautiful."

Her smile faded as her tears reflected the moonlight.

"I cannot give you the answers you seek," he said, "just as I cannot choose the life you offer. Though I care for you more deeply than you'll ever know, I left that decision behind long ago."

Her shoulders raised and lowered as she controlled her breathing. "It is Elgarroth. I know it is."

Vecnor rose with a sigh. "I made my choice. No one made it for me. My life is not mine to give. *That* is my truth."

"Fine." Eraim turned away. "Have your secrets." She headed for the campsite at a hurried pace.

A tear rolled down Vecnor's cheek.

He remained on guard for the rest of the night. As morning neared, he checked on the company. Only Gruelenor was awake. The krukari held something, and stared intently at the object. Next to Selanna, Eraim looked like a child fast asleep.

Gruelenor realized Vecnor's presence. After glancing at the resting bodies, the krukari approached. "Everything all right?" Though he spoke softly, his gravelly voice carried. Surprisingly, no one awoke.

Vecnor nodded.

Gruelenor's gaze shifted from the sky to the brightening horizon. It was obvious he had something to say.

"Is something amiss?" Vecnor asked.

The krukari visibly struggled with the words. "It's been so long since that battle in Kalmaar..." he said, finding his voice. "It's easy to convince myself you remain ignorant." Gruelenor sighed. "But you must have noticed... when..."

Vecnor raised a brow. "When you saved my life? Have I ever thanked you for that?"

Gruelenor held a wry smile. "I'm sure you didn't need any help from me."

"Don't fool yourself." Vecnor winked. "Everyone needs help now and again."

"Regardless, I see it in your eyes." Gruelenor faced Vecnor. "You know of where I come from."

Vecnor nodded once.

The krukari shook his head. "I allowed myself to believe only Nidor knew."

Gruelenor opened his hand to reveal an orange shard. It was a piece of the fire opal that once housed the paladin's soul. How had the krukari obtained it?

"He understood me," Gruelenor continued. "He helped me to lead a better life. And now he's gone. I had hoped he would teach Baylun everything he taught me."

Near the smoldering campfire, Baylun slept very close to Kiryanna, clutching his battleaxe.

"Your son is much stronger than his friends and family realize," Vecnor said.

Gruelenor chuckled. "He's almost as big as Nidor was."

"That's not what I mean." Vecnor turned to Gruelenor. "His spirit. His heart. Your father's lineage ended the moment you accepted Brazan with no plans to return."

Gruelenor attempted to show no emotion, but his eyes betrayed his surprise with the statement.

"You need not look over your shoulder anymore," Vecnor said. "You're respected, and you are loved. You carved a road of faith for your son, and he will flourish because of it. I'd say Nidor did his job quite well."

Tension visibly melted from Gruelenor's expression. And though it was obvious he had more questions, the krukari would never voice them aloud.

"I must go now." Vecnor motioned for Umbarc to follow.

Gruelenor glanced at Eraim. "Now?"

Vecnor nodded.

The krukari forced a grin. "Don't blame you. I detest parties too."

Vecnor kept his laugh silent. "You like to make everyone believe so. But you enjoy watching your family and friends have fun, no matter the cost."

Gruelenor almost smiled.

That was good enough for Vecnor. He didn't mind having shared information with the krukari—Gruelenor would tell no one of their conversation. After years of distrust for the krukari race, Vecnor needed to give credit where it was due. Gruelenor was a hero among men, and his son would surely exceed him. Perhaps their example would inspire others to follow the path they paved. Perhaps the world might change for the better.

"Will I see you again?" Gruelenor asked.

Vecnor shrugged. "All things come to an end." He gazed at the fading moon. "But you never know what the future holds."

He mounted, giving Gruelenor another nod, and clicked his heels to begin his journey home. Though Elgarroth had not called him, Vecnor dared not stay any longer. It would only cause Eraim additional pain.

❈ ❈ ❈

Vecnor arrived at the House of Elgarroth two weeks later. Elgarroth sat before the fire while Tux brushed Landolice.

"You are early," said Elgarroth without looking.

Vecnor dismounted. "There was no sense putting it off." He removed Umbarc's saddle. "It was cruel to remain."

Elgarroth smiled. "I see Eraim's future filled with happiness." He turned to Vecnor. "You have nothing to fear on that account."

That gave little comfort.

Vecnor sat across from the wizard. Tux approached with a tray holding two goblets and a large mug brimming with a foamy brew. In eight hundred years, the Salenti-elf had never served Vecnor—he didn't count the time he was recovering from their journey into Hell. Vecnor chuckled and accepted the mug.

Tux handed a goblet to Elgarroth before sitting with the final cup, and he raised it. "To victory. To the preservation of Vaeldor, and the end of Uustaag and Trannum."

"Here! Here!" Vecnor and Elgarroth chimed in.

Vecnor took a long swig. He wiped his lip and turned to the wizard. "Where were you? I had no idea what was happening outside the citadel."

495

"The magic emanating from Lormin Dmurr was strong." Elgarroth raised his brow. "Though I possess power greater than most, I could not combat the strength of a deity." A grin formed. "That is, not by myself. It was not until I employed the support of Arman that I penetrated the shield of silence."

"Did you see Merssa?" Vecnor asked.

Tux looked up.

Elgarroth frowned. "Once I broke through, I could not detect you at all. And I could not find Selanna. I had to use Eraim to see your companions fighting Uustaag. And then, suddenly, you were there." He gazed at Vecnor. "Where did you see Merssa?"

Vecnor wasn't sure what to say. He wasn't even sure where he had gone after being struck by the massive hammer.

Elgarroth studied Vecnor. "She saved you." He smiled. "Bless her soul."

"I believe I saw her on the battlefield," said Tux. "For a moment only, as a being of golden light. She rescued Vayla."

"That was the treasure Vayla unlocked," Elgarroth explained. "When she was at her lowest, believing all hope had abandoned her, Vayla opened a portal to the heavens; a corridor by which the gods could send their angels." The wizard paused, as if in thought. "Except, of course, for Nidor. Silcor was far-sighted, indeed, to have forged that paladin's soul when He did. But without Vayla, the Dale would not have been enough. Others were necessary, none more so than Merssa. It was her destiny. The reason for her existence."

Merssa was a busy paladin for having been dead for twenty years. As Vecnor recalled the warmth he felt while holding her hand, it returned, filling him with comfort all over again. She was watching him even now. A vision of Nidor replaced Merssa, the Silcor paladin slaying evil as it emerged into Vaeldor.

"I saw Nidor as well," Vecnor said, "defeating evil at the gates."

"Yes." Elgarroth lifted his pipe, and smoke issued from its bowl. "And with the aid of Merssa and a few others, the openings are no more." He looked at the darkening sky. "Now, it is over."

Vecnor gazed at his beer. "What's next? Do we vanish? Drop dead?"

Elgarroth chuckled. "Our time is at its end, but it is not so sudden. We will age, as we would have before taking our oaths."

Vecnor's heart raced. He would live another sixty years or more? Could he give those years to Eraim?

"Do not be hasty in planning your lives just yet." Elgarroth drew from his pipe. "The new Seer must assume her place before we are dismissed. And even then, our vows hold us to secrecy."

Vecnor pushed thoughts of Eraim away. "When does Selanna replace you?"

"Soon." Elgarroth turned back to the fire. "Very soon. And we need to prepare."

Elgarroth allowed Vecnor to fulfill his promise to Bornuk, and he journeyed to Darmhorng Castle and spoke to Queen Elloria and King Sullis. The queen happily promised to find the Kalmiran hero an occupation. Vecnor then returned home to prepare, in accordance with Elgarroth's wishes. Preparations included gardening, trimming trees, and sweeping out the house. In eight hundred years, Vecnor had never completed chores outside of chopping wood and serving guests. He figured it was Elgarroth's way of keeping him and Tux busy until Selanna's arrival. And it was probably a good thing. Vecnor couldn't avoid fantasies of riding to Salenti Forest to find Eraim and start their new home—that is, if she would still have him. She would outlive him by a couple of centuries, but he was willing to spend what time he had with her if she was open to the idea.

Several months later, Elgarroth made the announcement.

"Selanna approaches." He looked at Vecnor. "Please see to the wood." He turned to Tux. "You may wait around the back of the cabin."

Vecnor sighed.

He reported to the woodpile and grabbed the axe. The first couple of swings were as himself, as usual, and the tool crashed through the logs with ease. He expected the next cut to be less effective, when Selanna passed through the surrounding foliage, but the axe came down with equal force. He had not transformed into Tewlon. Had Elgarroth forgotten? He looked up to see the wizard rise while Selanna and Eraim dismounted.

What was Eraim doing here?

The small elf eyed Vecnor, working hard to stifle a laugh. Selanna seemed puzzled by his presence.

"Welcome," said Elgarroth. "Please, have a seat."

Vecnor lifted a stack of wood and entered the kitchen. The door remained open while he set the bundle next to the hearth, and he heard Elgarroth speak again.

"Are you ready for your new life?"

"New life?" asked Eraim.

"Now?" Selanna's voice was higher than usual, obviously unprepared for the question.

Vecnor saw a tray bearing five goblets of wine on the counter. Five?

Please join us, said Elgarroth.

Vecnor carried the tray from the house.

The conversation halted while he served Elgarroth and their guests. He then set a goblet on the log nearest to the cabin, and placed the tray on the ground as he took the final cup and claimed the spot opposite Tux's drink.

With a smug expression, Eraim sat a little taller. "I knew you were the wood chopper."

Vecnor could not withhold his chuckle, and he sipped his wine. He wasn't sure where the conversation headed, but Elgarroth saved him a journey by bringing Eraim to the clearing.

Tux accepted his goblet as he joined them.

"You will want to live here," Elgarroth said to Selanna.

Selanna looked from the wizard to Eraim and back. "So soon?"

"It is a job that has no holidays." Elgarroth held her with a level gaze. "And it is time that you got to it."

Selanna's eyes widened. "What about you?"

Elgarroth smiled. "My days in this world are not yet spent. I shall remain, retired as it is. But I will be available for counsel, if you find the need."

Eraim had stared with her mouth agape during the exchange. Her brows now furrowed as she stood. "What is going on?"

"Selanna is the new Seer," said Tux.

Evidently, the wizard had prepared Eslimil for the visit. So much for the oath of secrecy!

Eraim was thoroughly confused. "But the Seer—"

"Is in Tikken city?" Vecnor raised his brow. "That's the human seer."

Okay. This was a little fun.

Selanna frowned at Vecnor before turning to Eraim. "It is true. Elves have a seer as well. That is what Elgarroth is. That is what he has been training me to be."

Eraim glared at her friend. "How long have you known?"

Selanna hurried her response. "Not long. Just after our first meeting in The Jeweled Scabbard."

"But..." Eraim looked from Elgarroth to Tux to Vecnor. "What about Tux and Vecnor? Are they seers too?"

"They are my companions," Elgarroth replied. "They are with me. Here to serve me."

Selanna frowned at the wizard. "Companions?"

Elgarroth lowered his brow. "Did I not tell you? As seers, our lives extend beyond those of normal elves. I am just over a thousand years old, if I remember correctly. And it is essential we have companions. But we cannot be bothered with training new ones every time they pass on, so these two journeyed with me into Arman Forest to make their oaths. Their fates are tied to mine." He searched the sky. "I believe human seers can bond companions as well. All seers have the ability to enter Arman Forest, after all. Of course, the humans do not realize any of this, and it is not my place to tell them so."

"Companions!" Selanna held a devious grin. "That is how you learn so much. Tux is your spy!"

Elgarroth glanced at Vecnor. "And Vecnor is my strength."

Selanna looked like a child, impatiently waiting to open a gift. "Do I get a companion?"

Vecnor's heart sank. Selanna was going to choose Eraim. That was the reason for Eraim's attendance — Elgarroth had surely seen it. She was the obvious choice, and had Vecnor not allowed himself to get caught up in his dream life with the small elf, he would have remembered that.

Elgarroth spread his hands. "You may have two. But no more." He turned to Eraim. "But it appears to me you have both spy and strength combined into one."

Eraim blushed.

Elgarroth was right. Eraim was the most capable individual Vecnor had ever met.

"I do." Selanna nodded vigorously, staring at her long-time companion. "I choose Eraim, without a doubt." She spun back to Elgarroth. "But I shall still take a second, whether or not I am in need."

Before the war, Vecnor thought Nidor the best warrior to fill the role of Selanna's champion. But that was no longer an option, and he could think of no one else worthy.

Elgarroth lifted his brow. "Is that so?"

"Vecnor."

Vecnor had sipped his wine to hide his disappointment, and he now choked on the liquid. Could the oath bind him a second time? He looked at Elgarroth. "Is that possible?"

Elgarroth nodded, his smile unwavering.

The elf seer had known all along. Were Vecnor able, he might have been angry with Elgarroth. As it was, a small body packed with more muscle than most grown men knocked him from the log. Eraim kissed his forehead, his cheeks, his nose, and his lips. All traces of anger melted into the soil beneath him and vanished.

The conversation continued, but Vecnor heard little else. He grabbed Eraim's arms to settle her and kissed her deeply.

❊ ❊ ❊

Eslimil was happy for Vecnor and Eraim. Had he known Vecnor could serve a second Seer, he would have told the big man. Perhaps Elgarroth kept that knowledge hidden because it might have altered Vecnor's actions over the past fifty years. Only Elgarroth would know the truth. And maybe Selanna.

Selanna… What would the golden-haired seer do now? With Uustaag gone for good, there were no looming shadows over Vaeldor. When Eslimil accepted his duties with Elgarroth, the Enemy was on everyone's minds; and although it took most of Eslimil's life before the evil awakened, there were constant omens of things to come. What would be Selanna's greatest test? Whatever it was, Eslimil had faith in the silly elf. She would do just fine.

He inhaled deeply as Elgarroth and Selanna entered the cabin. It was the first breath of a free elf, and it tasted sweet. Not that Eslimil minded the past ten centuries—decades of challenges and excitement. He would not trade those years for the world. But now it was time he decided on what to do with himself.

Eslimil walked to Landolice's saddle. After grabbing his quiver, he settled on a soft grassy spot to inspect his arrows and think. The issue was that he had already been everywhere; seen everything. He knew the secrets of most kings, queens, and high-standing citizens. There existed no hidden paths he had not traversed, no castles he had not explored, and no lands he had not surveyed. Unless you counted the swamps, Tarn Arum Jungle, and the mines of Lornibur. But who wanted to explore those horrid places?

Eraim led Vecnor toward the back of the house. The height difference was comical. But love conquers all, right?

Love… That was it. The only path Eslimil was yet to travel. For centuries, he watched people grow, fall in love, and pass on. Never had he experienced the journey filling the gaps in between. Only three elves had ever caught his eye, all of them over eight hundred years ago. The pain of living through the disappointments were the only times he truly regretted joining Elgarroth.

The air suddenly seemed purer and the sky brighter. Eslimil would find himself a wife and have the life he had believed impossible. But would she be of Orlenfel? Salenti? Dakreal? Vermallon? Definitely not Maple Lore! Where would they live? How many kids might they bear? For the first time in forever, Eslimil felt giddy.

He slowed his breathing. One step at a time. He pictured an elf maiden awaiting his return from hunting with their son, a vision similar to his own youth. But was he teaching the lad to hunt? Or did he impart *other* skills? He had years to decide.

Eslimil smirked.

❁ ❁ ❁

Vecnor was alone with Eraim. Tux sat near the edge of the trees, inspecting those long arrows, and Elgarroth had taken Selanna into the house to show her around. How could the wizards accomplish the feat without entering and exiting a hundred times? Vecnor supposed Elgarroth could move from room to room.

"Come." Eraim dragged Vecnor toward the back of the cabin. "Let us walk."

Vecnor happily accepted the invitation.

"You let me go on and on about a home," she said as the clearing disappeared beyond the trees to the north, "and all along you had the perfect spot."

"Believe me," Vecnor chuckled, "if I —"

"No." Eraim held up her hand. "All is forgiven. It was mean how all of you kept this from me," she grinned, "but I told you I would figure it out."

"But you didn't…" Vecnor closed his mouth. Why risk angering her?

"That is why Elgarroth revealed everything." Eraim began skipping. "He understood how close I was to your little secrets."

Vecnor smiled and took her hand.

She looked up at him. "Are you human?"

He chuckled. "Yes. I was born in Kalmaar." He frowned at the memory. "It was not such a nice place then. I was extremely pleased to see Karrak's line take the throne."

A few seconds passed, and Eraim spoke again.

"So you have lived a thousand years?"

"No." He lowered his brow. "Tux was with Elgarroth from the beginning, well before they found me. Maybe eight hundred."

"And you are sure you can stand to live another eight hundred?" Her blue eyes anxiously awaited the answer.

He lifted her up and held her against his chest. "Surely you jest. The next thousand will be fantastic!"

She grinned. "This is going to be fun!"

Yes. It would be fun. There would also be journeys to make, perils to face, and evil to thwart. But there was no need to discuss those matters at the moment. If luck found them, those days were centuries away.

This Concludes

House

of

Elgarroth

But the journeys continue…

Look for more adventures in Vaeldor in the future.

Acknowledgements

As always, my deepest thanks goes to my wife, Justiina, for her continuing support and patience. To Ronnie, thank you for taking time out of your busy life to provide the maps. And once again, Mary J. Nichols provided invaluable assistance through the editing process. Thanks to all my readers that reach out with encouraging words; your support keeps me working on the next adventure!

About the Author

Ronald G. Bellar was born in Ohio and raised in Michigan, one of the middle children in a family of ten. He has degrees in electrical engineering and automated manufacturing, but his love for numbers led him to a life in tax accounting. His passion for medieval fantasy began at age 11, when he was introduced to *Dungeons & Dragons*, and it was cemented after reading *The Lord of the Rings* by J.R.R. Tolkien. He began writing when he was 15, but did not take it seriously until he was encouraged to do so later in life. After coaching football for 31 years, he retired his whistle to pursue his writing career, but his love for sports endures. He currently lives in Michigan with his wife and son.

Ronald G. Bellar has also written the *Fate of Vaeldor Trilogy*, including *Alas! The One that Evil Brings*, *Might and Strength of Evil Bone*, and *Eyes Open in Shadowy Hall*. And the adventures in Vaeldor will continue...

Look for additional novels in the future.

Prophecy of Trannum

As told by Seac the Seer

Power of five, united by one,
Forth on journey, defy the sun.
Summer tastes winter, darkness draws near,
Sleeping do wake 'neath shadow of fear.

From edge of old, bond does break,
At last revealed, One all did forsake.
Evil long subdued, the One long sought.
Centuries pass, power hard bought.

Alas! the One that Evil brings,
Takes the lands, takes the kings.
Forces gather, dark secrets unknown.
Death march begins from One's throne.
Under sunless sky, o'er blanket of cold,
Fall of strength by treacheries unfold.
Dark power grows, living join through death.
By might of Lords, Hallowed Land is wrest.

Many a hero, born to die.
Trial of time, the battles cry.
Companies four, to take the test,
Set forth on perilous quest.
Seek to end at dark throne,
Might and strength of Evil Bone.
Power shatters, dust does fall.
Eyes open in shadowy hall.

As told by Selanna

"Eyes of old are kindled;
Master returns from below;
Frozen righteous hand shall fall;
Sight is blinded in Shadow's wake.

Crystal of Doom, Air of Death;
Shadow's prize arrives at last;
Portals three, the Duke returns;
Savage land is broken.

The key! The key!
The Duke is leashed;
Release the minions,
March the hordes.

Shadowy hall, undisturbed;
Underlings hold the power;
Trap is sprung, treachery arises;
Scorching death avails.

Lords take flight;
March begins;
Borders crossed;
War is waged.

Within, without, the final stand;
Golden sun, Flame of Life.
Tools enriched with bones of dust;
Immortal to mortal, shadows fade;

Evil storm, fire cracks;
Gates are, the key;
Star affixed in holy hand;
Flame, not flame."

Glossary of Names

Andria (an-DREE-uh): Barbarian realm north of Harbnum.

Andrian (an-DREE-uhn): Barbarian native to Andria.

Anduiff (AN-doo-if): Krukari Death Lord. First Lord of Benasti Forest. Disappeared after his undead dragon was blasted from the sky by Wezlok.

Arbornum (AR-bor-nuhm): Militant city off Shield River. Guards the only bridge connecting Harbnum to Beit. Opposes the city Onzac.

Arduer (AR-doo-er): High Paladin of Arronaus in the High Order of Palidur.

Arkor (AR-kor): Younger brother of Vikur. Granduncle to Romik. Has only one arm. Governs Ironside Keep while Romik is away.

Arman (AR-muhn): Forest in northern Tenvale. Mysterious woodland known to possess magical properties. Resting place of Vou.

Arrikan (AIR-ik-in): Mountain ranger in northern Harbnum. Was married to Pallit. Mother of Magneer. Died of old age after the Necromancer War.

Arronaus (AIR-uhn-us): Deity of the sky.

Arubit (uh-ROO-bit): Giant ogre that moved from Orlenfel to Benasti Forest.

Balgorn (BAHL-gorn): River in Helmland. Also called Blood River.

Ballrik (BAHL-rik): Son of Vikur and nephew to Arkor. Father of Romik. Saved the realm of Nira from a demonic invasion by jumping through a gate to close it.

Barcum (BAR-kuhm): Name Vecnor gave to Umbarc when his horse shrinks to the size of a normal horse.

Barraday (BAIR-uh-day): City in southern Kalmaar.

Barrelda (buh-RELL-duh): Female Pavish barbarian.

Batorn (buh-TORN): Gulf north of Kalmaar. Also a breed of horse from the region of the gulf, known for their beauty and great endurance.

Battle of Balgorn: End of the Great War, when Welmirth defeated Uustaag at Lormin Dmurr by casting the warrior into the river.

Baylun (BAY-luhn): Krukari son of Gruelenor and Lorin. Half-brother to Romik. Cousin to Desser and Daymyn.

Bayn (BAYN): Marteese battlemage. Killed by the demon Ragab in Trannum's crypt.

Beit (BAY-it): Realm of northern Vaeldor. Ruled by evil.

Beitian (BAY-shun): Citizen of Beit.

Benasti (beh-NAS-tee): Forest in northern Kalmaar. Largely inhabited by evil tribes of hobgoblins, krukari, and ogres.

Benzon (BEN-zin): Capital city of Beit.

Blackfoot Goblin: Tribe of goblins unseen since the days of the Ancient Enemy of the North.

Borleen (bor-LEEN): Mountains separating the Desert of Fire from Tarn Arum Jungle and the fields north of the jungle.

Bormungdaher (BOR-muhng-DAR): Ancient dwarf king of Varlimor. Commissioned the construction of Palidur Bridge.

Bornuk (BOR-nuhk): Dismissed soldier in Kalmaar with a limp. Lives as a Bandit outside Barraday. Captain of Misfits.

Borse (BORS): Priest of Cafior. Marries Merssa. Father of Cavalor and grandfather of Vayla.

Bouldertown: Large village in northeast Harbnum.

Brazan (BRAY-zuhn): Journey taken by the princes of Benasti Forest to gain the skills necessary to defeat their father and claim the title of Lord of Benasti.

Brem (BREM): Marteese from Neja. Priest of Frayorna. Suffered permanent black spots on his skin from undead insect bites.

Brondor (BRAHN-dor): Deity of battle.

Bruulu Damiss (BROO-LOO duh-MEES): Ancient brand of mead from Holindale. Also called Nectar of the Gods.

Burmagaard (BER-muh-gard): Capital city of Kalmaar.

Burnod (ber-NAHD): General of Zurzak in Beit. Assists Vayla.

Cadorn (kuh-DORN): Death Lord destroyed by Merssa during the Necromancer War.

Cafdella (caf-DEL-uh): Village in Neja sporting rich soil.

Cafior (CAF-ee-or): Deity of the land.

Candermane (CAN-der-mayn): Waterfall in northern Varlimor Mountains. Also secret tunnel passing beneath the falls.

Cavalor (CAV-uh-lor): King of Marcove and father of Vayla. Adopted son of Merssa and Borse. Given to Selanna by Tarm when he was a baby and delivered to Merssa.

Chaluck (CHAHL-uhk): Castle guard in Kembald when Eslimil visited.

Charal (CHAR-uhl): Lake near the border of Selt and Nira, fed by the Echo Valley Rapids.

Charndova (sharn-DOH-vuh): City in Sardina, on the western edge of the pass through the Varlimor Mountains.

Clanghorr (KLANG-or): Ancient dwarfish battleaxe. Wielded by Greyor.

Coranthiar (kor-ANN-thee-er): Mountains across northeastern Vaeldor.

Council of Wizards: Group of eleven wizards, including the Seer, that rule over the free city, Tikken City. Responsible for keeping peace between nations, establishing a common language, and providing wisdom to kings and lords across Vaeldor.

Cramnil (CRAM-nuhl): Vircan soldier dismissed due to age. Captain of the Misfits.

Dakreal (DAY-kree-uhl): Forest in Philen. Home to Dakreal elves.

Dale Barbarian denizen of Holindale. The dark-skins.

Dandi (DAN-dee): Salenti horse belonging to Selanna.

Darmhorng (DARM-horng): Castle in Kalmaar. Home to King Radaam, then King Karrak, and then Queen Elloria and King Sullis.

Darmoor (DAR-moo-er): Militant city off Shield River. Guards the only bridge connecting Virch to Beit. Opposes the city Zurzak.

Darum Carumbor (DAIR-uhm cuh-RUM-bor): Ancient watchtower of Helmland during the reign of Uustaag.

Daymyn (DAY-min): Son of Solinin and Della. Cousin of Romik, Baylun, and Desser. Desire for power led him to betray his family in Darum Carumbor.

Delarrin (duh-LAIR-uhn): Young farmer-turned-soldier in Steadshire. Killed during the Necromancer War.

Dellabville (DEL-uhb-vil): Small village outside of Palidur. Hosted the second wedding between Merssa and Borse.

Dellen (DEL-in): Captain of the Guard in Tikken City. Killed by the demon Hezeb in Sistama.

Demoligius (dem-uh-LIDG-ee-us): Evil deity of fire and reptiles.

Denvale (DEN-vayl): City in Marcove on the eastern edge of the pass through the Varlimor Mountains.

Desser (DES-sir): Son of Magneer and Kalette. Mountain ranger captured by Pavish barbarians. Cousin of Romik, Baylun, and Daymyn.

Dimarr (di-MAR): Barbarian chief in Andria that possessed one of Trannum's orbs. Killed when Merssa destroyed the orb.

Dominelli (DAHM-in-EL-ee): Largest village of elves in Salenti Forest. Home to Selanna and Eraim.

Dragon Wars: Battle between dragons and all of Vaeldor. Led to the extinction of the giant reptiles when the wizards of Tenvale released Dragon's Fire, a devastating spell that also destroyed a portion of the Ladal Mountains. The region was renamed the Fire Hills.

Dresnian (DREZ-nee-uhn): Lorian elf soldier.

Dright (DRITE): Swamp west of Nomedd where Trannum placed thousands of the undead.

Driliz (DRIL-ehz): Krukari orphan from Charndova that began the Vengeful Deviants after claiming his freedom. Captain of the Misfits.

Dun (DOON): Title given to most things associated with the evil deity Thard'Dun, including Dun weapons, Dun Priests, Dun Soldiers, and Dun Lancers.

Dunarchin (DOON-er-kin): Undead created from a firstborn. Elite warrior, able to walk beneath the sun.

Dunuthar (DUHN-uh-thar): Death Lord.

Durl (DURL): Birth name of Cavalor.

Eastgate: City on the eastern border of Neja. Keeps watch over the only bridge crossing the Stony River.

Eimell (EYE-mel): Vermallon elf. Former scout for the Council of Wizards.

Ekland (EK-land): Barbarian territory north of Selt. Longtime enemy of Andrian barbarians.

Eklander (EK-lan-der): Barbarian denizen of Ekland.

Elgarroth Sandanari (EL-guh-roth SAN-di-NAR-ee): Elfish seer. Resides in the House of Elgarroth in Vermallon Forest. Mentor to Selanna.

Ellaville (EL-uh-vil): Village in northwestern Virch.

Elloria (el-LOR-ee-uh): Priestess of Brondor. Ascends to Queen of Kalmaar. Married to King Sullis.

Eraim (ee-RAYM): Salenti elf. Master of many talents and friend to Selanna. Wielder of Mithkahr.

Eslimil Tuxendora (EZ-li-mil ESLIMIL-en-DOR-uh): Legendary thief. Leaves the word "TUX" behind to take credit for his mischief. Spy for Elgarroth.

Faylun (FAY-luhn): Castle guard in Kembald when Eslimil visited.

Feddas (FED-uhs): Captain in Elloria's army in Burmagaard.

Fellna (FEL-nuh): Was married to Larman in Eastgate, Neja. Her son, Malen, now runs the inn.

Fendora (fen-DOR-uh): Kingdom in southwestern Vaeldor.

Fendorian (fen-DOR-ee-uhn): Denizen of Fendora.

Fenreil (FEN-ree-uhl): The new Seer in the Council of Wizards of Tikken City.

Fire Hills: Hills separating Vaeldor from the wilds north of the Tarn Arum Jungle. Once majestic mountains; destroyed in the Dragon Wars. Known for its reflective stones that make the terrain appear to be on fire when the sun sets.

Frayorna (fray-OR-nuh): Deity of the forest. Mother of Nature.

Fremar (FREE-mar): Scout captain in Elloria's army.

Galenfial (guh-LEN-fee-uhl): Deity of the elves.

Garaard (guh-RARD): Lake in Kalmaar, north of Burmagaard.

Garren (GAIR-en): High Paladin of Arronaus in the High Order of Palidur before the city fell.

Garthglen (GARTH-GLEN): Swamp in southern Moclen that held one of Trannum's orbs. Poluran led the expedition to claim the orb, but failed.

Gothnelli (goth-NEL-ee): Original name of the Silent Marsh. Elfish for hunting ground.

Gray Elf: Elf from Orlenfel Forest. Tallest of the elfish clans. Most known for their grayish skin, white irises on black eyes, and natural magical abilities.

Great War: The war between Vaeldor and Uustaag the Dark.

Grellmor (GREL-mor): Ancestor of Vikur and Arkor. Commissioned the construction of Ironside Keep on the pass through the Varlimor Mountains.

Greyor (GRAY-or): Dwarf from Morimont in the Varlimor Mountains. Wields the legendary battleaxe, Clanghorr.

Gruelenor (GREW-len-or): Krukari. Married to Lorin. Father of Baylun and step-father to Romik.

Guardians: Elves tasked with keeping watch over Helmland for the return of Uustaag.

Gruzim (groo- ZEEM): Death Lord destroyed by Vecnor. Father of Gruelenor. Grandfather of Baylun.

Harbanian (har-BAY-neeuhn): Citizen of Harbnum.

Harbnum (HARB-nuhm): Kingdom north of Sendorum. Protector of one of only two bridges crossing the Shield River.

Harnistae (HAR-nis-tay): Elder Lorian in Maple Lore Forest.

Helmland (HELM-land): Wasteland north of the Stone Eagle Mountains where the Ancient Enemy of the North resided.

Helni (HEL-nee): Queen of Fendora.

Hezeb (HEZ-ib): Demon possessing hundreds of teeth.

High Order: Organization of High Priests and High Paladins that govern Palidur. In New Palidur, they act as advisors for the Grand Paladin.

Holindale (HOE-lin-dayl): Barbarian territory south of Tenvale. Home to the dark-skins.

Horx (HORKS): Krukari prince. Son to Gruzim and Mayry.

Hubrid (HYOO-brid): Former High Paladin of Arronaus in Palidur. Died protecting the retreat of the city's last survivors before it fell.

Ironside (EYE-ern-side): Keep governing the pass through the Varlimor Mountains. Surname to Arkor and Romik.

Jerove (jur-OVE): High Priest of Cafior in the High Order of Palidur.

Jurak (joo-RAK): Krukari Death Lord.

Kalmaar (KAL-mar): Kingdom in eastern Vaeldor. Known for its strong military and dedication to the worship of Brondor.

Kalmiran (kal-MAIR-in): Citizen of Kalmaar.

Karlsum (KARL-suhm): Baron of Eastgate in Neja.

Karrak (KAIR-ik): King of Kalmaar. Died in Darmhorng Dungeon after he was freed by Selanna.

Kembald (KEM-bahld): Capital city of Marcove.

King's Rangers: Organization of mountain rangers that protect Vol Maren from monsters living in the Stone Eagle Mountains.

Kiryanna (keer-YAHN-uh): Marteese warrior in Neja. Bodyguard of Brem.

King Arman (AR-muhn): The largest lake in Vaeldor. Located north of Arman Forest.

Kodahn (KO-dahn): Ogre warrior in Orlenfel Forest.

Kolermane (KOHL-er-mayn): King of the dwarves from Morimont in the Varlimor Mountains.

Korban (KOR-bin): Bridge spanning the Squire River. Built by dwarves of Rornibur and named after their king of old. Made of rorbak.

Krahluk (KRAH-luhk): Gorilla-like monster from the world of Thard'Dun. Hairless with jet-black skin.

Krelnamir (KREL-nuh-meer): Paladin of Cafior that perished in Ironside Keep to save Vikur from Radaam.

Krukari (kroo-KAR-ee): One possessing both human and hobgoblin blood. Outcasts.

Ladal (lay-DAHL): Mountains separating Desert of Fire from Tenvale.

Ladonia (luh-DOHN-yah): Married to Lord Rholmar. Mother of Montac.

Lambrak (LAM-brak): Castle for the King of Marcove. Located next to Kembald.

Landerik (lan-DAIR-ik): Paladin of Brondor. Follower of Sullis. Largely blamed for Merssa's death.

Landolice (LAN-doh-lees): Batorn steed belonging to Eslimil.

Larman (LAR-min): Owned Larman's Brew in Ellaville, and then Larman's Haven in Eastgate. Family rescued by Merssa.

Lilli (LIL-ee): Salenti horse belonging to Eraim.

Lorian (LOR-ee-uhn): An elf from Maple Lore Forest.

Lorin (LOR-in): Wife of Ballrik and then Gruelenor. Mother to Romik and Baylun.

Lormin Dmurr (LOR-min duh-MER): Ancient citadel of Uustaag the Dark, Ancient Enemy of the North, in Helmland.

Lornibur (LOR-ni-ber): Ancient home to the dwarves. Original birthplace of the dwarfish race.

Lorylla (LOR-i-luh): Gray elf of Orlenfel. Daughter of Xorlunder.

Lothen (LOH-then): Forest on the border of Beit and Helmland. Home to the Guardians.

Maak Maak (MAHK MAHK): Giant, two-headed lizard (possibly a dragon) that lives in Lornibur. Defeated by Selanna, Eraim, and Greyor.

Macurak (muh-KYER-uhk): Captain serving under Vayla.

Magneer (MAG-neer): Mountain ranger. Son of Pallit and Arrikan. Marries Kalette. Father of Desser.

Mahlor (MAH-lor): Friend of Vecnor's from his younger days.

Mainin (MAY-nin): Bandit leader in southern Kalmaar.

Malgabi (MAL-guh-bee): Half-undead servant of Trannum. Killed by Gruzim.

Maple Lore: Forest along the Shield River. Home to the Lorian elves, a territorial race known to hold disdain for all other races.

Marc (MARK): Citizen of Marcove.

Marcove (MAR-kohv): Kingdom south of Kalmaar.

Marfesna (mar-FEZ-nuh): Ice demon employed by Trannum to spread eternal winter.

Marteese (mar-TEES): One possessing both human and elf blood.

Mayry (MAY-ree): Wife of Tarm and then Gruzim. Biological mother of Cavalor and Solinin. Desired power above all else.

Mees (MEES): Elfish word for alarm.

Melac (MEL-ak): Companion to Vikur and Poluran. Became wizard to the queen in Kalmaar. Sent to fight in the war by Queen Elloria.

Mentrial (MEN-tree-ahl): Forest in Marcove. Known to house bandits.

Merdain (mer-DAYN): King of Moclen.

Merssa Goldmace (MER-suh): Cafior paladin; hero of Palidur. Leader of the Necromancer War. Died while destroying Cadorn, general of the Death Lords. Married to Borse. Mother of Cavalor. Grandmother of Vayla.

Millord (MILL-ord): Stone Eagle dwarf from Rornibur. Cousin to Poluran. Died in Lornibur during the Necromancer War.

Mithkahr (MITH-kar): Ancient elfish blade possessed by Eraim.

Moc (MAHK): Citizen of Moclen.

Moclen (MAHK-lin): Kingdom west of King Arman Lake. Home to Tikken City and the Council of Wizards.

Montac (MAHN-tak): Son of Rholmar and Ladonia. Grand Paladin of New Palidur.

Mordan (MOR-duhn): Steward to the Council of Wizards.

Morimont (MOR-i-mahnt): Largest city of dwarves in the Varlimor Mountains and home to the dwarf king.

Morsum (MOR-sim): Elderly gatekeeper of Ironside Keep.

Muzmar (MUHZ-mar): Beitian commander in charge of small army bound for Lormin Dmurr.

Necromancer War: The war against Trannum.

Neja (NAY-shjuh): Kingdom south of the Stone Eagle Mountains. The Bandit Kingdom.

Nejan (NAY-shjuhn): Citizen of Neja.

Nelceana (nehl-shee-AH-nuh): Goddess of Water.

New Palidur (PAL-lid-er): Name given to Palidur after the city was rebuilt, a task led by Nilborg and Rholmar after the conclusion of the Necromancer War.

Nidor (NYE-dor): Paladin of Silcor. One of the dark-skinned barbarians from Holindale. Possesses special abilities involving fire.

Nilborg (NIL-borg): Priest of Soleran. Fought in the Necromancer War. Worked with Rholmar to rebuild Palidur, and renamed the city New Palidur. Assassinated by the Shadow.

Nira (NYE-ruh): Kingdom north of Kalmaar and south of Selt.

Niran (NAIR-in): Citizen of Nira.

Nomedd (NOH-med): Barbarian territory devastated by Trannum. Uninhabited.

Nomish (NOH-meesh): Citizen of Nomedd.

Norvec (NOR-vehk): Name used by Vecnor when posing as a human guard.

Olinin (OH-li-nin): Marteese wizard from Neja. Killed by Trannum while investigating the Silent Marsh.

Onivar (AH-nee-var): King of Virch.

Onzac (AHN-zak): Militant city off Shield River. Guards the only bridge connecting Harbnum to Beit. Opposes the city Arbornum.

Orlenfel (OR-len-fell): Forest in northeastern Kalmaar. Home to the gray elves.

Paknal (PACK-nuhl): Soldier in Norvec's platoon in Darmhorng Castle.

Palidur (PAL-i-der): Holy City in Sardina. Destroyed by Trannum's minions. Rebuilt as New Palidur by Nilborg and Rholmar.

Palidurian (PAL-i-DOO-ree-uhn): Citizen of Palidur.

Palius (PAY-lee-us): Warrior companion of Elgarroth. Perished in Sistama.

Pallit (PAL-lit): Mountain ranger. Married Arrikan. Father of Magneer. Killed by dunarchins in Trannum's stronghold during the Necromancer War.

Pavan (puh-VAHN): Barbarian realm of the northwest.

Pavish (PAY-vish): Barbarian native to Pavan.

Peltagarr (PEL-tuh-gar): City in northern Kalmaar off the Batorn Gulf.

Philander (FYE-land-er): Citizen of Philen.

Philen (FYE-len): Kingdom in southwestern Vaeldor.

Poluran (POH-ler-uhn): Stone Eagle dwarf from Rornibur. Former owner of Clanghorr. Killed by Radaam in Ironside Keep.

Radaam (ruh-DAHM): Death Lord possessing skills in both combat and sorcery. Disappeared at the end of the Necromancer War.

Ragab (RAH-guhb): Demon with many horns and bone spurs protruding from its skin. Possesses ram-like horns and a two-foot spike on its head.

Ralspen (RAHLS-pen): Lieutenant in Darmhorng Castle in charge of Norvec's squadron.

Raynek (RAY-nek): King of Nira.

Rholmar (ROHL-mar): Paladin of Arronaus. First Grand Paladin of New Palidur. Married to Ladonia. Father of Montac. Worked with Nilborg to rebuild Palidur and renamed the city New Palidur.

Rivercross: Large city in Virch near the Korban Bridge. Famous for its market.

Romik (ROH-mik): Lord of Ironside Keep. Son of Ballrik and Lorin. Older brother of Baylun. Cousin of Desser and Daymyn.

Rorbak (ROR-bak): Rare white stone native to the Stone Eagle Mountains. Used in the construction of Korban Bridge. Defies time.

Rornibur (ROR-ni-ber): City of dwarves in the Stone Eagle Mountains.

Rybeal (RYE-beel): Wizard that assisted Poluran in hunting Trannum's orb in Garthglen Swamp. Perished in Dright Swamp while saving his companions from an undead dragon.

Rybex (RYE-behks): King of Philen.

Salenti (suh-LEN-tee): Forest west of Moclen. Home to Salenti elves. Also a breed of horse that grows shorter and possesses long life and heightened intelligence.

Sard (SARD): Citizen of Sardina.

Sardina (sar-DEE-nuh): Kingdom east of King Arman Lake. Houses the free city of New Palidur.

Seac (SAY-ahk): The Seer. Member of the Council of Wizards of Tikken City. Assassinated by the Shadow.

Selanna (suh-LAHN-nuh): Salenti elf wizard. Friend to Eraim. Pupil to Elgarroth. The new elfish seer.

Selt (SELT): Kingdom north of Nira. Theocracy dedicated to Demoligius.

Seltan (SEL-tuhn): Citizen of Selt.

Sendor (SEN-dor): Citizen of Sendorum.

Sendorum (sen-DOR-uhm): Kingdom north of Sardina.

Shadia (SHAH-dee-yuh): Evil Goddess of Darkness.

Shield River: River separating the evil realm of Beit from the rest of Vaeldor.

Sikilaville (si-KIL-uh-VIL): Village within Urell Coast, south of Tall Pines Forest.

Silcor (SIL-kor): Deity of fire.

Sistama (SIS-tuh-muh): Elfish name for the Silent Marsh.

Soleran (SOH-ler-uhn): Deity of mercy and light. Defender of the Defenseless.

Solett (soh-LET): Wizard from Tenvale that possessed one of Trannum's orbs. Killed by Selanna.

Solinin (SOH-lin-in): Son of Tarm and Mayry. Killed by Gruzim in Nira.

Soren (SOR-in): Paladin of Soleran. Killed by Radaam during the Necromancer War.

Star: Batorn horse owned by Vayla.

Starrifix (STAR-i-fix): Powerful magical item once possessed by Uustaag the Dark, Ancient Enemy of the North. Key to the openings between Thard'Dun's world and Vaeldor.

Steadshire (STED-shire): Large village in Nira.

Stone Eagle: Mountains north of Neja. Home to Stone Eagle dwarves.

Stony River: Border between Virch and Neja.

Sullis (SULL-is): King of Kalmaar. Paladin of Brondor. Lost his sword arm in the Necromancer War.

Tarm (TARM): Duke that conquered Kalmaar and became king. Was married to Mayry. Killed by Gruzim. Biological father of Cavalor and Solinin.

Tarn Arum (TARN AROOM): Jungle in the deep south, beyond the Fire Hills.

Tedonis (teh-DAHN-is): Former compound of Merssa's make before the Necromancer War. Evolved into a city and was named after the original surname of Merssa.

Tenvale (TEN-vayl): Realm south of Arman Forest. Kingdom of Wizards, known for its strange laws.

Tewlon (TOO-lahn): Name used by Vecnor when in his elfish disguise.

Thalamir (THAH-luh-meer): Name used by Vecnor when in his dwarfish disguise.

Thard'Dun (thar-DOON): Darkest of all evil deities. The Dark One.

Tikken City (TEE-kin): Free city located in Moclen. Governed by the Council of Wizards.

Torrac (TOR-ak): Bronze axe wielded by Baylun. A birthday present from his brother, Romik.

Trannum (TRAN-nuhm): Ancient necromancer, corrupted after researching Uustaag the Dark. Destroyed at the conclusion of the Necromancer War and returned as the Shadow. Freed Uustaag.

Trethel (TRETH-uhl): River in Nomedd.

Tribenor (TRY-ben-or): Capital city of Sendorum.

Tux: Nickname of Eslimil Tuxendora.

Umbarc (UHM-bark): Andrian horse belonging to Vecnor.

Urell Coast (YOO-rell): Kingdom on the western shore of Vaeldor.

Uustaag (OO-stahg): Warlord of Helmland. Ancient Enemy of the North. The Enemy.

Vaeldor (VAY-uhl-dor): The continent of all known kingdoms.

Varlimor (VAR-lim-or): Mountains separating Kalmaar from Sardina. Home to Ironside Keep and Morimont.

Vayla (VAY-luh): Paladin of Cafior. Daughter of Cavalor and granddaughter of Merssa and Borse.

Vecnor (VEK-ner): Companion warrior of Elgarroth. Known as Black Rogue and Black Death.

Velgaad (VEL-gahd): Dwarfish Death Lord. Destroyed by Greyor during the Necromancer War.

Vennimor (VEN-i-mor): Paladin of Soleran. Founder of Palidur. Led the war against Uustaag in the distant past.

Vermallon (VER-muh-lahn): Forest separating Harbnum from Nira. Largest forest of Vaeldor and home to Vermallon elves.

Vikur (VIE-koor): Lord of Ironside Keep. Brother to Arkor. Father to Ballrik. Grandfather to Romik. Killed by Radaam in Ironside Keep.

Vircan (VERK-uhn): Citizen of Virch.

Virch (VERCH): Kingdom north of King Arman Lake. Known for its strong military. Guards only bridge between Beit and Virch.

Vol Maren (vahl MAIR-uhn): Capital of Neja.

Vou (VOO): Deity of magic. Provider of magical energy. It is said his mortal remains are buried in the center of Arman Forest.

Weblar (WEB-lar): Lieutenant in Darmhorng Castle.

Welmirth (WEL-merth): Ancient wizard that defeated Uustaag at the Battle of Balgorn.

West Palidur (PAL-i-der): City renamed by Rholmar when he was Duke of Philen.

Westessimer (wez-TES-sim-er): Lake located in Maple Lore Forest.

Wezlok (WEZ-lahk): Lorian elf wizard from Maple Lore Forest.

Wind of the Dead: A wind that raised the dead. Created by Trannum.

Wississtenance (wiss-SIS-tehn-ans): Magic words to hide Elgarroth's magic sack.

Wistin (WISS-tin): Father of Arrikan. Mountain ranger in northern Harbnum.

Wornduir (WORN-dye-er): Barbarian village in Andria.

Xorlunder (ZOR-luhn-der): Gray elf of Orlenfel. Killed by Gruzim during the Necromancer War. Father of Lorylla.

Yavell (yuh-VEL): King of Sendorum.

Yuris (YOO-riss): Lord in Kalmaar in Vecnor's younger days. Aspired to be king.

Zhokard (ZOH-kard): Means black warrior in the Andrian tongue. Creations of Trannum possessing black hearts. Neither living nor undead. Fought against Trannum in the Necromancer War. Bodyguards to King Cavalor of Marcove.

Zhomian (ZOH-me-uhn): Means black heart in the Andrian tongue. Creations of Trannum possessing black hearts. Neither living nor undead. Fought for Trannum in the Necromancer War.

Zreekan (ZREE-kuhn): Potato-shaped beings from Thard'Dun's world with one eye. Floats above the ground and has four tentacles. Nor arms or legs. Capable of terrible magic.

Zurkan (ZER-kin): Soldiers of Blood. Elite krukari warriors of Benasti Forest.

Zurzak (ZER-zak): Militant city off Shield River. Guards the only bridge connecting Virch to Beit. Opposes the city Darmoor.

Zutok (ZOO-tahk): Andrian chief of Wornduir.